Mesmer's Disciple
Copyright © 2012 by Edward Swanson
All rights reserved.

This is a work of fiction. While characters and locations may share names and descriptions with actual people and places, they should not be construed to be wholly factual representations.

No part of this book may be used or reproduced in any manner whatsoever without written permission, except in the case of brief quotations embodied in critical articles and reviews. For more information, e-mail all inquiries to: info@riverrunbookstore.com

Published by Piscataqua Press
An imprint of
RiverRun Bookstore

142 Fleet St | Portsmouth, NH 03801 | USA
603-431-2100 | www.riverrunbookstore.com

Printed in the United States of America

ISBN-13: 978-0-9885370-6-4
LCCN: 2012955089

www.piscataquapress.com

Mesmer's Disciple

Edward Swanson

Magic is justified of her children

Arthur Machen- *The White People*

Prologue

St. Louis, Missouri— late March, 1847

A madness enveloped the city of St. Louis, a madness made all the more ominous by its subtlety. For this particular brand of madness did not make itself known through omens ill-portending or howling mobs, but rather by whispered rumors of darkest sorcery and the sly smiles exchanged by the gentry in passing.

To the perceptive faculties of the inattentive nothing seemed amiss, but for the astute the hazy shimmer of the inscrutable was evident amidst the day-to-day routine of the populace.

All else remained unchanged; the steamboats still chugged past St. Louis on the turbid Mississippi, workers swarmed over the wharves and shipyards. Men and women came and went, casting off moorings to seek their fortunes out West.

Yet the signs of disquietude were there; most folks were simply too caught up in their daily affairs to notice signs so faint.

Among the minority who did was the man who now stalked the night woods just southwest of the city. In his day Marcel Durand had tracked and hunted both animals and men, and would have long been dead was it not for his uncanny ability to detect and interpret faint signs.

Such activities, those of both the mountain man and voyageur, had consumed his life for the past twenty-five years, weaving a tapestry of scars and powder burns onto his hide along the way. Trying years they'd been, although in them there had been much beauty, solitude, friendship, and glory. But several weeks past he had taken stock of his situation and realized that it was high time to bask in civilized luxury for a spell, if only to spend some hard-won cash and sleep in a decent bed. His body and mind needed a respite from the wild life and St. Louis, he reasoned, was a logical choice, for he knew some of the townsfolk from his youth and his stay there would be tinged with nostalgia.

Three days ago he had stepped off of a steamboat and onto the familiar wharves of St. Louis. So it was that he returned to civilization and found a black cloud hanging over the city of his birth.

And that rankled.

Long gone were the abundant prairies and the open, park-like woods that the red man had once maintained with the flame. Yet Marcel liked them all the more, for the dense understory of flowering dogwood, cherry, and redbud lent a wilder aspect to the forest. The larger trees, mostly burr oaks and sycamores, formed a second canopy some eighty feet overhead, and into one of the oaks he climbed with all the grace and swiftness of a feline. He perched upon a large, low-growing limb, propping himself up against the trunk.

Here he could be at ease once again, no longer hemmed in on all sides by people and buildings. Here his fringed deerskin smock and pants were not stared and snickered at by folks who couldn't even dream of the sights he'd beheld, the mighty deeds he had to his name.

Here was home.

Taking an already-packed clay pipe out of his breast pocket, he reached back and struck a match against the rough bark of the tree. With a deep, pensive drag, Marcel began reviewing the facts that he had gathered during his three days in the city.

Some people were acting in a manner that bespoke a conspiracy or secret society. Lord knew there were enough such groups in this country, and even more in Europe. Two days back he had tried to eavesdrop on a knot of men speaking furtively in a nearly empty tavern, but had been made by one of the fellows who hissed a quick warning to the others. The group dispersed with suspicious speed, with many a look askance being cast his way. He had observed other such groups since, always talking secretively in quiet spots. Marcel knew normal behavior when he saw it. That hadn't been such.

Then there was the peculiar matter of the city's elite, mostly the old French gentry and newly rich Yankee merchants. Marcel hadn't been two days in St. Louis before he noticed the knowing, surreptitious smirks and nods they flashed at each other as they went about their business. A keen observer of men, he knew well the subtleties of human emotion and interaction. This was not your average expression of recognition or salutation, but carried with it some sinister import.

More importantly, books and pamphlets were being exchanged among such men in stealthy fashion, often masked by handshakes or quick movements. Marcel had yet to get a hold of one, but he meant to, and soon. He felt that if a secret society had taken root in the city, the leading members of St. Louis were no doubt at its helm.

Marcel's strong French features creased with thought. Perhaps he was being a damned fool and nothing foul was afoot. Mayhap he'd been away from civilized people too long and had grown unaccustomed to their ways. But his instincts, which rarely failed him, suggested otherwise.

And just today, while speaking to an old friend, he had been informed of a marked increase in the population of the city's madhouse. Most people were not privy to this information, for the madhouse was located in a seedy, older part of the city that was generally given a wide berth. Yet it still stood that the population of the dilapidated stone building had swollen with the recent arrival of over twenty people suffering from violent seizures, delusions, and nightmares that were oddly similar in nature.

Marcel's friend told him that according to rumor this illness seemed to afflict only slaves and the very poorest of whites, so little notice was given to the situation. Consequently, the majority of St. Louis knew nothing of the hellish nightmares that wracked the bodies of the poor wretches, nor of strange words whispered in the dismal fastness of tomb-like rooms...

A last bit of evidence came just this afternoon. While walking along the wharves, he overheard the name, *Count Abendroth,* followed by, *surely you know of him- the mesmerizer.*

They had been two women of high birth speaking in barely audible whispers, but a lifetime in the woods and wilds had conditioned Marcel's senses accordingly. The canny mountain man harbored an inexplicable feeling that this information might prove to be the very key to the puzzle. He would find out the just who this Count might be, though it would behoove him to find out what a "mesmerizer" was before probing any deeper into this mystery, for that was a term utterly foreign to him.

Eventually, he eased out of the oak and made his way north towards the subdued glow of St. Louis's gaslights, a new development installed just last year from what he'd been told. It was with a twinge of regret that he left the forest, for he knew that only hustle, bustle, and far too many people awaited him back in town. Hardly enough room for a man to breath down there, let alone think.

Skirting an old Indian mound that rose eight feet from the ground, Marcel reflected on the passage of time. How long had it been since the Indians maintained these mounds, burying their dead in them or sacrificing to their gods? And how soon until the course of American civilization wiped out all traces of them?

A hideous sound cut short his musings, at once a roar and a shriek. In all his life, in all his experience, a more demonic and unearthly noise he had never heard.

Men being skinned alive made no such sounds; he happened to know that for a fact.

Again, the noise rent the night, sending a nearby flock of passenger pigeons rocketing out of their roost. It was beyond bloodcurdling.

The scream came not from the madhouse, for that was located in the heart of the city. Instead it came from west of town and not too far off from his present location. Marcel raced through the forest to find its source, even as the hairs on his arms and neck stood straight and his survival instincts screamed in protest.

He clawed his way through a dense patch of undergrowth and wormed through some clinging grapevine, gritting his teeth as he barked his shin on a root. As he broke through the tree line and into an expansive meadow, the burly woodsman sprinted in the direction from which he had last heard the sound. Once more his ears were assaulted by that hellish screech. Wincing, he pinpointed its origin: a large fortress-like structure of stone. This building was not one that he recognized from his youth, and there was something faintly menacing in its medieval appearance. It stood atop a hill about two hundred yards away.

Marcel made a beeline for it, intent on discovering the source of that anguished cry. For a fourth time it sounded, so intense in volume and terrible in nature that he abruptly bent over and was violently ill. Visions of hellfire and apocalypse flashed through his mind.

After all he had seen and done in life, a sound made him vomit? A sound?

And then—nothing. For five minutes he stood staring at the large stone building, fighting off the intermittent waves of nausea that assailed him. The night became astounding in its silence as intently he waited.

The stone building stood dark and solemn upon the hill, but he came to notice a faint orange glow emanating from a second story window. As he watched Marcel perceived movement in the room beyond.

Suddenly the sound of shattering glass met his ears and yells—normal, human yells—filled the air. The clouds parted at last, revealing a half-moon that dazzled the landscape with its pale light. This killed Marcel's night vision, but as the world shifted from shades of dull gray to shades of silver he saw a tall form tearing across the field right towards him.

With practiced ease and coolness, the mountain man smoothly drew his ten-inch Bowie knife from its belt sheath, holding the weapon in a firm reverse grip.

To his surprise the man began veering away from him, heading instead for the wood line to his left. Marcel caught a brief look at his face as he sped on by, and it was the face of a tortured soul. Torch-bearing men were crossing the field now, shouting for the fleeing man to stop and come back. As much as he hated to meddle in the business of others, he was determined to see what the hell was going on here. Turning on his heel, he loped into the woods, wraithlike in his movements.

The man came to a rest in a lonely little glade about a quarter mile into the woods. Chest heaving, legs giving way beneath him, he collapsed into a bedraggled heap on the long grass.

Marcel's moccasined feet made scant noise on the forest

floor as he came to the edge of the clearing. He watched the wretched figure twitch spasmodically, drawing in breath with great, ragged gasps.

As he watched, he became acutely aware that they were not alone in this moonlit meadow. Something unseen prowled the darkness surrounding the glade, and just then Marcel felt fear the likes of which rarely plagued him. He could not recall the last time he'd broken into a cold sweat, but did so now as his mouth dried up and his legs grew weak. As he stood stock-still, a jumbled chorus of seductive whispers drifted into his ears.

That he was in the presence of evil was obvious; indeed, nothing had ever seemed quite so obvious. He thought he caught a fleeting glimpse of a massive, shadowy *something* nearby, but it melted back into the night before he got a proper look.

Then a sibilant yet powerful hiss sounded from the woods just behind him and, heart pounding, hand aquiver, he drew his blade and prepared to face whatever in Heaven's name the thing might be, come what may.

Quite without warning, the fallen man rose to his knees, threw back his head and bellowed, "*Miserére mei, Domine! Miserére mei!*"

The voice carried a bit of that hollow roar that had accompanied the screams earlier. The specter, or phantom, or whatever that demonic presence had been was gone, as if exorcised by the man's shouting; he could feel the absence of its loathsome presence and it was a breath of fresh air.

Marcel frowned as he sheathed his knife. He remembered little of his early book learning, but had retained some Latin from attending Catholic Masses during his youth. The words the man had just roared into the night meant, "Have mercy on me, O Lord. Have mercy one me." The way they had been delivered caused a shiver to run down his spine. There was otherworldly desperation in those words.

He stared at the figure that writhed in a pool of hoary moonlight. After a final, violent convulsion, the man lay back and started breathing normally. With a deep breath of his own, Marcel moved in.

The fellow was ghostly white, but pastiness could not mask his handsome young countenance. Some small, shallow cuts flecked his face, tokens no doubt of the leap he took out of the window and his frantic run through the night woods. French was the dominant, if not sole race that comprised his heritage, Marcel would have bet. His clothes were stylish, finely tailored, and must have cost a pretty penny.

Dark eyes shot open. The mountain man felt a vice-like grip close on his wrist.

"Is this real?" There was terror mingled with confusion in those eyes, and the voice was extremely hoarse.

Marcel looked around the quiet glade, no longer occupied by that tainted shadow, and shrugged.

"I suppose," he answered in a gravelly voice.

"Where are they?"

"Huh?"

"Surely you saw them here?"

Marcel had indeed seen *something*, but did not wish to spook the fellow any further. "Ah, 'fraid not, mister. You all right?"

"I could have sworn I saw them just a moment ago, lurking shadows amidst the darkness?"

Those dark eyes bore right through Marcel, as if seeking some point beyond the horizon.

"Where?" the man asked breathlessly.

"Where what?"

"Where are we?"

"In the woods, friend. Just outside St. Louis. Let's get you out of here, eh?" Marcel leaned in to help him off the ground.

To his credit, the stranger suddenly seemed to shake off whatever it was that ailed him and put on a brave face. He rose unassisted and when he responded it was not with a shaky voice, but with a steady (albeit croaky) one that hinted towards refinement and education.

"That won't be necessary. I am just fine, thank you. Now which way to town?" The man acted as if he had not just woken up in the night woods with a perfect stranger at his side. It was pretty damn impressive.

"Thataway," said Marcel, pointing a thumb northeast where the lights of town barely filtered through the trees. The man thanked him again and began to walk off, but Marcel still wanted some answers before he left.

"You remember what you were just sayin', son? Somethin' about *things* with us here?"

The stranger's eyes widened for a moment. "Nothing to concern yourself with."

Marcel raised his bushy eyebrows. "Begging your pardon, *sir,* but I heard screams. Horrible ones. Came from that buildin' yonder, the one you fled. Care to explain?"

"Business, just business that I had there. They ah, slaughtered some lambs for supper and I fear that the noise was enough to wake the dead!"

His winsome laughter faltered under the mountain man's deadpan stare.

"Uh-huh," Marcel grunted skeptically. "Still don't explain why you came a'runnin from there like Ole Scratch was on your tail. 'Cause honestly, was only three clumsy fellers what lost your trail near as soon as they stumbled upon it."

Locking eyes with Marcel, the stranger spoke firmly and slowly. "*That,* my dear fellow, is no business of yours at all. I sincerely thank you for your assistance here, and if we meet again I will gladly buy you some drinks. But if you do not dispense with this line of inquiry then we shall have a problem, you and I. Good day. Night, actually."

Marcel Durand leaned up against a tree, arms folded, and watched as he marched resolutely into the dim aisle of trees. He had one more question, regardless of the "problem" promised by this arrogant dandy.

"What's the name, pilgrim?"

The fellow stopped and turned, the moonlight accentuating his sharp features. His irate expression softened, as he seemed to notice Marcel's knife for the first time.

"My name is Deas, Charles Deas. I am an artist from New York with a studio here in St. Louis. Anything else? I really must be going."

"Yeah, actually. You speak much Latin, Charles Deas?"

"Not a lick," he replied with a half-chuckle. "Mother tried to beat it into me and failed miserably."

And with that he vanished into the night, making a good deal of noise as he went.

Wiping his thick beard clean of drying vomit, Marcel came to the conclusion that this was no ordinary problem he faced. Something was missing from this picture. A big, mystifying something. His heart fluttered yet from the horror of that cry, a sound no mortal could have made or forced out of another. Now he happened upon a man, no doubt the origin of those sounds, who had spoken in a tongue apparently unknown to him while being stalked by some invisible specter. What he had encountered here tonight might well be at the center of the mystery that hung over his city.

Clouds drifted in front of the moon, plunging the glade into a Stygian darkness that brought terror even to the heart of Marcel Durand, whose acquaintance with darkness was more intimate than most. The forces of Good and Evil, of Heaven and Hell, were clashing in St. Louis. Marcel, moving quickly away from the spot lest those alluring voices return, offered up a rare, silent prayer that God might have mercy on those caught in between.

Part One

"A gateway of incredible adventure opened at his feet. He balanced on the edge of knowing unutterable things... an awful hand was beckoning."

Algernon Blackwood
Sand

Chapter 1

New York City— early April, 1847

It was with a spring in his step that Patrolman Andrew O'Farrell walked his beat on Lower Broadway. The sun had long set on an unseasonably warm spring evening, its fiery rays yielding to dull glow of the gaslights. Respectable society generally retired from this street at the onset of dusk, and in their place now stalked the darker elements of New York City; the whores, the pickpockets, the smugglers and street urchins.

Broadway, the most celebrated and refined of American streets by day, was by night a den of scoundrels.

Yes, Broadway at nighttime was enough to make the average man question his mettle, but Andrew O'Farrell harbored no such concerns. Two large, jagged scars on his forehead and a missing ring finger spoke of an intimate relationship with violence. Large for an Irishman at just over five feet ten inches, his one hundred-eighty pounds showed little evidence of fat. In fact, he was big for any American male— three inches taller than the average height of five-seven.

Having been on duty since six in the morning, O'Farrell had already made three unhurried sweeps of Broadway. A slow day had given way to an even slower night; at this point he would have welcomed some action. Stout was the truncheon in his belt, hickory in origin and delightfully wieldy. Should that fail him, the blackjack in his coat pocket would pick up where the club left off.

This would be his second year as a patrolman and it was shaping up to be a memorable one. Just last week he had acted on a tip and managed to apprehend Larry Flanagan, the notorious leader of an Irish gang called the Roach Guards, as he prepared to ransack a butchery in the Bowery. In the ensuing struggle O'Farrell sorely beat Flanagan and his two accomplices. Flanagan was suspected in four other recent break-ins in the Bowery, home to the rival nativist gang known as the Bowery B'Hoys.

That was quite a collar for a second-year patrolman. His fellow officers now held him in a higher regard, which came as profound relief. It was difficult for an Irishman to win the favor of men who regarded all Irish folk with suspicion, if not open contempt. But by arresting three high-ranking members of New York's most infamous Irish gang, O'Farrell had proven that justice meant more to him than the bond of blood. So among the other patrolmen and the English, Dutch, and German residents of New York's Sixth Ward, he enjoyed something of a celebrity.

On the flip side, he was now thoroughly despised by many of his countrymen for having a job that entailed meting out justice to a largely Irish criminal base. As expected, the Roach Guards had also taken the time to put O'Farrell on their shit list, so his name was mud throughout the Five Points, the Irish ghetto located south of the nativist-dominated Bowery.

But in truth O'Farrell was proud of his Celtic heritage, and often found his mind wandering back to his former home in Kilrush. He missed the lonely, rugged beauty of County Clare, home to the unique karst formations in The Burren and the soaring Cliffs of Moher.

Closing his eyes, he recalled the rich, almost indescribable blue of the Atlantic as seen from those cliffs, felt the warm kiss of the summer breezes upon his face.

New York was a good place to make a penny, to carve out a new future for yourself, but was a far cry from the majestic landscape that O'Farrell sorely missed.

It was nice to get away from it all like you could do back home, where a short walk would bring a body to the stone tombs and monuments that served as moldering tokens of the past. Many a stroll had he taken among those misty hills, but here he had to content himself with Vauxhall Gardens or Park Row. Tame, awfully tame to one accustomed to the vast wastes of western Ireland.

The life of the farmer had been good to him for a few years, before the Famine had brought Ireland to its knees. Everything changed with its coming. Stability and basic comforts were no longer realities during the Famine days. Lean, raw times they'd been and as close to Hell as he hoped to ever come.

America had been his only hope, and as he was a young man with no attachments he had secured passage to this country shortly after the Famine set in. He was determined to be a credit to his beleaguered race in this new and hostile land, to exceed expectations and overcome all prejudice.

And with his recent arrest of Flanagan and company, Patrolman Andrew O'Farrell of the Sixth Ward was well on his way to doing just that.

A lamplighter, identifiable by the nine-foot ladder he carried over his shoulder, huffed and puffed his way past O'Farrell as he made a beeline for a nearby tavern.

"Quittin' time, is it?" O'Farrell inquired lightheartedly.

"Damn right it is," responded the man, who had the look of a Dutchmen about him.

The Irish officer chuckled at the expectant expression on the portly fellow's face, inwardly wishing that he could follow suit. Chilly the night air was; he could use a dram to keep the cold at bay. But alas, he was an Irish police officer in a city that despised his kinsfolk through and through. Appearances needed maintaining lest he were to be lumped together with the other ne'er do well Irishmen.

It was a shame that those same people didn't take the time to notice the struggles faced by the Irish who came here. Most Irish immigrants arrived on these shores with nothing and took the jobs no one else wanted in order to get by, facing disheartening prejudice all the while. No wonder they got along so well with the blacks they lived alongside in the Five Points. That was adversity breeding strange bedfellows for you.

Few took note of the inspiring contributions made by Irish workers, either. The Croton Aqueduct, completed in 1842, had been built by mostly Irish labor. The impressive engineering feat ran underground for thirty-two miles from the Croton River in upper Westchester County to a stately Egyptian Revival distributing reservoir located at Fifth Avenue on 42nd Street. A sanitation crisis had developed in the city during the early 1830's, when a combination of filthy water, squalid tenements, and few sewers led to several outbreaks of cholera. Thousands died, but the paralyzing fear of cholera was now past thanks to the new supply of fresh Croton water that had helped increase domestic hygiene. Indeed, the nicest homes in the city now boasted running water and private baths, while the rest of the city contented themselves with the numerous public bathhouses that had sprung up. The Irish workers played a central role in that transfer of fresh water to New York City, but any praise had yet to reach their ears.

So on they worked, desperately reaching for the next rung on the social ladder.

A lone pig grunted loudly as it neared him, stopping by the policeman to sniff his recently polished boots. O'Farrell reached down and scratched the beast between the ears. His family raised pigs back home, and he'd always had a soft spot for the smelly, unsightly animals. Pigs roamed freely across Manhattan in both rich and poor areas. In fact, at night one was apt to see more pigs and dogs than people.

The people were there, however. O'Farrell's eyes roved the streets, taking careful note of each person occupying it.

A drunkard stumbled his way across Broadway, listing heavily to the right as he went. When he inevitably fell, he smashed into another sot who was sleeping on the sidewalk. A brawl ensued, but both men wore themselves out within ten seconds and leaned on each other for support.

If they were around upon his return trip, he'd arrest them, but he figured he would give them a chance to disappear first. Laughing, the patrolman continued his observations.

To his left, four loud, rough-looking men descended some old cellar steps that led to a bowling alley. If his memory served, that was a ten-pin alley, a game invented when the Legislature passed an act forbidding ninepin skittles for a while. What a strange country this seemed at times!

A modestly dressed couple walked past him, politely saying hello before walking down a similar staircase, although this one led to an oyster house. There people could pay for a private, curtained box in which they could sit, talk, and eat oysters in peace.

O'Farrell frowned slightly as he suddenly realized that the couple had said hello to him. This would not have happened before the Flanagan arrest.

It was as Captain Rawn had told him—just do your job, give them time, and eventually they'll see you for who you are regardless of heritage.

With a triumphant smile upon his lips, the Irishman strode confidently onward.

Two gaudily attired women of the night chatted as they crossed the street, no doubt heading to one of the brothels in the Five Points, where consecutive blocks of prostitution could be found. O'Farrell truly wished he could say that no self-respecting Irishmen would be caught dead there, but he knew that in truth it was the Irish who were at the heart of Manhattan's steadily rising vice. For while jobs were to be had, the money to be gotten from both petty and organized crime often surpassed that of a more respectable occupation. It was with a valid reason that so much crime was ascribed to the Irish.

And a crying shame it was.

O'Farrell continued patrolling his foot post, travelling uptown at a leisurely pace. To his left, a long way off down a road he'd forgotten the name of, he noticed a fellow patrolman slowly walking his own beat. Each raised a hand to the other in silent salute before resuming their patrol.

He passed the Astor House, a massive Greek Revival boasting Doric Columns, indoor gas lighting, and flush toilets. Popular entertainers and visiting luminaries all lodged here during their stays in the city. A symbol of American refinement, the Astor House was the place to stay if one was a wealthy visitor to Gotham.

Many buildings were being crafted in the Roman and Greek style these days, much to the dismay of New York's old guard. Both the Merchant's Exchange and Custom House were built in such architectural styles, while many of the old, sober Federal-style homes were being converted into ornate Italianate mansions.

The Irishman didn't care much for the building—too damn big, in his opinion. The thing took up far too much room, looming over him like some ancient colossus. Quickly crossing over to the east side of Broadway, he came to his favorite spot along his beat, City Hall Park.

A nearby gaslight illuminated the limbs of a massive elm tree that bowed gracefully over the wrought-iron park gate O'Farrell leaned against. Mighty oaks, maples, tulip trees and chestnuts also filled the park, spaced out in a very orderly fashion. Most of the trees had just begun to develop leaves, and here and there flowering dogwoods were beginning to blossom. It was nothing like the wild moorlands and craggy mountains that haunted his thoughts, but it was a breath of fresh air in a city as large as this.

Somewhere in there the Croton Fountain stood, built in 1842 to commemorate the completion of the Aqueduct. Music, laughter, and sounds of general merriment met his ears from across the park as folks filed into the beautiful Park Theater, which was located on the east side of the park. O'Farrell had seen many a play there himself, when the rates were reasonable enough for a middle class Irish immigrant to afford. Although as a policeman, he was often given greatly reduced prices on such things anyway. Better yet, there were certain places where he could dine, drink, and find entertainment completely free of charge. It was one of the many perks of the job.

With a smile on his lips, he turned and promptly stepped in a rather sizable pile of horseshit.

Cursing bitterly under his breath, he scraped off the bottom of his boot on the granite cobblestones. Horse manure littered the streets, for during the day omnibuses, coaches, hackney cabs, and private carriages dominated the main roads, all borne along by horses and mules. Street cleaners were supposed to remove it, but seemed to do a poor job. Being paid a pittance probably did not help inspire pride in the work.

On a corner O'Farrell passed one of the old wooden sentry boxes that dated back to colonial times. These days sentry boxes were little used by law enforcement, although some did sneak naps in them on slow nights. But back then, every adult male had rotated on night watch duty, and patrolled an assigned area with a sentry box located nearby. Of course, watchmen of old had tended towards incompetence, wore ridiculous-looking leather helmets and were generally laughed at by the public.

"While the city sleeps, the watchmen do too," had been a popular expression regarding the old nightwatch. Sentry boxes were often knocked over in those days by neighborhood youths, and even a rambunctious young Washington Irving had once tied a rope around one and dragged it behind his horse, much to the dismay of the watchmen trapped inside.

That was before the old Knickerbocker Aristocracy

dissolved and the crime rate skyrocketed. New York had come a long way since the merchants used to leave their wares outside at night, unguarded. There had always been some crime in the city, particularly around the sailors' haunts and brothels, but for the most part New York had been a safe place. Yet increased immigration and the concurrent establishment of slum districts offering cheap housing had given criminal elements a safe haven from which to strike out and a hive in which to multiply. Manhattan's population increased by five times from 1790 to 1830, with the old social hierarchies crumbling as the number of poor increased and the rich, no longer able to assert much control over them, began segregating themselves. By the 1830's New York's crime had evolved into a rather sinister strain as its law enforcement evolved alongside it and, some hoped, ahead of it.

Time would tell.

O'Farrell had arrived in America just in time to witness the reconfiguration of law enforcement in New York. In 1845, the New York City Municipal Police Act had finally passed after years of political wrangling. Modeled after London's own recently upgraded force, the Municipal Police supplanted the old night watch system with a semi-military day and night patrol. Its new forces were a visible presence in the city as they patrolled. That presence had the backing of political entities, as it was the aldermen of a ward who appointed its officers.

He had the good fortune of having an alderman who was free from prejudice against the Irish, and was eager to see fellow Democrats as policemen. Had O'Farrell been a Whig (few Irishmen were) he would almost certainly not have found such a job in New York, hotbed of Jacksonian Democracy that it was.

In times past, the policing efforts had benefitted from far greater public morality and the open support of the public as well. Now, patrolmen were cautiously loved by the rich and detested by the burgeoning population of poor folk.

As O'Farrell passed the northernmost part of the park, he was quite suddenly alone. This he enjoyed, for at such times it felt as though the city belonged to him. No hustle, no bustle, just him, the gaslights and the darkened buildings. Even City Hall, the stately Georgian building to his right, was quiet at this hour.

He inhaled deeply, basking in the magnificent solitude.

Manhattan wasn't all that bad when it was bereft of people.

Staring up the road, he found it hard to believe that this glorious Broadway eventually turned into a rough country road somewhere to the north. Too bad his ward did not extend that far, for he could have used a stroll through the country. An empty city was a good city, but was a city yet.

He checked his timepiece. Eleven o'clock. Time for one last, quick sweep through his section of the Five Points, where he was bound to find some respite from boredom before he was relieved at midnight.

Turning right onto Duane Street, O'Farrell took roughly a dozen steps before his eyes met with an alarming sight. Blocking the road ahead were twenty or so men, whom the patrolman immediately identified as Roach Guards by the blue stripe on the sides of their pants and the tall plug hats they wore. They were a motley, menacing lot armed with all manner of weapons. As his eyes swept across the gang, quickly taking in each man, he saw knives, cudgels, hammers, and billhooks, not to mention the various homemade implements that were in evidence.

Silently they fanned out, sweeping around until they formed a half circle around him. Standing before the rest, a stocky redhead addressed O'Farrell with a voice dripping sarcasm.

"Well, well, lads, now what've we here? 'Tis not the high and mighty Andrew O'Farrell 'imself, is it? Hope not, fer 'is sake. These night streets ain't a safe place fer a bloody turncoat."

O'Farrell ground his teeth. It was not so much the mocking tone and veiled threats as it was that grating Dublin accent that he'd always detested. The speaker's name was Thomas McClintock. Half Irish, half Scottish, rotten to the very marrow.

His heart pounded, but O'Farrell kept his voice calm and level.

"Evening, Thomas. I see you've picked up Flanagan's slack, then? Perhaps 'tis not me place, but I have to ask," he addressed the rest of the men, "how thin are you lads in the ranks that this is what you've dredged up for a leader? You know, if you find mud floatin' on the water's surface, you can be damn sure that it was stinkin' up the bottom not long before."

His words met with ill-stifled chuckles from some of the gangsters.

O'Farrell stared Thomas McClintock in the eye, a broad smile upon his face. It was a forced smile, one that threatened to evaporate, but Captain Rawn had always taught him that the best way to face a mob was with confidence, even if it's faked.

"Away with ye, pissant. I've got some patrollin' to tend to, and you and your louts are obstructing my path."

He focused on controlling his breathing, which had quickened upon encountering the Roach Guards. His hope was that his bravado would be enough to disperse them, for if there was a conflict he was on his own against twenty heavily armed men. Fit odds for Achilles, perhaps, but impossible for Patrolman Andrew O'Farrell of the Sixth Ward to overcome. Never had he faced such odds alone, nor felt such panic well up inside of him. There were other patrolmen on duty, but who knew if they would hear a call for aid? The Sixth Ward Stationhouse was located in the rotunda of City Hall, just a short walk away, but at this point to run was to be cut down or, should he prove faster than them, be labeled a coward. To stand, of course, was to face injury, perhaps even death.

He knew which fate he preferred.

"I fear tha' we'll be doin' a bit more than just 'obstructing'." A constant smile played around the lips of the newly designated gang leader, as if he could barely restrain his mirth.

"Bite the back of me bollocks, McClintock."

"You've brought it on yerself, man! You're a traitor to yer own blood! How the hell do you live with yerself? Tha' bloody butcher deserved whatever he got, and y'know it. Won't sell meat to Irish folk, the shit-stain won't! And he went an' beat some old woman what came beggin' for scraps t'other day. That's the man you'll defend?"

McClintock took a deep breath and strove to curb his temper. When he resumed speaking it was with a calm, impassive voice.

"Now Flanagan gets to rot in The Tombs and you get to rot in the earth."

Knowing what was coming and recalling his training, O'Farrell quickly backed himself up against the nearest wall. He drew his thirty-three inch truncheon, hand shaking as he did. Topped with heavy copper caps, these fearsome clubs had earned policemen the new nickname of "coppers."

"An' I don' suggest you yell for help," McClintock was saying, "ye bastard spawn of an Irish bawd, 'cause it's gonna be scarce as hens teeth in these parts."

And with that they advanced.

It happened so swiftly that O'Farrell barely had time to think about the pain he was to experience, or reflect on the magnitude of looming death. But such dark thoughts did enter his mind, if only briefly. A ripple of fear passed through him, and his mouth was suddenly bone dry. Rapid heartbeats fell like blows upon his chest. Yet as the gang drew nearer, shouting like savages, the knot in his stomach gave way to the boiling rage that has propelled many an Irishmen into hopeless battles.

McClintock, though he initially led the charge, fell back at the last moment and allowed several other Roach Guards to run past him. O'Farrell's vision became a jumble of snarling men.

His first blow was a massive sideways swipe that split the nearest man's skull across the forehead and sprayed the patrolman with blood. It was not the first life he had taken, but any kill at this range was a very grisly affair.

Men tripped over the fallen gangster, so the patrolman quickly lashed out again in something of a panic, aiming to crush another skull beneath one of the plug hats. Unfortunately, the Roach Guards stuffed their hats with wool to defend against that very move, so the club did little damage.

A small pick-like weapon pierced his cheek, knocking out a tooth as it did. The Irish officer crushed the offending arm with his next move, a sharp yelp complementing the hearty crunching of bone. Ripping the pick out of his cheek with a roar, O'Farrell blindly swung it into the throng. Men were now so close to him that there was little room to swing. He managed to land one more full-force shot, shattering a shoulder with his club, and then they were upon him and the long truncheon was no longer of service.

Blades pierced his torso; the initial cold of their steel quickly replaced by the warmth of his own flowing blood. Clubs and hammers smashed into his arms and head, but the fury was still upon him and on he fought, coming up suddenly with a wild punch that knocked out the front teeth of an attacker.

The truncheon had been ripped from his hand and lay useless on the ground, too far away to retrieve. Grappling with another man, O'Farrell bodily heaved him into some others and bought himself enough time to snatch the blackjack out of his coat pocket. He'd been driven hopelessly out of position; now he simply charged rather than wait for the gang's inevitable advance.

Roach Guards rushed in to finish him off, getting in each other's way in their haste. One fell right in front of him, so he gave that man a boot to the face, putting all he had into it.

His breath came in horrible, ragged rasps; he could feel himself weakening as his vision swam. Death would be a mercy at this point... pain stung his entire body, his lungs strained for air as he drowned in his own blood... he could lay down now and be done with it...

No—his departure from this life would not be made in that manner; no, he would rage to his last, ragged gasp against these swine who disgraced the Irish name. Driven by strength born of sheer desperation, his blackjack found the temple of an advancing Roach Guard, a swarthy black-haired man. O'Farrell felt the bone give way under his weapon, saw the eyes widen in shock before rolling upward.

A spiked club swished through the air and imbedded itself into the arm holding the blackjack.

Patrolman Andrew O'Farrell howled in pain and turned towards his attacker, who turned out to be McClintock. The redhead smiled with green teeth as he thrust a filthy knife into the patrolman's throat with his other hand, twisting the blade to widen the wound. With a quick wrench, the Irish gangster freed the weapon and stepped back.

O'Farrell, coat ripped by blades in numerous spots and covered in blood, swayed as if drunk. Still smiling, McClintock tipped him over with a lazy kick.

The gang leader leered into the glazing eyes of the patrolman as he bent over to rip off his copper badge. "Jus' so ye know, ye goddamn ball-bag, I enjoyed tha' immensely."

The Roach Guards collected their dead and wounded, each mobile member taking the time to spit on the fallen patrolman. Soon enough they were gone and all was silence.

O'Farrell was not yet dead, but he felt Death gaining on him with the passing of each second. The Roach Guards were gone—it was safe to move now. Not far ahead of him lay Broadway, so in a final act he began inching his way forward while trying to stem the flow of blood from his neck wound with his other hand. The metallic taste of blood in his mouth was overpowering. He didn't have long, he knew, for he was losing too much blood too quickly.

A dog sniffed his head as he moved. For a few moments it hung around, curious, but a loud cry of agony sent it scurrying.

Wounds white-hot with pain, O'Farrell dragged himself along the road. It was not with any particular purpose in mind that he did so; man's primal instinct to resist, to survive, was what urged him on to action. He did not even think to call for help.

As long as I move, I'm alive... as long as I'm moving, I'm still alive...

After a minute that passed as an eternity might, the dying officer reached Broadway, where his body no longer responded to the desperate urgings of his mind. His head lolled over to the left, giving him a view uptown.

The last thing he saw as he lay gurgling on the cobblestones was the lofty spire and cross of the distant Trinity Church.

Well, 'tis not the Cliffs of Moher, but for a last sight, it'll do. It'll do just fine.

And the darkness closed in on him with a silent rush.

Chapter 2

In a cool, dimly lit room in the rotunda of New York's City Hall, Captain Alvord Rawn of the Sixth Ward cast an eye over a neatly written letter. A sizable pile of similar letters sat nearby on his desk. Leaning close to an oil lamp, Alvord performed a preliminary skimming of the letter's contents, searching for any promising words or phrases. He was not disappointed.

"Hour of dire need," "no one else to turn to," and "handsomely rewarded for your efforts," certainly piqued his interest.

Now here was something to look into. Although he was a captain in the Municipal Police Department of New York, there was good money to be made on the side as a private detective. Better money than his seven hundred and fifty dollar a year captain's salary, truth be told.

Alvord sat in the room with fourteen other policemen, although it would have been difficult to tell that all present were members of the same quasi-military law enforcement organization. No uniforms were in evidence; each man dressed as he thought a man of the law should, utter nonconformity being the result. Some sported greatcoats and corduroy trousers, while others opted for wool shirts with frock coats. Top hats of felt, beaver, and silk graced the heads of most, in accordance with the dictates of current fashion.

Among members of the Municipal Police, uniforms were contemptuously dismissed as "servant's livery," an unnecessary appurtenance to men who prided themselves in their individuality. Was this to become London, where the bobbies were interchangeable manikins in fancy garb? No—this was Gotham, and personality would win the day. Only the copper badges upon their chests marked them as policemen, badges that did not even have to be displayed if the officer felt it unnecessary.

Some of the men chewed tobacco or puffed on cigars to pass the time, others read or played whist or chess, but the majority slept. In a typical forty-eight hour period, a patrolman would spend eighteen hours on patrol and fourteen on reserve before having sixteen to himself. Alvord had himself slept a few hours, but made sure to take some exercise too, and had also made good progress on Sir Walter Scott's *Ivanhoe*.

His desk was set apart from the others, commanding a direct view of the door. If ever an undesirable were to show up unexpectedly, Alvord could easily cover the door with the blunderbuss he kept strapped to the underside of his desk. As of yet, no one had tried to force entry into the stationhouse, but he privately relished the prospect.

By his estimation a leader of men should at all times be prepared to defend to the death those who acted upon his orders. Men needed always to respect and have faith in their commander; Alvord knew of no better way to garner both than through leading by example.

Decisive, indomitable example.

Running a hand through thick hair of darkest chestnut, he took a sip of his ale and regarded the letter once more. It read:

Respected Sir-

I call on your services in an hour of dire need, for my son's absence gnaws on my soul day and night, and I fear that if this absence is much further extended then my sanity will take leave of me. Others have refused my pleas; I write now for I have no one else to turn to.

Chiseled features that bespoke grave deportment grew more severe yet as Alvord frowned, pensively stroking his trim red beard. He had read some desperate letters before, but this one certainly took the biscuit. His eyes sought out the name at the bottom of the page. Mrs. Anne Izard Deas. The name Deas struck a vaguely familiar note, but Alvord was unsure of where he had come across it before.

Forehead crinkling with thought, he returned to the letter.

Several years ago my son Charles departed for the West, as his adventurous fancy dictated, and has been living there ever since. A painter of some renown, he keeps a studio in St. Louis, Missouri, from which he makes excursions into the frontier. This was the year he was due to come back, but this past fall and winter he sent letter after letter stating that he needed more time out there. He has yet to return. Money and letters he has sent steadily enough, but the latter grow increasingly peculiar. I no longer recognize my son's customary wit and affection in them; worse yet, there is constant mention of a Count Abendroth and how the man is helping him to mature as an artist, to "reach levels of artistic realization never before attained," as he put it. Charles has referred to this man as an animal magnetizer, which from what I've gathered is a practitioner of mesmerism.

Charles' latest correspondences have been marked by a growing strain of insanity and fanaticism; judging by his writing he has fallen prey to madness. I feel strongly that this "Count" plays a central role in it. My fear for Charles's physical and spiritual wellbeing grows daily, as his letters grow fewer and their content less lucid.

Thus far, none have been-

A frantic knocking on the door broke his concentration. A female voice shrieked in a foreign language, increasing in volume as the knocking quickly graduated to pounding. Rising to his full six feet one inch, Alvord grabbed his truncheon before making a beeline for the door. Though heavily muscled, he possessed long legs and reflexes that gave him unusual quickness for a man of his size.

He was the first to reach the doorway, with those patrolmen who were still awake close behind. Those who had been asleep hastily jumped out of the beds lining the far wall, pulling on boots and shirts. Club at the ready, the tall captain threw open the door to reveal a sobbing old woman clad in tawdry rags.

Alvord slipped past her to scan the hallway, making sure that this wasn't a trap of some sort. The gangs were getting bolder and bolder these days and it did not pay to underestimate their temerity.

The woman was quickly ushered into the stationhouse where she was given a seat, a blanket, and some tea. In time she calmed down and began talking, though occasional sobs still wracked her frail form as she spoke. Unfortunately, her speech was delivered rapid-fire in a guttural tongue.

"English, woman." Alvord firmly requested in a deep, resonating voice. It did not have the desired effect, so he turned to a short, barrel-chested officer with black hair.

"Schwarz, get over here. Sounds like German she's speaking, and I don't *spreche*."

The German patrolman came forward, knelt before the old woman and, taking her hands in his own, talked soothingly with her for a few minutes. The woman's words were punctuated by violent gestures and what sounded like curses. After her speech came to a close, Schwarz slowly stood and faced his captain, face grim. His voice, which barely hinted at his foreign origin, wavered as he spoke.

"O'Farrell's dead." Several gasps of shock followed the news.

Alvord felt a fiery surge of rage, but clenched his jaw and strove to control it.

"She saw it all from one of the tenements there. From what she described, twenty men, probably Roach Guards by the outfits, fell upon him as he turned onto Duane Street. That's his foot post, right? She says he put up a struggle, but they got him in the end. Says he crawled out onto Broadway and died there."

"She did not lend him aid once the attackers departed?" Alvord inquired with ill-concealed annoyance. He had taken O'Farrell under his wing when the young Irishman first found his way into law enforcement. He considered O'Farrell a brother, albeit an Irish and Catholic brother. It took self-mastery born of a lifetime of practice to stifle his churning emotions.

"She said that she only moved in once she was certain the attackers were gone, and by the time she got down to the street O'Farrell was dead. She recognized him as a patrolman and figured it would be best to come right here."

"How long ago?"

"*Wan ist das passiert?*"

The old woman thought for a moment. "*Halb stunde, ich denke.*"

"Half hour or so. She came as fast as she could. Apparently, there was no one else around that she could send here and she did not want to wake her neighbors, whom she fears. Also, she didn't want to yell and perhaps attract the gang's attention."

"Smart. Did she see the direction in which the gang headed afterwards?"

Schwarz posed the question to the woman, whose answer was accompanied by an emphatic shaking of her head.

"Nein. I mean, no. From where she was watching, she didn't get a look at where they went, but they didn't go out towards Broadway, or she'd have seen them."

"One final question: How did she get into City Hall?"

Schwarz inquired. "She says the front door was open and she already knew where the stationhouse was located. She encountered no one on her way."

"An open front door?" Alvord shook his large head in disgust. "They're just inviting trouble these days, aren't they? Ah, never mind it now."

Alvord walked over to the old German woman, gently placing his hand on her shoulder. His light gray eyes met her still-watering eyes of brown for a moment, and there was tenderness in his usually staid demeanor.

"Schwarz, offer her our profuse thanks. Tell her that she may remain here for the night, if she pleases. Additionally, inform her that she will receive a loaf of bread and some cheese for her trouble, which she can pick up midday tomorrow."

As Schwarz began relating the message, Alvord addressed the rest of his platoon. Although his face did not betray it, a boiling fury was taking hold of him. What he was about to do would engender great controversy, but would be done regardless. Of all the men in his two platoons, the most valiant and upright had been the young Irish lad who was now presumed to be dead. A lad in whom no observable character flaw could be found.

Vengeance screamed out inside of him, drowning out any thoughts of hesitation or proper procedure.

"Gentlemen, arm yourselves as you see fit. Be prepared to depart in three minutes."

With that, he strode over to the weapons closet behind his desk. All but one of his patrolmen followed him.

"Should we not go tell Chief Matsell of the news? He's still downstairs in his office, ain't he? This is one of his late work nights." The speaker was a young officer with sandy hair and piercing blue eyes.

"No, Hodgins, we shouldn't. He'll find out in due time. If we break news like this to him and a bunch of politicians, we shall never get out of here in time. This is not the time for shilly-shallying."

Hodgin's was looking a bit embarrassed, and Alvord felt for the Irish rookie.

"Under normal circumstances, the Chief needs to be informed of events of this magnitude forthwith. But we have an opportunity to bring justice to the filth who murdered O'Farrell, and their trail grows colder with the passing of each minute. Speed is of the essence."

Alvord truly wished the world were such that justice could override procedure. While efficient in many regards, the establishment of the Municipal Police Department in 1845 had brought with it a torrent of restrictions.

In the old days, he'd have marched upstairs into City Hall and announced Andrew O'Farrell's heartrending fate to all present. Some of them would have hungrily joined the hunt back then, politicians though they were. Indeed, some still might, but plenty of others would be restrained by regulations and fear of political backlash. They would be nothing more than bothersome impediments to action.

Alas, how the world had grown tame! New York was now too cultivated to be forthright in the dispensing of true justice, so justice had to grow clandestine in response.

Alvord flung open the arms closet and his men began grabbing their favorite weapons. There was none of the lighthearted banter that generally accompanied their mobilizing; most still struggled to process the news of their comrade's premature departure from this life. Blackjacks, truncheons, slung-shots, brass knuckles, and a few Colt revolvers were all taken down and made ready for battle. Normally guns were reserved for riots, but each man knew from the tone of their captain that there would be no holds barred this night.

Alvord also opened an old chest beside the closet, from which he began passing out hardened leather helmets not unlike the ones used by the fire brigades. These helmets had once been part of the old nightwatch's everyday gear, earning them the nickname of "leatherheads." While impractical for everyday use, they would save lives in a clash with a notoriously brutal gang.

As he distributed the last of the helmets, a hand tapped Alvord on the shoulder. He turned to find Dorsett, an old-timer who had helped train him, standing awkwardly before him. The man was fifty-five years old and it showed.

"Cap'n Rawn? Could I speak to you in private, sir?"

Alvord obliged him, moving a few steps away from the others.

The veteran patrolman looked sullenly at the ground, looking extremely disappointed with himself.

"Cap'n, here's the thing. The rheumatism is acting up, and I can't move like I should be able to. Even then, I just ain't what I used to be. Got this damned cough that I can't rid myself of, so I'm likely to give our position away if we're sneakin' up on anybody. I think it'd be best if I stayed behind." His lips tightened. "Don't like saying it, damn shameful it is."

"Dorsett," Alvord replied seriously, "I understand, and thank you for your honesty. There is still something you can do for me, in fact. The other half of this division will be returning from patrol within the hour. Don't tell them what has transpired just yet, lest they do anything rash, but tell them that they are to stay here until I return. Even if they notice O'Farrell's absence, keep your silence. Here, take this," ordered Alvord, handing him a small billfold. "Get them drinks."

The old patrolmen looked relieved that there was some purpose he could serve. "That I can do for you. If I thought I could help you boys out there-"

"I know it, Dorsett."

Alvord clapped the man on the shoulder and made his way to the weapons closet. He armed himself with a Hawken .65 caliber caplock pistol and the only sword in the arsenal. As he strapped the sword onto his belt, a quiet voice spoke.

"You realize, Alvord, that this is quite against protocol?"

The soft voice belonged to Sergeant Mitchell Turner, his second in command.

"To hell with protocol. I don't know about you, Sergeant, but it is my fervent wish to avenge the death of a fallen comrade. Rules will be broken, and we may come under some fire for our actions. But we must act, protocol be damned. If you don't wish to join me, so be it, but I don't suggest you try stopping me." A dangerous glint lingered in his unblinking eyes.

"Easy, Captain," said Turner calmly, his narrow face deadpan, "I just needed to know that you were aware of the consequences. I'm with you."

Alvord gave him a stiff nod of approval before sweeping past him. Grabbing his brown oilskin greatcoat and tucking his truncheon into his belt, he quickly reviewed his platoon. Rugged were the thirteen who stood before him, and not a coward to be found among them. Men he knew not only had his back but would also follow him to Hell's Gate. Mingled with some disbelief and fear, rage proved to be the dominant expression on their faces, and Alvord would see it duly indulged.

"We take the rear entrance out of City Hall to avoid detection. From there, it's to Grammery's Livery Stable for horses."

Captain Alvord Rawn, face masklike in its stillness, looked each of his patrolmen in the eye before speaking.

"Might as well leave the cuffs behind tonight, boys."

The assembled officers stared back at their captain, whose large frame stood outlined in the doorway. Broad in the shoulder, narrow at the hip, and with features that might have been hewn from granite, their captain was a man to follow in the darkest of hours.

Before leading his platoon out of the room, Alvord shot a sidelong glance at the golden lamplight that illuminated the papers on his desk.

Mrs. Deas's letter would have to wait, for there was killing to be done.

Chapter 3

The officers of the Sixth Ward had quietly absconded from City Hall and at the moment stood before the lofty doors of Grammery's Livery Stable on Chatham Street. Aside from being the closest to City Hall, this stable offered some of the best Manhattan horseflesh available. Its owner, however, could be a truculent one at the best of times.

Most city residents relied upon livery stables for transportation, although the recent increase in horse-drawn omnibuses provided another option for those who could not afford their own carriages.

"Stay here, I'll go around to his house and see if I can wake him. Be back in a bit."

Alvord left his men there, hoping to find Eleazar Grammery so that they wouldn't have to commandeer horses without his knowledge. Rounding the corner of the stable, he moved slowly in the murky darkness that his eyes were not yet adjusted to. Black clouds cloaked most of the night sky, their bulk obliterating any moonlight and starlight that might normally illuminate his path. Keeping one hand on the side of the stable, he stole as softly as possibly towards the small brick house ahead of him. Then something poked him quite hard in the chest, and he froze.

"That'll be far enough, m'boy."

Straining his eyes in the poor light, Alvord was barely able to make out the squat form of old man Grammery himself. Grammery's hands clasped a pin-fire shotgun, the barrel of which rested lightly against Alvord's copper badge. This was a rare weapon for a citizen of New York City to own, but the man had his life invested in the animals he owned, and was none too keen on losing them.

Alvord, none too keen on appearing startled, addressed Grammery in a thoroughly nonchalant tone. "Mr. Grammery. I do hope I find you well this night."

"Rawn? That you?" The man squinted through undersized spectacles.

"Right in one. I hate to trouble you at so ungodly an hour, but I have need of some horses. Your best, as it happens. But before we broach the subject of business, I'd be beholden to you if you would stop pointing that scattergun at my chest." Knowing that Grammery was by nature an irritable fellow, he kept his tone level.

"Well, I suppose you can have the horses, but it'll cost you. Woke me up in the dead o' night, you did. Rates'll double for that."

Diplomacy had gotten Alvord nowhere, so directness was the most logical next step. He hoped for the old man's sake that it worked, for after directness came decisive force.

"I really haven't time to dally, Grammery, and I doubt very much that we woke you as we barely made a sound out here. More likely, you were up due to the stomach trouble that's been ailing you."

The man frowned confusedly. "How'd you know that?"

"I noticed you clutching your gut spasmodically and the odor of ipecac still lingers on your breath. So, as I was saying, you saw us approaching and decided to try and intimidate an officer of the law with a gun."

Taking a slow step towards the frail oldster, whose gun was now pointed rather shakily at the ground, he added a dangerous edge to his voice.

"And, to top it off, you then try to charge us more than your usual rates? Matsell and City Hall will hear of this unless impending events transpire in my favor. Were I you, old-timer, I'd reconsider my position with all due haste. If not, I suggest you raise that bird gun and prepare to fire, because I'm taking those horses by fair means or foul."

"You menace me without explanation. All it takes is one shot, Rawn," stammered the stable owner.

He had guts, this one.

Alvord smiled, though there was nothing friendly about it. "I advise you make it a good one, Grammery."

The old man's distress was palpable as he licked his dry

lips and said, "You know what, Cap'n Rawn? Why don't you fellers just take what horses you need, and then come back and pay—the usual rates—in the morning? I'll send out some servants to saddle 'em up for you, should be ready to go in half a tick."

Alvord held forth his hand.

"There's a fellow. Nice doing business with you, Eleazar," he said with another shark-like grin. "Peaceful dreams, friend."

Atop their newly acquired horses, the patrolmen awaited orders from Alvord. Bringing his steed into a brisk trot, he exited the stable last after making sure that his men were properly outfitted.

"Murdock, Morris, you'll come with me to Broadway. We need to find O'Farrell's body and verify his death. Hopefully we'll find some evidence at the scene as well. As for the rest of you, stick together and head into the Five Points from the south. At the corner of Worth and Collect, you'll see a saloon painted bright green, run by some fat Irish blighter named Monahan. Inside, you will find a grotesque leprechaun of a man drinking himself into oblivion by dint of gin-slings. Goes by the name of Sleeth. Two of you go in and get him out of there, by force if necessary. He is an informant of mine. I need him out of that bar and ready to answer some questions. A bit further up on Collect Street is an old grog shop that took some fire damage last year—Hodgins, you probably know it from your beat. It is now deserted and will be a good place to interrogate him. Knock down the door if it's boarded up. We will meet you there within half an hour. Ride hard."

With a clatter of hooves Alvord was away, with Murdock and Morris close behind.

Galloping up Broadway, where shadow and gaslight vied for supremacy, Alvord's emotions ranged from transports of sorrow to tempests of rage.

O'Farrell was gone—*O'Farrell*, the twenty-three year old Irishman who had shown so much promise, who had been such a credit to his race...

He had trained O'Farrell himself, instructing him in combat, patrolmen-community relations, cultivating informants, conducting investigations, and the other skills that it behooved a patrolman to possess. The young man displayed none of the wariness that most Irish immigrants did towards native-born New Yorkers. Indeed, he had even shown scorn towards the degenerate sons of Hibernia that he dealt with each day. It must have been tough, trying to proudly represent your race while battling them in the process, all the while faced with the disdain of the native-born. In overcoming the prejudice and derision of so many, O'Farrell had been a shining example of what the Irish were capable of attaining in this country.

And it was that very race of people whose blood ran through his veins, the ones he sought to inspire and elevate through his own triumphs, who had seen fit to end his life. Backwards thinking if ever there was.

Alvord ground his teeth. Blood would flow freely for the sake of his good name.

It was a fine steed beneath him that had a bit of draft blood in it, and he could not help but liken this moment to the wars fought by his ancestors on distant fields in bygone days. Had they too felt this fiery rush of anticipation as they raced on massive chargers towards their foes?

Horses had not, of course, been entirely necessary tonight but they did afford he and his men a faster mode of travel, saving them from walking or running. Horses were also invaluable in breaking up crowds, should they manage to catch O'Farrell's assailants out in the open. And if things went to hell and they needed a quick avenue of escape, then horses were the appointed means. Perhaps it was the helmet on his head and sword on his hip, but horses just felt right in this situation.

City Hall Park flashed by him in a green blur as his horse's hooves clanged loudly against the cobblestones. The third Trinity Church, newly reconstructed in 1846, stood like a beacon ahead, towering over all other buildings in New York at an inspiring two hundred eighty-one feet.

"Up ahead!" yelled Morris from somewhere behind him.

A small crowd had gathered where Broadway met Duane Street. Alvord kicked his horse and gave him some rein. The beast lowered its head, flattened its ears, and tore towards the knot of people. He was no expert horseman, but in his day had done a reasonable amount of riding. To Chief Matsell he had proposed mounted troops time and again, but to no avail; the Chief hated horses and thought them an unnecessary expense.

Hauling on the reins lest his horse smash into the assembled people, he dismounted as it was still slowing, throwing the reins to the nearest bystander. Alvord, mouth dry and face drawn, knew what he was going to find as the crowd parted before him.

O'Farrell's body lay in a dark pool of blood, face mangled, bloodied clothes torn in countless spots. Alvord exerted his self-possession to its fullest, suppressing the hiss of anger that longed to escape his lungs. It did not become a police captain to lose himself to wrath in front of bystanders.

He noticed a grisly stab wound to the young Irishman's throat, and upon inspecting O'Farrell's head found a host of raised bruises and blood-encrusted cuts. The number of injuries on the head and body indicated a large number of assailants, as the old German woman had claimed, for one or two people did not usually mangle a body in this manner. This was the work of many, crowding around the patrolman to stab and batter whatever part of his body they could.

Alvord looked again at the once-handsome, now-wasted face of a man he'd been honored to know, a man he'd come to consider a friend despite the fact that he was both Irish and a Papist.

What a dark place Manhattan had become…

"We just found him like this about fifteen minutes ago, sir," said a man who looked quite wan but was trying to put up a brave front. "I sent a friend to City Hall, he should be arriving soon, said he'd run…"

"Quick thinking," Alvord commended him, trying his best to appear composed and not agitated that someone was going to break this news to City Hall before he had carried out his mission.

"I am Captain Alvord Rawn of the Municipal Police Department, and I ask one more thing of you. Get a carriage and have the driver bring the body within one block of City Hall, then wait for my return. The arrival of this body will cause an even greater stir and I need to be there when the body is displayed to those still at City Hall. Inform the driver that he will be handsomely compensated for his time. My men and I have some, ah, *business* to attend to but should be back within an hour or two."

The man considered this for a moment. "Rawn, eh? I

know well the name. I'll tell you what. I own a carriage myself, but I live on Fifth Avenue. I can go get it and transport his body in that. No fee will be required; one of your men came to the aid of my wife last month, so I owe that much to you."

Fifth Avenue, eh? The man must have been wealthy beyond imagination.

"Much obliged, sir."

Turning to his right, he saw Murdock and Morris silently emerge from the darkness of Duane Street. They were his best investigators, and with a bit more training they both could easily attain the status of marshal, the formal Municipal Police term for detective.

"Roach Guards, all right. Here you are-" Murdock passed a hat Alvord's way, lips tightly pursed and eyes blazing. His captain closely inspected it.

"Filthy plug hat stuffed with leather and wool. Roach Guards indeed. What else did you find at the scene of the attack?"

"Blood, busted teeth, a piece of scalp with some hair attached, and broken weapons," responded Morris. "Spread out over a fair piece of street, too. Must have been quite a fight."

"What of Andrew's weapons?"

Morris held forth O'Farrell's truncheon. Alvord took it, turning it over in his hands. Blood and a lighter, stickier substance caked the club, and the copper tip had some flesh and hair clinging to it. It was hard to believe that such scum as the Roach Guards could possibly take out such a tough, competent young man, but what was it that Tacitus had said?

Valor is of no service, chance rules all, and the bravest often fall by the hands of cowards...

"There's this, too," added Murdock, handing over a blackjack. The initial's A.O. had been carved into its leather. Again, blood clung to it; Andrew put up a fierce fight, as Alvord had surmised, and inflicted some serious damage judging by the appearance of his weapons.

Lifting up his leather helmet, Alvord ran a hand through his hair and loudly exhaled. "They had wounded or dead that they took with them, so they were moving slower than usual and might have been spotted. Like wounded wolves, they no doubt slunk back to their lair."

His head turned northeast towards the putrid shithole

that was the Five Points.

"Time to see what Sleeth can do for us."

Built atop an unstable landfill east of Broadway that had reclaimed land from the site of the old Collect Pond, the Five Points was a noxious, vice-ridden testament to New York's entry into a new age. For no modern city was complete without its slum district, and Manhattan's Five Points was hailed as the worst slum known to man. The complexities of urbanization had produced an ideal environment for the proliferation of poverty and crime.

"The St. Giles of the New World," was what Europeans had dubbed this, the most squalid region of New York, after London's own celebrated crime ward, St. Giles.

Having never been to St. Giles, Alvord could not be sure but very much doubted that it could hold a candle in the dark to the Five Points. In fact, European visitors would even venture into the Negro and Irish ghetto with police escorts to see firsthand that America had indeed surpassed them in urban decay.

The tremendous amount of gang violence that took place between the Bowery B'Hoys and the various Irish gangs in this section of the city had given rise to the nickname, "The Bloody Sixth Ward." To patrol here was to be respected by the rest of the city.

Alvord and his two men cantered down narrow alleys and lanes paved only in dirt, trash, and feces, scattering packs of half-wild dogs and pigs as they went. The pleasing, rhythmical clatter of horseshoes on cobblestones was replaced by a sickening squelching as the horses' hooves sank deep into the filthy street.

Beginning with the Old Brewery back in the 1820's, larger buildings in the area were converted into tenements that could house over a thousand people, most of whom where black or Irish. Countless ramshackle, wooden-framed tenements with little lighting and ventilation made for woeful living conditions; it was even rumored that gangs of feral children lived in tunnels under the buildings. The odor of animal and human feces was everywhere present, for sanitation and hygiene were alien concepts to the inhabitants of this place. Low-roofed saloons, grog shops, dancing halls, and houses of ill-repute also lined the streets, each of them filled to capacity on this night judging by the raucous noise issuing from them.

What a paradox. One could quite literally take a step off of Broadway, the very height of modern, urban refinement, only to enter a slum unequalled in degeneracy. It was hard to believe that while on Fifth Avenue Gothic and Italianate mansions were springing up at an unbelievable rate, here on Elm Street mankind seemed to be in a state of social regression.

It was said (if only half-jokingly) among New Yorkers that the Devil, if ever weary of Hell's scenery, could come to the Five Points and be refreshed by what he beheld.

As if to ward off the evil vapors that clung to the area, The Tombs stood just to the northwest. This Egyptian Revival jail and court complex was meant to counteract the lurid depravity of the Five Points. Often compared to an ancient Egyptian mausoleum in appearance, it did at times house many dead bodies, if only briefly. The "Bridge of Sighs" connected the main prison to the "Steps and String," as the gallows were often referred to. Public executions were frequent, popular, and on the rise in fact, for as the Five Points rotted from within it spawned legions of criminals who seemed destined for nothing more than a short drop and a sharp jerk. An enduring rock of justice amidst a churning sea of crime, The Tombs was a symbol of hope to the citizens of New York.

The waterfront was not far to the east, so as might be expected many a drunken sailor careened his way through the dark alleys towards a favorite watering hole. One of them was not quick enough in getting out of Alvord's way, and the massive shoulder of his horse sent the man flying into a pile of trash.

Taking a right onto Worth Street, the three coppers soon came to the old liquor store where they were to rendezvous with the rest of the platoon. They dismounted and tethered their horses to a hitching post, alongside the mounts of their fellow patrolmen.

Inside the others waited, forming a half-circle around a hideously ugly, gnome-like creature who conversed with himself in a sluggish tongue.

As they were in the heart of the Five Points, it would not do well to be overheard, so Alvord picked up the door, which had been knocked down, and set it back in place. It was a rather heavy piece of wood but he showed little sign of strain.

"Well then. How is our diminutive friend here doing?"

"Oiled to the gills, as usual," snorted an officer named Cartwright.

"Is that so, Sleeth? Do mine eyes deceive me, or are you in fact soused?"

The man called Sleeth sat in a chair against the wall, regarding Alvord with bleary, laughably unfocused eyes. When he spoke, it was with the very thickest of Dublin accents.

"Oh do shut yer accurs'd bone-box, yeh great lummox! I got a bunch o' fives a'waiting for ye right here, ye grim-faced blaggard!" Sleeth held up a feeble fist as he slurred his way through his sentences.

At the moment, Alvord had neither the time nor the patience for humor.

"Was ever there a threat so empty, Seamus? I must say, I expected a warmer welcome than that, old friend."

"I got your warm welcome right 'ere, laddy," boasted the besotted Irishman, grabbing his crotch.

He looked around expectantly, seeking approval in the form of laughter. He found none.

"For a useless drunkard, you've certainly got some dash-fire in you, Seamus. I have you here for one reason—information. I am going to ask a few quick questions and you will oblige me by answering them honestly and to the best of your ability. Savvy?"

"Look at me, pissed out o' me bleedin' tree and poor as Job's turkey and you come in demandin' information. Bold, laddy, bold as brass, 'tis. If'n I had me youth I'd put these maulies to work on yeh." Sleeth flailed one of his tiny fists in the direction of Alvord (who stood several feet away), accomplishing nothing but toppling out of his chair in the process.

Alvord look up as if seeking patience from above. There was no time for this ossified moron's blathering, yet the situation required delicate handling. "Look, Seamus, help me out and there'll be a decent reward in it for you. What say you?"

Hodgins hauled Sleeth off the floor and propped him back up in his chair. "Reward, ye say. I could do with a reward. Life can be awful tough for a misunderstood prodigy like meself. Too true, too true. What's with the helmets, by the way? Are ye out playing dress-up tonight? Rawny, you fellas remind me o' them lispy types you find down by the-"

So much for the delicate handling of this situation. Opting for another tactic, Alvord wrenched the little man out of his seat with one hand and smashed him into the wall. Hard. Outside, a horse stomped and whinnied its surprise.

"One more remark like that and the 'misunderstood prodigy' is no more. Where are the Roach Guards?"

Sleeth gulped loudly and seemed to sober up on the spot. "Alvord, ye know I cannot say. They'll torture me like bleedin' redskins, ye know they will!"

"I can promise your pathetic Irish ass protection and a bottle of Beefeater if you cooperate. If not, I assure you that death will seem a mercy compared to your life. Patrolman O'Farrell is dead and we've a score to settle with the Roach Guards." Alvord's gray eyes bored holes into Sleeth's.

Sleeth frowned and spoke in a disbelieving tone. "Not Andrew O'Farrell? Young Irish kid that patrolled here sometimes?"

"Yes. A cowardly reprisal has left him dead, body mangled, and the Roach Guards are to blame."

"A damn shame, 'tis. What a foine young gentleman 'e was. Alright, fer 'im I'll tell ye what I know. Jus' let me down." Alvord instantly obliged him and Sleeth slid down the wall and onto his ass.

"Quickly now."

Sleeth looked around the room, as if to make sure a Roach Guard wasn't among them eavesdropping.

"See, I was at the pub-"

"No surprises there," Cartwright cut in disdainfully.

"...and I did happen to overhear some interestin' discourse. This was early evenin', few nights past, mind you. Two fellas were talkin', real quiet like, but I did manage, inadvertently o' course, to hear what they said. Said tha' the Roach Guards needed a place to lay low late this night, after tending to some unspecified business. So t'other feller, older Bowery gent by the look of 'im, says tha' he knew of a place in the Bowery, on Mott Street, west o' the Bowery Theatre. Now it was odd that this Bowery guy was in the Points at all, so I listened real close t'what he said. The building he suggested was some kinda old slaughterhouse. Said he'd be only too happy to help out, 'cause 'e believed in what they were doin', said both communities would benefit from whatever was to go down. Truth be told, there's been talk of them Roach Guards doin' something big all week. Had I known it was offing O'Farrell, I'd of told ye, Rawn, believe me. That's all I know. Honest."

Alvord frowned, confused. The Bowery was home to nativist gangs that the Irish often did battle with. As a bastion of English and Dutch blood, the Bowery was the last place an Irish gang wanted to be found at night. Although if a Bowery higher-up had negotiated with the Irish, then what safer a place to hide from the law than in the very heart of enemy territory?

"I think I know where he's talking about," offered Hodgins. "Me'n Schwarz went up that way once to help out with a fire."

"Good," Alvord grunted. "Prepare to ride."

"Oh, and Seamus?" he said, tone mild.

"Yeah, Rawn, what now?" asked the drunkard sourly.

Alvord lashed out with a stiff right hook, striking the tiny informant in the gut. "Next time you give me lip I will cut out your tongue with my dullest blade. And if you just sent us into a trap, pray that Death finds you before I do. *Pray.*"

The Irishman panted on the ground, eyes wide.

"Come by tomorrow and retrieve your reward, it'll be waiting."

It took barely five minutes of breakneck riding to reach The Bowery, located at is was just north and east of the Five Points. They were now on Mott Street, outside a large old building that had been a slaughterhouse in times past.

This part of the city was far cry from respectable, but a definite upgrade from the Five Points nevertheless. Most of the roads were of crushed stone, streets were wider, and the buildings of more solid construction. Cheap dancehalls, dime museums, billiard salons, and rowdy theatres that hosted plays, animal performances, and boxing matches dominated the Bowery.

Working-class New York was glorified here; the aristocracy was lampooned daily and the virtues of middle-class America loudly extolled. The affluent made sure to give the Bowery a wide berth come nightfall.

Just across the street was a small theatre that had erected cheap wooden pillars in the Greek style as a mocking nod to high culture. Though it was late, music and other sounds of frivolity met the ears of the assembled officers.

For the patrolmen, this was not to be a night of merriment or lightheartedness. Dark deeds awaited them in that decaying slaughterhouse.

Murdock and Morris materialized out of the tenebrous night and quickly sought out Alvord.

"Captain Rawn," reported Murdock, "they're in there, all right. Second level of the building is just one big room; all the walls are torn down. So they've holed up in there, a little over twenty of them, doing some drinking and gambling, by the looks of it. Some wounded among them. Plenty of light from a couple of lamps, and no sentries posted from what we saw."

"Huh, complacent Irish swine," snorted Cartwright. Hodgins visibly bristled at the insult to his race, but offered no reply.

"Where did you observe this from?"

"We listened first for sound, then pinpointed its origin. We then took a staircase up the north side of the building and took a look through a window." Morris explained.

"Points of entry?"

"Three. One staircase leading up from the lower level, and two staircases leading up the north and south sides of the building that will take you to the room."

"Anywhere that they can escape to?"

One corner of Murdock's mouth curled into a vicious smile. "The windows, perhaps. But that's a solid twenty-five foot drop on a building like this. If they want to get out any other way, they'll have us to get by."

Alvord breathed deeply. It was getting difficult to concentrate now that vengeance was so close at hand. But he had to focus, for as much as he longed to lose himself to rage, the leading of his men was a vital matter. As if to serve as a reminder of that, one of them chose that moment to bend over and quietly expel his stomach contents. It was time to act, lest nerves overtake the men's anger.

"Turner, take four with you and go in from the first floor. Move with caution. Schwarz, take another four and go up the staircase on the south side. Hodgins, Cartwright, and Bishop, you're with me. We'll go up the northern flight of stairs. Get into positions from which you can quickly strike, but *do not act* until you hear me fire this." He patted the Hawken tucked into his belt. "Those of you with pistols, make damn sure that if you fire you are not endangering the life of a comrade. Hit hard, hit fast, and leave none standing. I want a historic body count, gentlemen."

He gave them all a stiff nod before heading towards the north side of the building. It was a sizable structure built with both stone and wood, dwarfing all nearby buildings. The stone stairs were just ahead, so Alvord and his men stole silently towards them, keeping close to the wall. Some moonlight now filtered through the clouds, but it was still dark enough that the officers were barely visible as they moved.

Mounting the stairs, Alvord drew and cocked the Hawken pistol, the smooth walnut of its handle filling his hand nicely. His boots made nary a sound on the steps as he slowly made his way towards the rough voices above. A lamp threw a faint glow out of the nearest window, so he dropped down and crawled past it. He could hear Hodgin's rapid breathing behind him, so he turned and issued a whispered order.

"Steady, Hodgins. Deep, quiet breaths. Try not to tense up."

The young man's face was set in a game grimace, but he did not quite have his emotions under rein. Alvord remembered well his first large-scale engagement, that knot in the gut that did not pass until battle had been joined, the nearly paralyzing apprehension. The Irish lad would learn and eventually overcome his nerves, just as he had.

Laughter from above met his ears, but it did not get to him at this point. It only added fuel to the fire that raged within, contained for now by his gradually faltering self-control.

There was a door at the top of the flight, so he stopped at it and signaled for his men to halt. Taking a peek through the window to his right, he saw that the Roach Guards were mostly clustered on the far side of the room, which was a large one. He cracked open the door and was just about to ease himself inside when he heard two voices nearby. Stepping back, he left the door ajar and strained to hear what was being said.

Chapter 4

"**Well,** tha' takes care o' tha'," declared a smug voice that Alvord instantly recognized as Thomas McClintock's. Not a logical choice in a new leader, by his reckoning. McClintock was hotheaded, ignorant, and utterly heedless of consequence.

Hence the impending slaughter that awaited him.

"And we didn't make out too badly, either. Only two dead and a couple o' wounded. Could've been a lot worse, ye know."

"Yeah, but some of t'other boys are real mangled, Thomas. Lifelong injuries, they'll have. You mark my words."

Alvord did not know who spoke those words, and didn't much care. He only let them talk now so that he might ascertain exactly how O'Farrell's death had played out. The voices moved away a bit, so he eased the door open some more. Lurking in the shadows, he caressed the Hawken and listened, though every fiber in his body called upon him to attack.

"Yeh shoulda come with us, yeh great puss. You coulda played a role! Feels nice to stick one to the coppers fer a change, I tell yeh! One less bloody turncoat Irishman walkin' the streets arresting 'is own kith and kin. Put up a decent fight, did O'Farrell, but we left 'im gaggin' on 'is own blood all the same. And Amen to tha'. Look ye here, I even got myself a nice little trophy outta the whole affair." A haughtily pointed finger indicated the burnished copper badge pinned to his chest, the one that Patrolman Andrew O'Farrell had once worn with such pride.

Alvord's head cocked to the side. So it seemed that not all of the Roach Guards were directly involved in O'Farrell's death. Oh well. They were all guilty of manifold, heinous crimes, yet the corrupt nature of New York's justice system allowed for their being put back out on the streets time and time again. But after tonight, none of them would ever darken the streets of his city again. He would personally see to that.

"Listen, robbin' rich folk and rollin' sailors and killing Bowery B'Hoys is one thing," insisted the other man. "But Lord a'mercy, Thomas, why'd you have to go an' kill a patrolman, huh? And in this of all wards? Rawn's bleedin' ward? What'll become of us? There's a small army of 'em and they're probably lookin' fer us right now, and they got clubs an' slungshots an' swords—"

"And pistols, too," interjected Alvord quietly, stepping out of the shadows and discharging his own into McClintock's face.

The Hawken reported with a boom like a thunderclap, and McClintock's head vanished amidst a spray of blood, brains, and bone. The acrid smell of gunpowder filled Alvord's nostrils, while a tingling warmth spread from his heart to the rest of his body. His vision sharpened, his breathing grew rapid.

Immediately following the report of the Hawken, a wild shout went up as his patrolmen spilled into the room of shocked Roach Guards, some wielding truncheons, others swinging blackjacks and slungshots. A few shots rang out as officers fired pistols at the gang members, who scrambled for their weapons and cover. The element of surprise accounted for a good many enemy deaths before the battle had even begun in earnest.

Alvord threw his still-smoking pistol at the nearest Irishman before drawing his sword and sweeping toward the main group of Guards. It was clear that the pack mentality was strong among them, for none knew how to act without instruction. For a moment they hesitated together in the center of the room, a snake without a head. But a hasty glance around told them that escape was not a viable option, and when that was established they charged as one with a savage cry of their own.

A snarling blond man swung an axe at Alvord, who caught the blow on his sword edge and swept it aside with contemptuous ease.

With a deft flick of the wrist, he brought the sturdy blade around and sank it into his opponent's neck. The sharp steel bit deeply, scraping on vertebrae as it was dragged downwards to unleash a torrent of lifeblood.

It was a heavy cavalry sword that Alvord carried, a model designed in England in 1796 that had seen much action during the Napoleonic Wars. The thick blade terminated in what was called a hatchet point, a strongly reinforced tip that brought balance to the weapon and inflicted horrific wounds. Often decried as a cumbersome blade, the heavy saber was nevertheless a fearsome slashing weapon in the right hands, and Alvord's hands were such.ABlvord's hands were such. Trained in the art by an old German swordmaster, his control of the slightly curved sword was exceptional.

He punched the next comer in the mouth with the sword's knuckle-guard, flooring the man in a spray of blood and teeth whilst barely losing a step. The fetid stench of the gangster's unwashed body assaulted his nostrils.

Another challenger came from his left, but was intercepted by Hodgins and Cartwright, who went high-low and brought the man crashing down. Soon their truncheons made meaty thuds as they pummeled his body with their metal-tipped truncheons.

Billhook upraised, a giant of an Irishman rushed him. Alvord made as if to block the wild overhand slash, but then retracted his weapon just before it made contact, at the same time taking a quick sidestep to the left. The man's curved blade met only air; as he stumbled past Alvord performed a neat backhanded swing that connected with the back of the gangster's head, and he smiled grimly as he did so. Some of the gangsters had taken a moment to slip on their padded hats but the majority fought without the benefit of that armor, his latest victim among them.

The inferno raged uncontrollably within Alvord, no longer impeded by his will. There was an intoxicating quality to it, of which he drank deeply.

The realization that Death might seek him out was present somewhere in the back of his mind, but he was not overly concerned. When he was a younger man, when he had a family to worry about, that fear would have had a strong hold on him. Yet now, thirty-six and alone, the fear of death found in him not a single foothold. These Irish hoodlums in blue-striped pants and filthy shirts were his inferiors, anyway. He was always a little faster, stronger, more coordinated and skilled than the best of them.

And if Death did single him out on this night, then so be it. The way Fate had been cruelly toying with him these last few years, death might not be a bad alternative to life.

All around him Roach Guards were being cut down by Municipal Police officers, who might have been initially outnumbered but like Alvord were fueled by rage at the loss of a brother. It seemed as if the officers were untouchable, while gang members fell like wheat before the scythe.

Across the room, Schwarz feinted high and went low with his club, striking his opponent on the outside of the knee. A high-pitched shriek rewarded this effort, but even as he landed an overhand blow to the man's collarbone it was clear that trouble was headed his way.

Three Roach Guards had just bowled over an officer and now fanned out, trapping Schwarz in a corner of the room. The rugged German juked right, as if to make an escape, but then stepped right towards the pursuing men, thrusting his truncheon like a rapier. Caught off guard and slightly off-balance from the sudden change in direction, one advancing man caught the club in the hollow where the chest meets the throat. He went down gurgling but the other two rushed in, knives upraised. Just before they reached Schwarz, a crimson sword appeared in one attacker's stomach with a squelch and a club demolished the skull of the other. The two went down to reveal Alvord and Hodgins, who quickly removed their weapons from the carcasses of their victims.

Hodgins's face was ashen and grim as he went about his task, but Alvord's was twisted into a bitter sneer. An unsettling gleam shone brightly in his gray eyes.

"Close call, eh, Schwarz?"

Most of the gang had been killed or incapacitated by this time, though some still fought on despite the hopelessness of their situation. Now multiple officers were facing off against individual Roach Guards, whose numbers had dwindled into single digits. In fact, shortly after aiding Schwarz, Alvord observed that only one enemy remained.

A wounded Irishman had backed himself into a corner and was lashing out at all comers with a nail-studded club, shrieking madly all the while. None seemed too keen on engaging the man, who had worked himself into a right old frenzy. Already he had injured one officer and knocked the helmet off another.

Alvord called for his men to back away as he positioned

himself in front of the gangster. As the man watched him warily, Alvord slipped off his leather helmet and tossed it to the ground. Sheathing his sword, he spread his weaponless hands mockingly.

A strangled scream tore from the Irishman's throat, heavy-laden with animalistic fury. He rushed the police captain, whose sinister smile only widened. The club streaked towards his face but found only air, for Alvord had neatly slipped under the weapon. Fluidly, he came up from the slip to deliver a thunderous left hook to the man's jaw, putting all of his two hundred and thirty-five pounds into it. The cracking of bone was audible to all present. Bending over, he hauled the Irishman up from the floor by the belt and the shirt collar. Breaking into a trot, he headed for the closest wall, and as he neared it hurled the limp body headlong into the bricks like a ragdoll. The Roach Guard's neck bent at an unnatural angle with a resounding snap before his body slumped to the ground

And with that, vengeance had been wreaked.

Chest heaving from exertion and anger, Alvord checked for signs of death and injury in his own ranks. Turner had an awful slash across the length of his forehead while a man named Crane gingerly cradled his bleeding left arm. Behind them Cartwright helped a cursing Murdock off the floor, but amazingly enough that seemed to be the extent of it. True, many of the men sported rising bruises or small cuts, but nothing of real consequence. Victory without price was an uncommon thing, so Alvord took a moment to silently thank the Almighty for his mercy.

"Crane, how's the arm?" he inquired.

"Rightly busted, feels like. Bastard got me with that spiked club. Got some real deep punctures too."

"Morris, wrap his wounds and make up a sling for him. Turner, all well with you?"

Turner smirked as he wiped blood from his face, answering between pants. "A lot better for me then it is for them, I'll wager," he said, indicating the bodies littering the ground.

"And that just leaves you, Murdock."

"Fine, fine, just got tapped on the chin and took a brief nap." His lips bled freely but this did not seem to bother him.

"Good." Alvord's chest swelled with emotion. Never had

he felt such pride in these men, who had proven themselves men in the truest sense of the word. "Well done, lads, well done. Now we ride to City Hall, collect Andrew's body, and see Matsell. But first, check every body, silence any who survived."

Plenty of whimpers and groans from the injured filled the room, causing the men to exchange shocked looks. At least half of the gang still drew breath, if but barely. Several of them implored Christ for aid and mercy, resulting in increased hesitation on the part of the officers. Killing in a pitched battle was one thing, but dispatching wounded men?

Their apprehension did not escape their captain's notice. Alvord's jaw clenched tightly. Moral analysis had no place in this rotting slaughterhouse; they needed to report to Matsell before all Hell broke loose at City Hall.

"Get to it and get to it quick," Alvord ordered, his voice cracking like a whip. "Bear in mind that these are the very swine who brutally attacked and murdered a comrade of ours not an hour ago. I don't want it to be one of you or myself next time. Were fortunes reversed, they would show you no such mercy."

He stared at his patrolmen, few of whom could meet his eyes. He spoke in a voice at once quiet and firm.

"It is up to men like us to right the wrongs of this world, and sometimes that requires unpleasant duties. Take our kind out of the equation and evil reigns unopposed. If you cannot bring yourselves to help me, then by the Eternal I will do it myself."

Marching over to a Roach Guard who was painfully crawling away from the officers, Alvord drew his sword and plunged it into the man's heart without breaking stride.

Conscious makes cowards of us all, a doubt-stricken Hamlet had lamented.

Well, Alvord thought to himself, *not me, not when I know that I'm in the right.*

Kicking over another body, he viciously stomped on the gangster's throat as soon as he detected signs of life.

About half his men fanned out to tend to the grim business, checking bodies and finishing the job when necessary. The other half, Turner and Hodgins among them, stood by and listened stonily as the frantic shrieks and pleas of the living gradually gave way to the silence of the dead.

Suddenly, a fallen Roach Guard leapt up and made a beeline towards the nearest window. Alvord swiftly drew his club with his left hand and hurled it at the man, missing by an embarrassing margin. The Irishman dove out the window with impressive grace as Alvord fiercely cursed his own inaccuracy.

"After him!" But Murdock and Morris were already in hot pursuit.

"Alright, we are done here- everyone else out too."

Before leaving, he walked over to McClintock's virtually decapitated body. Ripping O'Farrell's badge off the bastard's chest, he bitterly spat on his despised enemy. This was no honorable man that he had slain; there were plenty of animals with a better sense of dignity. As far as he was concerned, men like this weren't men at all but rather empty shells of humanity, devoid of the intellect and virtue that distinguished man from beast. Truly, this was the basest form of human life; if human it could be labeled.

The Hawken and poorly-cast truncheon he collected, taking a moment to right and extinguish a fallen lamp lest it start a fire.

His men gone, Alvord took a moment to survey the destruction wrought by their raid. Every mangled Roach Guard body told a tale of savage vengeance. Even if this night never graced the pages of history, it was not something that he'd soon forget. A statement had been made on this ground that all criminals would do well to remember.

Making his way to the staircase he had entered by, a soft noise caught his attention. Pretending that he hadn't heard anything, Alvord kept his course. Right before he reached the door, he dashed into the corner the noise had issued from. His hands closed upon a homespun shirt that tore when he yanked its owner out of the shadows.

"Whoa! Easy, yer Honor! I'd no part in it, ye've got me word!" The speaker was naught but a boy, a scared, whey-faced redhead who could have been no older than thirteen.

"I've dealt with killers younger than you, boy."

"Christ's wounds, I swear to ye I didn't do it!" he claimed in a squeaky voice that had not yet reached maturity.

"Blaspheme again and you end up as your compatriots," Alvord promised coldly, indicating the slain Roach Guards with a jerk of his head.

"Alright, alright, sorry. But I promise ye, I wasn't with 'em when they did it, ye've got me word. I ain't even a member yet, I just tag along sometimes... honest, ye've got to believe me."

"If I didn't believe you, *runt*, you'd have already joined your countrymen at Hell's Gate. Did you see it happen?"

"No."

Alvord believed him; maybe the kid just had an honest face, but he could detect no lie there. "You're coming with me nonetheless."

The boy's eyes widened. "You're takin' me in? What for, I told you I ain't done a blessed thing!"

"Habitual rascality. Let's go."

With the Irish lad in tow, he started down the steps. While he descended the staircase he counted the men assembled below. Upon reaching twenty, he drew his bloodied sword. He and his men numbered only fourteen. A sizable crowd of men waited below, but he could not yet determine if his patrolmen were among them. The Bowery, although a safer place for patrolmen than the Five Points, was no place to let one's guard down.

When his eyes adjusted to the dim light a wave of relief washed over him, for among rough-looking Bowery B'Hoys were the officers of the Sixth Ward. He quickly sheathed his sword and positioned himself in front of his young Irish captive.

Two fellows stood in front of the rest, holding the escaped Roach Guard on his knees with their knives at his throat.

The bobbies of London could often count on (and also demand) help from bystanders while on the beat, but this was far more unusual in America, where police were often viewed with mixed emotions by the public.

Odd it was, so cherished all the more.

"Will Poole. As I live and breathe!" Alvord extended his hand to the man on his left, William Poole. A local butcher-cum-gangster, Poole sported the typical Bowery "soap locks" hairstyle- long, greased curls that poured onto his shoulders and back. Although a shady character, he was a valuable ally of the Sixth Ward when it came to dealing with Irish gangs.

"Fetching helmet there, Rawn, if I may. Lookie what we found." He grabbed the Roach Guard roughly by his hair. "This filthy insect was scurrying about. We thought it best to crush it beneath our heel before we had a blasted infestation on our hands, but then we ran into your boys here and thought we'd reserve that pleasure for you."

Noting the copious amount of blood covering the clothing of the patrolmen, Poole grinned sadistically as he spoke.

"Yeah, didn't get too far, now did ya?" sneered Tom Hyer, a renowned boxer and leading brawler for the Bowery B'Hoys. He was the other man holding the luckless Irishman down, his trademark stovepipe hat in evidence.

"Gave him a tap that put 'is lights out, Rawn. Fine right hand, wish you could've seen it. A real sockdolager."

Alvord had trained and sparred with the burly Hyer in the past and knew what power the man could generate. The Roach Guard's nose was so much mush on his face.

"I'll use my imagination, Tom."

"What's his crime?" Poole inquired curiously.

Knowing that Poole couldn't give a damn about the death of an Irish officer, he ad-libbed.

"Public mopery with the intent to gawk."

A wave of laughter swept through the Bowery B'Hoys.

Hyer regarded the blood-spattered police captain with raised eyebrows. "Uh-huh."

"Well, sounds punishable by death to me," Poole exclaimed, smile broadening.

The surviving Roach Guard began pleading pathetically with Alvord, voice thick from his busted nose.

"Please mister, have mercy, take me outta here! I'm sorry about what happened to O'Farrell! Take me to The Tombs, anywhere! You heard 'em, they'll kill me, there's no way around it, sir! Please don't leave me with 'em!"

Alvord slowly bent to a knee in front of the sputtering Roach Guard. Here was a man that had participated in the murder of a close friend of his barely an hour ago.

"What fate do you think awaits if you fall into my hands, you bastard whoreson? Thank God above that you fell into their hands. Tell the Devil Rawn sent you, Irishman."

He rose lithely. "All yours, boys. Enjoy."

The Irishman's pitiable wail was lost amidst the hearty cheers of the nativists.

"I appreciate the help, Will. See you around. Gents," Alvord said, giving the other Bowery B'Hoys a wave.

"A rope, lads, fetch me a rope!" roared a jubilant Poole above the tumult.

A quick jerk of the head brought Alvord's men to his side.

"To City Hall, now. Time to face the music, boys," he said, leading the way to their waiting horses.

Where Chambers met Church Street stood the carriage containing the body of Andrew O'Farrell. The man from Fifth Avenue had kept his word, and waited a block from City Hall for Captain Rawn to rendezvous with him. It had been over an hour, and the fellow was growing understandably antsy. Once already a roving patrol of officers had passed by, no doubt looking for their fallen comrade or the men who had slain him.

Thankfully, they had given him a once-over and left it at that. Which was just fine and dandy with him. The last thing he needed was for the officers to find what was lying on the back seat of his personal carriage. That'd be a tough one to explain.

A faint yet unmistakable noise from the north caught his ear, the repetitious clatter of horseshoes upon cobblestones. Gradually the noise increased in volume until the patrolmen of the Sixth Ward charged into view.

At the forefront, on the back of a long-legged buckskin, was the officer who had identified himself as Captain Alvord Rawn. An unusual sight it was, a platoon of blood-spattered patrolmen galloping down Church Street right towards him. Thank God he knew these men, for intimidating strangers they would surely make.

The stern-looking captain swung off his horse and approached the carriage.

"I thank you for your assistance and cooperation, sir. I'd offer some monetary reward if I thought it necessary, but I daresay that a Fifth Avenue resident's chamber pots are worth more than I could possibly offer. Perhaps there is something else—"

The man grinned sheepishly. "No, no, you needn't do anything for me. It was the least I could do."

For an instant Alvord looked weary, distant, and quite older than his thirty-six years. "Perhaps there is hope for this city after all, then. We'll take Andrew's body and you can be on your way, sir."

He directed some of his men to retrieve it. "If ever you have need of our assistance, don't hesitate to drop by. If I could just get your name...?"

"Jonah Starbuck, Captain."

"Well, Jonah Starbuck, thanks again and fare thee well."

"I am genuinely sorry for your loss, gentlemen," said Starbuck to the officers before hopping into his carriage and signaling his driver to move. Horses whinnying, the carriage quickly vanished into the night.

"Give me a minute, lads," Alvord requested, dragging the young would-be Roach Guard over to the side.

"Listen," the boy started desperately.

"You listen to me, boy," interrupted Alvord, tone indicating that he would brook no interruptions. "I will make it quick and then you can be on your merry way. Where James meets Water Street is a shipyard. The man who runs it is named Marshall Tasker. Tell him that I sent you; my name is Alvord Rawn."

The boy's eyes widened at the name.

"Last I heard Tasker was looking for workers, even Irish ones. I suggest you go there tomorrow."

The redhead stared at him strangely. "You're an odd one, if ye'll forgive me sayin', sir. Ye ruthlessly kill off me entire gang like some avenging angel, then ye go an' direct me to a job? Why?"

Alvord's stared off into the shadows. "Because if ever your benighted race is to lift itself up from its miserable station in this country, honest work will be the appointed means. Not crime and shiftlessness. You're young— you deserve a chance."

"Well... I ah, I thank ye for that, Mr. Rawn. Yeah, maybe I'll go down to Water Street tomorra, then."

"Good. Then away with you, runt."

The boy turned to leave, but before he got too far Alvord hailed him.

"But just so you know, if ever I find you in the midst of a gang or committing a crime, I will come down on you with staggering finality."

Lips aquiver, the Irish lad attempted to reply, but the Police Captain's voice had turned to ice the blood in his veins. Quickly spinning away, he ran off into the night.

Slipping off his greatcoat, Alvord called over to his men,

"Some of you take off your coats or sweaters to tie together for a makeshift stretcher. Who will help me bear him?"

Hodgins, Morris, and Bishop came forward. Alvord could see Hodgins's devastated expression as he stared at O'Farrell's wasted, battered face. He knew that Hodgins would take this one hard. They had been close, he knew, two young Irish patrolmen on a platoon dominated by natives. That alone had forged a unique camaraderie between them

"Schwarz, once we get to City Hall, take some men from the Second Platoon and bring Grammery his horses back."

Like unofficial pallbearers, the four lifted the body of their fallen brother and started forward. City Hall was one block to the east, a distance that they covered in no time at all.

Alvord could see frantic scurrying ahead of them, which meant that the word of O'Farrell's death was indeed out. His own mobilization and subsequent assault on the Roach Guards had been completely unauthorized, so he was bound to face some censure and perhaps even punishment from his superiors. Despite this realization, it dawned on him that he didn't much care. The same sense of detachment that had taken hold of him after the deaths of his wife and children governed his emotions even now, when apprehension and fear of consequence should have held sway.

It was an unsettling revelation.

Soon enough they were mounting the steps of City Hall, a stately building that gracefully combined French Renaissance and Georgian architectural styles. Its façade boasted numerous pilasters and columns hewn from high quality Massachusetts marble. The potential flamboyance of the French style was tempered by the majestic accents of the English. City Hall was a structure that was downright inspirational in its architectural success; even in the inky darkness the stark white of its stone shone forth.

Passing underneath a soaring portico supported by rows of Doric columns, the patrolmen were met by a small crowd of shouting politicians and fellow patrolmen. Deaf to all the oaths, exclamations, and questions that were being flung around, Alvord led his platoon straight through the swarm and towards the silent man standing by the large, open doors of the building.

Chief of Police George Matsell, clad in a form-fitting frock coat of black felt, wordlessly helped them bear O'Farrell's body into City Hall. They came to a rest in the middle of the entrance hall, laying the dead Irishman's body on the marble floor. The politicians and other patrolmen mutely huddled around the fallen officer, with mingled shock, horror, and sorrow stamped upon their features.

Matsell, a short, portly, but sturdy man, stared down at O'Farrell's ravaged body with eyes sporting dark, saggy circles under them. Down his cheek a single tear ran, spilling onto his brown beard, but no other sign of emotion was visible.

He looked around at the people crowding the entrance hall. "I ask that all non-law enforcement personnel withdraw to give us a moment alone."

Quiet but authoritative, his order was dutifully followed.

Eyeing the blood-spattered (or in Alvord's case, blood-covered) clothing of the Sixth Ward's First Platoon, Matsell shook his head.

"I judge by your appearances and spontaneous absence that Andrew's death has been avenged?"

"Yes," Alvord affirmed.

"Did you incur any casualties of your own?"

"No deaths, a few injuries. Nothing life-threatening."

Matsell closed his expressive blue eyes and heaved a sigh that might have taken years off his life. "Good, good. But you and I need to speak, Alvord. My office, right now, I'd say. You have some serious explaining to do, sonny."

The Chief called everyone sonny, even Alvord, who was only a few months his junior and most definitely not a "sonny."

"You head down to my office, then, and I'll make arrangements for Andrew's body. As for the rest of you, it's back to the stationhouse at once. The Second Platoon is no doubt dying to hear of what happened."

"And no excessive drinking, either." He yelled after them as they departed. "There have been enough problems for one night..." he added, voice trailing off as he spoke so only he and Alvord heard the words.

Alvord shook his head. What man wouldn't drown his sorrows after such a night as this? Especially his own men, who had just emerged victorious from a fierce battle, avenging the murder of a dear friend and comrade. Matsell was always quick to lock up folks for inebriety, and loved telling others to watch their drinking, when he himself indulged aplenty in quality wine. The pot calling the kettle black, that was.

Before leaving, the Chief bent down and laid a gentle hand on O'Farrell's head. "Rest easy, boy. See you in greener pastures, one day."

Another tear rolled down his round face and off his bulbous nose, and Alvord felt himself getting a bit choked up too. Tears welled up in his eyes but he held them back, rectangular jaw firmly clenched, unwilling to display any sign of frailty. But this newfound sorrow was refreshing; it served as proof that he could still feet something other than hatred, rage...

Matsell led the way to his office, which was located in a basement room of City Hall. The basement was an unusual site for the Chief's office, but was currently the only available space for it. Unlike the Spartan stationhouse, this room was sumptuously furnished. Nail-studded leather chairs were complimented by a large desk of cherry and butternut wood, upon which sat several tall stacks of papers, a pewter water pitcher, and a dainty cup full of coffee. The walls were flush with small landscape paintings by Asher B. Durand, Thomas Cole, and Thomas Doughty, each work hanging in a gilt frame.

Seating himself in the chair behind his desk, Matsell put his head in his hands as he heaved another wearied sigh.

He locked eyes with Alvord before saying, "Please understand that I take no pleasure, none at all, in what I'm about to tell you, Alvord."

Alvord arched his dark eyebrows quizzically. This couldn't be good.

Chapter 5

"**Times** are fast changing, Alvord," Matsell explained tiredly. "I am not saying whether it is for better or for worse, but times *are* changing. Gone are the days when street-corner justice was accepted as a suitable mode of law enforcement. Your actions tonight were both hasty and outdated, and men in high places, myself included, simply cannot abide it. It is no longer conventional for a police captain to conduct a full-scale assault on a gang without the consent of his chief, however much you wish it were so."

"How did you know it was a gang, and a full scale assault?"

Matsell gave something of a snort. "A simple enough deduction, really. You and your men are covered in blood, and several of them have sustained significant injuries. Ergo, it must have been a large number of men you engaged, so a gang is the logical guess."

Alvord nodded, impressed.

"But as I was saying, Alvord, your actions warrant punishment. You know that you should have come to me before embarking on a mission of such magnitude."

"Let's be realistic, George, shall we?" Alvord cut him off as diplomatically as he could when the Chief went to take a breath. "You know full well that if I had come up here with the news of O'Farrell's murder on my lips that all of City Hall would have erupted into full-fledged pandemonium. Politicians of this age are not like the politicians of old, men who could momentarily put aside the importance of votes when it came to pressing matters—like avenging the death a city guardian, for example. So had I broken the news to you then, the ensuing political squabble would have ruined—"

"You presume to know too much, sonny. Think about it. You know as well as I that there were but a few politicians left in here two hours ago, just as you *damn* well know that I would have let you off the tether so that Andrew's death might be avenged. I'd have joined you, for Christ's sake!"

He did have a point, Alvord reasoned. It had been around twelve-thirty when the old German woman sought him out, so few politicians, be they Whigs or Democrats, would have been left in City Hall. And as for Matsell accompanying them on the raid, perhaps the Chief would have ridden at his side after all. But time had seemed so precious, the matter of settling the score so pressing...

Alvord had always liked Matsell, a short, round-faced man of solid character and tireless work ethic. A former justice of the peace, he had been elected to the position of Chief by Mayor William Havemeyer in 1845, when the Municipal Police Department had first been formed. Even if he was a bit sanctimonious at times, Matsell made up for it by being an active leader of men, something that Alvord heartily approved of. During the hellish fire of 1845 that consumed much of Lower Broadway, Matsell had personally directed the firefighting operations, competently commanding both his Municipal police officers and disparate elements of ragtag fire departments.

He had quickly earned the respect of both his men and City Hall, and from his humble basement office organized and directed the policing of all fifteen wards of Manhattan.

Adopting an even milder tone, Alvord held up his hands in placatory fashion. "It was not my wish to exclude you, George, or to skirt your authority. I... well, I was thunderstruck by the news, and after hearing what the witness said I figured that we still stood a chance at finding the Roach Guards and exacting revenge."

"Roach Guards, eh? Perturbed over the recent incarceration of Larry Flanagan, I presume?"

"Perturbed is putting it mildly. They waylaid O'Farrell as soon as he strayed from Broadway, attacked him *en masse,* and left him to bleed out on the cobblestones. Thomas McClintock led them."

Matsell reached into a draw and pulled out a cloth. Dipping it into a pitcher of water behind his desk, he tossed it to Alvord.

"So is that whose blood is marring your features?"

Alvord wiped his face, removing a surprising amount of blood. "Doubtful. I decapitated him with a Hawken from five yards out. This blood is from those I took with the sword."

"What became of the gang?"

"Killed to a man," Alvord promptly replied.

Matsell frowned. "No prisoners? You showed no mercy at all, then?"

Alvord's face instantly darkened. "When dealing with such swine, one's sense of mercy becomes somewhat blunted."

Shaking his head gravely and failing to suppress a shiver, Matsell rose from his seat. "I need to speak with your men and get their version of the story. Stay here, I'll return within half an hour."

Danger creeping into his tone, Alvord asked, "My own version is insufficient to satisfy your curiosity?"

Matsell coolly met his glare. "There was a time, Alvord, when I wouldn't have questioned anything you said, no matter how outlandish it might have sounded. But you've changed, man. I need the unadulterated truth, and I need to know what your men think of the events that have transpired. At the caution of repeating myself, I'll be back within half an hour."

He closed the door gently behind him and left Alvord sitting by his lonesome.

Alvord sat there fuming. If there was one thing he detested, it was being ordered around by men who were his physical and moral inferiors and George Matsell, redeemable qualities notwithstanding, was such.

A sigh escaped his lips. Maybe it was time to pursue private detective work as a sole means of income.

He had been involved in New York law enforcement for fourteen years now, and had been both a watchmen and marshal, or detective, before 1845 when the Municipal Police Department had been created. Truth be told, he had been a big part of the shift in attitude that both criminals and the public harbored towards the old nightwatch. Whereas once law enforcement in Manhattan had been a joke, after he had a year on the job people began developing a healthy respect for it. Alvord and several other like-minded men had forged a new, tough reputation for New York City's watchmen. That was before the establishment of the Municipal Police Department, before justice became impeded by innumerable regulations.

Yes, he had put fourteen hard years into this occupation, while Matsell had been a Chief for a paltry two and, worse yet, had not worked his way up from the streets.

Perhaps that was why things were not going as he expected them to. The man had no perspective, try as he may. Alvord had honestly anticipated something of a hero's welcome, having just annihilated an infamous gang whose hands were stained with the blood of a patrolman. A bit of chastisement—well that was perfectly predictable, but Matsell's open distrust was not something he had been prepared for.

How pathetic. In a proper world, he would have been hailed as a champion, a titan; the man who had successfully tracked down the Roach Guards in under an hour and had done what others didn't have the stomach for in laying them to waste.

It was just his luck that weak, indecisive men governed the modern world. As he often did, he told himself that he had been born into the wrong period of time. His skills were simply not valued in a world grown tame.

With a lithe movement he got out of his chair, comfortable though it was, and went over to the ornately engraved chestnut cabinet behind Matsell's desk. There was no lock, so he swung open the door to see what he could find.

A half-finished bottle of sherry sat wedged between numerous bottles of wine. Delicately moving wine bottles out of the way, he snatched the sherry and, pulling the cork out with his teeth, took a salubrious swig. Alvord hadn't consumed spirituous liquors in nearly two months, contenting himself with the occasional beer instead. Like Catholics, Episcopalians could choose to fast and give something up during Lent, and he had chosen booze. Lent had been over for a few days now, but he decided that perhaps abstaining from liquor might not be such a bad thing even outside of the Lenten season.

On such a night as this, however, he figured that it was fair to break his self-imposed rule.

Taking down another measure, Alvord looked over the paintings and prints that covered the walls. He was himself a fan of landscape paintings, particularly Thomas Cole's work.

The American Art Union was located just north of City Hall, and distributed a wide variety of prints in its effort to educate and enlighten Americans on the topic of art. As a member, Alvord paid five dollars a year in exchange for popular prints and art literature.

Next to a small pastoral scene that Cole had personally done was a print of "The Jolly Flat-Boat Men" by George Caleb Bingham, completed just this year. He liked Bingham's work; the man painted in a highly realistic fashion that afforded viewers a glimpse of everyday life on and around the Mississippi River. Below this work was the only other non-landscape painting, and this one really caught his eye.

It was a portrait of George Matsell in all his avuncular glory, but the style in which it had been painted was truly compelling.

Although he did have a taste for landscapes and some historical paintings, Alvord was no art critic. He found himself wishing that he possessed the vocabulary of one so he could more accurately describe this portrait.

Only Matsell's head and torso had been included in the painting, and were set within an oval that drew the viewer's eye right to him. His face and body were the only objects to hold color; the rest of the oval was of impenetrable black, while outside the oval the dull yellow of the canvas provided muted contrast. Matsell's head was tilted slightly downwards, lending a disquieting look to his face, and his eyes possessed a dark gleam that Alvord found difficult to look away from. The round blue and white orbs had been painted so that no matter where Alvord moved, they still seemed to be staring at him. The clothing, similar to the black felt frockcoat that the Chief wore now, melded into the blackness of the background while still maintaining its own individual hue. From a distance, this made his face appear to be hovering in a black void, bereft of a body. Every line of his visage conveyed a look of expectancy, as if he were waiting for some great and arcane secret to be revealed.

All in all, it had to be the strangest portrait he had ever come across. There was an air of darkness, perhaps even madness about it, subtle but detectable all the same.

Thoroughly intrigued, Alvord's eyes sought out the name of the artist.

C. Deas.

Deas. It was a man, a painter named Charles Deas that had been the focal point of the letter he'd been reading before the German woman had begun pounding on the stationhouse door. That was where he had heard the name before—Charles Deas was a frontier painter of significant renown, with famed works such as *Long Jakes* and *The Death Struggle* having secured his position in the American art world.

Coincidence was alive and well, then. He was suddenly overcome by a pressing urge to go finish reading that letter. A feeling that he could only describe as that of destiny crept over him, quite unlike anything he had ever experienced.

Heavy, rapid footfalls snapped him out of his trance. The door was flung wide and Matsell burst into the room, face considerably more florid than usual.

"Goddamnit, Rawn! If James Bennet and *The Herald* get a hold of this, we've had it! Had it, I tell you!" After a moment spent frantically groping for the right words, Matsell let out a vehement, "*Shit!*"

Two instances of blasphemy in one night from the Chief? Not exactly a good sign.

"Easy, Chief. Get a hold of what, precisely?"

Adopting a sarcastic manner, Matsell explained. "Oh, I don't know, Alvord. Perhaps *your order of execution* for the wounded Roach Guards? Or your turning over of one of them to the Bowery B'Hoys? Killing wounded men—have you gone mad, man?"

"To the best of my knowledge, my sanity is still intact."

"I tell you now- *hey*! Is that my sherry?"

"Ahh..."

"Well, never mind it now. Killing men in combat is one thing, but you just *executed* a dozen defeated men! Fitting behavior for savages, perhaps, but not men of the badge. Do you feel nothing at all, having committed such an atrocity?"

Alvord did, in fact. During the fight (or rout, more like) he had felt nothing but maddening rage. But after the red mists of ire had faded, a disconcerting knot developed in his gut. It was his conscience come to call, he knew, and now consequences both short-term and eternal raced through his mind as he talked to Matsell. How could he possibly reconcile what he had done with his faith? Could God ever pardon his sadistic rampage?

Yet he had made a decision and would stand by it.

"I feel nothing," he lied hollowly. Who was Matsell to judge, anyway? He hadn't been in that decaying slaughterhouse, hadn't heard the glee in McClintock's voice as he spoke of O'Farrell's brutal death.

Disbelief, mingled with a hint of pity and sadness, sat heavy upon Matsell's countenance. "Then I pray for your soul, sonny. I honestly do. Your men told me what happened in appalling detail. Most of them are disgusted with you, Alvord, now that they've had time to mull things over. Turner stated that he refuses to work under you anymore. I ask you—how did you summon the audacity to order them to dispatch the fallen Roach Guards?"

"I... ah..." He had no cogent answer for that one.

"And Hodgins is claiming that from what he heard, not all of the Roach Guards who were killed took part in the attack. Honestly, I can understand your initial assault on them, but the survivors of that fight deserved a trial, Alvord. This *is* America, after all."

"A trial? To what end? So that they can be cast back onto the streets after a spell, to steal and rape and claim innocent lives? You're quite correct- this *is* America, and it deserves to be safeguarded against social decay."

Matsell's voice grew soft. "Listen, Alvord. I realize that since the death of Katherine and your children—"

"*Enough!*" The command was snarled, and Matsell did indeed stop talking. "My wife and children are not a part of this discussion, so don't *dare* try to drag them into it."

Matsell patiently waited until Alvord's face resumed its normal pallor. "You see? There is a brooding ferocity in you that worries me, makes me question your ability to lead. Since those tragic losses I just mentioned you have become a different man, Alvord. Excessive violence has become your trademark, and I simply can't allow your actions to tarnish my reputation and that of the Municipal Police Department. Myself and others have simply worked too hard for this. You were once a man to follow into the blackest night. You still lead, and lead well at times, but you bring along too much darkness of your own."

Alvord's eyes bored relentlessly into his Chief's. "We are losing moral power over the criminal elements of this city, George. The Five Points is awash in theft, arson, rape, and murder, yet *I'm* being too harsh, *I'm* the one on trial? Can such a thing as excessive violence exist in this atmosphere?"

"Yes, it can." Matsell rubbed his eyes and heaved yet another mighty sigh. "As an officer, as Captain of the Municipal Police Department, your actions echo the moral standards of New York's law enforcement. It is bad out there I know, it's cutthroat and it's lowly, but it falls upon us to rise above it all. Tonight, you sunk to their miserable level."

"Merely fighting fire with fire."

For the first time since he had known him, Alvord watched Matsell's features twist into a bitter sneer. It lingered on his face but a moment before being replaced by a somber expression.

"You are firmly in the wrong, Alvord. You've brought embarrassment and sordid reputation to this department. I am forced to conduct an investigation of events concerning what happened tonight. I will require a written report from yourself and each of your men, and damn I hate to say it, but I will probably have to let you go."

Stone-faced, Alvord considered this new development. Fourteen years of loyal service come to this...

"Do what you must."

"Your alderman, Ragsdale, has grown tired of you too. There has been talk that he won't back you again, and after news of tonight's events reaches him there is no chance of it at all. We have enough favors owed to us that I can probably spare you formal prosecution, but your time as an officer of my department has come to close."

"Oh, *your* department, is it? Hardly. I may have lost my job, but you will lose this city, George."

Alvord took one last bitter swallow of sherry, grabbed his bloody oilskin coat and swept towards the door, which he paused at to utter a curt, "So long, Chief."

"S'long, sonny," Matsell replied miserably.

O'Farrell's body lay on a table in a basement room of City Hall not far from Matsell's office. Two patrolmen of the Sixth Ward's Second Platoon stood guard outside the door. They exchanged a hastily whispered discussion as soon as Alvord walked into view.

Alvord approached them calmly. "Bramson, Smith. I

require a moment alone."

"Yeah, sure thing, Cap'n," said Smith, clapping Alvord on the back. "You did the right thing out there, no matter how this plays out I know that much."

Bramson, however, hastily stepped out of the way, eyeing his Captain warily.

Why were some of his own men so appalled at what he had done? Surely they applauded the justice that he had brought raining down upon the heads of the Roach Guards? A brother of Bramson's lay dead as a doornail in the room beyond—would the idiot rather his death had gone unavenged?

He entered the room that held Andrew's body with due solemnity. A white cloth had been draped over it while preparations were made for his funeral and interment, and already the blood from his many wounds seeped through it. Alvord gently pulled the cloth back to reveal his bruised and bloodied face. From his pocket he withdrew Andrew's copper badge and reverently pinned it back onto the chest of its rightful owner. Resting a hand on the Irish lad's head, he bowed his own. A single tear slid unhurriedly down his cheekbone before his red beard checked its progress.

Bask in Heaven's glory, Andrew...

Chapter 6

The maze narrowed as Alvord wound his way through it. A nearly forgotten childhood fear of tight spaces reawakened with frightening intensity, as with every step his heart beat faster, his breath was drawn in with increasingly quick gulps of air. He could sense that an indescribable *something* that he really didn't care to meet lurked close behind him, so going back was no option at all.

A stale grayness dominated this labyrinth, so that even the damp moss that clung to its stone walls was colorless instead of a rich green.

Tendrils of mist swirled about the floor, vaporous serpents whose coiling and slinking appeared all too lifelike. One rose up right in front of him and seemed to look him in the face before gently deliquescing into nothingness.

There was a hint of light up ahead, so he began running towards it, thankful for the years of exercise that allowed him to move at a fast clip. The walls grew narrower still; a fearful thought took root in his mind that perhaps soon he wouldn't be able to move forward anymore, and would be forced to turn and confront the unearthly being that relentlessly stalked him.

Something tripped him up as he ran. Looking down, he recognized the mangled body of Thomas McClintock. Recoiling in shock, his hand touched the wall and something warm and wet oozed down his arm. Alvord smelt blood, and looking around found that it covered the walls and was suddenly the only thing that held color in the maze. And vivid color it was.

As he leapt over the dead Irishman's body, Alvord saw that more festering carcasses lay strewn ahead of him, obstructing his path. They were the Roach Guards he had slain last night, and each one triggered memories of his unfettered savagery.

After a sharp right-hand turn that he was barely able to squeeze through, the maze widened once again. Alvord breathed a sigh of relief, for in addition to walls wide enough to accommodate his broad shoulders, a large iron door stood at the end of the corridor. The light he had seen earlier glowed around it, haunting and ethereal. So there was a way out after all. He'd have to hurry, though; that *thing* behind him was gaining ground, he could feel it.

Sprinting over to the door, he turned the handle and pulled, but nothing happened. He tried pushing, but that yielded no results either. Panic, a sensation that had not plagued him since boyhood, began to well up inside his chest. For he knew that not even he could prevail over this fast-approaching adversary.

A sibilant hiss issued from just around the corner he'd rounded, galvanizing him into action. Alvord jumped with all he had, kicking off of one wall and then the other. This move allowed him to grab onto the top of the wall. He quickly scrambled up onto it, hoping beyond hope that he was out of reach.

From this vantage he looked out over the labyrinth in the direction from which he'd come. Eternity stretched before him, an infinite pattern of twists, turns, and dead-ends over which endless night presided. Glancing back towards the door, he saw that beyond it light shone, the only beacon of hope amidst profound darkness. There was his way out.

Running along the top of the maze, he leapt over the door, praying that salvation lay on the other side. As he jumped, he looked back and caught a fleeting glimpse of what had been chasing him, but no words could describe that nameless horror.

The ground he landed on was soft enough, and no pain flared up although it felt like he'd fallen as long as Icarus. Relief flooded his chest, for he could sense that the monstrosity had been left behind in the maze.

Yet aside from that knowledge, this new land offered little comfort. It was an expansive plain, perfectly bland in appearance and hot. Awfully hot. He started walking, hoping to find some indication of where he might be.

A broad river came into view, so he picked up his pace. Upon reaching it he dunked his head into its turbid waters in an effort to cool off.

Walking alongside the low gradient waterway, Alvord continued his journey, now and again walking through scattered groves of dead trees. In the distance, atop a grassy knoll, sat a large stone temple that looked to be vaguely Greek in style. He found himself inexorably drawn to its beauty and mystery. What was it doing here, on this cheerless savanna?

As he neared it, he saw cloaked figures moving about the shadows of the pillars.

When he mounted the broad stone steps leading up to the temple, he realized that the pillars weren't Greek at all, but something entirely different, something he didn't recognize.

Looking the building over again, Alvord gradually came to the conclusion that this structure far preceded any Greek temple. It felt ancient beyond calculation.

The cloaked ones froze as he drew near. Alvord paused, not knowing what to expect.

Without warning, they all moved in unison to either side of the hall, forming a gauntlet through which he could pass. And pass he must, for something across the temple had piqued his interest.

Behind some billowing, diaphanous fabric hung a painting, a portrait by the looks of it. Interested to see whom it depicted he decided to pass through the two silent rows of priests or acolytes or whatever they might be. With tentative steps he walked between them, and as he did their heads began shaking in all directions. These movements soon became blurred, too fast for a human neck to endure. And there were whispers, disembodied whispers that were jumbled together and indistinct yet so very seductive...

He felt a surging power in this room, like a buzzing current of electricity that stimulated all things, which he felt intensify as he continued walking through the two rows of cloaked ones. Suddenly a fantastic theory entered his mind as he passed by the people whose faces where concealed by their hoods—*They're being controlled by this force; they are devoid of will...*

Shaking off this unsettling revelation, Alvord closed in on the portrait, which hung above a marble altar. He positioned himself in front of it, moved aside the soft curtain, and scrutinized. What he saw made the breath catch in his throat.

It was Matsell's portrait he had seen in the Chief's office, the one done by that painter Deas! What the hell was it doing here, in this dateless temple?

He stared at it, making sure it was indeed the same one, but as he did so it began to change. Slowly at first, then more quickly as it progressed, the face morphed from Matsell's round one to Alvord's own strong, rectangular visage. Where Matsell's face had hung not one minute ago his own now sat, right down to his Greek nose and the small, neat scar on his left temple. It was like gazing into a mirror.

Forgetting for a moment the peculiarity of this whole situation, Alvord smirked.

Well, at least now the subject of the painting is actually deserving of the canvas.

Yet as he watched, it went beyond even that. His features began to warp into something that was still discernibly him but demonically twisted and distorted. It was as if his own features had been blended with that of Satan himself, the result being downright ghastly.

To his horror, the odious portrait tipped him a sly wink.

"It's about time, Alvord," the thing croaked.

It was eleven in the morning when Alvord snapped out of his nightmare in violent fashion. The bed sheets were thoroughly drenched in sweat, his pillows tossed clear across the room. He was quite out of breath.

Mouth bone-dry, he reached over to his bed stand and grabbed a pitcher of water, which he drained after splashing some on his face. He was sore from the events of last night, and moved stiffly at first.

The fear he had felt while in the grip of nightmare slowly wore off as he regulated his breathing and calmed himself.

Huh. So apparently he was no Theseus. Although whatever the Minotaur had looked like, it was undoubtedly more attractive than that thing he'd glimpsed in the maze but could not recall with much clarity.

What on this earth could provoke such fear in him? Nothing that he could think of. Well, perhaps sharks, in fairness, but he had been on land. And what place did the carcasses of the Roach Guards have in that shadow-dappled realm?

And the devilish portrait! How very incongruous the dream had grown in the end. Yet the power and vitality he felt circulating in that mysterious temple had felt so very real... ah, it was but a dream, nothing of any import.

At least, that's what he tried to tell himself as he washed and got dressed.

After a quick breakfast of tea, toast, and sausages, Alvord put on a black vest, his favorite frock coat of charcoal that hung slightly above his knees, and a black velvet top hat. Closing the door to his Church Street home, he looked back at the tidy redbrick structure. Unusually enough, he owned the entire building; these days few New Yorkers were able to do so, and those who could generally bastardized the sober redbrick and Federal buildings so as to erect the gauche Italianate mansions, French chateaux, and Gothic castles that he so despised. But that was not happening around here so much as it was at Fifth Avenue, Union Square, and Gramercy Place.

He liked his redbrick home; it was an unostentatious place of refuge in an increasingly busy, noisy city. It was also a testament to his financial success, for even upper middle class folks rarely had a whole house to themselves after the devastating Fire of 1835, which had destroyed much of Lower Broadway and driven rent rates skyward. But his dual income, that of the Municipal Police Department and the even greater sum of his private detective work, netted him anywhere from twenty five hundred to three thousand dollars a year, more than enough for him to keep both stories of his home.

Alvord began walking, reflecting on the time he had spent in New York.

He had first lived in this house in 1830, when he and his now-deceased wife, Katherine, were wed. What a glorious place Manhattan had been then; clean compared to today's standards, little violent crime, far less crowded. With the completion of the Erie Canal in 1825, the economic ascendancy of New York was secured. Job opportunities abounded and decent, hardworking families had populated the neighborhood around them, be they English, Dutch, German or Scots-Irish. All in all, a great place to settle down and raise a family, he and Katherine had figured.

Boston had been his home until his eighteenth year,

when his mother died of yellow fever and he and his elder brother Anscom decided to see what New York might offer in the way of jobs. Both found work with an enterprising merchant, but eventually thirsted for occupations in which action featured more prominently. Alvord found the night watch (and eventually the Municipal Police) while Anscom had opted for the high seas. He had not seen his brother in a while; Anscom had set sail for California aboard a merchant ship of his own two years ago and had left with thoughts of settling there with his wife and two sons. He went through with that plan; in their latest correspondence Anscom revealed that he and his family would be living in San Francisco, and that he was more than welcome to join them if he wished. He could sense his brother's concern, veiled though it was by careful wording. Anscom had beheld his darkness on more than one occasion, and feared what depths of inhumanity he might slip into now that he was well and truly alone.

Perhaps with good reason.

Stepping onto Broadway, Alvord headed for the nearest green grocer and purchased half a pineapple, a favorite snack of his. While chewing on the sweet, refreshing fruit, he made his way towards New York Garden. Upon reaching its shade and greenery, he seated himself on a bench tucked away amidst towering tulip trees and some thick coniferous shrubs that he could not name. A finely engraved silver timepiece appeared in his hand.

Noon. He still had some time to kill, but man alive was it hot, too hot to do much of anything aside from think. Shielded from the sun and his fellow man, Alvord lost himself in memory.

His expression, at first merely pensive, soon grew pained.

His recent past was riddled with loss and disappointment. Life had been kind to him until these recent years. His early married life had been blissful, more so than he could have imagined. Money came in steadily; he and Katherine had a fine home and a loving relationship. Life had been good, but soon soured. Katherine bore three beautiful children, all of whom were now deceased. Their youngest two had been girls, neither of whom lived to see their sixth year.

His second oldest, Bridget, had died just after she turned one. They found her in her truckle bed, dead for no apparent reason. The physician had expressed his deepest sympathies after he examined her, stating that sometimes children of this age simply died without any apparent medical explanation.

Little Isabel, the baby, was struck down at the age of five by cholera, that fell destroyer. The memory of that horrid disease and what it did to his daughter still caused him to grind his teeth and try to forever banish that recollection.

Tragedy heaped upon tragedy when shortly thereafter Katherine became stricken with consumption, and a volatile strain at that. While some people took years to cough themselves to death, Katherine had wasted away, had been *consumed*, in little over three years. Towards the end they were getting ready to move out West, where several physicians assured them the drier climate had cured other consumptives. Too late they had made those last-ditch plans. Katherine stoically died in their bed, in his arms, her once supple body reduced to a wracked, frail shadow of her former self.

"Consumption claims one in four deaths these days," the physician had sighed. Katherine did not deserve to be part of that statistic.

And just last year, his eldest child and only son, Elihu, ran off to fight in the Mexican War despite his father's insistence that he was too young and it was a foolish war anyway. But Elihu, intelligent and hardheaded at sixteen, had been filled with patriotic zeal and, caught up in the national fervor of expansionism, was determined to go seek glory and help expand his country's boundaries. Politics was one thing that they had never agreed on; Alvord feared that his son's last memory of him had been that of the thunderous fight they'd gotten into the night before the lad snuck away to war.

It was not that Alvord was anti-military; he was anything but. Benjamin Rawn, his father, had served with distinction in the United States Navy during the War of 1812 (despite his English birth). He had died in that service to his new country, and now his grandson had followed suit. The difference was that one had been a glorious defense of the homeland, while the other, in Alvord's opinion, was nothing more than the conceited flexing of expansionist muscle. The Mexican War, or Mr. Polk's War as Whigs were wont to call it, would show the nation and the wider world what lengths the more radical elements of the Democratic Party were willing to go to for the sake of land. Of course, some Whigs were benefitting from this conflict with the Mexicans as well. Politics- what a dismal farce.

But as always, young men would heedlessly rush off to death and glory while scheming politicians reaped the profits.

His first notification of Elihu's death had come from Horace Greeley's newspaper, *The New York Tribune*, in a list of slain New York soldiers. It had been a short list, for the Mexican War was one fought mostly by Southerners. Greeley himself delivered that paper to him, for he and Alvord were friends and he felt obligated to break the news personally.

Shortly after that, a personal letter from William J. Hardee, Captain 2nd Dragoons, had arrived. It told of how at the Battle of Resaca de la Palma, his son had fought nobly in E Company of the 2nd Dragoons, having ridden alongside Captain Charles A. May during the gallant, pivotal charge that silenced the Mexican guns and turned the tide of battle. They had retrieved what they thought to be his body; it could not be positively identified, like so many of the other men who had fallen to the fearsome artillery fire at close range.

Alvord still harbored hope that by some miracle his son had survived, that the body thought to be his was some other unlucky dragoon's. There was a chance, nothing had been definite...

Alvord checked the time as a crow's cackling stirred him from his reverie. Twelve-thirty; Ragsdale would be in by now. He left the park bench and his memories behind and reluctantly reentered the real world.

Arthur Ragsdale put down a freshly polished beer glass and cast a weather eye over his tavern's patrons. The Crow's Nest, situated at the corner of Canal and Elm, was a favorite haunt of sailors, and today's crowd was comprised mostly of seagoing types with a smattering of factory workers and merchants who were taking their lunch break.

Many of New York's aldermen owned saloons, taverns, and even brothels. The alderman of the city's most corrupt and violent ward was no exception. Here in the Bloody Sixth, Ragsdale could seamlessly blend a political career with a shady (and lucrative) business venture.

Aside from beer and liquor, patrons of the Crow's Nest could find whores and opium, the latter being in high demand these days, especially among sailors who had gotten a taste for it in the Orient. Opium was also commonly employed by physicians as a painkiller, particularly on the battlefield, but the stuff that Ragsdale sold from his bar was of a quality rarely found in New York. And used as it was by many people in either a medicinal or recreational context, Ragsdale found himself in the gravy.

After scanning the room for signs of dispute or discontent, Ragsdale told one of his workers to take over for him at the bar. Quickly he made his way up the sole flight of stairs to his office.

He opened the door, lost in thought. Absentmindedly stroking his impeccably groomed goatee, Ragsdale went to take the seat behind his large walnut desk and nearly fell down in shock when he found it to be occupied.

Alvord sat in the plush leather chair, boots casually propped up on the desk.

"Captain Rawn! You gave me quite a start there!" Even when startled, the man's voice was silk-smooth.

This was precisely the reaction that Alvord had been going for, though he did not let his satisfaction show. "Morning, Arthur. Chasing the dragon, are we?"

Between his fingers he deftly twirled a metal and wood pipe attractively engraved with Chinese symbols.

The alderman smiled. "No, no, nothing of the sort, Alvord. I *am* working, after all."

Alvord smiled back, as one might smile at a child caught in a fib. "Really? Because from what I hear, your use of opium is daily increasing, whether you are working or not."

He had never cared for Arthur Ragsdale, although deep down he realized that without this man's support he never would have gotten a job with the Municipal Police. Every patrolman, be he an officer or not, had to be appointed by the alderman of his ward and reappointed each year. Ragsdale had really helped him out over the years, and Alvord could trace his highly successful career back to the man. Yet he was a popinjay, a dandy, what with his outmoded claw-hammer tail coat, pea-green waistcoat, and cream colored trousers. He was trying to appear fashionable as only fops did—by donning stylish clothing from thirty years ago.

"You heard wrong, my dear Captain Rawn. While I have

acquired a taste for it, my business hasn't suffered. In fact, since I've started selling the stuff, my profits have increased twofold."

"Ah. And you're smoking it too, Chinamen-style. Whatever happened to the good old days, when you just diluted it in booze? You know, I hear tell that some even inject it using those hollow needles invented by that Irishman Francis Rynd."

Ragsdale returned Alvord's amused stare with an irritated one. "What can I do for you, then? Why have you come, and unannounced at that? Jolly tactless, you know."

"Yes, I do know, but I thought old friends like us might forgo the formalities. I don't suppose you happened to hear what occurred last night in the Bowery?"

The alderman grabbed a nearby chair and sat facing him. "I was informed of last night's events this morning. Quite an evening for you, eh? You look rather tired—get enough sleep?"

There was sarcasm in his tone, and Alvord could feel his blood begin to boil. He had no patience at all when it came to dealing with asshole politicians.

Recalling his nightmare, Alvord lied. "Slept like the dead. But for me, the interesting part was not so much the excitement of last night but rather in the aftermath. You see, Matsell disclosed to me some very interesting information upon my return to City Hall."

Ragsdale raised a thin eyebrow. "Such as...?"

"Such as the fact that you have stated several times that you no longer wish to support my position in the Department." Alvord regarded him intently. "Why is that, Arthur?"

Ragsdale lowered his eyebrow and smirked impishly. "Do you want me to come out and say it? Because I will, Alvord. Directness has long been a forté of mine."

He steepled his long fingers and continued. "Simply put, you are a bit too intelligent, a bit too independent, for a copper, Alvord. Too learned."

"A little learning is a dangerous thing."

"Pope," said Ragsdale, as if automatically. "See, there's the problem. The patrolmen of this age should not be quoting Alexander Pope. You know too much. You are too difficult to control because you are possessing of an intellect and you know the system, which you often exploit. So yes, for me your learning *is* a dangerous thing. It makes you less malleable. Additionally, you have been a constant source of vexation these last few months. And then there's the matter of violence. Oh, I've been reading the recent reports, all right, and have heard the tales firsthand as well. You are a loose cannon, Alvord, and I think it has much to do with your personal losses. It has clouded your judgment, man, made you unfit to lead. You are bloodthirsty; you've become a liability. Your annihilation of the Roach Guards last night will provoke a furor, believe you me."

"I am doing my best to safeguard this city against its criminal elements, Arthur, as is my sworn duty. You know what scum we deal with night after bloody night—no morals govern their actions. How else to deal with them if not by decisive, deadening force?"

"We use them," the alderman replied simply. "Like pieces upon a chess board, we use them. We placate, we satisfy, and we use, Alvord. Not that you would understand this particular brand of political ideology."

"Because I'm a Whig?" asked Alvord stiffly.

Ragsdale's eyes narrowed as his grin widened. "Nay. It has nothing to do with political orientation and everything to do with moral fiber, with character. But lend me your ear and I'll let you in on a closely guarded secret, old friend. Things are going to change, Alvord. This city's inner political workings are in a state of transition even as we speak. Tammany's going to consolidate power and will become downright machine-like in its efficiency. You know Fernando Wood, I'm sure? Well, with him at the helm, as he will soon be, New York Democrats will run this place with little opposition. And the Irish, whom you have been demonstrating undue malice towards lately, will be our army, our *pawns*. With you out of the picture we can convince the Five Points element to work in unison with City Hall and Tammany, free from persecution at the hands of nativist patrolmen. At the risk of sounding dramatic, a new age dawns."

"And how will you 'get me out of the picture?' By force?" Alvord laughed, a bitter, rumbling sound. "I know all of the shoulder-hitters that you have working for you. No three of those men are equal to the task of killing me. Nor can they be induced to even try."

And Ragsdale knew it. A devilish sneer formed on the

delicate face of the alderman.

"No. The nice thing about our society is how very civil it can be. No violence will be required. Your actions last night will go to trial, in which you will be accused of rabid anti-Irish sentiments and using your position in the Department to inflict excessive violence upon them. We already have the witnesses, as well as several men from your own platoon who will testify against you. Some corruption charges could be dredged up as well. You see, we don't want you as a patrolman and we certainly don't want you hanging around perhaps pursuing a political career of your own. We don't want you in this city anymore, Alvord, and we are legion. You cannot win."

Ragsdale paused and regarded him thoughtfully. "But honestly, Alvord, I like you. I *admire* you. I always have. Few men can boast of your distinctive blend of physical prowess and intellect. You really are something of a classical hero. In another place, another age, your name would have graced the ballads, would have filled the poems of the skalds. What's more, you're a no-bullshit man's man who stands by his convictions. That's why I've supported you all these years. It is just unfortunate that these very qualities have also made you something of an impediment to me. And so I offer you this—you will be formally prosecuted unless you resign today and leave this city for good. Take your talents elsewhere. Boston, Philadelphia, or perhaps even beyond to the frontier. Men of your mettle are at a premium on the frontier. So what say you?"

Alvord sat back in his chair, nodding faintly. "A grand design and no mistake, Arthur. I would most assuredly have impeded your progress. But as for corruption charges, you'll need to fabricate some because you'll find nothing. I've kept my nose clean; believe me, a nearly impossible feat in this vice-ridden place. You'll find nothing like, let's say Matsell's ties to Madame Retsell's abortion clinic and Josie Wood's bordello. And as for impending Democratic supremacy, there will be some left to oppose you, though I am gone. Horace Greeley and his crowd will resist you to the last gasp. *The Tribune* will reveal your corruption to the rest of the country, and you will lose the more moral element of your party."

Ragsdale pursed his lips. "True, true. He will be a tough one to deal with. But by empowering the lower classes, we will win the numbers game. Hordes of poor immigrants arrive here every month, and we Democrats will allow them to be heard. Well, eventually."

"So let me get this straight. The very people who built this city and made it great deserve to suffer so that these newcomers can prosper?"

"Chalk it up to *noblesse oblige*, chalk it up to political greed, but yes."

"Incredible," sighed Alvord, shaking his great head. "These newcomers that you'll blithely pander to have no sense of civic duty, and will engender the sort of urban degeneration that Jefferson foresaw. And just so you know, Arthur, I don't hate the Irish. Just the despicable ones, of which there are a goodly store in New York. And by empowering the filth, you will spawn more of them. Ill weeds grow apace. You will be overrun by them and whatever other race you decide to 'empower.'"

His former political backer merely shrugged his thin, velvet-covered shoulders. "I know your prejudice isn't radical. But radical anti-Irish sentiment will sound better in court, and we will use the 'filth' to our advantage. See you at the trial. Dress accordingly, please."

"There will be no trial. I shall leave." Tossing his copper badge onto Ragsdale's desk, he opened the door but stopped outside the doorway. "But were I you, Arthur, I'd cherish every dawn that I was fortunate enough to greet."

He slammed the door shut. Ragsdale sat at his desk for a long time, trying to laugh off Alvord's threat before coming to the sinking realization that he might be a dead man sometime soon.

The corrupt alderman quickly snatched up his pipe and sought serenity in oblivion.

Alvord moved down the stairs rapidly, his boots tapping out a fast rhythm on the creaking wooden steps. Once he hit the ground floor, he headed straight for the bar. A surly-looking bartend stood behind the counter, glaring at him.

"What d'ya want?"

"Friendlier service, for starters." Alvord made his way around to the other side of the bar, while the bartend stared at him. Walking past the confused man, he opened up a cabinet under the bar, revealing dozens of bottles containing various spirits. Grabbing three at random, he looked over his selection.

Cognac, Irish whiskey, and rum.

Splendid. Lent *was* over, after all. He turned to leave, but the bartend barred his way.

"Whoa there, what d'ya think you're doin'?" The fellow looked nonplussed, and also a bit scared.

"I was just leaving."

"Not with those you ain't!"

Alvord regarded the man curiously. "You're new here, aren't you?"

"Yeah. What of it?"

Whipping out one of the many spare badges he owned, Alvord spoke with authority.

"I am Captain Alvord Rawn of the Municipal Police Department."

The man's eyes widened.

"These three bottles are needed as evidence in an upcoming case involving Mayor Brady, several top-dollar whores, and a visiting Anabaptist preacher. Am I to take from your impudent tone that you intend to obstruct justice?" His glare was as fiercely serious as his voice.

"No, of course not!"

"There's a fellow."

Alvord moved past the man, but then stopped, turned, and regarded him thoughtfully.

"And just for the record, where were you on the night of Tuesday, March the thirty-second?"

The bartender's eye shifted back and forth as he fidgeted most uncomfortably.

"Ah, home! I ah, I was with... my woman, yeah—honest."

"Glad to hear it. And remember, we never had this conversation."

He marched resolutely towards the door, allowing himself one last look back at the fellow's slack-jawed wonder.

"*Halfwit*," he muttered to himself as he quickly exited.

Chapter 7

The sunlight stung his eyes as he reemerged from The Crow's Nest. The dreary bar setting contrasted mightily with the bright whirl of activity that was daytime New York.

Looking around, Alvord noticed a servant putting milk bottles on Ragsdale's doorstep. The alderman's home was connected to his bar.

Seeing a raggedly dressed kid up ahead, he hailed the boy, who scurried over to him.

"Yes, sir?"

"How would you like to make a shilling, son?"

The boy's brown eyes widened and his mouth dropped. "Honest?"

"Honest. But I need you to do something for me."

"Sure. What might that be, sir?"

"You see those two milk bottles over there by that door?" He pointed to the door that led to Arthur Ragsdale's home. "Go take a piss in those bottles and a shilling shall be yours."

The boy's desire for money clashed with his suspicion. "Won't I get in trouble for that?"

Alvord showed him one of his old badges. "No, you won't. See, this is police business."

Shrugging, the boy accepted the coin and eagerly ran towards the bottles. Alvord waited until the boy began the deed, then moved on.

Walking at a brisk pace, he headed for Broadway.

He had to dodge plenty of fellow pedestrians who couldn't seem to walk and pay attention to their surroundings at the same time. Several times, he simply walked straight into people, mostly wealthy folks who expected him to get out of their privileged way. It was tempting to use a carriage or omnibus to travel, but he enjoyed the exercise that walking provided.

As busy as the side roads were, Broadway was bustling beyond description. Rich men in tailcoats, workmen in drab trousers, women in stifling dresses and bodices; all hurried to get to where they were going, evading people and pigs alike. Hot corn girls stood on street corners, offering hot corn for sale and, for a bit more coin, delights of a carnal nature. Newsstands and pushcarts cluttered the streets, while patrolmen conducted ladies across the perilous road.

A wide variety of vehicles plied Broadway. Hackney cabs, private carriages, double-tandem mail coaches, phaetons (for speed-demons), and large-wheeled tilburies all rocketed down the street. Brightly painted omnibuses, with fees ranging from two to four cents and the capacity to hold up to twenty passengers, were drawn at much slower speeds by lumbering draft horses. Coachmen, both white and black, were easily identified by the striped linen and straw caps they sported.

Alvord crouched slightly, turned his face downwards, and blended in with the crowd so as to avoid the notice of the patrolmen, who would be of the 2nd Platoon of the Sixth Ward. At six-one, he was half a head taller than most men and therefore easy to spot. He didn't feel like answering any questions they might have about his actions last night. Or perhaps he simply did not wish to perceive the look of fear and perhaps disgust in their eyes...

As Wall Street was the business center of Manhattan, so Broadway was its entertainment district. Come evening, it would be even more crowded with people filing into Mille-Colonnes Café, or Contoit's, the ice cream specialist. Although Niblo's, on the corner of Prince Street, undoubtedly drew the biggest crowds. The magnificent structure was a German-style establishment boasting an opera hall, concert hall, and a ballroom with the ability to seat one thousand people.

He stopped by an Italian, one of the few in the city, who was playing a barrel organ and urging his leashed monkey on to its quaint dances. He gave the thankful man a small sum and bent down to pet the monkey, which appeared cute and tame enough until it bit his hand surprisingly hard. Swatting then spitting on the beast he continued walking, carefully crossing to the western side of the street. He had one more stop to make today but it was close to his own home, so he stopped at his redbrick to drop off his recently purloined booze.

Alvord put the finishing touches on some fake documents that detailed the reasons for his being in St. Louis. According to them he was being sent on a mission by the Municipal Police Department. The letters stated that Charles Deas was needed back in Manhattan for questioning regarding an official matter that could not be revealed. Should Deas attempt to use St. Louis law enforcement to prevent his leaving, these papers could count for a lot. Surely a few country bumpkins would balk at such thorough, official-looking documentation?

With a quiet chuckle he stamped a steaming pool of red wax with the official seal of the Department, which he had stolen from Matsell's office last night. Why not strive for authenticity?

His chore concluded, he stepped onto Franklin Street, which was but a stone's throw from his home. Arching elms provided some shade and pedestrian traffic was much reduced, coach traffic nonexistent. Some newspaper venders made their voices heard as a few chimney sweeps chatted loudly nearby, but all in all this area was refreshing after enduring the roiling madness that was Broadway. This neighborhood was familiar to him, similar to his own in both architecture and the social standing of its residents. Although here on Franklin Street, some silver and gold finery appeared on the doors of residents aspiring to refinement.

Vanity of vanities, all is vanity, thought Alvord, shaking his head.

His destination, Sixty-three Franklin Street, lay up ahead, but before he knocked on the door, he wanted to read over Mrs. Deas's letter one last time. Several times this morning he had already done so; he hated looking foolish or uninformed. A letter such as this one he was inclined to read multiple times lest he forget any part of it.

Respected Sir-

I call on your services in an hour of dire need, for my son's absence gnaws on my soul day and night, and I fear that if this absence is much further extended then my sanity will take leave of me. Others have refused my pleas; I write now for I have no one else to turn to.

Several years ago my son Charles departed for the West, as his adventurous fancy dictated, and has been living there ever since. A painter of some renown, he keeps a studio in St. Louis, Missouri, from which he makes excursions into the frontier. This was the year he was due to come back, but this past fall and winter he sent letter after letter stating that he needed more time out there. He has yet to return. Money and letters he has sent steadily enough, but the latter grow increasingly peculiar. I no longer recognize my son's customary wit and affection in them; worse yet, there is constant mention of a Count Abendroth and how the man is helping him to mature as an artist, to "reach levels of artistic realization never before attained," as he put it. Charles has referred to this man as an animal magnetizer, which from what I've gathered is a practitioner of mesmerism.

Charles's latest correspondences have been marked by a growing strain of insanity and fanaticism; judging by his writing he has fallen prey to madness. I feel strongly that this "Count" plays a central role in it. My fear for Charles's physical and spiritual wellbeing grows daily, as his letters grow fewer and their content less lucid.

Thus far, none have been willing to help me, but several of the men I've approached have suggested you as someone to strongly consider. All patronizing aside, I have been told repeatedly that you are the best detective on this island.

It is therefore my wish that you undertake a journey to St. Louis to retrieve my son. I realize that this will require great sacrifice on your part, but you will be handsomely rewarded for you efforts, of that I can assure you.

If you be willing, I should like to meet with you to discuss the terms of business.

With fervent hope—

Anne Izard Deas

Below was the woman's address. Alvord knew that he should have sent word before showing up at her house, but the desperation in the letter and his own precarious situation in this city made him dispense with the strictures of formality.

He tapped the door's knocker three times, taking a step back while he waited for a response. No ostentatious gold or silver accents to be found on this door, he noted with approval. Shortly thereafter, a young man in black and white servant's livery answered the door.

"Can I help you, sir?"

Alvord held forth the letter. "Last night I received this letter from Mrs. Deas. I am the Captain Rawn indicated here." He pointed.

The servant carefully scrutinized the letter. "If you would wait just a moment, I shall go inform Mrs. Deas."

A servant, eh? She had some money then, this woman. Not that money was the sole criterion on which he was taking this case. He could certainly relate to her fear of losing a child. When Elihu left for war, the anxiety regarding his safety had been ever present. Perhaps it was in part that understanding that drove him to seek out Mrs. Deas.

The door opened again, and beside the servant now stood a regal old woman. In her youth she must have been strikingly beautiful, in a French sort of way. She wore a cashmere frock with taffeta ruching, a brown velvet jacket with a high neck frill, and a black velvet bonnet with rose silk trim. Age had not bent her form, nor diminished the fierce light that shone in her eyes. Yet immediately Alvord could tell that sorrow had taken its toll on her, for dark bags hung under those eyes and her expression, while dignified, bore the unmistakable signs of strained nerves.

He swept off his top hat and bowed. "I am Alvord Rawn, ma'am."

Despite her apparent anxiety, she gave him a sharp, appraising look, her dark eyes sizing him up good and proper. She then held out her hand and he elegantly stooped to kiss it.

"Pleased to make your acquaintance, Mr. Rawn. I thank you for your admirable promptness. Do come in."

"I must apologize for not sending word before my coming here, but I read your letter last night and it struck me as most urgent. I do hope this is not a bad time for me to drop in."

"No trouble at all. I prefer a prompt, if unannounced response, rather than none at all, which sadly is what I have come to expect from private detectives on this island. Two did actually get back to me, Crawford and Harris were their names, but only to give me a nay and drop your name."

"Crawford is an outright coward," Alvord replied with a dry chuckle, "and Harris has a family to worry about and so takes only local jobs."

"I see."

She led the way to a nicely furnished parlor. The servant had silently disappeared at some point, leaving the two of them to their conference.

"Lovely home you have here. I live in a similar redbrick, though the interior is not nearly so nice or spacious."

"Where is it that you live?"

"Not far from here, on Church Street."

"This is a pleasant area, and for me this house is perfectly situated. Close enough to Broadway to be convenient, far enough away to enjoy the tranquility of a quiet neighborhood. Mulled claret, Mr. Rawn?"

The servant reappeared behind Alvord as if by magic, holding a bottle and two small glasses.

Although as a rule he didn't drink before four P.M., Alvord relented for the sake of civility. "I'd love some."

Mrs. Deas took a slow sip before she spoke.

"It was not always that I could afford such a place. My husband came from a prominent slaveholding family in South Carolina, so the early years of our marriage were blissful and we lacked for nothing. But alas, he passed when Charles was a youth; times were tough for some time. Luckily, one of my daughters married into wealth, and she and her husband have been very generous to me. Charles too sends money. Charles actually lived in this house before departing for the West, so I have only come to live in it of late. I once lived in Ulster, on the Hudson, before my children urged me to come here, yet the conditions were not nearly so comfortable. I am very blessed to live like this."

Alvord nodded understandingly. He instinctively liked this woman. Maintaining his intent silence, he allowed her to continue.

"Well, right to it then. To begin, please pardon the panicked nature of my letter, but I needed something that would grab your attention."

"In that you succeeded. No worries, Mrs. Deas, I see your logic."

"As you know from that letter, Charles was due back from St. Louis this year. Now, I know my son better than any. If he said he was coming back, he'd be back by now. But he...he has changed this past year, as is evidenced in his recent letters to me. Something dark is restraining him, and I now know that his interest in the occult is playing a central role."

Alvord leaned in, intrigued. "By the occult, you mean...?"

"Astrology. Séances. Ancient powers that mankind might once have wielded. Since his youth he has been fascinated with the arcane and the darker side of nature."

She hastily added, "Of course, it has never consumed him in the past. It was but a single facet of his complex personality. Actually, his mystical side was part of what made him such an interesting person. Now, it seems that his fascination with the occult has found fertile grounds in St. Louis. I fear that I have lost him to it."

Her voice broke for the first time, and she shuddered visibly.

"Forgive me," she asked, clenching her jaw and gripping her hands together tightly.

"I quite understand."

Quickly enough she composed herself. "So, he left New York in summer of 1840, and I don't think he was ever so happy in all his life. City living, first in Philadelphia and then here in New York, simply didn't suit him and left him terribly dissatisfied. True, he was elected a member of the National Academy of Design at an unusually young age, soon finding favor with the American Art Union, but his eyes strayed ever westward. In the summer of 1840 he left for the Wisconsin Territory to visit his brother Edward, who was posted at Fort Crawford. The woods and wilds of the Old Northwest brought him great joy, elation even, and after his time there New York just didn't cut it anymore. He decided to settle for a while on the fringe of American civilization, in St. Louis, Missouri. In St. Louis he could both venture onto the frontier and find wealthy patrons looking for artwork. He frequently sends work back here to the American Art Union, where his paintings are much in demand. But his work has grown strange of late, apocalyptic even."

The portrait from his nightmare flashed through Alvord's mind. It was a momentary occurrence, a fleeting vision quickly shaken it off.

"And you think that the animal magnetizer whom you mentioned in the letter is to blame?" Alvord carefully measured his words. "I mean not to be blunt, but could it not be that a woman is keeping him there?"

"No, no. Trust me, he would have told me if that were so. And his letters, which you can have if you take the case, will clearly demonstrate his growing insanity. No woman could produce so drastic a change in Charles. Then there is the matter of this Count Abendroth he makes frequent mention of. Charles calls him a "mesmerizer" or "animal magnetizer," and insists that this man is helping him to enhance his artwork and has opened a door to new realms of artistic aspiration. His words, mind you. It has become clear to me that this mesmerizer is corrupting his mind and work; through my research I have found that some instances of animal magnetism go horribly awry, engendering dreadful consequences for the patient."

After a flavorful sip of claret, Alvord spoke. "It is my understanding that in Boston these animal magnetizers, or mesmerizers, are quite common. They are essentially faith healers, correct? They claim to use some form of energy to restore balance in the body, I believe."

"That's correct. They are not nearly so common here in New York, and it was actually a European phenomenon long before it reached our shores. But whatever the case, it is in St. Louis, and my son needs to leave that place forthwith for the sake of his mind and soul. The last few letters he wrote to me were so very bizarre, so horribly unsettling..."

Alvord saw the pain etched in lines of her face, and made his decision right then and there. "Tell me, are there any daguerreotypes of him, or perhaps a small portrait that I could borrow? I shall have need of at least one recent image so that I can positively identify him upon my arrival in St. Louis."

Mrs. Deas face lit up, and her words were spoken with joyous disbelief. "So you will take the job, then? You will journey to Missouri and retrieve Charles?"

"Yes. I depart tomorrow."

"This won't interfere too greatly with your job with the Municipal Police?"

"Ah, shouldn't be much of a problem, actually."

"Bless you, Mr. Rawn, bless you! My prayers for you will be frequent."

His red beard twitched ever so slightly. "That is worth a lot, Mrs. Deas. I thank you for that."

She handed him a bundle of papers that had been lying on the table. "Here is everything you will need to know about my son. The location of his studio out there, his history, personality, prints of his works, and also recent images of him—anything that I thought could be of use. There is also some literature pertaining to animal magnetism."

Impressed with her competency, Alvord leafed through the file and was quite satisfied with what he found. He was just about to inquire as to payment when she held forth a small burlap bag. Alvord took a peek inside only to look up in shock.

"Ma'am, I have been doing private detective work for some time now. I realize that I will be traveling across the country, but this amount is still quite excessive."

"You get half now, half upon your return with Charles."

"Mrs. Deas—"

"I will brook no argument."

Alvord recognized finality when he heard it.

"Very well. Now, it seems probable that Charles will not want to come back. If that is the case, then...?"

The steely glint in her dark brown eyes grew in intensity. "Then bring him back by force. Bring him back kicking and screaming and shouting his defiance to the four winds, but bring him back. My son needs help, Mr. Rawn. He has callously ignored my pleas to come back to New York, and his letters indicate mounting insanity. That is simply not the son I raised, the man I know. Do whatever needs to be done, but bring me back my son, proper procedure be damned."

That was something Alvord could appreciate.

She was breathing heavily as she finished speaking, her eyes blinking rapidly. With a deft movement, she hoisted her glass and drained it.

Alvord could tell this meeting had reached its end, so he too made empty his glass and handed it to the servant. "It will be done, Mrs. Deas."

They moved out of the parlor and towards the door, which the servant was suddenly holding open.

Damn, but that kid could move.

As he stepped out onto the stoop, Mrs. Deas put a hand on his shoulder for a moment, stopping him.

"This Abendroth strikes me as a most sinister and manipulative man. If you should cross him, I cannot promise that things will not get violent, Mr. Rawn."

Alvord chuckled mildly at that. "Violence, Mrs. Deas, is not something that I shrink from."

Tipping his hat, he left.

Part Two

"It is absurd to pretend that evil is not infective; it is as infective as measles or scarlet fever, and often as fascinating as a full meal to a hungry man."

Hugh Walpole
Above the Dark Tumult

Chapter 8

The scenery had become a source of major disappointment. Alvord had never ventured into this sparsely populated part of the country, and had anticipated a splendid landscape. But alas, the eastern Pennsylvania countryside was perfectly bland in appearance, bereft of any of the pastoral glory that he hoped to find.

It did not help that the train he rode was hurtling along at breakneck speed. But even so, the view was rarely extensive and what little he could see was far from scenic. A wall of trees, more like. When the tracks did cross open ground, miles of stunted trees, burnt stumps, and unsightly villages met his eyes.

Train travel was something new for him. Although Manhattan did boast a "street railroad line," it was in reality little more than an outsized, glorified stagecoach drawn slowly along tracks by horses.

The individual train cars actually reminded him of the familiar New York omnibuses, although on a larger and somewhat grungier scale. Unlike an omnibus, however, there were separate gentlemen and ladies' cars, and a Negro car as well. Contrasting with English trains, there was no first and second-class to be found, although the gentlemen's car was noticeably more elegant than the other two.

Riding in them was every bit as uncomfortable as riding in an omnibus, what with the incessant jostling and rattling of the tracks. Actually, in combination with the shrieking of the brakes, those factors probably made for an even more unpleasant mode of conveyance. Yet it was speed that he needed to get him to St. Louis, and trains took the biscuit in that regard. So as long as the train did not get derailed (already there had been several collisions with livestock) or its boiler did not explode, Alvord would be making impressive progress across the country.

Tobacco smoke hung heavy in the air of the gentlemen's car that Alvord sat in, making an already unpleasant trip all the more unbearable. Men puffed on pipes and cheroots, adding to the noxious cloud of smoke. Worse yet, the windows were small and barely opened at all, allowing little fresh air in.

He detested smoking, a widespread habit in America that had always struck him as patently pointless. What possible satisfaction was there to be found in inhaling bitter smoke into one's lungs? More unseemly yet to him was the habit of chewing tobacco; men spat vile tobacco juice all over the train with scant regard for where it landed.

Staring out the window, his eyes grew unfocused.

He had not stayed for Andrew O'Farrell's funeral. That bothered him, but there had been no other option. New York was a dangerous place for him to be, and he needed to make good on his promise to Ragsdale that he would depart rather than face trial. This also brought him to the sinking realization that once he left New York for good, he would no longer be able to easily visit the graves of his family, as he had each week. It was their memory, rather than their headstones that were most important to him, yet the thought of not having their graves close by was a depressing one. Before leaving, he'd brought fresh flowers to the four headstones. While standing before them, doubts about his mission crept into his mind; doubts he knew would take root should he linger in New York much longer.

So he left the morning after he spoke to Mrs. Deas, and was now going west to St. Louis, the gateway to the West, on a mission to rescue a disturbed artist from his obsession with the occult and a strange phenomenon known as mesmerism...

This trip had real potential.

At first he thought he'd sorely miss New York, but this adventure stirred in him almost childish excitement.

Some of his patrolmen he missed, yet Matsell had mentioned that a number of them were disturbed by his behavior during that wild and vengeance-filled night. And the knowledge that some of his own men were willing to testify against him was a shocking revelation. He wondered which of them had offered to do so.

To Hell with them. Men willing to testify against him were not men worth thinking about, yet he could not help but bitterly recall the pride he'd had in them after they'd wiped out the Roach Guards.

Misplaced pride, that was. Although in fairness, fault could be laid on him for failing to recognize the consequences of his actions.

He considered what life would be like now that he was no longer a patrolman. There would be much to miss, for sure. The excitement of leading men, his many informants and the interactions he'd had with the colorful characters he dealt with day to day. And, even though he knew it to be blatant arrogance, he had to admit that he'd miss having a reputation. To cultivate that delicate balance between fear and respect had taken him some time; at first new, exciting, and intoxicating, he had quickly come to accept it as part of his identity.

Wherever he ended up relocating after he brought Charles Deas back to New York, he would have to forge his reputation anew in a strange land. Law enforcement might have use for him elsewhere. Or he might opt to lead a quiet, anonymous life. Maybe he would go to California and try to track down his brother Anscom.

Or perhaps...perhaps he would simply find a place where few men ventured, where the aspens grew tall and the valleys spanned wide and the soothing lilt of mountain brooks would sing him to sleep each night...

A thousand paths unfolded before him—it remained only for him to put foot to one.

Trying to find his balance amidst the constant vibrations of the train, Alvord took a deep pull from a bottle of Lord Chesterfield Ale, which he had acquired in Philadelphia. Brewed by a man named D. G. Yuengling in Pottsville, Pennsylvania, it was a damn fine thirst quencher on a hot day such as this. Plugging the top with its cork stopper, he held its dark green glass up to the light.

Capital stuff; he wondered if he would be able to find it in St. Louis. It was early for him to be drinking but hell, he was on holiday (sort of), and needed *something* to get him through this wretched train ride.

He would take the railroad as far as Harrisburg,

Pennsylvania. From there the railways were fragmentary, of shoddy construction, and often unpunctual, used mostly for the transportation of coal and lumber. Stagecoaches would bring him as far as Pittsburgh, at which point canal boats and steamboats would become the most expedient modes of transportation. But for now it was shit for scenery, crowded conditions, and an ever-growing cloud of vile tobacco smoke.

Lovely. He took another hearty swig of ale.

A quick glance out the uncurtained window told him that still, no breathtaking views were to be had. He rested his head back against the plush cushion of his seat. As was his custom, Alvord discreetly observed each of his fellow passengers from time to time. Most were of the generic, unremarkable variety of men, although one had the face and eyes of a fighter while another with red hair had met his gaze with amused mien.

Two people could comfortably fit in each seat, but Alvord sat alone; he had deliberately slapped on his "brooding face," which he always found to be a useful deterrent against unwanted company.

For unwanted company there was. Two young honeymooners had come stumbling into the car some twenty minutes ago, and already the pair was making quite a nuisance of themselves. That they were drunk was obvious; both struggled to walk efficiently and giggled tipsily as they chatted without interval. But what really peeved him was that the woman, girl really, was switching seats at an incredible rate. She would whisper to her man, who would then proceed to get up and inform another passenger that his wife had grown rather tired of her vantage and fancied a different view, and wondered if he would be willingly to relinquish his seat to her.

In those words, time and again. And, as was customary when a woman requested a seat, the man would graciously get up and move. Alvord was all for chivalry, but this drunken wretch was hardly deserving of it.

By the young man's attire and manner he was strongly reminded of Arthur Ragsdale, and an unfavorable comparison it was. Popinjays were simply not his cup of tea.

He did his best to ignore the raucous pair and began to read his newspaper, *The Anglo-Saxon*. It was not long, however, before their idiotic shifting about brought them in close proximity to him.

The young dandy stood by Alvord's seat and waited to be acknowledged.

He wasn't.

Opting for a more direct approach, he addressed Alvord in a voice that might have been smooth had it been plied by sober tongue.

"Pardon me, sir."

Turning the page of his paper, Alvord ignored him and started reading about internal improvements in Ohio.

The newlywed reached out and tapped him on the shoulder. "*Pardon me*, sir."

Alvord slowly turned his head towards the fellow. "What?"

"You see, my wife," he indicated the giggling girl, "has grown rather tired of her vantage and fancies a different view. I was wondering—"

"If I'd be so kind as to relinquish my seat to her?"

"Why, yes! What say you?"

"Ah, *no*." And he turned back to his paper.

A frown of dawning comprehension appeared on the man's face. He looked back at his wife and then to Alvord.

"No?"

"I think not." The former police captain didn't even bother to look up.

"You call yourself a gentleman, do you? Don't even have the common decency to give a lady a seat?" The florid-faced fellow spat his words.

Alvord looked back at the man balefully. "I do, actually, but your wife is hardly a lady. Not in that state. I highly recommend that you and she seek out some coffee or water, and quick. You are making a right old nuisance of yourselves; the other passengers, including myself, grow irritated."

The man took a step back in shock. Swaying as he tried to balance in the jolting train, he balled his fists.

"Stand up and face me like a man, you ill-conditioned cur!"

"Sit down, boy," Alvord growled from his seat, locking eyes with the indignant fop, "before I put you down."

The coldness of his gray eyes and lurking menace in his voice caused the man to reconsider his position. At last he returned to his seat, collected his wife, and left the car. The other passengers were all looking at Alvord, mostly with smiles on their faces. To decline a lady (even a soused one) a seat was not something that most of them would have done, but they all enjoyed it when he had done so. For while everyone loves confrontations, few wish for an active role in them.

A clean-shaven man with dark red hair combed into a wild, windswept style got up and took the seat across from Alvord. He was the man who had drolly noticed Alvord's assessment of the car's passengers earlier.

"Well now, that was nicely done," he praised.

"Thank you. Irish?" Alvord inquired.

The man's smooth, honest-looking face broke into an even-toothed smile that revealed a gold upper canine. "Why yes, I do have that distinction."

He spoke with a mild but detectable Irish accent, yet there was something else there too, higher education perhaps. Alvord had already given the man a once-over, but sized him up more thoroughly this time.

The Irishman had a crafty sort of face, free from freckles despite his red hair, with a slightly hooked nose and dark green eyes. There was intelligence in those eyes, Alvord felt, and the clothing he wore bespoke wealth and refinement. Dressed in Continental fashion, he sported a nicely tailored black tailcoat and a white waistcoat with a wide, upturned collar.

The man chuckled. "You finished analyzing me there? A touch disquieting, 'tis."

"Sorry, I have a habit of doing that; it probably stems from fourteen years spent in law enforcement. Clothing, posture, countenance- such things can tell you much about a person."

"Indeed. Such things told me that you were not going to move for the sake of that tipsy lass's fancy. What would've gone down had that chap pressed matters?"

"I'd have given him a proper thrashing. What would you have done?"

"The very same."

With a smile, Alvord extended his hand. "Alvord Rawn."

"Quite a name. I'm Finnbar Fagan."

"I declare! With a name's as Irish as inebriety!" said Alvord jokingly.

"Oh you might joke, but deep down you wish your name

was as poetically rich as mine. This is your typical Anglo-Saxon jealousy of the Irish race."

Alvord raised his dark eyebrows. "Jealousy?"

"Well, Ireland has long produced the finest breed of man, and English folk have ever been jealous of the fact. Yes indeed, the perfect blend of grace, wit, intellect, creativity, mysticism, ire, and faith can be observed in the Irish form. It's tough to be humble but Lord knows we try."

A jocose grin slid onto his face, but Alvord could tell that Finnbar did believe what he said, at least in part.

"Come now. Even you, a proud son of Hibernia, must concede that the driving force behind the march of Western civilization has been the blood of England?"

"Well, you English have accomplished a mite, in fairness, but 'twas Irish mercenaries that did a fair bit of the fighting that won you your empire. And in the sixteenth and seventeenth century, Ireland was a veritable training ground for English men-at-arms. Kept your skills honed, we did. As the old proverb went, *'He that will England win, Let him in Ireland begin.'*"

Alvord nodded. "That's precisely what my ancestor, Sir Walter Raleigh did. Went to Ireland and won himself some land and a reputation during the Second Desmond Rebellion."

"Not Raleigh! Our ancestors fought, lad!"

"How so?" Alvord asked, intrigued.

"I'm from Cork. My mother was a Barry, and Raleigh captured Barry Castle back in the day. He came just after that bastard Humphrey Gilbert had satisfied his bloodlust. Every bit as brutal as the Romans had been was Gilbert. But after him came Raleigh, as a youth, and was a far more just, if not wilier opponent."

"Yes, he did have a knack for handling obstreperous Irishmen."

"Obstreperous Spaniards and Italians, too. After the Siege of Smerwick, he slaughtered the Spanish and Italian mercenary troops that had aided the Irish."

"Actually, he only oversaw that. In his later writings he revealed his disgust with the whole affair. But as a soldier, he had little choice. Earl Grey was the man who issued the order."

Finnbar nodded. "Very coincidental then, our meeting."

"Quite."

"So you are Cornish? Raleigh was."

"A bit. Most of my family is from Cumbria."

"The Lake District, eh? That explains the dark hair and light beard. You see a lot of that up there. Northwestern England is the nicest part of the country, breeds hearty folks, too."

"I visited the place once, in my youth, and I hope to go back some day. A lonely land, it is. Hauntingly beautiful, fit haunt for the gods."

"Wordsworth himself couldn't have put it better. I'd say you've got a touch of the poet in you."

Alvord laughed. "Mayhap, but I doubt it. Where were you educated, Finnbar?"

"Trinity College in Dublin. It shows, then?"

"Forgive me, but it is not every Irishman who speaks intimately of Sir Walter Raleigh and William Wordsworth."

The Irishman looked Alvord over a little more carefully.

"No, I don't suppose it is. But while we are dealing in generalities, I must ask—why do all American homes, stores, and apparently trains have a stove burning even in the hotter months?"

He gestured towards the glowing stove in the center of the car that burned hot with anthracite coal.

Alvord shrugged. "Can't rightly answer that, actually. I guess in America we have such an abundant supply of coal and wood that we don't feel the need to conserve it."

"I declare, you Americans burn more wood in a single day than there is wood in all of Ireland. Now don't get me wrong, I like me a good fire, but not on a day such as this."

Wiping sweat from his brow, Alvord exhaled loudly. "Nor I."

Reaching into one of his valises, he removed his last bottle of Lord Chesterfield Ale and offered it to Finnbar.

"Ale?"

Grinning slyly, he accepted it. "Wouldn't be very Irish of me to decline, now would it?"

He took a swallow and his face lit up. "That's a fine dram of stuff! Where'd you find this?"

"Philadelphia. I do hope I can find it in St. Louis, though."

Finnbar folded his arms and leaned back in his seat.

"So, The River Queen is your destination too?"

"You yourself are St. Louis bound?"

"I am, but first I have some quick business to attend to in Harrisburg. So perhaps we'll meet again along the way, or in St. Louis."

"Sounds good. I will be staying at the Planter's Hotel, look me up when you arrive."

"Alright then."

And they drank and chatted lightly as the iron horse sped them west.

Chapter 9

Now this was more like it. At last the landscape satisfied Alvord's yearning for pristine wilderness. Mighty virgin timber established a dense canopy at least eighty feet overhead, through which little of the midday sunlight penetrated. In between the enormous oak, beech, and hemlock trunks the forest floor laid surprisingly clear of brush and undergrowth, making for good visibility. Here and there giant, moss-covered boulders reared skyward like some gnarled creatures of fairytales. Out of swamps rose ranks of blasted trees, standing sentinel over the stagnant waters.

Alvord had passed through big woods country once before, while on his nuptial tour in New Hampshire, but those woods had been far thicker than these. Sections of this Pennsylvanian forest were so open that they almost felt park like.

Unfortunately, the stagecoach that transported he and seven other passengers through the Alleghenies rattled and shook with such violence that the observation of one's surrounding was no enjoyable task.

Macadamized roads, ones paved with crushed stone, were a rare blessing in this part of Pennsylvania. Oftentimes the unpaved coach roads were riddled with epic ruts and jagged rocks, which hampered progress and occasioned bone-jarring jolts. Sometimes they encountered corduroy roads; logs thrown across wet areas to settle, but more often than not the road was a mere dirt track though the dark, silent aisles of trees. He could have taken the Cumberland Road, which was macadamized, but this road (if such it could be accurately labeled) was both closer and more direct a route.

It struck Alvord as incredible that some politicians were eager to acquire more territory for the United States when the territory already gotten was in dire need of internal improvements. Like roadwork, for starters.

The constant bumps did not seem to dampen the spirits of the other passengers, most of whom were engaged in passionate discussions ranging from cotton to banks to the Mexican War. They were well dressed and seemed respectable enough, but Alvord was not of the temperament to blithely trust in the character of people he barely knew, nor engage much in idle conversation.

The seats were luxurious, yet the coach was slightly too small to comfortably accommodate its eight passengers, though had Alvord been of normal proportion this might not have been an issue. Once he had asked the coachmen if he could sit outside with him, but the filthy, tobacco-spitting driver glibly told him that that was not happening. Coachmen had a terrible reputation as being sullen, taciturn bastards, and it seemed as though this particular man did all he could to reinforce the notion.

Alvord suddenly noticed the stagecoach coming to a gradual halt. Wondering if there was a downed tree or water to negotiate, he leaned out the window to find out. What met his eyes was neither, but an altogether more unwelcome sight.

Up ahead four mounted men sporting burlap sacks over their heads blocked the road. Two held shotguns, while cutlasses filled the hands of the others.

Dammit. As if this trip wasn't miserable enough. He ducked back into the coach and looked at his fellow passengers. So enthusiastic was their discourse that they had failed to notice the gradual slowing of the vehicle. All but one. A young, plain-looking brunette who had refrained from most of the discussions was looking intently at Alvord. He met her intelligent gaze, at which point she leaned closer to him.

"We are coming to a halt. What is going on, sir?"

He spoke in a quiet tone. "I mean not to frighten you, but highwaymen are blocking the way."

The girl's face remained steady. "It is what it is. Being frightened won't help matters, now will it?"

As she spoke, the coach creaked to a stop. Alvord gave her an encouraging nod but had little time to be impressed with the girl's sangfroid, though he certainly was. Hastily he addressed the others.

"We are being waylaid by highwaymen. Do any of you have guns in your possession?" The news elicited many a shocked gasp. Looking them over, Alvord realized that only the young brunette could be counted on to remain level headed in this situation.

"Why yes, I have a gun," answered a thickly bearded man with a monocle.

"Good. May I have it?"

"Oh, you mean right now? It's on the roof, with my other luggage."

"And a fat lot of good it's doing us there." Alvord's jaw clenched. He kicked himself for not having purchased a gun of his own yet. The various weapons he had used as a patrolman were the property of the Department. He had snuck back into the stationhouse and purloined his truncheon before leaving New York, but he figured that stealing a gun would have been audacious to the point of stupidity. Yet at the moment, he wistfully conceded that the blunderbuss strapped to the underside of his old desk would have lent him a nice edge in this situation.

While the people around him began to enter the early stages of panic, Alvord reached into the valise he had kept with him. The rest of his baggage was strapped to the top of the coach, and was likely to be taken if he did not act and act shrewdly. His hand closed around the familiar handle of his truncheon. Running a hand along the smooth hickory, he allowed himself a small, grim smile. Put a weapon, any weapon, in his hands, and no situation was completely without hope.

Quickly, he secreted the club into his belt and covered it with his greatcoat.

The doors of the coach were flung open by rough hands, and they were gruffly ordered out of the carriage. Alvord complied; the time for action would come soon enough.

The passengers huddled in a group, staring anxiously at the four highwaymen. Alvord did the same, but his was a calculating stare, not a frightened one.

The four men were a motley crew to be sure, with ragged clothing, unwashed faces, and a putrid stench emanating from their beings. They had taken off their masks and stood leering at their hostages. Alvord interpreted this as a bad sign; the only reason they would have for removing the masks was if they intended to kill each of their victims and were unworried by thoughts of identification. Three of the ruffians were white; one appeared to be a half-breed Indian. All were lean and relatively short. Not men to be feared, had they not been armed to the teeth.

One of them approached the knot of passengers. He kept his shotgun leveled at Alvord, who did his best to look inoffensive. Despite his efforts, he was clearly the most formidable of the group, for aside from his large size his appearance had an ineradicable sternness about it.

"Well, well," the man sneered at them, "what a splendid little group o' folks! Does me heart good to see such upstanding citizens."

He smiled to reveal black teeth and shriveled gums.

The coachman was over to the side with a cutlass to his throat. "Just get on with it," he requested angrily.

"Shut it!" ordered the half-breed, who gave him a tap on the skull with his sword's pommel. The coachmen grimaced gamely, glaring death at the man.

Alvord noticed the composed brunette watching him closely. He tipped her a quick wink.

She saw him make a blurring pass in front of his mouth with a closed fist, but could only guess as to the purpose it served.

"So then!" spoke the tallest highwaymen, who appeared to be the leader of the group. "Let's see what you ladies and gents have in yer pockets, and then we'll have a look-see at your baggage, eh? Tell ye what—if we likes what we find, we'll let you live, though you'll have to walk your couth arses out of here.

"'Cept for you," he pointed a filthy finger at the young brunette, "you're comin' with us, m'dear."

The man with the monocle gasped in shock. "Come now, surely we can come to some sort of—"

The highwaymen slammed the butt of his fowling piece into the speaker's gut, laughing scornfully as he did so.

He signaled the other two whites to move in on the passengers. As they approached Alvord began to cough uncontrollably, moving away from the others.

"Hey. You there, consumptive. Belay the coughing." One of them walked over to him and gave him a hard shake, warily keeping his shotgun on Alvord's broad back.

"Sorry, sorry," Alvord choked, but was overtaken by another series of hacking coughs.

To the highwayman's profound amazement, a silver coin fell from his victim's mouth. He picked it up, dumbfounded.

"Look ye here, fellers! Bastard spat up a coin! A Silver Liberty Dollar!"

The others gathered round, weapons now pointed at the ground.

"What?" spat the half-breed disbelievingly.

"Watch 'im!" As they did, several gold and silver coins spilled from Alvord's mouth onto the leaf litter.

"What the...?" their leader breathed. It was the last thing he did.

Alvord came up with his club held in both hands, driving its copper tip into the man's sternum with tremendous force. Blood shot out of his mouth as he went down, but before he hit another shot caught him on the back of the head, splitting his skull. His gun went off, carving a crater out of the forest floor next to Alvord's foot. The other shotgun-wielding highwayman raised his weapon, but too late. The arm holding the trigger was crushed by a ferocious downwards swing, the elbow rendered useless. The butt of the club came round and turned his nose to mush.

Suddenly Alvord took a swift step back, and the half-breed's cutlass swished through the air where he had been standing a moment before. He curved a left hook into the man's pockmarked jaw. A loud popping sound followed, and the ruffian collapsed with a loud exhalation. Turning his attention back to the wounded highwayman with the shotgun, Alvord saw the brunette sneak up behind the screaming man, a fist-sized rock in hand. She rapped him sharply on the top of the head, bringing him down.

The remaining highwayman jumped over the still-twitching carcass of his leader to engage Alvord. Alvord was impressed—most men would disperse after losing their accomplices and leader. But he was not impressed enough to let the man live.

An unanticipated jab from the former police captain split the man's lips, but he kept coming, wielding his cutlass with considerable skill. He was good, but even with a club

Alvord was his better. His footwork alone had the man tripping over his own feet and slicing nothing but air. With deft moves Alvord turned aside the rusty blade, riposted powerfully each time to inflict grisly wounds. Faking a downward slash, the desperate highwayman went for a thrust, but his opponent sidestepped and delivered a terrible backhanded blow to the side of his neck. A swift kick to the gut lifted him from the ground, and an open-handed strike to his chin sent his crippled body sprawling. He lay among the dirt and leaves—bloody, unconscious, but breathing.

His vanquisher moved in to deliver the *coup de grace*.

"*Stop!*" A shrill voice implored him. It was the brunette.

Alvord stared at her, eyes blazing.

"Please leave him, sir. He's no longer a threat. Let's just be on our way, *please*."

He snorted mirthlessly. "Leave him? So that some other unsuspecting victim can fall to his blade? Did you hear what they intended to do with you, girl?"

The girl's brown eyes held his penetrating stare, though they were watery and her lips did tremble. He knew that she was shocked by what she had just seen and done, yet she spoke slowly and firmly.

"Yes, I heard them. But are you not better than this, better than them? You have done what needed to be done, and for that we will all be ever grateful. But don't sink to their wretched level, I beg of you. Please sir, can you not see that this is unnecessary, excessive?"

He stood there, breathing heavily and gazing hypnotically at the prostrate form of the highwayman. The hair on his arms and legs all stood erect, and he could feel the raw power coursing through his body. In the grip of wrath, his instincts told him to destroy the foul caricature of humanity that lay gasping before him, but a persistent voice inside his head said that the girl was right. He was better than this. He had enough blood on his hands.

Turning toward the young woman he drew near her, his beard tinged with gold from the sun. He owed her much—she had helped him beyond her knowing.

"Thank you." His voice wavered, as if barely controlled, but grew smoother as he continued.

"I am quite impressed by your aplomb in the face of

danger; you were remarkably heroic in your actions. This world could use more like you."

The girl blushed at the compliment. Recalling the brave actions and wise words that spoke to her noble character, Alvord was reminded of his late wife Katherine. A more complimentary comparison he could not think of.

After retrieving his coins he stuck his club's tip into the dirt and twisted it, clearing the trusty weapon of blood. "Come now, let's get back into the coach, everyone."

"Who are you?" the man with the monocle wanted to know.

"No one of any importance," replied Alvord, stifling a grin.

Without warning, the half-breed popped up, sword upraised. Alvord immediately turned to face him, but the deafening report of a shotgun came before he engaged the man.

The half-breed went down, clutching his gut. The coachmen stood behind him, the shotgun still smoking in his hands.

"Tough 'un, that half-breed. Let's listen to the gentleman here and get going, shall we?"

The passengers obediently filed into the coach. As Alvord went to get in, a hand restrained him that turned out to be the coachman's.

"Nice trick there with them coins. Care to ride up front?"

Chapter 10

The steamboat spewed foul-smelling smoke into a darkling sky as it chugged its way up the Mississippi. St. Louis lay only eight hours upriver and Alvord could hardly contain his excitement. Normally a staid man, he found himself stifling smiles and trying to slow the rapid pulsing of his heart. Yet he had good cause to be in such a state, for soon he would set foot on the wharves of The River Queen, the St. Louis that George Caleb Bingham had painted with such fondness, the city that stood on the threshold of the vast American frontier.

He thought of all the trappers who had passed through St. Louis on their way to the Rockies, the exploration parties that had used the city as a staging ground for their expeditions. Louis and Clarke, Fremont, Pike, Ashley's Hundred; all had walked the hallowed ground he himself would soon trod. The ripe renown of their deeds had always made him yearn for the wilderness and now, as he fast approached the city that had been so instrumental in the exploration of the West, he felt as merry as a troubadour.

Minus the gaudy attire, of course. And the musical aptitude.

So eager was he that he momentarily forgot the mission that had brought him there.

Incredibly, the journey from New York to St. Louis had taken a mere twelve days. Alvord had assumed that a trip halfway across the country would take closer to a full month, yet the speed of the trains and steamboats surprised him. Granted, he had traveled almost non-stop since leaving Manhattan, but it still stood that Americans had impressively fast modes of transportation at their disposal. What other nation could easily navigate so immense a wilderness?

At each major city along the Ohio River, he had stopped

to take a quick look around. After all, when would he ever be out this way again?

Pittsburg he had enjoyed his time in. The people were somewhat sullen and seemed disinclined to talk to strangers, but the city itself was a credit to America's burgeoning manufacturing industry. Many iron, brass, tin, and glass products were shipped east and west from Pittsburgh, and the timber industry was another thriving aspect of the local economy. The primeval forests of the western Alleghenies provided ample work for the axe, aside from providing nice scenery for travelers. Excepting the Second Court House, a sizable Greek Revival that sat atop Grant's Hill, the architecture was dull and often an eyesore. It didn't help that in 1845 a fire had swept across part of the city, causing nine million dollars' worth of damage and leaving hundreds of smoldering buildings in its wake. Peculiar how both Pittsburgh and New York had suffered physically and economically devastating fires that year. But in Alvord's assessment, the Pennsylvania city would rebuild and continue to prosper, for the whole place had an air of optimism and tireless work ethic about it.

Cincinnati had been pleasant; there was real potential there. The citizens were polite and cheerful, showing great pride in their city. As well they may. The streets were all well paved, which came as a surprise since macadamized roads were scant elsewhere in Ohio. Houses of red and white graced the streets, which were incredibly clean. Oddly enough, this "rural city" had fewer pigs roaming its streets than New York City, the very height of urban achievement. It was hard to believe that just fifty years earlier, this hollow in the hills had been a frontier town where folks barred their doors at night against ravening wolves and panthers, and even Indians. Since then, the town had evolved into a respectable city with stately private residences, lush gardens, and well trod footpaths shaded by lofty elms.

And even Louisville had been—well no, actually, Louisville had been a dingy hellhole. Far too much traffic on the river there, and the waters had been both murky and trash-filled. Everything in that city, from the homes to the young trees planted along the streets, had been covered by a fine layer of coal dust, which was a result of the widespread use of bituminous coal in the city. The populace wore clothes soiled by the stuff, even the wealthy.

These rapidly developing western cities surprised him in their size and advanced industries. He had been expecting small, struggling, and unsightly cities still clawing their way out of the wilderness, but was pleased to see that progress was the catchword of these places.

Returning his mind to the present, Alvord spat into the river and sighed. It was hot—breathless in fact. Alvord had shed his outer coats until all he wore was a thin white shirt with several top buttons undone and the sleeves rolled up. A bit risqué, he knew, but how else was a man to keep cool in this accursed heat?

This western steamer was devoid of all the comforts offered on eastern canal boats. On a canal boat, no man sat until every woman had a seat, but the veneer of civility wore thin out west, it seemed. On a canal boat there would always be a well-stocked bar, comfortable rooms to sleep in, and even a barber. The booze was still present on the steamer (though in diminished quality), but the rooms were miserable, and he had seen neither hide nor hair of a barber. Negroes and the poor were relegated to the lower decks, while those who could afford it secured grimy little rooms that stank of fish and mold. Four meals had been served each day aboard the canal boat, including such luxury items as tea, coffee, salmon, shad, liver, pickles, steak, and black puddings. Uncharacteristically, he even found himself longing for the cheerful conversations and good company that had accompanied those savory meals. Here on the steamer, the people were taciturn to the point of being rude, dirty, and often quite malodorous. Dinner had been a miserable affair, with foul food items and river water to drink, if one did not want watery ale or lethal whiskey. When his dinner mates did speak it was scurrilous in the extreme, and grew more colorful and boisterous as the consumption of alcohol increased. Rowdy bands of Irishmen roared out the lyrics to bawdy songs and sawed on fiddles with earsplitting enthusiasm. Some even discharged guns into the air in the throes of their drunkenness. Alvord liked a drink as much as the next man, but was disdainful of those who let themselves get too sloppy in public.

Alvord had taken leave of that cacophonous inner deck

some time ago, and now leaned against the railing of the boat. Glad of the solitude, he stared at the eastern shoreline. He had situated himself near the rear of the boat, as the crewmen had advised him to do, for if the engine was to explode then it was the front of the boat that would be destroyed.

When he asked the men how frequently that happened, he had received only sly smiles in reply.

He was impressed with the crew, a mix of whites and free blacks. They worked as a seamless team, the blacks showing greater skill and work ethic than Alvord had ever witnessed in New York blacks. He had yet to see any crewmen scolded by a superior for slacking or botching a task.

Constant was the need to fend off floating tree trunks with staves, and smartly they went about the task. The lookout was by far the most remarkable crewman aboard, though. Just by looking at the riffles in the water and the shifting of the current, he could determine where sawyers, the fallen trees stuck to the river's bottom, were located. Alvord had watched the man closely and eventually tried to spot the sawyers himself, a task at which he found himself quite adept.

A small farm appeared on the shore, a motley collection of ramshackle cabins and stump-studded fields. He was told that wheat was the primary crop of this area, but the visibility was too poor for him to make out what these particular folks grew. A little girl, dressed in tattered, dirt-stained clothes, stared at Alvord from the river's edge. He raised a hand in salutation, a gesture unreturned. There was a haunting quality to her pale, thin face as she stood there limply holding a cloth doll. It was almost as if she wanted nothing more than to swim out to the steamer and leave that unproductive farm forever behind. Alvord held her stare until her receding figure was nothing but a white speck in the distance, and said a silent prayer for her wellbeing.

A flooded forest reared out of the water near shore. Called snags by the crew, they were a serious hazard if totally submerged, capable of ripping out the bottom of a boat. Alvord hoped no such misfortune befell them, for he was none too eager to bail ship and swim for it.

And with good reason—the water was absolutely filthy. It was a dull brown, and in the wake of the steamer had a disgusting layer of reddish scum floating on its surface. He had heard that the Mississippi wasn't the cleanest of rivers, but hadn't expected this.

But its sheer majesty made up for its unsightliness. Upon reaching the Mississippi, Alvord had been awed by the size and scope of The Father of Waters. His familiar Hudson River, even at its widest, was hopelessly dwarfed in comparison. At times, this river was over two miles wide, churning with froth, dead trees, and a variety of man-made debris. Riverbanks were few and very flat, and marshy more often than not. Mosquitoes abounded along the Mississippi, as did the frogs that were already beginning their raucous salute to the encroaching dusk.

Where the shore wasn't marshland, it ranged from stunted forest to some of the mightiest timber he had ever laid eyes on. He didn't envy the men and women who would hack out an existence from those woods. Felling one of those great oaks or hickories would require an entire day's work. It suddenly dawned on him what a privileged and comfortable life he had led; here he was complaining to himself about the conditions of the steamer when there were people pitting themselves against the wilderness in a desperate bid to succeed by the labor of their own hands. What reckless impulse or dire situations could drive people to settle where before only savages had trod? Whatever it was, it would breed rugged people, as it ever had on frontier land.

Alvord moved to the other side of the boat, so as to observe the setting of the sun. The last few nights, clouds had obscured it as it sank, but tonight would be clear. According to the crew, sunsets were often spectacular on the river.

"Hey Alvord," a familiar voice hailed, "What's the matter? You don't deign to mingle with we commoners inside?"

Alvord held his surprise in check. "You said it Finnbar, not I."

They shook hands, smiling.

"How long have you been aboard? I'm surprised I didn't see you before now."

"Since Evansville, lad. Took ill right before I boarded, and spent the last two days in me room, if you could call it that. Haven't spent so much time in the fetal position since Mother Fagan's womb."

"A lovely visual." Finnbar did indeed look peaky, with

hollow cheeks and pasty skin.

"And while I'm on the topic of complaints- have you dared taste the water they serve on board? Tastes like—"

"Somebody took a drunken piss into a cup of mud, I know it."

"Well, I was going to put it in a slightly more poetic way, but yes."

"I hear the Indians drink it aplenty. Think it's healthful."

"Sadly mistaken, the poor bastards."

"You're feeling salubrious now, then?"

"Fit as a fiddle. Which, by the by, those countrymen of mine are making a jolly old racket with. 'Tis a disgrace to their blood, the way they're carrying on in there. They loudly proclaim themselves Irishmen and in doing so drag the Irish name through the mud."

As if on cue, a gun suddenly was discharged by the front of the boat, followed by whoops and howls of laughter.

"They certainly are a spirited lot."

Alvord actually felt for him; how difficult it must be to belong to a race despised by so many. He watched Finnbar, who stared with intense green eyes into the murky waters.

"I'm going to change the perception of my people, one day." He spoke slowly and seriously. "One day our race will assume a position of respectability in this world of ours, where the Irish are now scorned as dogs. It'll take time, but it'll happen."

A short black crewman struggled past them, heavy laden with ropes. As he passed, he bumped into a man going in the other direction.

"Watch it, boy!" snarled the man in a heavy Southern accent. He was tall, this gent, and ostentatiously attired in a claw-hammer tail coat of blue, a buff waistcoat, and breeches, which had been out of fashion for several decades. Over it all he sported a black leather riding coat that reached his ankles, and a silver-tipped cane was clutched in his hand. It was sweltering but he hardly seemed to notice, as he had a black felt top hat on.

The crewmen bowed his head in apology. "My mistake, sir. I'm sorry for that."

"Yes, well one would reason that a lifetime of servitude would result in more polished work skills."

The black man's nostrils flared as his eyes widened in anger. "I happen to be a free man."

"Aye, nigger, in a white man's country. Know thy birth, boy." And with that he stomped off into the darkness, his knee-high boots creaking something terrible.

The crewman stared after the disappearing figure, and for a moment Alvord thought he might drop his load and charge after him. Finally, he merely shrugged, shook his head, and got back to work. Alvord was not so sure that he could have exercised the same restraint.

"What a bloody prick!" Finnbar exclaimed angrily.

Another crewman, a white man, gave his black messmate a conciliatory pat on the shoulder before addressing Alvord and Finnbar. "I ask that you don't judge all of we southerners by the actions of a few arrogant slave-owners. We ain't all like that, believe me. Race tensions between whites and niggers is commonplace here, but some of us try to rise above it, 'specially in a situation like this where we're working side by side."

Whereas Alvord had found the other man's accent irritating, this man's voice had a soothing, mellifluous Southern quality to it.

"As a frequent victim of prevailing conceptions of Irishmen, I can assure you that I don't judge groups based on the untoward actions of one man," Finnbar promptly answered.

"I thank you for that. Hope you enjoy the rest of your trip, gentlemen," said the man gratefully, and he departed.

The sun was hidden behind the trees, and began radiating the rich purple, red, and gold aura that Alvord had been waiting for. He and Finnbar stood in reverential silence as the colors intensified and broadened across the horizon. It was magnificent—blazing, illuminating the earth in red and golden hues. The landscape, lifeless just a moment ago, was born anew amidst the otherworldly glow that infused every leaf, every blade of grass with a rich golden luster. River water that had been a thick, dull brown now shone a rich purple and yellow. The clouds overhead were few but equally brilliant in their coloration.

It was a fleeting beauty, however. Soon enough the colors faded, and the afterglow proved brief. The reds and golds were gradually replaced by a monotonous blue-gray that shed little light on the river.

"That," Alvord stated firmly, "was something."

As the blue-gray faded into a definitive grayness, the steamboat's paddles fought arduously against the slow, weary, but inexorable current of the river as it chugged its way north to St. Louis.

Chapter 11

Some of the more restless men aboard the steamer leapt for the wharf before the vessel had even been made fast. All were successful in this but one, who cracked his face on the wooden pier and started floundering pathetically in the frothing water of the Mississippi. He was fished out before he drowned by some of the dockhands, cursing a blue stream and trying to stem the flow of the blood that seeped down his forehead. A black porter attempted to apply a rag to the wound but tripped as he did so, knocking himself and the injured man back into the water.

Alvord shook his head bemusedly as he watched the proceedings. What a flock of morons.

The steamer had been due to arrive in St. Louis before sunup, but had gotten caught on a sandbar in the middle of the night. Several labor-intensive hours later the crew (aided by Alvord, Finnbar, and several other passengers) managed to free the vessel, so they ended up reaching St. Louis at eight in the morning.

After the boat was properly tied up, Alvord stepped onto the bustling wharves with Finnbar at his side. Both men grasped the handles of their valises, which they would have to carry themselves unless they wished to entrust them to slow-moving porters.

"No more foul meals and watered-down ale aboard that floating heap, eh Finnbar?"

"And good riddance!" Finnbar happily proclaimed, spitting on the steamer with unbridled joy. "A more miserable craft did never defile the waters!"

The captain shouted a fiery insult from the upper deck, prompting the Irishman to raise two fingers in impolite salute and respond in kind.

"Kiss me bollocks, you pig-ravishing primitive!"

Leaving the boat behind they walked towards the city. As it was mostly men on the wharves Alvord, half a head taller than most, moved for no one, so Finnbar had only to walk in his wake to ensure easy travel. For those without the benefit of Alvord's height, width, or might, traversing the wharves was a nightmarish affair, with constant jostling and bumping into others. It was mostly blacks and whites they encountered, with a smattering of Indians, Mexicans, and even the odd Chinaman.

Along the river a veritable forest of steamer chimneys and flagstaffs towered over the levee. Boats were constantly coming and going, dropping off cargo, mail, and travelers. The waterfront could accommodate three hundred steamers, and the din of the crews, the passengers, and the rotating paddles was incredible. Shouted orders and oaths were punctuated by the strident whistle blasts that heralded each revolution of the steamships' paddles.

The sun blazed with savage intensity, and the humidity was unlike any that Alvord had ever experienced. The steamer had provided some shade, but shade was simply not to be had along the waterfront. The sun beat down upon he and Finnbar unmercifully as they walked. He could feel himself sweating through his undergarments, and did not doubt that his outer layers would soon be similarly drenched. It was quite obvious to him that he was ill-suited for this climate. Mopping at the sweat rolling down his face, he continued his undeviating march towards the levee, where stone warehouses sat in tidy rows and the milling horde seemed slightly less dense. With a quick glance behind him he saw that Finnbar was still close by. To become separated here was to be separated for a tidy spell. The River Queen was a city of over fifty thousand people, and it seemed as if the entire population had decided to concentrate itself on the waterfront area this particular morning.

Finally, they were beyond the levee. Finnbar reappeared at Alvord's side, dripping with sweat yet looking exhilarated all the same. The pair stopped alongside a gunsmith's shop and rested in the sparse shade of a young locust tree. With keen, roving eyes they took in their surroundings.

Horsemen and carriages flashed by them pell-mell, while lumbering oxen and mules propelled carts heavy laden with a wide variety of goods. Alvord slipped off his waistcoat and deposited it into the larger of his valises. Finnbar followed suit, breathing a sigh a relief as he did so.

"Well, with that wretched tribulation behind us, I think we can finally start enjoying ourselves on this holiday."

"Speaking of holiday, what brings you, a proud son of Erin, to this stifling frontier outpost anyway? If you don't mind my asking."

"I'm going to reinvigorate Irish literature," responded Finnbar offhandedly while still observing the city.

"A herculean task," Alvord ribbed.

"But in order to do so," continued Finnbar, undismayed, "I need some worldly experience. I desire to "see the elephant," as you Americans are fond of saying, to see it all. The British Isles I've seen, Brazil and Uruguay too, but I felt that in the American West I would find the sort of literary inspiration I have longed for."

"So you're an itinerant writer, eh? Most interesting." This was not your typical Irishman, Alvord concluded. After working alongside the man to free the steamer and having spoken to him through much of the night on various topics, Alvord had determined that Finnbar was an exceptional man, Irish though he might be. Although perhaps he was wrong to impose limitations on the man on the basis of race alone. Having worked with Irishmen on the force, particularly Andrew O'Farrell, Alvord was beginning to re-examine his ingrained suppositions regarding the deficiencies of Celtic blood.

"And what business do you have here?" Finnbar wanted to know.

"Let's just say that I'm a New York Police Captain being paid to reunite a lost sheep with his flock." As he was no longer a copper that was a bit of a lie, but he did not feel like explaining his whole story.

"How very biblical. An evasive explanation but it sounds exciting nonetheless."

"It should prove to be."

Finnbar threw his head back and chortled, but did not press any further.

St. Louis was situated on a small hill, which Finnbar and Alvord slowly ascended via Walnut Street. The ground rose in a gentle swell, so the climb was none too taxing. The roads were macadamized, but miserably so; an inferior strain of limestone had been crushed and laid atop the foundation of leveled dirt, and was riddled with cracks and threw up a choking white dust.

At the corner of Walnut and Fourth, a crumbling two-story fort met their gazes.

"Strange. Looks Spanish," remarked Finnbar.

"The Spanish gained St. Louis in the Treaty of Paris of 1769, and held it until the Louisiana Purchase of 1803. In true Spanish style, they tried to rework the city to fit the Spanish model, but the city stubbornly maintained its French identity. Indeed, the oldest part of the city is still French in architecture and tongue, and the social elite here are mostly descended from the early French settlers. But from what I have read, the recent improvements and expansion has been distinctly American in nature."

The Irishman looked impressed. "You know your history."

"History is a valuable and oft-neglected weapon."

Finnbar chuckled appreciatively. "Might have to quote you on that someday."

Peering past the old fort, Alvord could see a five-story building that dwarfed all structures around it. "I believe that is the Planter's Hotel. Charles Dickens stayed there during his visit. I'll be lodging there myself. Do you have a certain destination in mind?"

"I was told that an Irishman from Cork keeps a small but fashionable hotel up on Olive and Twelfth, so I'm bound by blood to patronize his establishment. I have business to attend to today and tonight, but what do you say we meet for drinks sometime tomorrow?"

"Sounds good. I too have things that need doing. As talk has it, some good taverns are to be found on Market Street. What say you to meeting..." he consulted the small map he'd purchased aboard the steamer, "at Market and Eleventh tomorrow at four? City Hall stands just north, on the corner of Chestnut and Eleventh."

He held the map out for Finnbar to see.

"Alright. Four it is. Until then, Alvord."

They shook hands and parted ways.

Alvord would have thought it impossible, but somehow the heat of the Planter's Hotel surpassed that of the street. The place was classy and aesthetically pleasing, but that was hard to notice when you were dripping sweat onto the marble floor. Dropping his valises with a thud, he rested his sweaty palms against the table. The desk clerk looked up from his work, and started when he saw Alvord's florid, dripping face.

"By Jove, are you alright, sir?" he inquired, Kentish accent in evidence.

"Fine. Just ill-acquainted with heat of this intensity, is all. I would like a room for one, please."

"Very well then! Have you a preference as to what floor you stay on, sir? We currently have rooms free on the fifth, third, and second floors-"

"Is there some sort of cellar room that I could stay in?" Alvord interjected distractedly.

"Good Heavens man! Why on earth would you seek lodgings in the cellar?"

"It will be significantly cooler down there. I can't abide this accursed heat."

"Sorry, but the cellar is for storage only," the man told him, giving him a concerned look. "There are no furnished rooms down there."

Alvord sighed. "Hmm. Well, I guess I'll take something on the second floor, then."

"Capital! We can have your room ready in ten or so minutes. How many days will you be staying?"

"I will pay for three now, though I may be here longer."

"Very well. Chambermaids are available to clean your room each morning at ten o'clock, if you'd like."

"No thank you. I will notify you when I require a maid. Is there a balcony for this room?"

The Englishman frowned. "You mean a gallery?"

"No, I mean a *balcony*."

"Sorry, only rooms on the fifth floor are equipped with *balconies*. I can secure one for you now. While it is made ready, I suggest you go into our dining hall for a sideboard breakfast."

"You mean a buffet breakfast?"

"No, I mean a *sideboard breakfast*."

"Whatever the case, which way to the food? Decent victuals have been in depressingly short supply lately."

After Alvord paid, the desk clerk conducted him through a tall gilded door and into an expansive dining hall. With a barely audible moan of expectancy, Alvord made a beeline for the smoked eels.

After a hearty breakfast Alvord stood in front of the mirror in his room, stripped to the waist. For a moment he observed his powerful and well-defined form, but averted his eyes after a spell lest he be guilty of vanity. Perfunctorily, he went through his daily ablutions, using the large washbasin that had been provided. He trimmed his beard with the scissors he kept in his hygiene bag. Unkempt beards were unbecoming of a gentleman in his estimation, so he always made sure his own was uniformly short.

The bed was large and comfortable too. Despite its neat appearance, Alvord was still skeptical as to its cleanliness. Hotels and boardinghouses were often ridden with lice and fleas, and he was none too keen on becoming host to the tiny vermin. He soaked several small cloths in lavender extract and laid them down on the bed. It would drive any lurking vermin away, at least in theory.

Lastly, he changed his clothes (his first outfit was thoroughly sweat-soaked), making sure to dress lightly and in light colors. He decided to forgo the waistcoat-top hat look, opting instead for trousers and a white dress shirt with the sleeves rolled up. Thus attired, he stepped out onto the balcony; he had decided on the fifth floor after all, for he wanted the balcony so as to have a view of the river and the lands beyond.

The hotel commanded an impressive view of the Illinois side of the Mississippi, which was more desolate than the Missouri side. Some small farms made patchwork out of the forest along the river, but by and large wilderness presided over that region. A sizable island lay between the two shorelines; somehow Alvord hadn't envisioned it like that. He had anticipated a massively wide river unbroken by islands. Yet there sat one, with another off to the south, close to the city and the waterfront area. The Mississippi itself teemed with activity, with all manner of craft plying its waters.

Alvord looked down upon the frenzied madness of the waterfront. It didn't seem quite so bad when you were far removed from it.

To the north a large, round hill could be seen above the

rooftops. He figured that must be Big Mound, the largest of the old Indian mounds still found in the city.

To his right the cupola of the Courthouse reared up over the roof of a hospital, but above even the cupola soared the steeple of the Second Presbyterian Church. Now there was an impressive building.

Pleased with the view, he went back into his room and gave his face a final splash of water, trying to fortify himself against the heat.

He allowed himself a nap, which he took in an armchair that faced the door, as was his wont. Two hours later he rose, refreshed and prepared to work.

After nearly two weeks of continuous travel, it was time to pay Charles Deas a visit.

The artist kept a studio on 97 Chestnut Street. Alvord stood outside the building, taking a good hard look at it. One last time he checked the address from the piece of paper given to him by Mrs. Deas. The plain, two-story structure was of wood, with no obvious architectural style to it, but stately and clean nonetheless. Deas rented out the upper story, so Alvord opened the front door, walking past the entrance to the main floor to mount the staircase. At the top of the stairs was a narrow hallway that ended at another door, which he loudly rapped on.

Nothing. He knocked again, this time calling Deas's name. Ear to the door, he listened intently for a voice or footsteps. Satisfied that Charles was out, he reached for his lock pick and sprung the primitive lock in a few minutes time.

A quick look around told him that Charles Deas had little concern for tidiness. Easels were set up willy-nilly around the main room, while parchment, canvases, pencils and paintbrushes littered the floor. The nearest window was open, allowing a pleasant breeze to circulate through the room. A piece of paper blew off a nearby table and scuttled into Alvord's boot. Picking it up, he examined the charcoal sketch that it contained. It was crudely executed, but he recognized it nonetheless.

Long Jakes, first exhibited in 1844, was a quintessentially American work that appealed immensely to people like Alvord, who relished stories of the American frontier and the characters that populated it.

Intrigued, he looked around the room and found several oil versions of the sketch hanging on the far wall. He took a good long look at the best of them. The painting depicted a sun-scorched mountain man in a bright red calico shirt and fringed buckskin leggings astride a mighty black steed. Both the horse and rider appeared to have heard something behind them, and the trapper's firmly clutched rifle betokened an imminent encounter. The rakishly angled hat on his head and the casual position of his body in the saddle suggested a composed man of action who was undaunted by whatever challenge might come his way. The trapper and horse dominated the foreground, while in the distance craggy peaks soared skyward and a vast forest carpeted the dark valley below.

Alvord recalled reading about the painting in *The Broadway Journal* three years ago, where it had been hailed as a huge financial success. And no wonder. The colors were bold, the detail incredible, and it pictured a white man facing the desolation of the American wilderness with only his rifle and horse for company. Indeed, looking at the work triggered an impulse in Alvord to jump on a horse himself and ride deep into Indian country.

Walking around the room, he examined the other works, some of which were rather tame genre scenes, others of which were brimming with conflict and action.

One showed a drunkard walking the chalk, a popular sobriety test in taverns and aboard ships. Another entitled *The Trooper* depicted a mounted duel between two cavalrymen amidst a gloomy, menacing landscape of slashing rain and towering cumulonimbus clouds. A number of them showed rather quotidian scenes of Indian life, although he did favor one of Sioux Indians playing lacrosse. Alvord found himself enjoying most of the works he passed, even if some of them were vaguely sinister.

Deas had painted some landscapes that were akin to Thomas Cole's, yet there was something noticeably darker and ill-boding about them. They could actually be likened to a fusion of Cole's style and that of John Kensett's, another popular landscapist of the day.

Alvord looked at them more closely. Something about those jagged cliffs and dead, vine-choked trees just wasn't right.

And the clouds and skies were ominous too, in ways that Alvord simply couldn't explain. It seemed to him that the whole tone of these landscapes was one of impending doom.

One scene portraying voyageurs plying the gloomy waters of a river was equally unsettling, with that same eerie landscape and ominous sense of expectancy. He recalled that Mrs. Deas had warned of her son's love for the darker side of nature, and these paintings served as a worrisome confirmation of the fact.

Alvord passed into another room, larger than the first, and was confronted by an enormous canvas on which a desperate battle raged.

It was called *The Death Struggle*, and it had been completed in 1845. Precariously poised upon the edge of a sheer cliff were a white trapper and an Indian. The former was mounted on a frothing but gallant white steed while the savage sat astride a demonic-looking black horse with its tongue lolling and its head flung wildly back. For both men death seemed inevitable, although the white man's horse was making an unlikely leap for a nearby rock. Impending plummet notwithstanding, the two men were locked in mortal combat. The bloodied Indian doggedly bear-hugged the trapper, who was desperately holding onto a dead tree limb above his head with one hand. The white man, unlike his foe, sported no visible injuries, while both the black horse and the Indian atop it were bleeding profusely. Laughably enough a beaver, caught in a steel trap and held in the trapper's hand, was viciously sinking its teeth into the arm of the red man who just couldn't seem to catch a break.

Alvord took a seat in a comfortable armchair and regarded the piece once again. There was something about the way in which the dark horse's eyes blazed and the nostrils snorted fire that conjured up images of Hell and the Apocalypse. With its red irises and wild posture it might have been Satan's own mount. The scenery was quite compatible with the violence in the foreground, for ominous black clouds shrouded the sky and ragged buzzards zoomed towards the conflict. In the distance it appeared that two mountaintops were aflame and sending smoke wafting into the darkening sky, reinforcing the sense that catastrophic events were unfolding beyond the present struggle of the combatants.

It was a scene without hope, and it summoned

gooseflesh to Alvord's arms.

Gazing around the room, he noticed a nail-studded, crimson-colored door to his left. An instant later he stood in front of it, turning the doorknob. It was locked, sure enough.

Alvord paused a moment, listening to make sure that nobody was coming up the stairs. After a few moments he reached for his lock pick.

"You'll be needing this to get through that door," said a smooth, amused voice behind him.

Doing his best to appear unsurprised and unconcerned, Alvord turned around in what he hoped was a casual manner and found Charles Deas leaning up against the doorway. He pointed a flintlock pistol his way with one hand and held a sizable iron key in the other.

Alvord instantly recognized him from the portraits and daguerreotypes Mrs. Deas had lent him, although he looked hard worn, sick maybe. Despite this he was still ruggedly handsome, dashing even, with dark flyaway hair spilling onto his long, ovular face. His features were decidedly French while not entirely excluding the possibility of other blood. A slightly hooked nose and severe eyebrows gave him a somewhat stern air, but Alvord could detect a humorous twinkle in the man's eyes and mouth.

"Hello there, Charles. I needn't tell you that it's rather rude to sneak up on people unannounced."

"Ho, ho, hark the bold hypocrite," chuckled Deas sarcastically. "You enter my studio without so much as a by your leave, then chide me for sneaking up on you? By name, no less. You're quite lucky that I'm not the 'shoot first, ask questions later' type."

Alvord smirked. "Saw that portrait you did of George Matsell. It was a good likeness of the man. Dark and disturbed, but good."

Deas strode forward and sat in a chair facing Alvord, flintlock still focused on his chest. He remained silent for a moment, and then frowned.

"Matsell, eh? I did that when I still in New York. Justice of the Peace, no? Portly, ruddy-faced fellow?"

"Right in one."

The artist's lips curled into a sly, but still tired-looking smile. "Dark and disturbed, eh? Well, to the untrained eye of the vapid layman, I suppose it seems so. But truth be told, that was my first *real* artistic achievement. In that painting I first transcended my old puerile works of creative mimicry and broke into a new sphere of artistic consciousness. How did you come to see that portrait, mister?"

"He was appointed Chief of the Municipal Police Department, and I worked under him as Captain."

"Worked?"

"Turns out I didn't do enough to curry political favor in New York, and was ousted for a number of reasons, some legitimate, some concocted."

Deas nodded understandingly and broadened his smile.

"Bloody politics, eh?"

"Bloody politics," Alvord affirmed with quiet laughter. He did not know why he shared that information, but he supposed he needed to get it off his chest at some point.

Deas motioned with his pistol, indicating that Alvord take the chair across the room. The fact that Deas still hadn't asked for his name and didn't seem in a hurry for the information said a lot about him. He wasn't the panicky type, this painter, at ease as he was with a total stranger who had just broken into his home. Of course, the gun in his hand could only serve to boost his confidence.

"May I be so bold as to ask why you broke into my studio?"

"May I first ask how you stole upon me so quietly? I am generally not so easy to stalk."

"My boots have soles of India-rubber which grant me near silence in movement, hence the silence. I saw your form through a window as I was coming home, so figured it would behoove me to act with caution."

"Good man. My own boots have such soles."

"Who are you?" He shot the question, finally weary of all the evasive banter.

"Alvord Rawn."

"Alvord Rawn. I do believe that I recall the name from my time in Manhattan. Yes, Rawn the copper, I remember now. Alvord- isn't that a surname?"

"Yes it is, but my mother thought it would make a fetching first name and I rather agree with her. It is generally a Cumbrian surname."

Deas tipped back in his chair and pursed his lips pensively. "I've met many a man with two first names, but you sir are the first with two last names."

Alvord tipped back in his own chair and steepled his fingers. "Now to business. I was sent here by your mother, Ann Izard Deas. Roughly two weeks ago she contacted me. You see, aside from being employed by the Municipal Police, I did private detective work on the side. Now that I am no longer affiliated with the Department, I can devote myself wholly to the detective aspect. In short, she sent me to request your return. Demand it, in fact. Ensure it."

Deas's face was a rigid mask of shock. "*What*...are you mad, man? She paid you to travel halfway across the country so that you could order me home on her authority! I'm a grown man, nearly thirty years old. I can make my own decisions, thank you very much!"

"Those last few letters you sent her were maniacal, Charles, do you realize that? You seem like a decent fellow—what kind of state were you in to write such rot? All this talk of Count Abendroth and mesmerism and heightened consciousness—its madness, and it has her worried. Downright terrified, truth be told. So do us all a favor, and pack up your things so we can leave in a timely fashion. What say you?"

"Don't slander what you don't understand, Alvord," whispered the artist with narrowed eyes.

"Will you cooperate or not, Charles?"

The painter looked Alvord in the eye and grinned pleasantly. "In two words, my dear fellow—*Piss off.*"

"Ah. I feared you'd be intractable. Oh well. I will not stoop to beg for your compliance. We can do this the hard way, too."

Deas looked taken aback, seeming to notice Alvord's size for the first time. "Hard way?"

"Yes. In that instance I handcuff you to me for the return trip and have all your belongings shipped back east on a mail steamer. If you prove defiant, I will periodically dose you with opium and enjoy a quiet trip home. Upon arrival, I will then deliver your bedraggled ass to your poor mother, who is no doubt fretting about you as we speak. Then I proceed to collect the second half of my pay and we never meet again, unless of course you choose to flee, in which case I might be hired to track you down for a second time. Savvy?"

The man visibly gulped, but tried to put on a tough act. Alvord was impressed.

"That's all good and well, but what if I were to beat you to the door and vanish into the frontier for a spell? What then?"

Alvord's face betrayed the immense amusement he felt with curling lips and a dreamy look in his eyes. "Then, my friend, things really get thrilling. Because then I'll come after you on the frontier and it'll be like something out of a bloody Cooper novel. I'd enjoy that beyond telling, boy."

"And if I involve the law?"

"As far as you're concerned, I am the law." A tad dramatic, yes, but what was life without the occasional theatric moment?

"And if I choose to resist?" he asked, waving the pistol in Alvord's direction.

"I would advise against it, unless of course you think you can out-violence me. That flintlock only affords you one shot, and that's not nearly enough. Anyway, you are not a killer, Charles. I can see that plain as day. A game individual, but not a killer."

Running a hand through his thick hair, Deas sighed before looking up again. "So how are things back east, anyway?"

"Same old. New York is still bustling and overcrowded and reeks of pig shit and unwashed bodies. And your mother is still a wreck, as she has been for months. You'll see for yourself, soon enough."

Deas peered skyward, as if seeking divine guidance, then regarded Alvord seriously. "Alright, listen. I ask that you give me a few days to get my affairs in order, and then I will go with you. I am not pleased, believe you me, but for my mother I'll do this. Her letters to me were a bit pleading in their tone, but I guess this really puts things in perspective. Huh, perspective—art humor, eh?"

Alvord did not crack a smile.

"Ah, perhaps not? Anyway, I'll return home with you. But first, I want to get to know the fellow I'll be travelling with. Let us go dine. Drinks are on me."

With a glance at his timepiece, Alvord clucked disapprovingly. "Barely even noontime and you're seeking booze? Very well, it seems to be the way of things here in the West. Do you know anywhere we can get a decent steak?"

"I know the very place. Rivington's, over on Market Street. It ain't Delmonicos but it ain't bad."

Rising swiftly, to showcase his unusual speed and coordination, Alvord spoke slowly and deliberately to his ward.

"If you run, I'll catch you. Fight, you'll lose. Don't make me regret doing this with civility, Charles."

"You've got my word, Alvord. But it's for my mother, not for fear of you."

Alvord believed him, for his eyes told no lie.

Chapter 12

Market Street proved to be every bit as crowded as the waterfront. Wagons and caravans were being loaded with supplies in preparation for journeys west. Merchants, porters, slaves, workers, and a smattering of trappers passed them by in a whirl of frenzied activity. Above it all the clamorous din issuing from the nearby lumber mills and iron foundry was readily detectable. Even by New York standards, this was a mite congested.

Alvord walked briskly alongside Deas, blinking in the dust and stifling heat.

"How do you deal with such a climate?" he asked of Deas, who seemed quite unaffected by the temperature.

"You grow accustomed to it."

Alvord very much doubted this. He had always favored cooler climes, and now found himself longing for the icy sting of a winter wind. In cold temperatures, at least one could bundle up, but in oppressive heat one could only strip down so much. Seemliness obstructed comfort in that regard, unless you belonged to a primitive race. He had read that some tribesmen in New Guinea wore naught but gourds over their manhood. Imagine that!

"I somehow pictured more Indians in the city," Alvord commented with a hint of disappointment in his voice.

"Used to be more, but when General Clarke gave up the ghost in '38, the tribes stopped coming here on annual pilgrimages. He had a way with the red man, did Clarke, and they would come from all over to negotiate with him. Used to get a lot of Sacs, Fox, Shawnee, and Osages here performing dances and rituals for money, I've heard. There are still plenty of old Indian mounds around the city. In fact, Big Mound is located just over on Broadway and Mound Street; the thing has got to be thirty feet high and at least a hundred long. And tribal representatives from the Indian Territory still pass through on their way to Washington. You'll see Indians around, but not in the numbers they once appeared in. Plenty of half-breeds in the city, but not quite the same thing, is it?"

"Not really. Some Delawares actually still reside in Brooklyn, Staten Island, and the Bronx, but they are few in number and have been thoroughly acculturated."

Deas sadly shook his head. "A doomed race, the red man. Catlin was right, you know—we would do well to document their fast-fading culture now, before it is lost forever. I personally try to pay as much attention to detail as possible when depicting Indian scenes. I owe them that much, for they have always treated me with respect."

Up ahead a slave auction was underway. The pitiable Negroes were confined to massive pens where potential buyers could observe them while sellers hovered around extolling the virtues of their slaves. Prospective purchases were taken out of the pens and made to stand on auction blocks for closer inspection.

Slavery had been outlawed in New York City in 1827, so the grim reality of human enslavement was not something Alvord regularly came into contact with. He had seen slaves in his day, but never before had he observed men, women, and children in shackles and iron collars, standing listlessly in cages whilst corpulent plantation owners appraised them like common farm animals.

Noticing the blatant disgust and anger contorting Alvord's features, Deas nudged his elbow. "Those slave pens belong to a man by the name of Bernard Lynch. Wealthy fellow, highly influential in the city."

"Money and influence obtained through the bondage of one's fellow man. Truly sickening."

"I agree, but that's not what I was getting at. Listen, just so you know, St. Louis is *rabidly* anti-abolitionist. Whereas you say fellow man, they say subhuman beings born for bondage. Fellow by the name of Elijah Lovejoy ran an abolitionist paper here called the *St. Louis Observer*. When he spoke out against the savage burning of a free black named Francis McIntosh in 1836, pro-slavery mobs threw his printing press into river and forced him to relocate to the Illinois side. For defending *one*

Negro, Alvord. Although in truth McIntosh did slay two deputy constables, so I can understand the anger and perhaps he got what he deserved. The slave trade is a booming industry here, and plantation owners all along the Mississippi flock to St. Louis to purchase slaves. Even free blacks enjoy few rights around these parts. It is a tad shocking at first, I know, but sadly enough you grow used to it, just like the heat."

His words were rewarded by a look of deepest contempt.

"Hey!" he exclaimed, holding up his hands, "I know how it sounds, but it's simply the way of things out here. Some of them don't have it that bad, they can actually earn money with which to purchase their freedom. And not all are whipped and mutilated when refractory, as often you hear in the North. In fact, I've spoken with slaves who genuinely adore their masters, as astounding and sick as it may seem. I still don't agree with it, Alvord. Believe me. Not that black folk should be equal to whites; of course they shouldn't, yet they do not deserve to be slaves. But while you're here, you would do well to keep your opinions on slavery to yourself. I sure as hell do."

They walked for a while in uncomfortable silence.

"You are a Whig, then?" Alvord asked.

"Right in one. We are few out here, but well organized and smart. And we know that it pays to keep relatively quiet, for the time being anyway."

"What paper should I buy in these parts? I have not read a decent one in a while."

"Only Whig paper is *The Missouri Republican*. Everything else is Democrat trash."

"I'm sure the Democrats would disagree."

A group of mounted Dragoons trotted briskly through the crowd, sabers clattering loudly at their sides. One raised a hand in salute towards Deas, shouting something that was lost amidst the clamor of the crowd.

"Friends of yours?"

"You might say that. Three years ago I accompanied them to Fort Kearny and points beyond to visit and basically intimidate the Otoe and Potawatomie, who had been behaving badly. Some real good men among those dragoons, never saw one of them show the slightest indication of fear during our trip, though there was peril aplenty."

They continued their slow advance up Market Street,

shouldering their way through the thick crowd.

"I hear a lot of German being spoken here. What sounds like German, anyway. I sometimes confuse it with Scandinavian tongues."

"Yes," answered Deas, "we've got loads of German immigrants in St. Louis. Parts of the city are now referred to as 'Dutchtown'."

"But they are Germans, not Dutchmen. The Dutch come from the Netherlands, I have never understood why so many Americans refer to Germans as Dutch..."

Drifting towards the right side of the road, they freed themselves from the main knot of foot traffic with a final surge forward. Deas took the lead, but stopped when a commotion broke out ahead of them.

Alvord immediately recognized the main player in this incident—the arrogant, cape-wearing man from the steamboat who had nastily insulted the black crewman. The man had roused his ire then, and did nothing now to cultivate his redemption. That he was soused was obvious, from his slurred speech to his staggering walk. He was with an equally drunk friend and attended by two slaves, whose large brand marks Alvord could see from twenty yards off. Their master wended his sloppy way down Market Street, roughly pushing people aside, lashing out with his cane at intervals, and making a general nuisance of himself. As they watched, the man aggressively shouldered a woman out of his way while snarling something about the inferior classes.

That simply did it. Alvord's hatred of slavery and dislike of this bastard popinjay heated to a rolling boil.

Deas also stiffened, let out a snarl, and took a purposeful stride towards the man, but in a flash Alvord was in front of him.

"I've got this," he assured Deas cheerfully.

He walked up, slapping the man soundly in the face before hip-tossing the drunkard into a nearby watering trough. Floundering pathetically, he shouted garbled insults at his assailant, who merely dunked his head back under the water. The man's friend made as if to seize Alvord but was intercepted by Deas, who landed a solid, thudding punch to his midsection and threw him to the ground, where he lay wheezing.

"Let us abscond before a crowd gathers," suggested

Alvord, satisfied with the results of their actions. Smoothly, he and Deas melted back into the throng.

Three minutes later they were in the dimly lit interior of Rivington's. Both ordered steak with potatoes and beer.

"You threw a decent right hand there, artist. There's nothing quite like righteous indignation, am I right?"

Deas chuckled. "For starters, you *are* right. Furthermore, just because I'm an artist doesn't mean I have to be a craven bitch. You shouldn't paint with such broad strokes, Alvord. Trust a painter on that."

"I suppose not." He raised his tankard in salute. "To the dismantling of popular notions of artists."

A pretty redhead served them their food; her coquettish glances at Deas being rewarded with a roguish wink. After she departed, they drank and ate in silence for a bit. Washing down an unseemly mouthful with a gulp of beer, Deas spoke.

"So who *are* you?"

"We've been over this. My name is Alvord Rawn."

"I know that, and like I said I recognize the name. But what sort of man are you, what do you do?"

Alvord took a moment to consider that. "Well, as I said I am a former New York Police Captain who fell victim to 'bloody politics' as you phrased it. At present I am pursuing my private detective work as a sole means of income. I am a staunch Whig and friend to Horace Greeley. I used to entertain notions of going West to explore, to play the mountain man, I suppose; now that I have nothing to keep me in New York I just might pursue that dream."

He chose to omit the fact that he was under strict orders to leave New York or face prosecution.

"I've ventured onto the frontier quite a bit," said Deas, "and trust me, there is no better place for exploration, reflection, and self-discovery. St. Louis is merely the gateway to the West, Alvord. Beyond this frontier city lies a vast land, sparsely peopled and magnificently diverse in its terrain. I was myself confined to cities in my youth. It was not until I visited the immense wastes of the Wisconsin Territory that I truly felt myself whole. The West was exotic, alluring. But it is more than that. It is an exhortation of my soul, the wanderlust that drives men to seek out the dim and ancient hollows where few before have trod."

Deas's dark, hollow eyes radiated a bright gleam of enthusiasm. Alvord leaned back, trying to visualize what the artist passionately described.

"You should see it out there, around Fort Crawford and Winnebago. Dismal, primeval swamps stand as mute witnesses to Nature's secrets. Ancient groves of soaring pine lend the forests all the reverent atmosphere of a cathedral. I journeyed once to Lake Michigan from Fort Winnebago, and it is like an inland ocean of fresh water—wild, utterly pristine, and yet unsullied by civilization's inroads. And further west, along the Missouri and the Platte, the glorious immensity of our country's wilderness truly becomes apparent. A man can see forever, walk among savages and herds of buffalo, and fall asleep to the lugubrious yowling of the prairie wolves. The air you breathe out there just seems freer."

"I will soon find out, I think."

"But you have nothing back in New York? No family to support, no friends you'd miss?"

"I am a widower and my children have also gone to meet the Lord. And as for friends, well, I do have some, like Greeley, and some of them I'd definitely miss. But New York grows ever more crowded, ever more crime-ridden. I've read enough Edward Gibbon in my day to recognize social decay when I see it. New York will go the way of Rome. I could not stand idly by while my city stagnates, then declines. I just couldn't do it."

He did find himself missing his men. They had become his family really, after his wife and children had passed. Upon his return to New York he'd see them once more, but after that? It was unlikely. Who knew what Destiny had in store for him? Suddenly, Alvord felt as if he was living a life utterly devoid of purpose, and an indescribable loneliness took hold of him. His lips grew thin, his expression stony.

"I am sorry to hear about your family," spoke Deas quietly, and he looked it.

He signaled the barmaid for another round. When they arrived, he hoisted his tankard in salute this time.

"To new beginnings, then."

Several rounds later, Deas stared into his nearly empty glass of absinthe and frowned.

"Have you ever drunk deep of this stuff?" He had switched to the bright green liquid after a few beers.

"No. I do enjoy it, but mostly in a small quantity after dinner, just to settle the stomach. It is unwise to overindulge in that particular potation."

"Have a round of it, on me."

Alvord hesitated for a moment, then relented. "Fine, but just one, and if a little green fairy starts fluttering 'round my head you've had it."

After they received their drinks, both men stared at the strange green absinthe as it swirled around in their glasses.

Deas laughed hollowly. "You know, I use to think that this was the only thing that would open up doors to new worlds of artistic potential, but I know now that no mere drink can rival the powers that lie dormant within us all."

"Is that so?"

"Ever heard of mesmerism before now? Or animal magnetism, as it is also known?"

Alvord let out a brief rumble of laughter. "I was wondering when you'd bring that up. Your mother says you've become a monomaniac on the subject, and after seeing your recent letters to her I am inclined to agree."

The painter's pupils dilated as his eyes sought out some point in the distance, as they had done when he had spoken of the frontier.

"If you experienced the miracle of magnetism you would understand, my friend. Cosmic truths would be revealed to you, you could unleash unrealized potential, achieve things that would stagger your mind. I owe my artistic progression to mesmerism, which has led me to realms of consciousness and inspiration I never knew to exist. It is so much more than just the simple faith healing it is wrongfully touted as in America. Powerful practitioners like Count Abendroth acknowledge and utilize animal magnetism to its fullest extent, and believe me you would be dumbfounded by its effects."

"By wholly putting myself at the mercy of another? I think not. Anyway, how does simple hypnosis allow you entry into a higher consciousness? Your mother gave me literature concerning this mesmerism, and frankly I'm not buying it."

"Skepticism is to be expected from the uninitiated. But if you won't take my word for it, I'll make a believer out of you by tonight. Count Abendroth will be performing at his chateau this evening, and I am bringing you to the showing with me.

Prepare to be astounded, Alvord. You will be downright thunderstruck by the magnitude of his achievements and will hunger for the secrets behind his power."

The walk back to Deas's studio was a quiet one. Alvord had demanded that the painter stop talking about mesmerism and Count Abendroth about halfway through their return trip. The artist had maintained a sullen silence ever since. His talk had grown fanatical with incredible and rather startling speed, and Alvord had no patience for such ravings.

Yet as offended as he might be Deas invited him up to his studio all the same. Alvord accepted, wishing to look upon some of those paintings again, particularly *Long Jakes*, *The Trooper*, and *The Death Struggle*.

A moment later he was seated in the same armchair gazing at *The Death Struggle*, stroking his red beard pensively.

"What say you?" demanded Deas as he grabbed a half-empty bottle of absinthe from his own stock.

"Highly realistic, inarguably epic, but something about this work strikes me as hellish, Charles. Why all the doom-laden imagery, when the struggle itself is foretelling of imminent disaster?"

Deas looked upon his work, eyes brimming with the irrepressible pride that will come over artists when considering a favorite creation.

"I told you that Matsell's portrait was my first truly original work, mere portrait though it was. I broke the mold when it came to portraiture, but found it difficult to apply that new style to genre scenes, landscapes, and epic works like these. Enter Count Abendroth. The Count took a keen interest in my work soon after he set up shop here, and kindly offered his services when I admitted that my art was lacking a certain *je ne sais quoi*. Under his tutelage my work matured into what you see before you, into what you'll find beyond that door."

Alvord followed his pointing finger and his eyes came to rest on the nail-studded door of crimson.

"And just what *will* I find beyond that door?"

A slow, disconcerting smile crept onto the painter's face. "I would be disinclined to show most, but then again, you are a most inquisitive man. You proved that by breaking into my studio and examining my work uninvited. So for the sake of intellectual inquisitiveness, I'll satisfy your curiosity. You sure you want to see my most original works?"

"Yes. I am rightly interested in what lies beyond that door."

"Really? Some of the subject matter might prove...*shocking.*" Deas asked, with something creepy hovering around his eyes and lips.

Alvord rolled his eyes and spoke dryly. "Yes, and I can hardly stand the suspense. So get on with it and don't make me repeat myself again."

Deas paused, thinking hard. "Later tonight, I think. After you see the Count's performance and the miracle he achieves, I think you'll understand how he can lend power to my talents and allow me to take my work in an entirely fresh direction. In short, you will appreciate it more."

He walked over to a large canvas covered by a cloth. "I will, however, give you a foretaste of my new work by allowing you to see this."

With a flourish, he whipped off the covering.

"It's called *The Prairie Fire*. My most recent painting. What do you think? In my opinion it's my best yet." He smirked peculiarly. "The best that I've presented to the public, anyway. I displayed it in early April, at the Mechanics Institute Fair."

Like *The Death Struggle*, this oil painting contained a scene charged with peril and doom. The crackling flames of the prairie fire chased three characters across the canvas. In the forefront, a pale, mad-eyed horse reared in a classically heroic manner. Atop it were two figures. One was a young man whose face was turned away from the viewer, creating a sense of inaccessibility. In his hand was clutched a musket, which he raised towards the raging prairie fire behind him as if in salute. With his left arm he held a pale, dark-haired woman who had clearly just swooned; her disheveled helplessness lent to the desperate feel of the painting. Next to them was an old man whose terror was etched into every line of his face. He sat astride a dark horse whose head and neck melded into the murky dark of the distant horizon. With a frantic gesture he pointed forward, urging the younger man onwards, but it seemed that the latter was caught up in some dreadful fascination with the blaze that threatened to consume them. The tall prairie grass added a feeling of claustrophobia to an already-eerie work.

Alvord stared at the canvas for a long time without speaking. Between the blazing fire, blanketing smoke that swept across the plain, and the jagged lightning tearing at the sky, Nature itself was creating a wild scene. But it was the look of utmost horror on the face of the old man, the limpness of the female form, and the apparent exhilaration of the young man that really gave him a chill.

"So?" asked the artist eagerly.

"Is this a work that 'The Count' helped you with?"

"Only a bit. I've learned to control and focus some of the power that he unleashes within me."

Alvord nodded towards the young man in the painting. "Why the exhilaration, instead of fear for himself and the others?"

"Ah. I received similar criticism before. Alvord, don't you understand, do you not see it? There is a glory, an awful glory, in the furious powers of Nature. Some, like myself, can appreciate this but most never stop to consider just how awesome natural disasters can be. Is there a greater force than an earthquake, a flood, or a twister? When I see something like a prairie fire I see the Almighty, Alvord. I see the darker side of the Almighty offering we few who know to look a glimpse of raw, ancient power. So yes, the young man is enthralled by the prairie fire, as I was when first I beheld one."

He paused for breath and a deep draught of absinthe.

"We men foolishly think ourselves supreme in a universe governed by beings that could snuff us out like so many candles. Our arrogance and materialism has led Mother Nature to conspire against us. For all our technologies and advancements, for all our intellect and philosophy, we are still at the mercy of the illimitable powers of the natural world. The threat of catastrophe that looms over us is but an avenging angel at the end of its fraying tether."

After staring at him for a moment, his guest got up abruptly.

"Yours is a diseased mind, boy."

Deas's pale, handsome face twisted into a bitter sneer, then relaxed. "After tonight you will understand, friend. Meet me here at seven-thirty. We'll see Abendroth's performance tonight."

"Very well," Alvord said, and left.

Chapter 13

The night air was mercifully cool, and a refreshing breeze blew gently through the forests and fields. Stars, in their far-flung legions, were just beginning to make an appearance in the rapidly darkening sky. To the northeast the moon loomed just above tree line like a burnished scimitar, slightly obscured by the dull yellow glow of St. Louis's gaslights.

Deas and Alvord made their way across the western section of The Common, an area of over two thousand acres that was divided into land parcels and variously used as farmland, grazing land, and communal woodlots. They were several miles west of the main city, and heading even further west. As few houses or cabins had been erected this far from St. Louis, the paved road they had begun on gradually degenerated into a rough, dirt coach road. Glad to be free from the confinement of the steamboat, Alvord had insisted that they walk to Count Abendroth's, and it was a nice evening for it.

Behind them another group walked along the same path, chatting noisily about the recent and resounding American victory over the Mexican army at Cerro Gordo.

"We would do well to keep our wits about us—there are ruffians back here that throw snuff in your eyes before taking the boots to you and stealing what you have."

Deas cast a furtive glance around him as he offered this information.

Alvord eyes scanned the shadows. "We call them sneeze-lurkers in my line of work. Old line of work, more properly put. Smart way to go about robbing someone really, disabling the eyes like that. It is tough to fight effectively when momentarily blinded, and even harder to get a good look at one's assailant."

"Too true. Not too long ago I was aboard a coach that was waylaid by three men while en route to the Count's. Had it not been for his bodyguard, who was traveling in the same direction, I'd have been in a considerable amount of trouble."

"And in what manner did this bodyguard intercede?"

Deas gave a hollow laugh. "He killed them all with a saber in rapid succession. Never seen aught like it."

"Huh."

No fear of sneeze-lurkers found lodgment in Alvord, who had finally purchased some weapons. One of them was a rare Colt Walker, which had been jointly designed by Samuel Colt and Samuel H. Walker, an Army Captain who had recruited Colt to aid him in the making of a new and more powerful revolver for use in the Mexican War. Six .44 caliber rounds were housed in the revolving chamber, which could be accurately unleashed at targets as far as fifty yards away. Not bad for a pistol.

His other purchase was a novel weapon known as the Elgin Cutlass Pistol, designed in 1838 by the United States Navy for the purpose of boarding enemy vessels. The .54 caliber percussion cap gun was equipped with a Bowie knife blade that protruded from under the barrel. The blade was twelve inches in length, though only about half that length stuck out past the barrel's end. Such versatility was what had drawn him to the weapon; if he did end up seeking his destiny on the frontier, this gun would be perfect for Indian fighting (at least by his reckoning). The storeowner had given him a special holster for it, one that had been specifically designed to accommodate the blade along with the gun.

Neither had been cheap, but he would rather pay more for a quality weapon than less for an unreliable one. Thrift did not enter the equation when it came to purchasing something that could save your life.

As of now the four-pound Colt was tucked into the capacious inside pocket of his gray frock coat, and there was reassurance in its weight.

On his belt was strapped a ten-inch blade comprised of Finnish steel but actually crafted in Saxony. Its ornate silver handle bore many inscriptions that had need of translation. Having seen and heard plenty of Germans around town, Alvord figured it shouldn't prove too difficult.

Emerging from a towering grove of ash and sweet gum, they found themselves at the edge of a sprawling, verdant prairie. The soft wind rustled through a rippling sea of big bluestem and switchgrass, wafting an agreeable, straw-like scent towards them. Rolling hills undulated into the distance and atop the largest was a fortress-like structure made mostly of stone. Leading to the building was a path paved in crushed white stone. Torches thrust into the ground on either side of it lit this path. Thus illuminated it rolled out before them, a giant, fiery serpent winding its way around the knolls.

"Our destination?"

"Yes, Alvord. Feast your eyes upon the manor of Count Abendroth."

He did so. "I am strongly reminded of Norwich Castle, though it's much smaller in scale and subtly Gothic in its architectural style."

"Looks downright portentous outlined against the darkening horizon, no?"

"A bit. We will need lanterns for the return trip. I very much doubt the moonlight will be enough to travel by once we leave the light of these torches. Should've thought of that before we left."

"Abendroth will lend us some."

Immediately upon finishing this sentence Deas's head snapped to his left, towards the forest's edge.

"What is it, Charles?" Alvord's right hand instantly strayed to the smooth handle of the Colt.

Deas pointed towards the dark forest of arching, vine-laden maples and locusts. Alvord's eyes scanned woods with a few quick sweeps, and it was not long before he saw what had attracted Charles's attention.

Leaning up against a tree trunk fifty yards away was a short, stocky figure whose casual pose suggested utter comfort in the dark fastness of a night forest. Shadows obscured his face, but he seemed to be staring at Deas. Alvord noted the occasional flare of a pipe's glowing contents. Whoever the man was he simply stood there, watching, and before Alvord thought to call out to him he slunk into the shadows, making nary a sound as he went.

By this time the group traveling behind them had caught up, nearly bumping into Deas and Alvord for lack of attentiveness.

"Is something the matter?" one of them asked in a

cultivated voice.

"No, it was nothing," Deas informed them coolly, "just a coyote, that's all."

"A coyote, you say? Perhaps I should start traveling with the assurance of a gun at my side."

Deas and Alvord waited for them to move on.

"That is the fourth time I've seen that man watching me," said the painter slowly. "Haven't the foggiest notion as to who he is, either."

"I say we get to the manor. Could be a group of rogues out there, and their eyes will be adjusted to the night while ours are not due to the torches' glare. So let's move." The Colt was out and at his side.

Deas nodded vaguely, still peering intently into the forest. "Alright, let's go, but somehow I don't think its ruffians."

Soon enough the pair stood before the wide doors of Count Abendroth's manor. Comprised of some dark stone that Alvord could not identify, the fortress-like building rose three stories and exuded an aura of antiquity. For a moment a dim memory of a strange temple atop a hill near a muddy river registered in his mind, but it was as fleeting as it was vague.

Light shone through the windows of the first story, yet the upper two remained dark.

Deas tapped the grotesque dragonhead knocker, which sounded a hollow, reverberating clang. Shortly thereafter, the door creaked open and a dour middle-aged man dressed in servant's livery admitted them into the manor.

"Two dollars is the admittance fee, Master Deas."

"As always, my good man. Here you are, and that will cover my friend here as well."

"You know the way, sir."

"Thanks, Ezekiel." Deas patted the man on the shoulder and led Alvord through a narrow, dimly lit hall towards a door on the other end.

Two whole dollars. This performance had better be worth it.

With a push, the artist opened the door. A bizarre sight met Alvord's eyes.

An assemblage of eighty or so well-dressed men and a few women sat quietly in a high-ceilinged room. Marble of a dark green with frequent white flecking comprised the main building material in this chamber. It was constructed in the style of an amphitheatre, with half the room being devoted to a rising series of stone benches that swung in a gentle semi-circle, the other half an open space below with a raised dais in the middle.

Those gathered were sumptuously attired in the manner of the haughty when attending a church service. Alvord, having anticipated the formality of the occasion, had dressed accordingly but not nearly so richly as the others. His was a nice but not flashy outfit. He wore his favorite frock coat, one of charcoal that hung just above his knees, a black satin vest underneath, and a removable black collar on his shirt under that. The trousers were the same charcoal color, his boots a highly polished black (although the walk over had taken a bit of the shine from them). Having decided to forgo a top hat or derby, he had oiled and neatly combed his dark chestnut hair.

Deas headed for the stairs and he followed. As was wont to happen, Alvord's size and severity of countenance drew more than a few speculative glances. All such looks were met with flinty gray eyes and an unsmiling expression. He did not much care for folks who stared.

Deas, on the flip side, received pleasant salutations and even slaps on the back as they climbed the rows of stone benches. Finally, he settled down about halfway up the amphitheatre benches, where few others sat.

"We'll want a good view," he stated excitedly.

Some quiet talk could be heard, the topics varying from real estate and slavery to the war and the ongoing construction of the Illinois and Michigan Canal in Chicago. Others thumbed through pamphlets and books and seemed to be entranced by what they read.

Alvord ran his hands over the smooth marble of the bench.

"I feel as if I am in ancient Greece. How long until we get underway here?"

Deas check his timepiece. "Shouldn't be long now."

As if on cue a man, elegantly clad in black save for a white cravat, entered the room. A hush fell over the crowd, reverential in its speed and absoluteness.

His movements were smooth, his posture upright and regal. With easy strides he came to the dais, which he mounted, facing the crowd with his hands clasped behind his back.

He was not a large man, perhaps of average height but slim, with a narrow, pale, and somewhat saturnine face free of any facial hair. Alvord placed his age somewhere in the early forties. Nothing in the man's physical appearance was overtly imposing, but as time wore on his fixed stare became unsettling, almost suggestive of madness.

From his hypnotic gaze to his imperial stature, there could be no doubt- this had to be Count Abendroth.

In his wake loomed a man of gigantic proportions. Alvord reckoned that the fellow stood a good three inches taller than him, with a broad span of shoulder and a thick chest. He estimated that this man tipped the scales at two hundred and eighty pounds. A greatcoat of midnight blue covered his form but did not disguise his thick limbs and powerful structure. If he had to guess Alvord would say that the man was a German of some sort, with hair of golden blonde and a square, muscular face.

A sheathed sword hung at his side; recalling Deas's story, Alvord reasoned that this must be Abendroth's bodyguard. There was an air about him, not so much of arrogance but rather assured confidence. His steps were slow and calculated, his gaze predatory as he took in the assembled crowd slowly and completely. As his eyes swept upwards, they met Alvord's. The giant's head cocked slightly to the side as he paused to observe Alvord's face and form. His assessment lasted but a moment before he continued his review of the congregation. Alvord noticed that his eyes did not stop again as they had for him.

There is something about being a man of the warrior caste that at times provokes a body into a baseless aggression towards a total stranger, an instinctual reaction towards a perceived threat. Such was the feeling that gripped Alvord when he looked upon the giant bodyguard. Alvord had no quarrel with the man, did not even know the fellow, but a knot formed in his gut as the blood pumped hotter in his veins. If ever contest were to transpire between them, could he prove himself superior to the giant who stalked about so assuredly?

A certain menace hung about this man, and Alvord's primal side reared its head in response.

With a deep breath he quelled it. It was a prideful, hotheaded notion that needed to be suppressed.

"That's Otto Volkmar, the Count's bodyguard," whispered Deas, not taking his eyes off of Abendroth.

"Ah." Not a name he'd soon forget.

"Welcome," said a voice, satin-smooth and urbane. It had the quality of being at once soft and everywhere, as though it were spoken directly into one's ear yet reverberating around the room all the while.

Alvord knew it was Abendroth, but the man's lips barely moved and he was far away, he should be speaking in a loud voice to be heard by all...

"Welcome and thanks to all for coming tonight," he continued in a cultured London accent. "For those of you who are first-time visitors, I extend to you a personal greeting. I am Count Abendroth, and I am a practitioner of animal magnetism, or mesmerism, as it is also known. Some of you may have heard of this phenomenon before, others perhaps not. But let me assure you—after tonight you will never doubt its reality. But alas, talk is cheap. Let me begin by demonstrating the sanative use of animal magnetism, as it is in this capacity that it is most commonly applied."

From a side door two sturdy men led a black woman towards the dais, and they had their hands full trying to restrain her. Banshee-like shrieks and ghoulish howls tore from her frothing mouth, setting the hair on Alvord's arms on edge. Skeletal fingers clawed at the eyes of her detainers, who dragged her writhing body before the dais.

Abendroth looked her over, face devoid of emotion.

His penetrating stare shifted from her to the crowd. That silken voice somehow made itself heard even over the piteous howling of the crazed woman.

"There is a force that flows throughout the cosmos, invisible to the human eye and utterly undetectable to most people. Through the ages, this fluid has been known as the universal or cosmic fluid, but to we magnetizers it is animal magnetism. This fluid flows freely through all things, including people, and afflictions such as this poor woman's are merely the result of an imbalance of this fluid within the body. If balance is restored, her health can likewise be restored. The question for a long time was this—can animal magnetism be willfully channeled by man?"

As if to answer the question, he swiftly raised his right hand and directed it at the woman, palm outstretched.

This was all very sudden; Alvord had been expecting a slow dimming of the lights and many theatrical pauses in the demonstration. Instead this Count, if Count he truly was, seemed eager to get to the meat and potatoes. Alvord approved.

The woman's frantic efforts at escape ceased with the rising of Abendroth's hand. He peered unblinkingly into her eyes from the dais, reaching down to place a gentle hand on her forehead.

"By channeling my own powers into her, and becoming master to the grossly imbalanced animal magnetism within, I can restore her sanity. When animal magnetism ceases to flow freely and evenly through the nervous system, organs malfunction, fluids grow stagnant, joints stiffen, and any number of ailments can wrack the unbalanced body. Yet all this can be undone, balance can be achieved.

"But," he said, and the woman slumped onto the marble floor, "first we must reach the crisis, the point at which the illness is intensified and the imbalance is forcibly exorcised from the body."

He stepped back and closed his pale hand into a tight fist, pointing it at her prostrate form. In immediate response to this, the woman started emitting sounds the likes of which Alvord had never heard. She convulsed violently, kicking, punching, and shrieking all the while. Abendroth's eyes, Alvord could see even from this distance, were a particularly vivid shade of green and stared pitilessly at the woman's wracked, tortured form.

Alvord looked at Deas, who was leaning forward in his seat, watching with what approached enthrallment.

A man in the front row leapt forward and headed straight for Abendroth.

"That is my property!" He proclaimed in an indignant shout dripping with that accent Alvord had come to associate with Southerners. Volkmar stepped in between the man and his master, leering at him with challenge in his eyes. The angry fellow stopped dead in his tracks, looked at Volkmar, then to his slave, and back to Volkmar again. He took a hasty step back.

The Count opened his fist and the horrible sounds and spasms subsided. "Your slave will be fine, Mr. Latour. Take your seat and give me but a moment."

Latour meekly did as he was bid. With a smooth movement, Abendroth got down from the dais and lay both hands upon the woman's limp head as the two assistants held her up.

Her head jerked upwards abruptly and with a loud gasp she drew breath.

"Everything is now in working order. Her nervous disorder is no more, thanks to the healing powers of mesmerism."

"Speak, woman," he ordered mildly. "How do you feel?"

"I... I'm fine. Just fine, mista. Wha' happened here? Where am I?"

"Don't worry your precious head over that."

Latour rose and collected the slave, but stopped upon close examination of her. "*What*? Look at this! What did you do, Abendroth?"

Abendroth raised a thin eyebrow. "Are you unsatisfied with you slave's newfound sanity, Mister Latour?"

Latour turned her towards him in reply. "Her eyes are blue, damnit! How in the hell are they blue?"

The people in the first few rows gasped in shock as they too beheld the hue of her eyes. Alvord peered down from his perch, but was too far away to detect any change in them.

"A small price to pay for a now-functional slave, wouldn't you agree?"

"But...wait, how on God's green earth was this achieved?"

The Count tut-tutted, shaking his head. "First hell and now God's green earth, eh? You should make up your mind, man. The changing of eye color is a rare but not unheard of side effect of mesmerism, particularly in traumatic episodes. Now please, no more questions. If her condition deteriorates, bring her back, but right now the show goes on, Latour."

With that he turned back towards the crowd. "That was but a small and standard demonstration. You can find dozens of men in this country and many more in Europe who are perfectly capable of curing a simple case of hysteria. Yet healing, while a noble and worthwhile use for mesmerism, is but a glimpse through the keyhole on the door of human potential."

He turned, mounting the dais once more, and spoke with unabashed pride. "Before the pioneer in mesmerism, the great Franz Anton Mesmer, died in 1815, I was his final disciple. By this time he had been scorned by modern science, shunned by the fearful intellectual circles that were secretly jealous of his gift, his power. As a young man I, having heard tales of his awesome talent, sought him out upon the desolate shores of Lake Constance, nestled in the foothills of the German Alps. Years of reclusiveness granted him the time and environment to refine his skills and realize his powers to their fullest extent. All that he knew and learned was passed on to me, the sole disciple he accepted in his lonely latter days. What you will see next is an example of his later doctrine, which states that while in the mesmeric state some people are able to tap into a higher sense of perception. A lucky few are particularly sensitive and receptive to animal magnetism, going into the deepest possible trance while mesmerized. Their five outer senses go into abeyance as a far more potent one is unleashed, a sixth sense capable of the miracles you will now bear witness to."

Despite initial skepticism and reluctance to take the man seriously, Alvord found himself eager to see what would happen next.

The mesmerizer pointed to a woman in the front row, and beckoned her forward. "With your husband's permission, of course."

She approached hesitantly after being urged onward by her husband, looking quite pale and vulnerable.

Abendroth gave her an encouraging smile. "You needn't fear. You will not be wracked by paroxysms of madness or pain. I have detected an aura around you, ma'am, one that indicates a heightened receptivity to animal magnetism. In addition, it appears that you are suffering from a slight head cold, and it is generally only the sick that can experience the purest form of mesmerism. The cosmic fluid runs strong through you, so with your cooperation I would show this audience just what you, with my guidance, are capable of."

She glanced back at her husband, who nodded energetically.

It seemed strange to Alvord that any man would consent

to his wife putting herself at the mercy of another, especially one with strange powers. Yet at the same time a quiet but persistent voice told him that this was nothing more than clever stagecraft. That slave could have been faking, the whole thing could be nothing more than a well-executed hoax...

"To demonstrate that I can elicit the dormant powers in her through animal magnetism would be simple. The laying on of hands is an aspect of the practice that most never graduate from. This wooden partition," one was quickly dragged in from another room, "will separate us, yet still I will influence her actions."

With no further ado, he had the woman seated on one side of the barrier and he went on the other. Raising his hands, he began making strange oval and horizontal patterns in the air before him. This continued for well over two minutes with no discernible reaction from the woman. People in the crowd started fidgeting and conducting hushed conversations, expressing doubt and annoyance.

Quite suddenly the woman's head slumped onto her chest. She seemed asleep, for her body grew limp and her breathing slow and deep.

"What I am about to do is what Mesmer himself explored while in exile. His new doctrine asserted that some men and women under the influence of animal magnetism could activate perceptive faculties that are otherwise quiescent. Thus activated, these faculties result in the unveiling of cosmic truths, and the means by which we humans gauge reality becomes obsolete. Mesmer struggled with this, for he always considered himself a scientist. By the same token, he wished to steer clear of the occult. For him, the problem with this theory was that he could no longer distinguish where true science left off and occult knowledge took over. So I leave it to you to decide—are we delving into true science here or brushing up against the super or preternatural?"

The patient's head snapped up, eyes still shut. She sat there, face calm as a millpond, as if awaiting orders.

The Count reached down and picked up a pack of cards. He pointed to a man in the crowd and waved him forward.

"I will pick a card and show it to you. You will write it on this piece of slate and display it to the crowd."

Selecting a card, the mesmerizer held it towards the

man, who wrote it on the slate with a piece of chalk and held it towards the audience.

Two of hearts. Alvord shifted in his seat. Was this charlatan really going to bore them with a card trick?

"You have all seen it?"

The crowd nodded in unison.

"What card, my dear?" he asked the listless woman.

"Two of hearts," she responded in a voice bereft of emotion.

This was done four more times, with the woman answering correctly and without hesitation. Alvord was decidedly unimpressed; all this could have been arranged before the show. Someone in the crowd could be signaling to her.

"She is now in a state of consciousness between sleep and wakefulness, and while in this mesmeric trance is capable of fantastic things. But to prove that this is not a mere hoax—"

One of his assistants brought forth two tin containers.

"We need two volunteers. One of these substances is ammonia, the other a smelling salt. You needn't inhale deeply and get the full effect, but I want you to make sure that they are genuine."

Two men volunteered and sniffed the substances, which sent them reeling backwards.

"Real enough for me!" one of them sputtered between coughs.

The assistant took both over to the patient and stuck each one under her nose for thirty seconds each.

"Breath deeply," the Count commanded her. She did and amazingly this did nothing to stir her from her reverie. Alvord began to reconsider his position of doubt.

"The trance has taken firm hold of her," the Count said, "and now her potential might just be limitless."

"Be seated," he commanded. "Now sink into yourself, immerse yourself in the sixth sense and the animal magnetism which both surrounds and inundates."

He gave her a moment, during which she slumped even more.

"Now," he ordered, "kindly read some of the minds of those in the audience."

At this Alvord had to stifle a snort. Deas glared at him,

but Alvord could not help himself.

"That man there," the woman said, pointing to a man off to her right, "is thinking about how he wishes to develop his own powers of mesmerism. He has read the pamphlets and books on the topic that are in rapid circulation. He is desirous of becoming one of your devotees."

The accused man recoiled in surprise, looking to his left and right and shaking his head in an artificial manner, a half-hearted attempt to convince his friends otherwise.

"That woman," she continued, "feels as if this whole showing is unsavory, odious to the soul. She does not think it was wise of me to bend unto your will. She fancies this pure deviltry."

The woman in question gasped loudly, staring at the mesmerized patient in numb disbelief.

It was all Alvord could do to keep from rolling his eyes. All of the people around him seemed highly impressed with what was an obvious instance of trickery, but not him.

"And that man right there," she accused, pointing directly at him, "believes that this is nothing more than clever stagecraft."

Alvord stared at the woman, amazed that she had in effect read his mind. Her eyes were closed- there was simply no way she could have observed his incredulity, obvious though it might be.

Abendroth, however, merely chuckled. It was a most sinister sound. Peering up at Alvord, he spoke.

"So, we have a skeptic in our midst, eh? Let us see if we cannot persuade him to reconsider his stance."

Chapter 14

All eyes turned his way in the leaden silence that followed. It was a most awkward situation—why had he agreed to come here again?

Deas regarded him with angry disbelief, appearing both offended and embarrassed.

"Well," Alvord said loudly but civilly, "you must admit that this whole performance hasn't been exceedingly convincing. Surely you will concede that what you have shown us *could* be faked by clever means."

Abendroth nodded solemnly. "Perhaps to the cynical eyes of the nonbeliever, yes. However, I am quite confident that what you shall see next will firmly dispel any lingering doubts."

He turned to his volunteer. "Now please, my dear, would you perform five handsprings across the room?"

The woman did so with blurring speed, her many skirts swishing loudly. Some began to mutter—this was hardly couth. But they were captivated and let Abendroth continue.

"Now back-handspring back to your former position." And it was accomplished with the same gymnastic finesse.

An anvil was wheeled in on a cart and brought to rest in front of her.

"Otto, kindly lift that out and place it at her feet," Abendroth requested.

The giant bodyguard hoisted it up, but with definite signs of strain. The anvil made a loud clanging as it was deposited onto the marble floor.

"Will someone else please come forward and try to lift the anvil themselves before we proceed?" Abendroth looked around, patiently waiting.

One man, short but powerfully built, waddled out onto the floor and succeeded in lifting it a few inches before he collapsed in a panting heap.

"Pick it up," Abendroth commanded the patient.

Alvord could not believe his eyes when she did as bid and did so without the slightest indication of effort. Volkmar was more than twice her size and no doubt twice the strength of the average man. Yet amazingly, this woman had lifted the anvil, face demure and evincing no signs of exertion.

"Sir," he asked of the woman's husband, "is your wife possessing of any musical aptitude?"

"Why yes. She plays the piano with exceptional dexterity. Her singing voice is also second to none."

"Has she any experience with the violin?"

"No, none at all. Just the piano, as I said."

"Splendid."

One of the assistants brought forth a violin and placed it in the woman's hands.

Abendroth raised his arm, closing his eyes as he directed his palm towards her.

With a deft movement she drew the bow across the strings of the violin. What followed was the most haunting song Alvord had ever heard. It conjured up recollections from his trip to northern England, where the fog hung low over desolate lakes and untrod ways. Where crumbling ruins evoked memories of forgotten peoples who once staked their claim to a barren, unforgiving land. The tune flowed on, telling of tragic loss that actually brought a tear to Alvord's eye. This he wiped away with all due haste, for he was not the type to put his emotions on display.

The song drew to a melancholy close, leaving behind nothing but faint reverberations of the strings' final strains and the hushed stillness of the audience.

"So as you have seen, aside from an ability to tap into hidden powers of the mind, those under the influence of animal magnetism are capable of feats of strength and dexterity that normally they could never hope to achieve. But some, like this brave woman you see before you, can go beyond even that. With my guidance, she can spiritually enter a realm where past, present, and future meld into one. In this state the soul becomes one with animal magnetism, and the results are perhaps the most astonishing phenomenon mankind has ever stumbled upon. Cosmic revelations are experienced; laws of the universe and the miracles of creation that normally defy even the greatest human mind's abilities to comprehend. And, most interestingly, some receive revelation regarding lost civilizations and glimpses of those yet to come."

Standing before his patient, Abendroth narrowed his emerald eyes and raised his hand, again making strange yet oddly fluid motions in the air.

"This is, you should know, the greatest extent of my power and therefore the greatest extent to which the powers of animal magnetism can be used."

Alvord shook his head. What shameless self-effacement.

The mesmerizer returned his attention to the woman, who sat in a stiff, upright position. As he continued his motions, she slowly began to slump in her chair, chin resting on her chest.

"Open your eyes." She did so. "What do you perceive when you look upon me?"

"I cannot make out most of your form," she replied in that same hollow voice, "for the glow emanating from your hands and head is too intense."

"Good. She is now in a state in which she and I are communicating animal magnetism to each other. As she receives mine I will bring her even deeper into the realm beyond consciousness."

His hand motions ceased, and slowly he drew his right hand into a fist.

"Have you done as directed?"

The woman, her form still slouched, answered. "Yes. I have pierced the veil."

"And what it is that you see?"

"A lost and ancient island civilization, buried in the sea south and east of here, advanced in ways we cannot understand. Whispered tales of its existence and destruction persist today, though they get more wrong than they do right. Inner conflict wrought by the Sons of Belial resulted in political and military disunity, ultimately leading to mutual destruction. The few survivors that remained fled to ancient Egypt and Central America. In over a century some will locate ruins of this forgotten civilization, though the world will be unwilling to accept it."

"Delve deeper, push onwards. Is there anything else that

you see and understand? Anything regarding the future of mankind?" Abendroth's eyes and face betrayed his excitement.

Alvord began to sense something in the room, a presence of sorts. There was a sound, a barely audible susurrus of jumbled whispers that seemed to be everywhere at once. The flames of the candelabras and torches flickered wildly, as if stirred by a wind. And a sensation washed over him whereby a static energy could be felt buzzing in the air, giving him goose bumps and raising the hair on his arms and neck. It was at once a welcoming and repellant feeling, unlike anything he had ever experienced.

For the first time, the woman's face became animate as a deep frown creased her brow. "Darkness. Peril. Wretchedness and desolation. Rivers of blood churning and frothing with the innards and limbs of the fallen."

Alvord began to feel sick as she continued. He also felt that dark presence more keenly now, and heard a darkly seductive hiss that seemed to be right behind him...

Her voice grew shrill. "Dark beings of untold power stalking an earth where no sun rises! Agony without interval! Horror without name! Oh please, no, *God no*—"

The tin containers holding the ammonia and smelling salts were suddenly flung across the room as if cast by an unseen hand. Several of the torches nearest her flared up dazzlingly before losing their flames altogether.

The Count snapped his fingers and she snapped out of her reverie, breathing rapidly and visibly shaken. She clutched her chest with one hand and her head with the other. Red-faced, her husband got out of his seat and embraced her.

"What did you do to her?"

The Count seemed quite untroubled by the venom in his words. "Rest assured, your wife is just fine. Better, in fact—no head cold anymore. She's just had a bit of a start, is all. Am I right, ma'am?"

She stood quickly and sought to compose herself. "Yes, Arno, he is right. I am fine. A bit confused and breathless, but fine. I don't rightly remember what happened, in truth."

"And your head cold?" Abendroth interjected.

"Gone. Cured!"

"Good. That is all for tonight, I think. I do hope that you all enjoyed this demonstration, and next week there will be another. But as you head home tonight, I would ask you all to meditate over what you have seen. Even for you skeptics out there, I know there were points at which a wind of true belief swept across the monotonous plains of your mind. Our outer sense and our logic prove wholly insufficient when it comes to perceiving what lies beyond the veil of the supernatural. There *are* forces and powers in the universe that resist all efforts at scientific categorization. Remember: *With an application of will we are capable of more than what we can possibly fathom.*"

Alvord sat in his seat for a few moments as the crowd began to leave. The dark presence he had felt was gone; all that remained was an awestruck audience and a feeling in his gut that there was something demonic at work here.

"C'mon, Rawn," urged Deas, "I would make introductions."

Still trying to wrap his head around what he had just experienced, a slightly dazed Alvord followed the artist down the steps of the amphitheater towards Abendroth.

"Count Abendroth!" Deas greeted him reverentially, bending over in a most obsequious bow.

"Charles!" the Count happily exclaimed. "I see you've brought a friend."

"I have indeed. Alvord Rawn, meet Count Abendroth, a friend of no small importance."

The Count extended his hand, which Alvord clasped in what amounted to a very incompatible handshake. The Count's was small, long-fingered, and frail, while his own was large and somewhat meaty.

Alvord noticed that Abendroth was maintaining eye contact far beyond what was necessary in a simple greeting. So he made sure to hold that hypnotic stare until the mesmerizer broke it off quite suddenly.

"Ah yes, the skeptic." Abendroth's pale, almost cadaverous face twisted into a slight smirk, those cat eyes of his reduced to slits. "Well, have I swayed your opinion, or do you remain unconvinced of the powers of animal magnetism?"

"In truth, what I saw tonight has given me much to think about."

"Good. If all I manage to do is provoke deeper thought on the subject, my job is done."

Looking Alvord over, the Count continued. "I sense a very

strong aura radiating from your being—your potential would be great, were you inclined to submit to my guidance. Ah, I note immediate suspicion flooding your eyes. Fear not, my intentions are good. It would just be a downright shame for one with such potential to remain skeptical of the very thing that could open his mind to fantastic wonders. How about this, then—two days hence, drop in say mid-morning, and we will take a tour of my manor and grounds as we discuss my power, and how you might develop yours. There are a good many things about mesmerism that I did not touch upon tonight."

Taking a second to consider it, Alvord realized that he fervently wished to get to the bottom of all this, to uncover what dark forces lay at the heart of mesmerism.

"If I am still around, I might just take you up on that."

"What brings you to St. Louis, Mr. Rawn?"

"I am here on police business, to take Charles back to New York. His presence is needed in a legal matter of which neither he nor I can speak."

Abendroth lips curled in a very unpleasant manner. "Oh."

Alvord had always prided himself in being able to tell a good lie when necessary, but felt that Abendroth had instantly seen through this one.

Deas gestured towards a group of twenty or so men standing off to the side, some talking quietly, others looking at Abendroth expectantly.

"Am I to infer that you are holding a meeting tonight, Count Abendroth?"

"Yes, as a matter of fact I am."

The way in which Deas's eyes lit up at the confirmation of his question was most unsettling.

"Alright then, Charles," Alvord interrupted brusquely, "how about we head back to town?"

"Alvord," began Deas in a very diplomatic tone, "I am staying behind to meet with the Count and some others. I will see you tomorrow, then."

Alvord could tell by his expression and the quality of his voice that he was staying, and that was final. Not wishing to cause a scene, Alvord relented.

"Yes, I suppose you will. Do behave yourself, Charles."

The Count looked from one to the other, a slightly

bemused look on his face. "Did I miss something?"

"Nothing at all," Alvord assured him, "I was just leaving. I bid you gentlemen goodnight."

Chapter 15

Chary though he was of leaving Deas with Abendroth, Alvord was resigned to the fact that his protests would fall on deaf ears. Moreover, keeping Deas happy would increase the likelihood of his coming back to New York peacefully. The last thing he needed was for Charles to experience a sudden change of heart and make a bid for freedom. Although tracking the artist across the West in a sporting game of cat and mouse did hold its appeal, ultimately taking the man back against his will would be a monumental hassle. He would be forced to drug the artist upon capturing him, and the legality of that was somewhat dubious. Downright unlawful, more properly put. Patience in this scenario would be a virtue well worth the wait.

But Alvord had no intention of leaving without first snooping around a bit. Having espied a tree growing close to the south side of the building on his way in, he reasoned that its limbs might grant him access to a second-story window. He wished to find out just what activities Abendroth had in store for the group that stayed behind.

The audience left Abendroth's manor in herd fashion and Alvord calmly followed suit, trying to look as innocuous as possible. Upon exiting through the front door, he separated himself from the crowd with a swift sidestep that landed him in the shadows just beyond the yellow glow of the torchlight. Edging along the building, he hoped that his eyes would soon adjust to the damnably faint light afforded by the sliver of waxing moon.

He reached the southeast corner of the manor, and peeking around it saw the massive tree, which grew even closer to the building than he had previously thought. Its many low-growing branches made for easy climbing, and within a few seconds he was twenty feet high. Perched upon a branch, he smiled amusedly. How long had it been since he'd climbed a tree? Not since his early youth, which had been some time ago. Yet the ability to climb had not deserted him with the passage of time, and he was quite pleased at how nimbly he had swung and leapt his way up the tree. Grabbing a leaf, he examined it and determined it was an oak, though different from the oaks found in New York.

Carefully he eased out onto a thick limb, peering through the screen of leaves. A second story window was located another five or so feet above him, through which shone light. He strained his ears but could make out no voices.

Perfect. That would serve as his entry point. With a few lissome but careful maneuvers Alvord reached a height of thirty feet. The window was now slightly below him, which was good because a well-aimed jump would be necessary to actually get to the window's ledge, as the branches did not reach all the way. The limbs were strong enough to walk out on, but suddenly the thirty-foot fall that could accompany that act seemed positively dizzying.

A gentle breeze rustled through the leaves, and he paused as its warmth swept over his face. A legion of frogs sounded their throaty calls from a nearby swamp, loud but not loud enough to drown out the doleful whoop of an owl.

What a queer situation this was. Never in the most fanciful of his dreams did he imagine himself in such a position—thirty feet high up a tree, poised to break into the castle of a mesmerizer on the outskirts of St. Louis? A dry chuckle escaped his lips. If only the boys back in the Sixth could see him now!

With a deep breath he steeled himself for the walk out along the branch and the subsequent leap.

Another chuckle interrupted the stillness and Alvord nearly took a spill, for it was not his own.

"You know," said a gruff, uncultured voice, "for a city-dweller you ain't half bad at playin' Injun."

A hasty snatch at an overhead limb was all that prevented him from losing his balance altogether. Alvord's heart raced; he hated being caught off guard, for shock was a tough emotion to conceal. But he tried anyway, replying in what he hoped was a casual manner.

"City dweller, eh? And on what do you base that astute

assumption?"

A second bout of gruff laughter came from a dense clump of leaves that shielded the man from view.

"Well forgive my sayin' mister, but you're rightly dandified. Elegant clothes you got there, real elegant. Easterner, if I ain't mistaken?"

"You are not. But trust me, friend, there is a big difference between being elegantly attired and being a dandy, the same difference that is found between proper grooming and sheer vanity. If you would do me the courtesy of showing yourself, I would happily assess the garb of he who is so quick to judge."

He—a dandy! Of all the preposterous accusations! He could already feel the flow of blood quickening in his veins. A line had been crossed.

A squat figure emerged from the leafy darkness, moving with a swift ease that he would not expect in someone this high up a tree. The man leaned up against the trunk, staring at Alvord with heavily hooded eyes.

His attire indicated both his livelihood and character. A fringed buckskin smock hugged his powerful torso, while fringed buckskin pants of a vaguely European style covered his legs. He wore moccasins nicely decorated with beads and quillwork, which came almost up to his knees. All in all, he looked every inch the mountain man of the 1820's and 30's.

"And you said *I* was good at playing the Indian? If I squint, I see a savage before me, and a rather unkempt one at that. Your beard has need of a good trim." These were bold words, for the stranger could be friend or foe and might be armed.

The man came closer, and Alvord took in his face at a glance. He looked French, with thick dark hair and a matching beard. A prominent brow and deep-set eyes gave him a somewhat primitive appearance, but there was a gleam of shrewd intelligence there, too. What looked to be a powder burn scarred the flesh next to his right eye. Watching him move, Alvord also noticed that he was slightly bowlegged.

He realized that his eyes had grown accustomed to the faint light now, for he could now see in detail, albeit colorless detail.

"Careful now," the trapper cautioned with a laugh, "your

ignorance is showin'. Most Injuns can't grow the barest trace of a beard. And listen, I didn't invent this here outfit. It's just practical, is all. Damn comfortable, too."

A large bone-handled Bowie knife hung on his hip, but the man didn't seem overly aggressive. In fact, his voice was quite easygoing. Still, Alvord did not make a habit out of trusting perfect strangers. He kept his eyes peeled for any aggressive or sudden movements.

"Fair enough, friend."

Alvord extended his hand. His left hand was poised to grab the silver-handled knife in his belt should the man make any sudden moves.

He didn't, and held out his own hand.

"My name is Alvord Rawn."

"Marcel Durand."

Ah. He had been right, the man was French. "I notice you don't pronounce *Durand* as many men of French heritage in this area would."

"Well I'm American, ain't I?"

"Good man. So Marcel, how did you come to be in a tree in St. Louis in the dead of the night?" He reflected on how peculiar a meeting this was.

"I could ask the same of you, Al, but I'll oblige ye. I'm here spyin' on this Abendroth feller, plain and simple. Man's evil. Tainted."

Alvord had never been called "Al" in all his life, but found that he didn't mind this scruffy fellow doing so.

"The very thing! Talk about a chance meeting, eh? Two fellows operating alone, climbing the same tree with the same purpose in mind. I believe that Fate has us right where it wants us. I myself just bore witness to Abendroth's power and it was a vivid presentment of evil. At first I was highly skeptical of the man's alleged gift, but now I am convinced of it and its demonic origins."

Marcel frowned. "Demonic, good word fer it. You got in there, did you? Now that's somethin' I could never hope to do—they only admit highfalutin' folks."

"I noticed. Abendroth caters to a very affluent crowd. By the by, are you stalking a man named Charles Deas? I saw a person staring at us from the wood line as we approached this place. He resembled you in proportion and dress."

The two men spoke with each other frankly, each sensing that the other was a straight shooter and perhaps even a kindred spirit. Alvord considered how sometimes you could read a person you've just met better than someone you've known for years.

"That was you with him? Huh, should've recognized you by your form. Big feller, y'are. Well yeah, I've been followin' 'im around lately. Why d'ya ask?"

"I'm being paid by his mother to bring him back to Manhattan, whether he wants to go or not. She fears that his obsession with this mesmerizer is unhealthy, which it is, and might even lead to physical or spiritual harm, which it may."

"Huh. Smart lady. What he presents durin' his show is nothin' from what I've overheard others describe of his weekly performances. It's what goes on afterward, on the second floor, that's the real issue. You want demonic? Look ye no further. I've witnessed things through that window that staggered my soul, no exaggeration."

"You have seen Abendroth and Deas through this window?"

"Few times, with a mess of other gents with 'em. They don't always use this room."

"How did you come to know Deas, anyway?" It was an obvious question that he couldn't believe he'd overlooked.

Marcel gave a hollow laugh. "Late March I was takin' some fresh air out in the woods at night when I heard screams comin' from this castle of a building. Never in all my born days have I heard the like. Cut through my soul, hell, even made me hack up my supper. Bein' the fool that I am, I wanted to find out what was making the sound, 'cause I was pretty sure the Four Horsemen was unleashed upon the earth, and I figgered that would be somethin' worth seein' 'fore I died. I ain't kiddin', still gives me nightmares. Anyways, from outta this window comes a'fallin your Mr. Deas, hits the ground and took to runnin' like the Tempter himself was on his heels. Followed the lad, I did, to a small glade where he collapsed. And then, well, sounds strange I know but something was there, something purely evil."

Alvord recalled with a chill the presence he'd felt towards the end of the performance.

"I couldn't see it, but I heard it all right. That... *thing* was right behind me and I figgered I was a dead man, but then Deas up and hollered in Latin, which afterward he claimed he didn't speak. The phantom was gone, and all that was left was a confused Deas. Odd it was, like he was a timid boy one moment, whisperin' to 'imslef, then snapped out of it and turned right haughty on me. Since then I been keeping an eye on 'im, seein' as how he's known as a good man in the city and a topnotch artist. Well, maybe I also figgered he could lead me to the heart of this mystery what's been wrapped around this city, too. An' he has."

Alvord stoked his beard pensively. "Do you recall the words he spoke in Latin?"

"Yeah, gave me a chill, them words. He yelled 'Have mercy on me, Lord, have mercy on me.'"

Clenching his jaw, Alvord glanced at the window. "Well, that settles it. I'm going to find out what goes on behind closed doors here."

In reply, Marcel guffawed loudly. "Ho, ho! Bold feller, ain't ye? You know that he's got a Prussian in there even bigger'n you? Hulkin' brute, seen 'im round town a few times. Hard to miss 'im, really."

"I am decidedly unconcerned. You might content yourself with watching from afar, but I'm going in. Perhaps I'll see you around, Marcel."

Marcel looked at Alvord strangely, nodding his shaggy head slightly in what appeared to be approval.

"Aw hell. Alright. I'm with you, Al. You've got the bark on."

"I am unfamiliar with the phrase."

The mountain man smiled broadly, revealing a missing lower incisor. "Means you've got balls, son."

"*Ah.*" A bit crude, but a compliment was a compliment.

"Well, we doin' this?"

"Just a moment. I need to know—why exactly are you staking this place out? What are you looking to do, what is it you hope to achieve?"

"Fair enough. This here's my city, place of my birth. I returned here 'bout a month ago after not seeing the River Queen for many a year, and as soon as I do so, I notice that somethin' just ain't right here."

"That mystery you mentioned being wrapped around the

city?"

Tight-lipped, the mountain man stared off in the direction of St. Louis for a moment. "You ain't noticed it? Some folks is actin' strange, like something big is comin'. They sense it now like they didn't before. What'd you call it, a pall? Yes sir, there's a pall hanging over this place. Upper classes been skulking about at night, there's been talk, too. Some seem to think that Abendroth is training them for some greater purpose, and I've seen them with him gathered in this room. Choteau, Calvi, Solard, Labeaume—all the old money, the city's gentry. I've been tryin' to figger out what all this is about, but I took ill two weeks back and been laid up 'til recent. Yesterday I come across some pamphlets and literature what's been circulatin' among the city aristocracy—nicked it out of some unwary gent's pocket."

He pulled something from his shirt pocket. "Have a look."

Alvord took it, reading the title aloud. "*A Handbook to Practical Mesmerism.* By Count Abendroth. My God, he's instructing them."

"This animal magnetism they're practicing strikes me as evil, and I've heard what hellish sounds issue outta this place come nightfall. Ain't human. And I've seen people twitchin' and thrashin' around after being mesmerized, like their soul's was ablaze and tryin' to claw their way outta the bodies. Also, the city madhouse is gittin' mighty full of slaves and poor whites these days; rumor has it that Abendroth is experimenting with 'em, driving 'em to insanity with 'is powers. Somethin' is at work here that I can't quite piece together. The answer to this here riddle is in this fortress, but until tonight, well, I been cautious. Time to buck up, throw caution to the wind and get to the bottom of this. If people like me, like you, can't find it in 'em to stand in opposition to shit like this, who will?"

His speech broke off abruptly, his breathing a bit heavy as he fidgeted uncomfortably. "I'll shut my trap now, that's more talkin' than I done in some time."

Alvord considered Marcel's information. What had begun for him as a relatively straightforward retrieval mission was rapidly developing into a far more complex issue. Occult madness had gripped St. Louis, and for some reason he, like Marcel, felt an obligation to uncover just what insidious designs might lie at the heart of this ever-deepening mystery.

"Your mindset echoes my own. We are not like most, we are...superior people, and for that very reason sometimes it falls on us to grapple with things others would not fain to look upon."

With a firm nod to Marcel, he stole forward towards the window, using higher branches to stabilize himself. At a certain point the branch they were on began drooping under their combined weight. The window ledge was about seven feet away and slightly below them. Alvord took the last few steps quickly, making damn sure that he didn't look down. As he launched himself into the air, he felt his stomach drop and his limbs grow weak with fear. But in a moment his feet were on firm stone and he was looking into a square, dimly lit room. The shutters were open so all he had to do was slip inside, which he did after scanning the room and ensuring that it was unoccupied.

He glanced back just in time to see Marcel leap cat-like from the darkness onto the ledge. The trapper eased into the room, his moccasins making scarcely a whisper on the stone floor. Alvord moved with equal silence, glad of the India rubber that formed the soles of his boots. Keeping to the shadows, of which there was no shortage in this room, the pair headed for the nearest door. Furnished in a very Spartan manner, the room gave no overt indication of what its purpose might be. A pair of chairs and a single table stood near its center, and a large chest sat in one corner.

"Might be worth looking into," suggested Alvord in the best whisper his deep voice could muster, indicating the chest.

No lock impeded their designs, so in a flash its contents were exposed. A bizarre array of objects were stored inside. Wands of differing woods, magnets, leather restraints, glass bottles containing water—no rhyme or reason to it, as far as Alvord could tell. He and Marcel exchanged puzzled looks and moved on.

Up ahead was a door that Marcel eased open. The hinges must have been well oiled, for it gave not the slightest squeak. A long, medieval looking corridor lined with gleaming torches stretched before them, with other passages leading off to the right at intervals. Faint fragments of speech floated out of one, so after making sure the coast was clear they crept towards the source.

Peeking around the corner, Alvord saw that this passage

terminated in a spacious, high-ceilinged room. The twenty or so men who had been waiting for Abendroth after his performance were gathered inside, their backs to the entrance. He could not yet see if Deas was among them.

Abendroth was speaking, but just what he was saying was unclear. They needed to be closer.

Several alcoves housed suits of armor along the wall nearest Marcel and Alvord, so after a brief consultation conducted entirely by hand motions they crouched low and followed a line of shadow to the closest alcove.

No one detected their movements, although Alvord could have sworn that Otto Volkmar cast a momentary, questing glance in their direction.

The light from the many torches and candelabras did not quite penetrate the alcove. As they crouched behind the armor, Alvord caught a strong whiff of Marcel's body odor, which was rank even when measured against the standards of the day. Washing was by no means a common occurrence for most people, but the middle and upper classes often used perfumed oils and water to offset natural odors. Were he a gambling man, Alvord would have been willing to bet that Marcel had neither heard of nor made use of either.

Doing his best to ignore it, he peeked around the armor and observed what was going on. A man stood above a seated female slave, a wooden wand with what appeared to be magnets on it pointed at her skull.

Abendroth's voice cracked the air like a bullwhip.

"You're losing her, Gibault. *Focus*. Focus or you will lose her like Lynch did his."

The mesmerizer sat in a chair nearby, one foot propped up on a stool.

Beads of sweat testified to the man's attempt at focus, although the woman struggled all the more.

"She's struggling too much, Abendroth. Do something!"

The Count shook his head scornfully. "Dose her with more magnetized water, Calvi. Half a bottle. Gibault, you hold her there or she'll end up a hollow shell."

Another man darted forward and, forcing open the woman's mouth, poured some water down her gullet. He held his hand to her mouth and pinched her nose to ensure that she swallowed it.

She instantly relaxed. Gibault breathed a sigh of relief before screwing up his face in concentration.

"Now, make her rise and walk across the room." Abendroth watched closely, those green eyes staring unblinkingly like those of a snake.

The woman stood and took a few shaky steps forward. Gibault's eyes were shut, his wand raised and pointed at the slave's frail form. Without warning, she fell to the floor and began writhing in ways Alvord did not think humanly possible. A sound tore from her throat, the most inhuman, unearthly cry he had ever heard. The presence that Alvord had felt during the Count's demonstration could be felt again, the feeling that something huge and unseen was flying around the room in slow circles.

"Out of the way," demanded the Count quickly, "*get back*, Gibault."

The woman's flailing body neared a wall, and as Alvord and Marcel looked on in utter disbelief her wracked limbs began clawing their way up the wall. Then it seemed that she was no longer climbing, but was actually adhering to the stone itself, all the while roaring inhumanly in some unknown tongue and thrashing like a landed pike.

The Count directed his hand towards her, eyes closed and lips thin with concentration. At first she barely reacted, but soon her face relaxed and slowly her body slid down the wall.

"I almost had her," panted a ruddy-faced Gibault, "I almost had her that time."

Abendroth leered at him. "*I almost had her?* A regular comedian, you are. Not even in the rosiest of your delusions did you 'almost have her.' I can see that instructing you lot will take the whole of me."

He paused, getting his breathing under control. When he continued, it was in a calm, level voice.

"I am wrong to be so harsh. You are all being thrown headlong into this. These patients are not unwary subjects, they know what's coming, and dealing with recalcitrance always comes with a certain degree of consequence. Yet such training is vital to your success, to *our* success. Were this standard mesmerism, I feel quite confident that each of you would excel. But the fact of the matter is that you will generally not be mesmerizing willing subjects, and politicians will be far harder to hold mental dominion over, trust me. Politicians, even if taken by surprise, will have more mental defenses at their disposal than a baseborn slave. You *must* learn to overcome initial resistance, or the results can be severe."

He indicated the slave woman, who lay motionlessly on the cold stone of the floor. Abendroth paced back and forth distractedly, hands clasped behind his back.

"The only advice I can offer is this—there is a point at which you can feel the animal magnetism flowing from the refractory patient in a stronger wave than what you are administering. This is defiance born of sheer despair. To counteract it, you must not fight against the ebb and flow, but rather absorb the subject's own pulse without straining against it. All the while, keep your own waves of animal magnetism going strong, for after their initial pulse most people will be mentally dried up, utterly at your mercy. Weather the tumultuous but short-lived storm and victory is assured. Keep your breathing regular. Administering magnetized water and using magnetized wands will aid your efforts, and in some cases will immediately render the power of your subject ineffectual. Now, before Charles and I have our private session, who would like to have one more go at it?"

It was at this point that Alvord had the misfortune of brushing up against the suit of armor behind which he and Marcel crouched. The helmet, a pig-snout basinet, snapped shut with an extremely loud clang that reverberated around the room.

"Let's go, shall we?" suggested Alvord in a loud whisper, and he raced towards the corridor that led to their place of egress. He and Marcel kept to the shadows, moving like wraiths.

Men began shouting and milling about; the resulting confusion provided good cover. Alvord heard Abendroth yell, "After them!"

He caught a glimpse of Otto Volkmar drawing his sword and shoving men out of his way.

Not tonight, Alvord thought to himself. *No doubt there will be another day.*

At a dead sprint Marcel led the way into the room they had entered by, and with a wild whoop leapt out of the window. Alvord could hear men not too far behind him as he too jumped for it.

His downward progress was checked by a branch that took him hard in the chest, knocking the winding out of him. Wheezing horribly, he dropped to a lower limb that he was able to grab onto. Several gunshots rang out from overhead, and bullets tore through the foliage around him. With a downward glance he determined that roughly fifteen feet separated him from the ground below, and preferring a fall to a gunshot wound let go of the branch. Grabbing at other branches around him, he wildly strove to slow his descent.

The ground met him with considerable force, driving the butt of the Colt into his hip and side. But bullets still flew and there was no time to tarry. He dragged himself off the ground and started running. Spotting Marcel up ahead, Alvord fought against the pain and picked up his pace. Soon he ran alongside the mountain man through the tall prairie grass. At one point they glanced sidelong at each other and began laughing uncontrollably, like boys fleeing from the scene of some petty crime.

"We could've stayed and fought," panted Marcel when they had come to a rest at the wood line.

"Just as well that we didn't—too many of them in there, he had at least ten assistants not including Volkmar and then there were the twenty or so men he was instructing. Better to bow out this time around."

Marcel stretched his left side, grimacing slightly. "That was some fall, huh?"

Looking the man over, Alvord wondered just how many wild chases he had been involved in on the frontier, how many brushes with death he'd endured in his day. "At least there were branches to slow our descent. Now, did you see that slave crawl up the wall? Or am I delusional?"

"*Hell* yes I saw it. I ain't overly religious, but demons was unleashed upon that woman. What else could do that to her?"

Alvord thought about it for a moment, coming up with nothing. "I...I don't know. Marcel, what know you of law enforcement in St. Louis? Can they be trusted—should we tell them of this, seek their help?"

The mountain man scratched his beard reflectively. "Can't rightly say. I think a man by the name of Bogardus is sheriff these days. Supposed to be a sturdy one, not sure if he can be trusted, though."

"We may have to enlist his aid in this one. If we were dealing with an ordinary criminal...did you feel it in there? That presence?"

"Damn straight I did, just as I did in the woods that time. Never felt aught like it. It just feels, well...*evil*."

"Abendroth needs to be stopped. As if animal magnetism itself wasn't bad enough, I fear he has more worldly motives too. He mentioned something about mesmerizing politicians, I wonder to what end?"

Shouts could be heard back in the direction of the manor, and torches flickered around the entrance like so many lightening bugs. A search was being conducted, and they were the targets.

Marcel gave a derisive snort. "Those blunderin' fellers ain't findin' us, and that's a fact. We should probably head back into town though, just get outta their clumsy way. I could go fer a drink, how 'bout you?"

"I normally would, but midnight draws apace and it's been nonstop travel for me these last two weeks. But I'll tell you what— am to meet another acquaintance tomorrow around four o'clock at Market and Eleventh, and from there we'll be hitting some taverns up along Market Street. You should join us; we can plan our next move. My friend, an itinerant Irish writer, would be overjoyed at the chance to converse with a genuine mountain man."

"Sounds good."

They began jogging slowly eastward, leaving behind Abendroth's manor and the insanity its walls contained.

Chapter 16

St. Louis by night was a far less crowded but altogether more lurid place. Drunken men discharged guns into the air as they staggered out of taverns, raced horses up and down the streets, and roared the lyrics of bawdy ballads as they hit their choice watering holes. Whores were on the prowl, peddling their wares in the windows of brothels and out on the streets, primped and preened and clothed in all manner of garish attire.

Alvord walked by these people with utter detachment. Sometimes it truly bothered him, how little he had in common with most, but tonight other thoughts held sway in his mind. Like what nightmares might lie beyond the red door in Deas's studio, for instance. Having witnessed the madness that was mesmerism firsthand, and recalling the painter's statement that Abendroth used that force to enhance his art, Alvord needed to see how the mesmerizer's corruptive influence affected Deas's recent work. He had witnessed things tonight that defied even his most concerted efforts to explain away. He had seen a woman scurry up a wall, for God's sake!

It disturbed him that he actually yearned to see how the darker side of mesmerism could be translated into art. He had been granted a glimpse of it with Deas's paintings *The Prairie Fire* and *The Death Struggle*, but Deas hinted at far more shocking subject matter contained within that locked room. Deas's hidden artworks would, no doubt, buttress his belief that sinister forces lay at the heart of Abendroth's power.

Yet he could hear Deas's earlier statement all the while, telling him, *"You will be downright thunderstruck by the magnitude of his achievements and will hunger for the secrets behind his power."*

In labeling the mesmerizer's power as demonic, was he merely trying to explain away powers that he felt no man should have? Did he himself secretly crave such supernatural gifts?

Five minutes later Alvord stood before the crimson, nail-studded door. Only horrors could exist beyond, but they beckoned most seductively. Reaching into his pocket, he withdrew the large iron key that he'd nicked from Deas's pocket while at Abendroth's demonstration.

Turning the lock was the work of a moment, and the door creaked open dramatically. The room beyond lay dark and still before him, so he lit and hoisted a nearby candelabrum before moving on.

Heart fluttering slightly in anticipation, Alvord pressed further into the room, which was long and narrow in design with not a single window in evidence. Several large candles stood at intervals along one wall, so he lit those as well. Their yellow glow floated over twenty or so paintings, and Alvord let out a startled gasp in spite of himself.

Words failed him utterly. For a time he just stood there dumbly, turning in place as his awe-stricken eyes wandered over the paintings. Earlier today he accused Deas of having a diseased mind, and in doing so had made perhaps the biggest understatement of his life. How a man, in even his wildest imaginings or moments of revelation, could conceive of such monstrous, apocalyptic subject matter was simply beyond him. So this is what Deas described artistic maturity as, the achievement he was brimming with pride over?

Mad, he was. Stark, raving mad.

The largest canvas depicted a naked man falling into pitch-darkness, surrounded by grotesque serpents that tore savagely into him as he fell. Abject horror was stamped upon his features as he extended one hand upwards, like he was trying to claw his way back up. Blood and entrails provided the only color; all else was depicted in a neutral gray or an inky black.

Alvord checked the title: *A Vision.*

And a ghastly one if ever there was, this grisly Hellborn visioning. Another entitled *Apollyon Unbound* featured a colossal angel struggling mightily against the spiked, golden chains that bound him to the bottom of a pit ablaze with brimstone. Unlike *A Vision,* this work Deas had imbued with vivid color, taking great pains to show the scorched flesh of the roaring being, the bloody stains around its mouth, and the scattered entrails of human corpses strewn about its feet. The chains, upon close inspection, showed cracks and looked as if they would be torn asunder before long.

Apollyon, Alvord knew, was the powerful angel that Revelation asserted would break free from the bottomless pit in the end times to bring ruin to the earth.

A Nightmare Alvord found to be the most disturbing of these hellish works. Clad only in a rather revealing white robe, a woman lay chained to a rock while hideous impish creatures stuck her with tridents and wickedly lashed her frail form with whips. Blood ran freely down the rock to which she was chained, and several of the imps sat beneath, lapping it up. The expression she wore suggested eternal pain and anguish that transcended the human mind's ability to fully grasp.

Alvord found himself frequently checking behind him and casting quick glances into the ill-lit corners of the room. Several times he swore that he heard whispers.

Don't be a damned fool, he told himself. *There's nothing there.*

Another voice chimed in- *Are you really so sure of that?*

Other works were tamer, though still in keeping with the dark theme of the netherworld. One showed a legion of fallen angels in Pandemonium, soaring upward in frenzied flocks as if soon they would be shot of Hell and unleashed upon the world. Another was simply a set of eyes, staring hypnotically from the murky dark of the canvas. Their shape and coloration indicated madness and malice, and sounded the very depths of pure evil.

One painting, *Stygian Shores*, Alvord actually found to his liking. In it a man wandered along a desolate stretch of shoreline, peering uncertainly at the impenetrable blackness of the expansive River Styx, which coursed languidly over jagged rocks. Here and there misshapen forms just barely rose above the water's surface, watching him. A sense of isolated hopelessness pervaded this painting, but it was mild in comparison to the others.

Obviously, Abendroth's malign influence had polluted Deas's mind to the point where only apocalyptic themes had any value to him. Death, desolation, Hell, the end times—Alvord did not know why the Count exerted his influence over Deas to produce such abominable works, but surely he was behind it.

He had felt it twice tonight, that lurking presence that made itself known when Abendroth's mesmerism strayed towards the dark side. It was otherworldly in the very darkest of ways, and powerful enough to break through the veil that separated this world from the next. That it was demonic he was sure, but he did not venture to guess how Abendroth managed to summon it.

Frowning deeply, he agonized over the question that had been nagging him since the demonstration—how could a mere man wield such power? And what sinister forces did he conjure up and unleash when exerting that force?

Why would someone whose powers could work so much good instead delight in dabbling with the occult? If he himself possessed that power, the good he could do...

Whatever the case, one thing was clear—he had to get Deas out of this city and beyond Abendroth's influence as soon as possible. He would let the painter settle his affairs, and then it was back to New York posthaste.

However, there was always a chance that Abendroth would attempt to interfere with their departure. Deas was one of his elect, right there in his inner circle, after all. If things deteriorated and got ugly in a hurry, it would pay to know whether or not he could count on local law enforcement to help him. The Count had already infiltrated the city's patrician class; how hard would it be for him to control the law in this frontier city? The man's power over others seemed almost limitless.

Speaking of power over others, he recalled that just before he and Marcel had been made, Abendroth mentioned that politicians would be the targets of those men he was training in mesmerism. What nefarious designs did the man have in mind that involved the mesmerism of politicians by his disciples? Could it be that he sought a position in government?

Perhaps it would not be enough to just remove Deas from Abendroth's clutches. The mesmerizer's powers were otherworldly and moreover he abused them; who knew how many spent souls cried out for justice since dying by his hand?

Then and there Alvord determined that he would kill the mesmerizer, putting an end to his diseased fancies and whatever other insane plots he had in mind.

With a last look around, Alvord snuffed out the candles with his fingers and left that room of artistic insanity behind him.

    Alvord placed the iron key on a table and walked back to the Planter's Hotel at an express pace, for not since his boyhood had the night seemed so menacing.

Chapter 17

Dawn had established itself some ten minutes ago, casting the first feeble rays of sunlight onto the Mississippi. It was not quite six o'clock, but even at this time the waterfront area resounded with the noise of honest toil. Lumber, steel, and other cargoes were moved and organized in preparation for loading. Yelling men and chugging steamboats interrupted the dreams of those living near Front Street, and many a grumbled curse was cast upon the workmen.

Three miles south of the city, on the dirt road called Carondelet Avenue, Alvord jogged past carts, wagons, and carriages. They rumbled by him on the road, along with men and women on horseback. Those without the benefit of animal labor walked along in that loping, leisurely fashion that Alvord presumed to be the appointed mode of walking in the South. These people moved at a nag's pace, half the speed of your average New Yorker.

Having been confined to trains, coaches, and steamboats for over two weeks, Alvord relished the growing burn in his legs. True, it was Sunday and therefore not a day he'd typically exercise, but he had simply been cooped up too long. His destination, the village of Carondelet, lay four miles south of St. Louis. Once there he would turn around and head back upriver to the River Queen. An eight-mile run would give him ample opportunity to run himself ragged.

It was nice country through which he passed, with the river to his left and anything from farmland to deep woods on his right. All manner of craft plied the water, though along this stretch small sloops seemed to be the most popular vessels. But steamboats chugged along too, and a good many canoes, rowboats, and rafts transported people up and down the river as well.

The Federal Arsenal came into view, a square, stately building set back from the road and surrounded by park-like meadows and woodlands. Both infantry and mounted troops drilled in front of it. Alvord could just make out the sternly rapped orders of the officers.

From the Missourians he passed Alvord received many a bewildered look, for recreational running was by no means a common thing. Exercise might be common enough among the middle and upper classes back east and in Europe, but he reasoned that in a frontier town it could be viewed as extremely unusual.

For many, every day involved strenuous exercise. Farmers and laborers performed grueling daily tasks that kept them strong, and had no need of exercise regimens to stay fit.

As a patrolman Alvord had not received work-related exercise aside from occasionally cracking skulls or running down fleeing criminals. So years back when he first got on the job, he developed a daily exercise regimen to stay in top physical condition. Always he strove for balance between speed, power, and endurance.

Both Franklin and Jefferson had stressed the importance of taking exercise (and would have done well to follow their own advice), but horseback riding, battledore and shuttlecock, and dancing had taken the place of the running, swimming, and strength training advocated by the two Founders. In Alvord's mind, exercise should not be masqueraded as a pleasurable activity; training should be tough, even brutal in its intensity, pushing the limits of physical and mental endurance. A country's strength lay in the vigor and tenacity of its people as much as in its leaders' capacity to command, so it stood to reason that a sense of physical excellence ought to be instilled in the citizens of the American Republic. In the United States could be found the purest example of republicanism and civic freedom—it deserved a superior breed of people that could be called upon to defend those precious liberties.

But for Alvord there was more to it than that. He had an inborn drive, an individual need, to better himself. He was naturally endowed with impressive speed and power, but what good were those gifts if not developed to their greatest extent? He trained hard and considered himself elite, yet knew that plenty of men reckoned the same. There were no doubt men somewhere out there who trained harder than he, whose overall physical prowess surpassed his own; perhaps Otto Volkmar was among them. That did not sit well with him.

So he trained like a man possessed.

Cresting a small hill, he caught his first glimpse of Carondelet. It lay in a natural amphitheater of gentle knolls, a pastoral paradise of rolling crop fields and elm-besprinkled meadows. Wildflowers were present in riotous abundance, carpeting the hillsides in rich, diverse colors. Near the river neat, white houses sat clustered around the town's center. To the west, larger homesteads were perched atop the hills, with the land around them displaying that perfect aesthetic balance of field and woodland; enough fields to signify progress, but enough woods to retain a wilder aspect as well.

From this vantage he also noticed a round, castle-like building atop the bluff closest the water. A massive red flag hung limply from its tower in the still morning air. Incongruous was the first word that came to Alvord's mind, for when compared with the other structures this one was outsized and wholly out of place. Then, recalling the tourist pamphlet he'd read, he realized that it was the Montesano House, a medieval style structure that served as a theatre and place of amusement for St. Louis residents.

Hopefully, these were more chaste amusements than the ones provided by Count Abendroth.

He came to rest under the umbrageous elms that shaded the main street, seeking respite from the searing power of the now fully-risen sun. The sun's dazzling rays lent luminosity to the silver maples and sycamores lining the shoreline, so that even the opaque muddiness of the Mississippi took on a nice luster. Bald eagles and ospreys circled lazily above the river, and as Alvord watched one of latter tucked into a steep dive, flattening out at the last second to neatly scoop up a sizable fish. A group of children stood knee-deep in the muddy water, fishing in the far less spectacular method of man, while further out a group of older men fished from a raft. George Caleb Bingham's painting *The Jolly Flatboatmen* seemed to have slid off the canvas and right onto the Mississippi.

Breathing raggedly, Alvord gazed wistfully upon them. How pleasant it would be to float down the river free from care, idly fishing the day away. Instead, he had four miles worth of return trip to look forward to, an ever-deepening stitch in his side, and a dull ache in his right shoulder.

Ah. Better to dispel such thoughts before they too firm root. Wiping the sweat from his brow with an equally sweaty arm, he allowed himself another minute of rest before doggedly heading back up the dirt road.

Forty minutes later he lurched onto the southernmost extent of Front Street, a little-used section of road that afforded him some privacy. Alvord decided to conduct the remainder of his regimen here. He did not breathe but rather wheezed; never before had he trained in such inescapable heat. Even the shade offered little relief. Though lightly dressed, every article of clothing he wore clung to him most uncomfortably, saturated with sweat.

That he was not built for this climate was obvious, but then again he was descended from stock whose native range never experienced extreme heat.

Beginning with push-ups, he moved on to shoulder presses, using a broken piece of wooden spar as a weight. He then switched to behind-the-neck presses, before standing the spar on end and lifting it straight up into the air with his arms extended, using his chest and arms as well as his shoulders. Curls were the last lift, after which his upper body was thoroughly exhausted.

Back in New York he exercised in an informant's livery stable, where he could do pull-ups off the rafters and rope climb in addition to his other exercises, but he did not feel comfortable enough here to ask some stranger if he could exercise in his stable. Such a request would only be met with suspicion, and he hoped to keep a low profile while in St. Louis. Suspicion could easily lead to annoyance, annoyance to open animosity. These Southerners were a tempestuous lot; he'd heard and read many tales of their predilection for issuing duels. The last thing he needed was for some hot-blooded buffoon to challenge him. Killing a man would be a rather poor way to avoid attention.

Strength training concluded Alvord headed towards a deep creek he had passed. Swimming would complete his regimen and serve to cool him down, something he was in dire need of. A bridge spanned the width of the creek, from which he performed a neat ten-foot dive into the crystalline water.

The creek merged with the Mississippi some one hundred yards ahead, slowly winding its way through patriarchal groves of cottonwood and willows. Cottonmouth snakes, he'd been informed by one of his fellow steamboat passengers, were to be found in small numbers around St. Louis, but were by no means common. Hot as it was, he was willing to risk an encounter with one if it meant cooling off a bit.

For a moment he merely floated, basking in the glory of the crisp water. The sun filtered lazily through the verdant, interlocking limbs that formed a canopy over the creek, tingeing the shaded groves with a golden glow. It was hard to believe that bustling St. Louis lay just north, full of churning steamships, yelling men, and braying beasts of burden.

Beginning with a slow breaststroke, Alvord eventually transitioned into an overhand stroke that brought him to the confluence of the creek and the Father of Waters. Upon meeting the bigger river, the clarity of the creek became instantly obliterated by the roiling muddiness of the Mississippi. He eased out into those murky waters, swimming against the current. The river proved to be far colder than the creek, but was still nice given the heat of the sun. Although slow moving, the Mississippi's current bore down on him with relentless power. Realizing the futility of his actions and not wishing to get swept too far downstream, he headed for the shoreline.

A man fished in the shallows nearby, watching Alvord make his way towards shore.

"Saw a shark in there once," called out the fisherman matter-of-factly.

The last fifteen feet of his swim Alvord concluded with speed born of primal terror. Not many things under the sun could awaken true fear in him, but sharks were among the exceptions.

"What the devil would a shark be doing in a river?" Alvord demanded.

"Huh, beats me, maybe it felt like doin' a bit of exploration." The man appeared to derive immense satisfaction out of Alvord's obvious unease.

Alvord keenly scanned the surface of the river, with its floating trees and filthy foam. "Could a shark even survive in there?"

"Huh, if one made it here from the Gulf o' Mexico, I guess so. My brother down in Carondelet once saw a fin himself, and over in Cahokia, Illinois some feller lost a cow to somethin' as it waded out into the water... shark, I'd imagine."

"But... children swim in this river, men float down it on flimsy rafts..."

"Yep, and folks do the same in the ocean, where you find even more o' them devil fish, don't they?"

Alvord considered this. "Valid point. Well, take care, and were I you, I wouldn't wade too far out."

The man cackled, revealing crooked but very white teeth. "Ain't you a cautious one? Look, me and this here river go way back, friend. I got this muddy water flowin' through my veins."

"I very much doubt that."

"Anyways, if she wants me to become shark-bait, hell, so be it. Lord knows I've taken my fair share from her. Suppose it stands to reason that I gotta give something back one o' these days.

Casting his eyes over the mighty river, Alvord nodded understandingly. "An ideology most peculiar, but I confess I kind of like it. Good day."

Weary from exercise, he dragged his sore and dripping self back towards the Planter's Hotel.

He made the nine o'clock Mass at St. Paul's Episcopal Church in the nick of time. It lay just west and south of the Planter's Hotel, on Fifth Street where numerous other places of worship stood. By this time the heat bordered on unbearable and Alvord spent the Mass slowly sweating through his clothes. But it was nice to sit in a pew again, and after Mass concluded he went back to his room in a reflective mood. He could have stayed for the tea and cake that was offered afterwards, but he was not the type to do so among all strangers. Had Katherine been with him she'd have dragged him there, forcing him to interact with his fellow man in spite of his disinclinations. But alas, she was not here, and he was uncomfortable doing so alone.

Having not gotten nearly enough sleep the past few days, he determined that he would indulge in a nap from eleven to noon, but before he drifted into the mists of slumber he read from his copy of the Book of Common Prayer for a while.

When he awoke, the first thing he noticed was the cavernous rumbling of his stomach. At four o'clock he would be meeting Finnbar and possibly Marcel, but he wasn't entirely sure he wanted to go that long without a meal. A leisurely glance at his timepiece engendered a hurried leap out of his armchair. It was two-thirty; he had overslept by two and a half hours. Not that it really mattered, but still, he hated violating his self-imposed schedules. Plus, while a one-hour nap on the Sabbath was perfectly acceptable, he felt quite sure that three and half hours of sleep midday approached sloth.

And sloth, he reminded himself, could be found on a rather notorious list of seven sins that any God-fearing man would do well to eschew.

After getting properly dressed, he took down a glass of water to purge the dryness from his mouth, and headed for the door.

He placed a hand on his stomach as it rumbled again. He simply had to have a bite before meeting Finnbar and Marcel.

Leaving the hotel, Alvord took Fourth Street south to Market. Turning east, in the direction of the waterfront, he walked towards a restaurant on the corner of Market and Third that had caught his eye yesterday.

The quaint white and brown building bore the name "The Bavari Inn," and Alvord, privy to the pun, decided that the owner of the establishment had exhibited a healthy dose of wit and deserved business. Additionally, he figured that with a name like that the food would be German cuisine, and he was interested to see what kind of dishes German's made. German restaurants existed in New York, but he realized that he had never ventured into one.

Upon opening the door his ears were met with the sounds of drunken revelry. Nothing too rowdy, but noisy nevertheless. Most of those present spoke in guttural German tongues, and dressed in Continental fashion. A bar stretched the length of the left wall, at which many men stood drinking and talking. Twenty tables sat evenly spaced around the room, most of which were full of laughing, feasting Germans. In the room's center a large table contained a dozen men engaged in a very serious discussion conducted in rapid speech, while next to them others leisurely smoked pipes and played cards. All in all, it was a very cozy place, welcoming in its atmosphere.

Alvord made his way towards the far wall, where stood a small, unoccupied table. Looking around more carefully, he decided that aside from a cheerful feel to it, the place had a touch of sophistication, too.

Exquisitely engraved pewter plates could be found hanging on the walls, reflecting the flickering candlelight. Shields bearing various emblems also graced the walls, and axes, halberds, and swords were hung as well, sharing the wall with mounted deer antlers. Above Alvord's head was a pair of massive two-handed swords, their broad blades crossed in a visually pleasing manner. He wondered at the degree of strength and training it would take to effectively wield so mighty a weapon.

The ceilings were low, the chandeliers bronze and elegantly wrought. Not nearly as bright as most restaurants or taverns, the dim lighting of this place lent it an ambience that was all the more welcoming.

A blonde of what could only be exceptional pedigree swiftly approached his table, menu in hand. Alvord placed her age at around twenty. A green bodice accentuated an already-prominent chest and a white skirt swished around her ankles as she moved.

"Hello," she greeted him in a velvety contralto heavily laced with a German accent, "My name ist Valda Eberhardt. I haff a menu here, but I am afraid zat it is in German. Ve are working on getting von in English, but it is not yet ready. I can, however, explain ze various meals."

"That would be much appreciated. But how were you sure I was American?"

She smiled broadly, revealing faint dimples. "Forgive me, but you dress unlike a German or European, and carry yourself differently as vell."

"Observant of you. That you are an immigrant is obvious. Where did you learn English?"

"My vater and I lived in London for three years before moving to St. Louis. I learn much English there."

Alvord regarded the menu, none of which made a lick of sense to him. "So, it seems that you will in fact have to explain the meals."

Valda leaned closer, pointing to the items she described.

In his experience, Europeans were wont to get much closer to you than American decorum allowed for.

She smelled absolutely delightful and looked even more alluring close-up, but Alvord quickly quelled any untoward thoughts. Every time another woman appealed to him he could not help but feel as though he were callously betraying his dead wife. Katherine, aside from being a rare beauty and a superlative wife, had been graced with unshakable poise and self-control, something that he yet aspired to and now applied.

"So," Valda explained, "this first one ist Schnitzel vith mushroom gravy, spatzle, and a potato pancake. Schnitzel ist breaded veal, and spatzle ist an egg noodle."

That sounded extremely appetizing. "Hmm, I like the sound of that, but I'll listen to some more."

"Very vell. Next ist Sauerbraten, a beef roast marinated in vinegar, wine, and spices before cooking. It comes with potato dumplings and red cabbage. The locals around here call it 'sour meat,' and eat much of it. Then ve haff Rouladen, vhich ist a piece of very thin rump steak from ze Hirsch, I mean deer, rolled up with chopped pickles and onions, some bacon, and smeared vith mustard. It is served vith either spatzle or dumplings, and—"

"Alright, I'm sold. You can stop right there, I'll have that. With dumplings."

She laughed and, withdrawing the menu, asked, "And to drink?"

"What, in your opinion, is the finest German beer you serve? I have heard a great many things about the beer your people brew."

With pursed lips she thought about it. "Vell, ve haff many good beers, but I think Spaten is the best. It is brewed in Munchen, Bavaria's capital. A very old brew."

Alvord nodded approvingly. "Good enough for me. So, you are from Bavaria, then?"

"Ja. Sorry, I mean *yes*. Though it has been five years since I haff lived there."

"And the people here," he gestured around the room, "are they mostly Bavarians?"

"Some are, yes, but many others, too, like Prussians, Saxons, Hessians, and Austrians. From all over the German Confederation, really. Ve Bavarians can barely even understand some of the others, the dialects vary so much!"

"How strange."

"So, I go get ze beer then, and place your order, sir." And off she went with a loud swishing of skirt. It was all that Alvord could do to keep from staring.

Instead, he reached into his shirt pocket and withdrew the locket that contained Katherine's miniature daguerreotype. Looking at her face and form, outlined as they were against a dark background, quickly banished any thoughts of other women. She had been the rarest of beauties, with those high cheekbones and hair that lingered somewhere between blonde and red. Lively and intelligent, green eyes alive with curiosity and wit, she had been the ideal spouse for him. His time with her comprised the happiest years of his life, and he cursed himself now for being subject to the basest of his desires.

He knew he would never remarry; to do so would be a betrayal of the bond he and Katherine had shared and still did, to a certain extent.

For there were times when she haunted his dreams in the most vivid of ways. And sometimes when walking down busy streets he fancied that he glimpsed her regal form amidst the jostling crowd. That she watched over him he was certain.

A tankard of frothy beer hit the polished wood of the table with a thud, stirring him from his reverie. Valda stood off to the side, waiting for his assessment of Germany's finest brew.

"Thank you," Alvord said, raising the tankard to his lips.

"By Thunder," he thundered, "this is the beer that all others should be judged against. Do you brew this yourselves?"

Valda, pleased with his reaction, shook her magnificent head. "Ve do not, I'm afraid. Ve haff no knowledge of zat. My vater owns this restaurant, and thought German beer vould be valued in America, where, it is known in Europe, men take their beer seriously. Ve can order it now, but when ve first came he had Spaten and some other beers stored in... in, I cannot think of ze name. Giant barrels?"

Alvord took another gulp before replying. "Ah, you mean hogsheads. Yes, some can hold over fifty gallons of fluid. A wise man, your father. And by the by, you might try to get that 'th' sound into the word father. No pressure, just a friendly suggestion. I have been wondering about this place—with all this armor and weaponry and silver finery, don't you have trouble with local ruffians, especially being immigrants? This place is a veritable gold mine of antiques. What deters them?"

The German beauty turned and pointed at a tall, hulking man with long auburn hair done up in a ponytail. He stood behind the bar, polishing glasses. Alvord had noticed him on the way in, taking note of his heavy musculature.

"I see. Your father, is he?"

She nodded. "Ve had trouble early on, but they learned qvuick to let us be. My vat—*father*, Rudolph, was forced to beat some of them qvuite badly."

Alvord chuckled. "Good man."

Valda left, having other tables to tend to, leaving Alvord to tuck in. The Rouladen exceeded his wildest expectations, a perfect marriage of tender venison, pickles, and bacon. The dumplings he also found to his liking, their peculiar consistency quite unlike any other food. He asked Valda to extend his compliments to the cook, who turned out to be her mother.

Even when feasting, Alvord's police instincts were at work. Every second mouthful his eyes would look up from his plate and dart around the room, searching for anything suspicious. On one such sweep, his eyes met those of Otto Volkmar, who leaned casually up against the bar where thirty seconds before he had not. The Prussian gave him a slight nod, a salute that Alvord returned with the raising of his tankard. The towering bodyguard must have recognized him from Abendroth's performance.

Valda's father Rudolph slid a frothy beer glass to the Prussian, who struck up a conversation with him.

Damn. Germans were known as a large people, and those two were a testament to the belief. Alvord was used to being taller than most, but the Prussian stood a solid three inches above his six-feet one inch. Rudolph was only slightly shorter than six feet, and was quite thick in the chest and shoulders. If a healthy stream of Germans kept immigrating to the States, then the already-brawny stock of America would grow larger and stronger yet. True, half of them were Catholics, but then again Andrew O'Farrell had been as well...

As he turned his attention back to his food, he glimpsed something out of the corner of his eye that did not seem right.

His head instantly snapped to attention.

A man outside stared at him through one of the windows, squinting his eyes in the manner of someone straining to make something out more clearly. When Alvord held his gaze, his mouth opened in a furious snarl and he headed for the door.

Alvord sighed, for he was reasonably sure that he recognized the man, what with his cane and swishing cloak.

Confirming his suspicions, the slave-owner from the steamer *Sultana* shoved the door open and stared daggers at him from across the room. It was fair to say that he hadn't appreciated Alvord's dunking him in the watering trough yesterday, or Deas slugging his friend in the gut.

Shoveling another bite of Rouladen into his mouth, Alvord watched the man as he stomped towards his table with a manifestly peevish look on his face.

So much for keeping a low profile...

Chapter 18

The man strode across the tavern with an imperious mien. He sneered at the Germans who occupied the bar and tables, obviously repulsed at the sight of immigrants. Cane rapping with each stride, he positioned himself squarely in front of Alvord.

"*You,*" spat the man, voice dripping with malice. "I hoped I'd find you."

"Well," replied Alvord drily, "in that you've succeeded. Though honestly, I must register my surprise at the fact that you actually recognize me, given the state you were in yesterday."

The man's sneer deepened. "You humiliated me. In front of my slaves, in front of my friend, and in front of the citizenry."

"My heart breaks for you." Cool demeanor notwithstanding, Alvord's right hand crept towards the Colt, lest the man make any sudden moves.

The Southerner crept closer, speaking in a brasher tone. "No matter. All has fallen into place."

Alvord noticed that for all the man's rage, he stood perhaps five foot five and a stringy five-five at that.

"You would do well to simply admit fault and leave. You were ossified, unruly, and abusive towards women. You were in the wrong, not I. I merely did what any man with a proper sense of justice would have."

"Your arrogance knows no bounds. You haven't the slightest inkling as to who I am, do you? The name is Richard DuPont, one you will come to remember, Easterner."

"Listen," Alvord replied, taking a small sip of beer, "if you plan on doing something, exacting some revenge, then I suggest you get on with it. I am trying to enjoy an exceptionally fine meal here."

By this time all chatter had ceased in the restaurant; all eyes were on Alvord and his aggressor. Volkmar and Rudolph watched him intently from the bar.

"And who are you, you ill-mannered swine, that you don't have time for me?"

"I am Alvord Rawn, and allow me to be blunt," Alvord snapped, losing patience altogether. "I am not given to badinage of words with my inferiors."

The popinjay's eyes narrowed maliciously. "Inferior? We'll see yet who the better man is."

"And what, pray tell, do you have in mind?"

"A duel." The man hissed the words as if they were a dread pronouncement, but Alvord remained unmoved.

"Now we're getting somewhere!" he proclaimed cheerfully. "So, are you in strict adherence to the Code Duello, or do you deign to dabble in swordplay?"

His enemy snorted derisively. "Pistols, swords, it makes little difference. Choose your weapon, you bitch's whelp—all roads lead to you gurgling in your own lifeblood."

"I choose swords, then." Alvord announced, rising quite suddenly to his full height. "These swords."

His antagonist's eyes followed Alvord's pointing finger, coming to rest on the massive greatswords. The man's lips parted in astonishment.

"You jest."

Alvord took the swords off their racks and tossed one to him by way of reply. The man caught the weapon with both hands but still failed to steady it, and the tip of the blade went thudding into the floor.

"But, but, these are barbaric weapons! They are ancient!"

"There's many a good tune played on an old fiddle."

"I shall not entertain this warped fancy; face me on my own terms if you won't be civil about this." His gaze kept roving from the oversized sword clumsily clutched in his hands to his enemy's large form.

Alvord saw this and gave a shark-like grin. "Come now! You issued the challenge. You, in an act of supreme temerity, allowed my choice of weapons, yet now you rescind? Oh, there's comedy there! You might put up a good front, and are no doubt the biggest toad in the puddle back home. But let me assure you, I hail from a far larger pond. So now you have no pistol to hide behind, no fancy footwork to save you. It is just you, me, and twelve pounds of cold steel."

The man's resolution wavered noticeably. "I will not! Your challenge is beyond the pale! This is barbarous, uncivil!"

"Kind of like standing twenty paces apart and discharging pistols into each other's hearts, no?"

The man's swagger and haughtiness had long deserted him, and his growing panic became obvious to those gathered, some of whom began to snicker disdainfully. Volkmar joined in.

"Face me like a man!" the slave-owner demanded in something of an assertive stammer. He glared death at the chuckling patrons of the Bavari Inn.

Alvord raised his sword with one hand, letting the candlelight dance playfully along the length of its broad blade.

"I daresay it does not get much manlier than this."

"I... you *have to*—"

"Kindly remove yourself from my line of sight, you pugnacious little shit-smear."

"Ja, go," said a deep, authoritative voice, which turned out to be Rudolph's. He had come around the bar and was standing nearby, pointing to the door. "NOW."

The exasperated fellow dropped the sword with a loud clatter, turned on his heel and flounced out of the room, cape swirling most dramatically.

"My apologies," Alvord offered to Rudolph, "I did not mean to make a scene in your restaurant."

"Ah, ist no matter," Rudolph assured him with a wave of his hand, "He vas the von vhat brought it in here. You are velcome to stay."

He returned to his bar and the room was soon abuzz with chatter. Many glances were snuck at the big American who wished to fight with those monstrous swords. Some even saluted him with their drinks.

Alvord hung his sword back up and turned to collect the fallen one. His way was blocked by Volkmar, who held the sword's hilt towards him. Close up, it became apparent that he stood closer to five inches taller than Alvord, and was thicker in the chest and shoulders. The man's clean-shaven face was a square block of bulging jaw muscles and heavy bone structure, topped with neatly-combed blonde hair.

"Would you have really fought him with these swords?"

he asked in a resonant voice slightly tinged with a German accent.

"Damn straight," responded Alvord with the shadow of a grin, taking the sword and putting it back.

"May I?" the Prussian asked, gesturing towards the empty seat across the table.

"Please do."

"Otto Volkmar."

"Alvord Rawn."

The two shook hands.

"The sword you carry, is that a Swiss-made Walloon?"

"You possess a keen eye, Herr Rawn."

Alvord eyed the blade appreciatively. "A larger sword than what is normally carried these days."

"Indeed it is—but in all modesty I am a larger man than is normally seen these days. I prefer even heavier swords, specifically broadswords, but to carry one of those around in this day and age would be most outlandish. What is it you are drinking?"

"Spaten, actually. First time I've had it, but I'm already developing quite a taste for it."

Now that he and Volkmar were in close proximity, exchanging pleasantries, the tension he had felt towards the man slowly faded. Yet the realization that this was the man who guarded Abendroth, the man he would likely have to fight to get at Abendroth, remained fixed in Alvord's mind.

Volkmar nodded approvingly. "We Germans are known for three things. Good breeding, good steel, and good brewing. Superior stuff, is Spaten.

"Zwei mal Spaten, bitte," he politely requested of Valda.

The Prussian gave her an appraising look as she strode gracefully towards the bar. "And speaking of good breeding... what say you?"

Alvord could not help but cast his eyes her way. "Can't argue with that. Say, where did you develop your English? Your voice carries only the barest suggestion of German origins."

"I was taught English as a child, and later lived in England for several years."

Valda brought them their drinks in odd clay mugs, ones with metal lids that had to be flipped open.

"What are these called?" asked Alvord, experimentally

flipping open the lid with his thumb.

"Steins. This way you don't spill precious beer. A fine instance of ingenuity, no?"

"I'd say so. They should give these to the Irish; those people are always slopping beer all over when they drink. Probably those vigorous hand gestures they employ in discourse."

"Hah," Volkmar sneered, "inferior people, the Irish. A fiery race, heedless of death, but they have no organization and are no match for the blood of England, which unless I'm mistaken is mostly the blood of Angles and Saxons."

"It could be argued," said Alvord fairly, "but there is also much Viking blood in certain parts of the country, as well as Celtic and Pictish. I myself have some Cornish ancestry, which is Celtic and Iberian. But mostly, my line is of Saxon and Viking origin."

"And what of the Normans?"

"They did not mix much. William's top men ruled over our island, but mostly despised our race, language, and culture. Sir Walter Scott's *Ivanhoe* deals with that. Some Norman immigration occurred, but not nearly enough to dilute our blood."

Volkmar nodded understandingly. "I hear that the Irish in New York City are wild, like the Indian tribes out here almost. Do you know that to be true?"

"I am actually from Manhattan, and dealt with them in my old line of work."

"Which was?"

"Law enforcement. I was a captain in the Municipal Police Department of New York."

Volkmar looked him over again, more closely this time.

"But you do that no longer?" he asked carefully.

"I do not."

"Why is that, if I might ask?"

"Perceived excessive violence. I was deemed too much of a hazard. And politically, I stood against what New York is fast becoming."

Volkmar leaned back in his chair and crossed his mighty arms. "A man willing to stand for his principles, eh? So then, you dealt with these feral Irishmen until recently?"

"Often. And harshly. There is much gang warfare in New

York, and as a patrolman you frequently find yourself in the thick of it."

"Are they all red-haired, Catholic animals?"

Alvord instantly thought of Andrew O'Farrell, whose noble character and sense of duty had culminated in a hopeless, brutal struggle against men whose blood was his own.

"No, not all of them. Their Celtic blood is inherently weaker than our own, but a number of them overcome that. Even with their popish religion, some of the best men I've known were Irish."

The two men sat drinking for a while, and talk grew desultory. Volkmar eventually brought up dueling.

"You know, I have never understood the point of a pistol duel. How does that really determine who the better man is? You stand there like a buffoon, either waiting to be shot or shooting at a man who is not defending himself. Swords, now there is a way to settle disputes. One needs skill, speed, strength, strategy, and fortitude to succeed. Is that not the measure of a man?"

"I could not agree more."

"I sense that you are trained in the art of the blade?"

"As a youth I fenced quite a bit. When I got on with the Department I was instructed in the way of the sword by an old German sword master, went by the name of Maximilian Schuller. Aside from rapiers and sabers, he also instructed me in the use of the broadsword, antiquated though that fighting form is. He owned copies of these manuals; I want to say he called them *Fetchbuchs*."

Alvord abruptly realized that he might have spoken too freely, for if Volkmar knew of them then he understood Alvord's training, which invariably influences style.

"Ah yes! *Fechtbuchs* are very old sword fighting manuals; few have the privilege of studying them today."

"But you have?"

He grinned slyly. "I have. A fight between us would be most interesting, I am thinking, as we are of somewhat similar size and have a similar background in training. *Most interesting.*"

The vapors of a malevolent curiosity hung around Volkmar's words.

"While in the Prussian army," he continued, "I ranked

first in the broadsword tournament." He paused to take down some Spaten. "With sabers I did well too, but with rapiers I was out of my element."

"Well, men like you and I are large targets for small, lightweight thrusting swords."

"That is true, and rapiers are for *untermenschen* anyway, inferior men. Not as bad as pistols, but still, some spindly-armed bitch can pick you to pieces, striking the most feminine poses all the while. Fighting with sabers and broadswords requires real men, and is therefore more honorable."

Alvord hoisted his stein. "To we proud standard-bearers of the past."

They clinked mugs and drank for a while in companionable silence.

"Is Friedrich von Steuben a well-known figure in Prussia?" Alvord wanted to know.

"Yes, quite so actually."

"Though many of my countrymen have forgotten, we in the States owe much to Prussia, for from your land came von Steuben. Had it not been for his drilling and training of our troops at Valley Forge, we may not have had the discipline to overcome the British on the battlefield. He essentially turned the ragtag Continental Army into a proper one."

"Yes, the Prussian army is elite, and always has been. Even when our rulers are weak, the men in the ranks remain strong. Frederick the Great showed that with proper leadership, Prussia can rise to become a dominant force in Europe. Though a sodomite, and a lover of Jews and Catholics, he knew how to run a country."

"He was a sodomite, you say?"

"Yes," replied Volkmar, shaking his head perplexedly. "His father actually had his lover beheaded in front of him when he was young."

"Huh. That'll get you chasing skirts instead of breeches. You mentioned you served in the Prussian Army. You see any action?"

"No. That is why I left, and made my sword for hire."

"Which is how you came to serve Count Abendroth?"

"Yes, which is how I came to see a large man with dark hair and a red beard skulking around his manor late last night."

Alvord's guts immediately twisted into a knot, but he did his best to keep his face impassive. The cordial nature of their discussion was instantly replaced by a weighty tension.

Volkmar's dark blue eyes bored into him coldly, with a faint flicker of amusement providing the only visible sign of emotion.

"Hmm," Alvord replied, stroking his own red beard, "well I'll keep my eyes peeled for anyone fitting the description."

"Please do," requested the Prussian with a wolfish smile, rising from his chair and draining his stein. "I am not telling my master of this, as he has enough to worry about, so I am taking a personal interest in it. And should you find the man fitting that description, kindly let him know that should he ever darken my master's doorstep again, his swordsmanship will be put to the test."

"I will advise him to keep his blade well honed," said Alvord, a dangerous edge to his voice.

The bodyguard gave a mirthless snort, threw down some Prussian *thalers* on the table to pay for Alvord's meal and their drinks, and then swept out of the restaurant.

Alvord watched him go, realizing that someday soon he would probably be forced to kill the man, if he proved equal to the task. Surely he would try to prevent him from killing Abendroth, and only one would walk away from that battle. He wondered a moment if Lady Fortune would smile upon him in that titanic undertaking.

Polishing off the last frothy dregs of his beer, he got up and left shortly thereafter, offering compliments and a brief goodbye to Valda and Rudolph.

Caution must now become the catchword of his existence, for one misstep could lead to mortal danger. In his two days in St. Louis he had made two enemies, one of little concern but a threat nonetheless and the other formidable in the extreme.

Amazing. Just amazing.

Leaving behind the convivial atmosphere of The Bavari Inn, Alvord went north on Market Street, towards Market and Eleventh where he would meet Finnbar and Marcel. The road sloped upwards and his legs ached something terrible, sore from his morning run. He stuck close to the buildings along the road, taking advantage of the shade they afforded, meager though it was. For the umpteenth time, he wondered how people could function in such searing heat.

The Colt rested reassuringly in his waistband. As he came to the corner of Market and Fifth, Alvord made a mental note to never stray from his room without the assurance of a weapon, for who knew when either that popinjay or Volkmar might make an attempt on his life? And on top of it all he had to make certain that Deas remained compliant and willing to depart within in the next few days, and blissfully ignorant of his plan to dispatch Abendroth.

His vigilance must never waver, for—

Something thudded into the back of his skull with tremendous force, and for a moment he saw only incoming stars and colors he had never known to exist. Hard contact between his face and the gravel of the road snapped him out of it; he regained his consciousness if it had in fact taken leave of him for a moment. He heard yelling, felt the pain begin to tear at his head. Instantly he sought to get up, but boots began beating him back down. Some of the bastards were wielding clubs, too.

Covering his head with his hands, he rose powerfully, throwing men off of him. They swarmed him again and punches, kicks, and club strokes found every part of his body, some blows inadequate, others viciously efficient. Alvord was encircled by a tight ring of snarling men, one of whom was Richard DuPont and all of whom clamored to get at him. Their numbers and enthusiasm actually led to their getting in each other's way, providing Alvord with a second's respite. Seeing a gap in their ranks amidst the chaos, he threw himself into an agile sideways roll that brought him outside their circle. Then he was up and throwing punches with the very worst of intentions.

His Colt had been knocked from his waistband in the initial assault, or else he'd have let fly at them with that. But fists were all he had now and fists would have to do.

It seemed that he faced a dozen or more men, a few of whom wielded wooden clubs. At least that's what he thought. His vision, blurred and darkened around the edges, failed to serve him properly. But he really didn't care about numbers, for his blood was up.

The first three men turned on him, brandishing fists and

clubs with exuberant cruelty. Their hurried swings he skillfully ducked, countering with a blurring series of hooks and uppercuts that brought all three crashing down in a matter of seconds, unconscious and broken.

Then the rest of the ravening pack was upon him again, and he found himself fighting for his life.

It was a beating such as he'd never had. Punches found his face and ribs while clubs tore at his back and legs. Alvord had not lost a fight since his youth, but realized pretty quickly that he was destined to lose this one. That first blow to the head had really sent him for a loop, rendering his reflexes sluggish. But on he fought, doggedly and desperately.

Grabbing the nearest man by the hair, he gave him his hardest right hand to the throat and then, using the gurgling bastard as a shield, plowed through the group in an effort to reach a building and get his back against a wall.

In this he was successful, though he took much punishment doing it. He slammed the man headfirst into the wall of the dry-goods store that he then got his back against. A wild punch immediately found his chin, and he staggered before savagely boxing the man's ears and head butting him, crushing his nose in an explosion of red. He could feel the warmth from the fine mist of blood that spattered onto his face. Another man stumbled over the limp body of his friend and Alvord's arms shot out, sending him soaring into a nearby hitching rail that snapped on impact. Two club strokes landed on his ribs and neck, and a kick took out one of his legs. He crashed to the ground, and his assailants immediately went about stomping him again. From between one man's legs Alvord perceived Volkmar in a fleeting moment of clarity, observing the fight as he casually leaned up against a wagon.

A kick smashed into his mouth, and he tasted the metallic tang of blood. Suddenly he reared up and, grabbing a man's incoming foot, twisted the ankle fiercely, feeling the tendons crunch, before swinging an explosive kick into his groin. If only he could grab one of those clubs, he could make a better go of it... but all around him was roiling activity and there was simply no time to look for one.

Every part of him was riddled with pain, but the worst of it lay in his head and back. Even his rage was insufficient to totally block the lancing pain, which surged at times to truly agonizing levels. His frustration mounted too, for each time he sought to mount a decent attack a mass of men were upon him.

Another blow from a club put him down, but he sprung back up immediately. The noise that generally accompanied a fight was eerily replaced by an intense ringing that drowned out all else. Men closed on him, trying to tackle and drag him down while another caught him a calculated stroke to the temple. He grabbed that man by the collar with his free hand, sending him sailing into the wall with a flick of his arm. More men piled onto him, punching and kneeing and cursing all the while. Under their combined weight he began to sink to the ground.

Summoning the last reserves of his strength, he exploded upwards and flung out his arms, throwing men off of him like a buffalo shaking off harrying wolves. One man still clung to his back like a limpet, so he lunged backwards and crushed him between his body and the wall, effectively dislodging him.

He could feel himself weakening, and knew that soon neither his wobbly legs nor burning lungs would support him sufficiently. Six men were down, but another six at least remained standing, too many for him to contend with in his present condition. Determined to go out on an aggressive note, he charged the regrouping men with an animalistic roar, tackling the nearest. Driving his shoulder into the man's gut, he lifted him off the ground before slamming him back into it. The man lay under him, gasping horribly. The startling realization dawned on Alvord that he would not be able to drag himself back up this time, but he attempted to regardless.

Three well-aimed kicks to his midsection brought an end to his efforts.

Chalky was the gravel that clung to his torn lips, mingled with the salty flavor of his own blood. Body alive with pain, he lay sputtering on the ground, striving to move but struggling to translate his thoughts into action.

"Get me that noose, Jackson, and let's find us a sturdy limb!" said a gleeful but breathless voice that Alvord instantly recognized as DuPont's. He could hear, but everything sounded so very far away, so garbled...

"Tough bastard," panted one of the other men, looking around at his fallen friends.

"Bastard being the operative word," spat the popinjay, his cape torn and cane broken. "Now let's have ourselves a lynching!"

"I think he killed Hornsby!" cried out another man.

"Let's string him up quick-like, then we deal with our losses."

He turned to say something to one of his other accomplices but walked straight into a hard right cross swung by a furious Finnbar.

Marcel too dashed into the fray, bowling over one man before wildly pouncing on another. The remaining assailants, some nursing injuries and all thoroughly winded, were no match for Alvord's friends, who made full use of the element of surprise.

The Irishman drove home a fine shot to a man's gut. The man hunched with a groan only to receive a swift knee to his nose. Two others came at him but he hastily snatched a club off the ground and laid into them with it, displaying considerable skill.

Marcel eagerly engaged the rest. The mountain man was a brawler born, overcoming his opponents with a combination of deft throws and well-placed haymakers.

DuPont took a shot from Marcel, rolled and tried to make a run for it, but a partially recovered Alvord instinctively lunged, grabbing his enemy by the knees and bringing him crashing down. Crawling on top of him, he threw a series of crippling punches into DuPont's face. That accomplished, Alvord attempted to rise but achieved only a shuddering stumble. Wheezing hoarsely, he lurched sideways and would have gone down had not Marcel grabbed him.

"By the way," said Finnbar disdainfully to the pulped mess that was DuPont's face, "1804 sent word. It wants its wardrobe back."

One of the fallen men leapt up and sprinted past Finnbar, who failed to grab him in time. He flew up Market Street but did not make it far.

Otto Volkmar stepped out and met him head on, crushing him with a devastating punch to the sternum that brought the man to his knees, spewing blood. Grabbing him by the collar and belt buckle, the giant Prussian hefted his limp weight into the air, spun him around, and drove him headfirst into the road. The man twitched wildly, his neck at an impossible angle. His movements a blur, an unsatisfied

Volkmar drew the Swiss Walloon and drove the sword into the man's heart.

Locking eyes with Alvord for a moment, Volkmar sneered, spat on the man's wretched carcass and left.

"What the hell was that about?" Finnbar asked in amazement.

Marcel, meanwhile, unsheathed his Bowie knife, grimly staring at a fallen enemy whose arms were rigidly stretched towards the heavens as if grasping an invisible rope.

"Don't," requested Alvord, who could just barely support himself. "Please, stay your hand."

"Maybe it ain't my place, Al, but these fellers was fixin' to lynch you in what I'm guessing was cold blood. I could give 'em all the dag right now and be done with it."

"I've got enough blood on my hands," Alvord panted dazedly, "The law can deal with them. Let us leave."

A crowd had gathered 'round by this time, forming a half-circle around the scene of the fight.

"Fine showing there," Alvord heard one man say through the mists of semi-consciousness, "You fellers get him off to a physician quick-like, we'll say nary a word as to his location. Has to be a good sort if he got on DuPont's bad side, and his fightin' alone has earned him postponement from dealings with the law, at least for today."

Marcel grunted his appreciation to the man as he threw one of Alvord's heavy arms across his shoulders.

"Well," said the Irishman briskly, "you look a fright, my friend. Let's get you to the nearest tavern for immediate treatment."

Chapter 19

The walk to The Bavari Inn passed with all the speed of an eternity. Alvord's vision swam; several times he felt sure he would vomit, but managed to keep his stomach contents where they belonged. He was reluctant to show just how battered he was, though never before had he been quite so battered. Those clubs and kicks had damaged his ribs, which were bruised if not broken, and his head was one throbbing mass of cuts and rapidly-rising bruises. White-hot pain stabbed at his arms and hands, which had borne the brunt of the attack while protecting his skull.

"You all right?" Finnbar and Marcel asked in unison as they supported him, both realizing just how seriously their friend was injured.

"I'm good." But he wasn't and wouldn't be anytime soon. Still, he forced his legs to move.

"What in the hell happened to him?" inquired a shocked voice that turned out to be Deas's. Alvord saw him as if through a rippling sheet of water.

"Who're you?" Finnbar shot back.

"Charles Deas, a friend of his. I heard the commotion and thought I recognized him from across the road. So once again, I ask what happened?"

"Good question, really. What did happen, Alvord? Marcel and I were chatting when we saw the commotion from our meeting spot, and decided to check it out. Made it in the nick of time too, I might add."

Alvord struggled to walk and talk at the same time, and spoke thickly, his swollen jaw granting his mouth only limited movement. "And for that I thank you. Slave owner we saw aboard the *Sultana*, Finn. Saw him again yesterday, Charles and I roughed up he and a friend of his after we saw them abusing some women. He saw me in this tavern up ahead and sought revenge. Challenged me to a duel and let me choose weapons, so I chose two-handed swords, which he declined. He left, and must have rallied the some friends who jumped me once I left."

"'Some' friends?" Finnbar scoffed. "There were over twelve men there, Alvord. That bastard must've really doubted his ability to take you out. Huh, a bigger bollocks never put his arm through a coat. Mayhap we should've sent him to the Lord."

Marcel examined Alvord closely. "I gotta say, Al, they really did a number on you there, pack-running cowards that they were."

Alvord grunted in reply.

"Although, in fairness, you did a number on them too. 'Specially that last one you got a hold of."

Finnbar snorted derisively. "Yeah, that rancid ball of shite surely got his."

"I saw some folks heading off to find Sherriff Bogardus shortly after you left," mentioned Deas. "He's a strict one; those men will be dealt with harshly, I'd reckon."

"You know Bogardus well?" inquired Marcel innocently, and Alvord could tell he was probing for information.

"You could say we belong to the same social club," responded Deas cryptically.

Through the haze of semi-consciousness, Alvord heard and processed this, grasping the fact that the Sherriff could not be approached in regards to taking down Abendroth. So much the better. Organized law enforcement often impeded the designs of true justice anyway; he knew that all too well.

The door to the German tavern swung open to admit Alvord and company.

"*Mein Gott!* Ve saw you approaching, vhat on earth happened to him?"

Finnbar offered a quick explanation to Valda in surprisingly fluent German while they ushered Alvord towards an empty table. Alvord's mangled appearance occasioned many a startled gasp.

"There you go, lad, just ease back onto the table there. Does anyone know where the closest physician's practice is?"

"Not necessary," Alvord assured him. "I just need some

time. And maybe some booze. Although, if there be any bandages around I could use some."

He could tell that nothing was broken expect perhaps a few ribs on his right side. And perhaps a knuckle or two. All a physician would do therefore was dose him with laudanum, an alcoholic drink containing up to ten percent opium. Having once developed a slight addiction to opium after breaking an arm, Alvord wanted nothing to do with the stuff. Anyway, he could clean his own cuts and had ointment back in his room to prevent their getting infected. The ribs he could have anyone bandage.

"You sure, Rawn?" asked a concerned Deas.

"Yup," responded Alvord through tightly clenched teeth.

"God," the artist said in a hoarse whisper, "he looks a fright, doesn't he?"

"Heard that, Charles. Very encouraging, thanks."

He leaned his head over the table and spat a stream of blood. A quick probing of his mouth with his tongue assured him that all his teeth remained in place. He had never lost a single tooth to fights or decay, a fact of which he was immensely proud.

A large form appeared next to him.

"Drink this," ordered Rudolph.

An ambrosial liquid was poured down his throat, stinging his split lips. But it warmed his body and momentarily caused him to forget about some of the pain.

A ring of worried faces hovered overhead. Realizing that his current position was pretty pathetic, he slowly sat up with a pained grunt. He got off the table and gingerly eased into a chair, unable to suppress a grimace as he did so.

"My, my," grinned Marcel, "ain't you a tough 'un to keep down."

Alvord ignored the compliment and drank the rest of the liquor Rudolph had given him.

"Capital stuff. What is it?"

"*Sechsamtertrophen.*"

"Come again?" asked Finnbar humorously.

"Hell, nothin' needs a name that tough to say," Marcel commented.

"Ist schnapps—an after dinner drink."

"Best liquor that ever passed my lips."

Rudolph poured him some more, and Alvord took another fortifying gulp.

"Rawn," said Deas seriously, "I mean not to startle or dishearten here, but I cannot recognize you, your beard and size aside. You're in rough shape—how will you be fit to travel?"

"Where is he travelling?" queried the Irishman.

"He and I are travelling back to New York, after I settle my affairs here."

"Ah, so you're the one he was sent out here to collect?"

Deas chuckled. "The very same."

"Put your head back," Valda firmly demanded of Alvord, delicately placing two cool steaks on his face. "These vill help. I vill fetch ice from ze cellar too."

She came back with ice, which she applied to his arms and hands, then proceeded to clean the cuts on his skull. The brass washbasin she used to dampen her rag soon grew red with vaporous clouds of blood.

"I was fortunate," Alvord said to no one in particular. "The clubs they employed were long and narrow. Had the clubs been stouter and their arms stronger I might have gone down for good after that first shot."

"Got the drop on you, did they?"

He paused for another sip of *Sechsam...* schnapps. "That they did, Marcel. Waylaid me something fierce. Felled me with that first blow, they did, now that I think it, it was probably DuPont's metal-tipped cane. I got back up to make a fight of it, but they were too many, and I too concussed."

"You ruined a good many of their days though, looked like you may have killed one of them, too. And by the way, that was a beautiful Liverpool Kiss you administered there."

"A Liverpool *what*?"

"Oh, might be more of an English term," reasoned the Irishman. "Head-butting is what you would call it here across the pond, I suppose. Liverpool sailors and dockworkers employ it aplenty in bar fights, hence the name. But whatever the case, I saw that as we hurried over. Nicely done."

Marcel reached behind him and pulled something from his belt. "This Colt yours, Al? Found it on the ground at the scene, figgered I'd grab it just in case."

"Yes, thank you." The schnapps helped with some of the pain and a pleasant buzz strove to supplant his headache, but his back began tightening up on him, sending waves of pain radiating through his body. His left knee ached horribly, too; though if he thought about it too much, *everything* ached.

"It got dislodged from my waistband early on, lucky for them. I must say, they were tough men. In my experience, most groups will disperse after you put down a few of them, but those fellows were intent on taking me out regardless of losses. So, you two have gotten acquainted with each other, then?"

Finnbar's sly face lit up boyishly. "Marcel was regaling me with tales of the frontier. Riveting stuff, 'tis."

"Hold on!" blurted a startled Deas, pointing an incriminating finger at Marcel. "You, you're the one who's been tailing me lately, aren't you?"

"Yep."

"May I be so bold as to ask why?"

"Well, you apparently don't recollect, but we met in the night woods southwest o' here few weeks back. You'd just fled from Abendroth's castle. Ring any bells?"

A look of epiphany slid onto the artist's face. "That's right! My memory of it is a bit hazy, but I do remember a squat, ugly fellow in buckskins. But why have you been following me since then?"

Marcel took out his pipe and began absentmindedly filling it. "Cause I hear tell that you're a decent feller and one hell of an artist, and I figgered the mesmerizer has sinister designs fer you. Shoulda heard those screams you were lettin' rip that night, inhuman they was. So I guess I been keepin' an eye on you to make sure no harm came your way, 'cause as an artist you're one o' them vulnerable types. I also thought by following you I could learn more about Abendroth, who strikes me as an evil bastard."

"Define 'vulnerable'," Deas requested amusedly, eyebrows raised.

The mountain man did not hesitate. "Sensitive. Emotional. Strange. Thinkin' too damn much about unimportant stuff. Perfect prey fer one like the mesmerizer."

"How very flattering. So how did you come to meet Alvord?"

"Met last night, right before we snuck into Abendroth's castle to spy on 'im."

Deas stared at Marcel before turning his disbelieving

gaze to Alvord. "That was you two last night! What a daft move, Rawn! You're lucky you weren't caught. Volkmar would've killed you!"

Alvord removed the steaks from his face and spat out another dollop of blood. "That is one of two possibilities."

"Do not underestimate that man. And certainly don't underestimate Abendroth. They are not men to be trifled with."

"We saw what went down there, Charles. He is training those men for a purpose. What is his endgame?"

"Considering that we will be gone in a few days, it is nothing to lose sleep over. It does not concern you, and soon enough it will not concern me either. I told Abendroth that I plan to depart in two days' time."

"But what is it that you go to him for? What do you need him for? I know this concerns your art, but how do his powers aid you in producing paintings?" Alvord decided not to mention that he had seen Deas's private collection of paintings after breaking into his studio.

A sudden, fleeting darkness swept over Deas's face, like the shadow cast by a fast-drifting cloud. "It is in the past, now. I will have to learn to work without it. My mother was quite right, I have grown infatuated with mesmerism, and I need a return to normality. My art will either flourish or wither, but it will do so free from Abendroth's corruptive influence. After reading her letters to me I realize that in truth, he is simply using my talents for his own twisted end. I am done. Though Heaven should fall, I am done."

Finnbar, who had been listening intently, broke his silence. "While I am loathe to profess ignorance of any kind, what is this mesmerism you talk of? And who is Abendroth?"

Deas and Alvord both started explaining, but were interrupted by a man who had been eavesdropping on their conversation.

"Pardon me," said the man in a cultured British accent, "but did you just say Abendroth? As in Count Gregory Abendroth?"

Deas eyed him suspiciously. "You know the man?"

"No, but I know all too well of him. That man is evil incarnate."

"How so?" Alvord leaned forward, intrigued; any new knowledge of the mesmerizer could be of use.

The man saw Alvord's devastated visage and started. "Upon my word! Are you alright, sir?"

"I am about as salubrious as I look. Keep talking, please."

The gentleman took a seat at their table. He was nondescript through and through. No identifying marks lay upon his face, no facial hair or striking features. In fact, his bland appearance was such that Alvord realized he would forget the man's face as soon as they parted ways.

Even his voice seemed to lack character. "Are any of you aware of his story? His *whole* story?"

"He rarely mentions his past, except to speak of his apprenticeship under Franz Anton Mesmer." Deas seemed very interested in what this man had to say.

"There is reason for that, trust me. I resided in London until recently, and I can recall when first he made himself known to the city's social elite. It was said he came to London from Germany in 1843, seeking followers. Gained quite a following too, as many bored aristocrats found the powers of animal magnetism, well, *mesmerizing* if you'll pardon the pun. He set up shop in a grand estate, never telling anyone where he acquired the funds. Beginning with simple demonstrations of animal magnetism, Abendroth gradually moved on to more elaborate displays, far surpassing anything that other practitioners were capable of. By this time Europe's infatuation with the art of mesmerism had simmered down, but now it seemed that it was poised for a grand revival. He was a showman born, and had a way of attracting followers. Whispers could be heard of god-like powers and descents into realms of consciousness where no man was ever meant to stray. Some even said that his power extended to other souls, which he could control and, if need be, separate from their hosts. Soon enough other magnetizers decried his methods as devilish. He grew unpopular in many circles. Yet at first this failed to faze him. He had a giant Prussian bodyguard who, as it were, dealt with anyone who posed a threat to his master, and Abendroth amassed many an enemy, mind you. In London there exist a number of secret societies, some you might be familiar with and others that are far more... *esoteric*. His forceful attempts to infiltrate these societies were met only with suspicion and eventually violence. He supposedly offered members of these societies power over others and riches to boot. It seemed that many were willing to throw in their lot with him. Some others decided to band together and find hard evidence against him that might hold water in court. For rumor had it that a number of crimes could be traced back to him, from sudden instances of insanity to missing persons and even mysterious deaths."

"If I might lend credence to your argument," offered Alvord, "the local madhouse has seen a recent influx of insane persons."

His musings were met by a short, thoughtful silence.

The stranger absently toyed with a thick black ring inlaid in gold that encircled his finger. "Then it's happening again. He is making another go of it. Back in London it came to pass that no definitive evidence was found against him, and for a while he gained followers and influence, much to the chagrin of his detractors. But in time he dug himself a hole. It turns out that he had been incessantly harassing two celebrated English artists, both known for producing works of an apocalyptic nature. Their names were John Martin, a painter and mezzotint artist, and Francis Danby, another painter. Both were notorious for painting scenes portraying instances of Old Testament vengeance on an unrepentant mankind, and even depictions of Hell itself. Apparently, the mesmerizer is a collector of such paintings, and thought that with his powers he could bring the sublime aspect of their work to a whole new level."

At this Deas ran a hand through his hair, staring fixedly at the floor.

"Martin and Danby?" he whispered to himself.

The man continued. "Abendroth seemed determined to take them into his fold, but they strongly resisted these efforts, startled by whatever it was that he offered them. His harassment eventually took the form of threats, with no effort made at veiling them. The artists contacted the authorities, who finally took the claims of his evil activities seriously and went about disbanding his cult.

"He remained in London for a spell, those societies I mentioned remaining ever vigilant against his aspirations to power. It was determined that Abendroth still operated, but on a smaller and quieter scale. Unwilling to abide this, we—*they* rather, ran him out of England, burning his manor to the ground. Many men were lost in the attempt, some rendered insane by Abendroth's occult deviltry, others butchered by the Prussian. But in the end it was accomplished. Abendroth was wounded and fled, to where it was not known. Until now, I suppose."

Again the man spun his ring around his finger nervously.

"And these societies," Alvord asked somewhat dryly while eyeing the ring, "you wouldn't happen to know anything about them, now would you?"

The Brit glanced at the ring on his finger before answering straight facedly. "No, I wouldn't. How long has he been here?"

"Perhaps two years," replied Deas. "His manor was under construction for nearly a year before that."

"He constructed a manor? So he is here and here to stay?"

"So it would seem."

"Well then, gentlemen," said the fellow in a tone that implied his wish to leave, "good day."

He put on his white beaver top hat and got up.

"Wait," requested Alvord. "You've got connections, I'd put money on it. You know firsthand what a menace this man is. Help us take him out."

This elicited a startled look from Deas, but Alvord could not waste this opportunity.

The man shook his head slowly. "The wise man seeth the plague when it cometh. Only tragedy awaits those who oppose him, I've seen it before. It is not mere physical harm you risk, but the fate of the soul as well. Were I you, I would depart this place posthaste. All of you. Measures may be taken against him once this news reaches the Old World, but until then he will corrupt all around him."

"Why did you relate this tale to us if you did not plan on doing anything about it?" Alvord already knew the answer to this. He had dealt with this type in the past—fervently hoping for a matter to be resolved, and totally unwilling to have a hand in it.

The fellow looked at him gravely. "Because the more people who know what that man really is, if man he can be called, then the better chance there is of destroying him, as such you are set on attempting. Best of luck, gents."

"What are you doing in America?" Finnbar asked,

regarding the man curiously.

The man let to a hollow laugh. "Ironically enough, I seek a change of scenery and peace of mind."

He left hastily, leaving the others to ponder his grim words.

"Odd that we would encounter a man so well-acquainted with Abendroth's shadowy past," Alvord said slowly and half to himself. He knew that Fate had come a'knocking as often she did—when you least expected it.

Finnbar tipped back in his chair and asked, "So what exactly is the mesmerizer doing in St. Louis?"

Alvord and Marcel quickly explained everything to Finnbar, and filled Deas in on how much they had seen in Abendroth's manor.

"So," said the Irishman afterwards, "you mean to tell me that this 'animal magnetizer' can render folks empty shells of humanity? I'd have figured by the name that he simply had an unwholesome attraction to farm animals."

"The reality of animal magnetism is a grim one, Finnbar. It has its sanative purposes, but Abendroth is capable of far darker feats. He is also using the local aristocracy for some end which, Charles, I would really like to know about."

"Yeah," Marcel added, "and would you like to fill us in on how he had some slave crawlin' her way up a wall, speakin' in tongues?"

"Wait, *what*? Crawling up a wall?" Finnbar was rightly flummoxed.

"Oh yeah," explained Alvord quickly, "that can happen too."

Deas heaved a careworn sigh. "As I said, it is not our problem. It will never succeed anyway; he's a fool to think it will. Too many variables, and fools for disciples."

"I am killing him regardless."

"If I don't get him first," added Marcel.

"I am not saying that he doesn't deserve it. But what of the law?"

"You let slip that Bogardus is in league with Abendroth. Since we can't go to him for help, we act swiftly and leave behind no evidence. I have seen what Abendroth's powers can do to people. I will not leave this city until I've put a bullet through his heart."

"That is your business. I have no emotional attachment to the man, now that I realize I was but his pawn. Do it if you must, but if you lose, or get caught, I leave for New York without you."

Alvord considered his words. "Fair enough. But you know better than I what that man is, what unholy powers he abuses. Justice has been a guiding principle in my life and I aim to bring it raining down upon Abendroth's head. The people he's driven insane, that Negress he had crawling up a wall and writhing in pain; do they not deserve retribution? I will not abide that outrage, nor will Marcel."

"Nor will I, for that matter," added the Irishman. "Aside from having a stereotypically Irish love for conflict, my involvement in this undertaking would add considerable zest to me memoirs. Taking down a rogue animal magnetizer—how many can make that boast?"

"Of this you are sure, Finnbar? This is not to be taken lightly. Injury is likely, death possible."

"There's that English blood, not quite willing to believe that an Irishman can make his own decisions. I'm with you boys."

Alvord arranged his swollen, bloody lips into a smile. "You're an odd one, Irishman, but we're glad to have you along."

"Now are *you* sure you'll be able to manage? You must be hurting something terrible, no?"

Alvord wiped some dripping blood from his face. "I will manage, worry not. It looks worse than it is."

"We leave in two days' time, Rawn," Deas informed him. "I have told Abendroth, and he seems okay with it. Tomorrow night is the city's eighty-third anniversary celebration. It will give me an opportunity to sell some of my works, and to let my local patrons know of my departure. Some will hopefully want my new address in Manhattan, so they can place future orders."

"Very well. We will take care of our business by then. Tomorrow evening at seven, we will meet here to plan our next move."

"Alright," said Marcel and Finnbar.

Finnbar signaled for Valda to come over. "Well then—eat, drink, and be merry, for tomorrow we die! Well, possibly. First round's on me, boys. Order up—sky's the limit."

Drink flowed freely, as did talk. Deas and Marcel discovered their mutual love of the frontier, and Alvord and Finnbar discussed English and Irish literature before speaking at length about the future of Britain's empire. Alvord spoke of his time as the captain of Manhattan's roughest platoon in the city's most lurid ward, though he omitted the part about getting fired. That would require much explaining, and his jaw ached terribly when he spoke. He had already shared his story with Deas and worried that the artist would blab, but Deas just listened and kept that information to himself. For that Alvord was thankful.

Valda appeared with bandages, which Alvord had Marcel tightly wrap around his ribs to reduce movement. Though initially painful, this lent him some much-needed relief.

Rudolph joined them with massive steins of Spaten once the place slowed down a bit, and before long his German-rich English seemed far more decipherable. He spoke of his homeland, telling them of the political and social tensions that he felt would soon come to a head.

The men (Alvord aside) played hood skittles, a smaller version of ninepin bowling played on an enclosed table. Marcel reigned supreme, and even when he switched over to his left hand still smoked his competition. Once their demeanors graduated to the more amusing phases of drunkenness, they engaged in games of Devil Among the Tailors, or table skittles. A small wooden ball hung suspended from a horizontal post attached to an upright one. Nine miniature pins sat below, and by swinging the ball in an arc around the post one sought to knock the pins down. Several of the matches were so pathetic that they degenerated into bouts of rowdy laughter.

Alvord generally did not allow himself to consume so much alcohol, but he felt as if he were among friends for the first time in ages, feeling none of the vulnerability that often accompanied drunkenness. The fact that the booze was helping the pain was also a major factor in his uncharacteristic inebriety.

Marcel snickered as Alvord described his encounter with Richard DuPont. "So that dandified prick had the gall to challenge you to a duel, eh?"

"He did. And let me choose weapons."

"Are those the double-handed swords you challenged

him with?" Finnbar pointed to the giant swords hanging across the room.

"Yes."

Marcel raised a skeptical eyebrow. "Can you use them swords? Even fer a big feller like you they're a mite oversized."

"When I have occasion to use one, you'll find out."

"Those swords vere used by ze *Landsknecht*, a mercenary group in ze sixteenth und seventeenth century. Von of my ancestors served vith zem. Ze were called *Doppelsonders*, double soldiers, und received double pay. Savage fighters, feared throughout Europe. *Zweihänders*, those swords are called—two handers."

"Some weapon to fight a duel with," laughed Finnbar.

"What is it with Southerners and dueling, anyway? I've heard that it is still commonplace."

"Well Al," explained Marcel, "Southerners is testy folk, believe in honor to the point of vanity. And most of 'em ain't cowards, neither, and are willin' to fight. But it's most common among richer folks. I am surprised that all them rich men attacked you, though. That first feller must have figgered you fer a rich man yourself, roughly equal to 'im in status, otherwise he'd have just send a bunch of lowly henchmen to deal with you. But to issue a challenge and then personally waylay you with a bunch of other dandies at his side, he must have really been pissed. As fer me, well I never did see the wisdom of pistol duelin', but lots of folks seem to favor it."

"Hell," Deas added, "Bloody Island was so named because it was the appointed ground for duels. Most famous was probably the duel between Benton and Lucas, folks still talk of that one..."

"When I was a boy, growing up here," reminisced Marcel nostalgically, "there were no islands by the waterfront, just a few small sandbars. The river ran strong then, seventy feet at its deepest. Now the river is divided in half, and I see that the Engineer Corps is constantly dredging the west side of it, to prevent loss of flow."

Talk wandered again, with Deas receiving many questions about his art and Finnbar about his writing. Many a toast was made and many a cup drained, and spirits soared as the sun slunk lower in the darkening sky.

At nine o'clock Finnbar rose and stretched. "Alright, lads.

I hear there are some first-rate bawdy houses in this place. Who's with me?"

"I'll go," grunted Marcel.

"My vife vould not approve," Rudolph assured him.

"Charles?"

"I'm not in the habit of paying for it, Finn. G'night. Like I said, you and Marcel should stop by tomorrow, say early afternoon. I'll show you my work."

"Will do. How about you, Alvord? You fancy extending the night?"

"I think not." He detested whores and whoremongering.

"Somehow I figured. What's your rationale?"

"Brawl with a pig, you walk away with its stench."

Finnbar made as if to reply, but then cocked his head to the side amusedly.

"I suppose there's a certain puritanical logic to that."

Alvord gingerly rose from his seat. "Night all."

Gritting his teeth against the searing pain, Alvord climbed the seemingly endless stairs of the Planter's Hotel. Upon entering his room, he kicked off his boots and took a good look at himself in the mirror. As he suspected, he was an almighty mess. His beard hid some of the bruising, but his forehead and upper cheeks formed a throbbing mass of bruises. The white of his left eye glowed red from impact with either a fist or club.

He was in no shape to fight; his body was riddled with pain and his movements were quite limited. While he had talked big tonight, the knowledge that he would be forced do something extremely dodgy had been nagging him.

For there was only one option. After wrestling with the notion all evening, he had arrived at the same conclusion time and again.

On the morrow he would go to Count Abendroth for healing.

Chapter 20

In the barroom of a brothel located in the old French section of the city, Finnbar casually tipped back in his chair as he took in his surroundings. Every once in a while, if he observed a particularly humorous instance of human interaction, he would smirk ever so slightly and break out a small, leather-bound book on which to scribble notes. The brothel, as it happened, was the scene of many such an interaction.

Finnbar was no amateur at observing the ebb and flow of life, and little escaped his keen notice.

Riverboat men and factory workers poured on the charm with drunken disregard for dignity, maladroitly vying for the attention of the extravagantly dressed whores.

Cards were dealt by swift fingers and checkers deftly placed onto game boards. Card games were associated with vice and unwholesome gambling, so those with solid reputations to uphold opted for checkers.

Nearby a verbal argument erupted into a fistfight, albeit a rather pathetic one. Both combatants had reached the stage of intoxication that rendered coordination all but unattainable. Before long they leaned on each other for support, wheezing loudly. Laughter broke out and Finnbar heartily joined in.

A writer's job was never really done by his estimation, for truly understanding the myriad subtleties of the human condition required constant scrutiny.

Sipping on some potent yet pleasantly smooth Monongahela rye, he watched Marcel descend the nearest staircase, his fringed buckskins wildly out of place amidst frockcoats and top hats.

"Still walking, I see."

"Yep."

"So... she know her trade?"

"Ain't gentlemanly to say."

The Irishman laughed, running a hand through his crazily-spiked, dark red hair. "And who says chivalry is dead? I had myself a blonde, fiery little thing..."

Marcel grabbed the bottle of whiskey and took a deep pull, spilling some of it onto his thick beard.

"So, give any more thought to that trappin' expedition I mentioned?"

"Well Marcel, it would provide me with a unique opportunity to travel this land. 'Tis not everyone who has the privilege of journeying alongside a seasoned mountain man. How old were you when you started trapping?"

"I been trappin' since my youth, but when I turned fourteen I up and left St. Louis for the West as one of Ashley's Hundred."

"William Henry Ashley?"

"Uh hu. Loved the land and the life, so I spent most of my life out there and up Lake Superior way. This is the first time I been livin' within civilization's confines for more than a few days. Gettin' antsy, too."

He pulled out his pipe and went to light its contents, but his match ignited explosively. Sparks flew past Finnbar's face, and an evil, sulphurous smell lingered upon the air.

"What the shite!" the startled Irishman exclaimed. "Gotta watch out for those old Lucifer matches, doncha?"

"Goddamn, I hate when they flare up like that. Anyway, you should think this over real careful like. First we trap this area I know of in Michigan's Upper Peninsula, then head northeast into Ontario at some point. Whatever the case, we head south to ride out the winter of '48 here in St. Louis. Friend of mine knows of a family back east what's looking to head out Oregon way come early spring of '49. He and I'll be leadin' the wagon caravan they'll travel with."

"I'll mull things over, all right. But I think I'm in," he paused and chuckled lightly, "should we survive this mesmerizer business, that is."

Regarding him seriously, Marcel spoke with measured words. "What's yer story, son?"

"Pardon?"

"You've either been to war or your outta your damn mind. Although I'm kinda thinkin' it's the former. No normal feller would willingly get involved here, having little knowledge of the matter and no stake in it at all. Even the Irish don't like fightin' that much."

"What stake do *you* have in it?" The Irishman shot back.

"Simple. This here is my city, place of my birth. It's my duty to protect it. Plus, I seen firsthand the dark side of mesmerism, I know the influence Abendroth can exercise over folks. I've heard talk around town—some others is savvy to it too, but none are willin' to stand against it."

"And Alvord? Why is he so eager to steep his hands in the mesmerizer's blood?"

Marcel was silent for a few moments, thinking carefully. "Understands justice, Al does. And he's worried that Abendroth will prevent Deas from leavin', I can tell. So again, is it war, insanity, or both?"

Finnbar smiled broadly, gold tooth gleaming. "You got me. War, 'twas. Like many of my brethren before me, I sought the madness of battle in a foreign land. In Uruguay, a civil war broke out in '39. European Empires like England and France got involved, so disenchanted with life and seeking excitement I fought under Britain's banner. We supported the *Blancos*, the federal forces of Manuel Oribe. Fought skirmishes mostly, but then in '42, at the battle of Arroyo Grande, I got my first taste of a full-fledged battle. My side won, handedly too. But it was a hellish experience all told... didn't much care for the killing, either. Although once battle was joined and me blood was up I didn't think about it much. 'Tis afterwards that the memories come back to haunt you. It occurred to me after that battle that my talents would be better applied to writing, but I needed worldly experience, I needed to observe and understand mankind and behold the wonders of nature. The United States struck me as the best place to start. So I left that sweltering, wretched continent to its wars."

"And now?"

"And now, after my travels are concluded, I will place Ireland on the cutting edge of the modern literary scene. Intellect will become our weapon against the English. Myself and some associates of mine are using our God-given intellectual strengths to bring about a renaissance of sorts on our island. But if I can enjoy a few adventures during my peregrinations, I will do so before hunkering down for a life of boring scholasticism. I'm only twenty-six; I have plenty of years left, God willing."

The mountain man puffed pensively on his pipe for a while.

"So what d'ya think of Al?"

"Hail fellow, well met by my reckoning. And a tough bastard to boot. You see him during that scrap? He took shots that would've laid low a bull. And then, even though beaten to hell, he managed to intercept that last fellow. Really knocked that one into a cocked hat, didn't he? Fights savagely, does Alvord. I wholeheartedly approve."

"Yeah, savage as a meat axe. And then afterwards he carried on like he wasn't nursin' broke ribs and a cracked skull. Intent on takin' out Abendroth too, despite 'is conditon."

"That's how you gents met, eh? Spying on the mesmerizer?"

"Yep. Met up in a tree that served as a good vantage."

"Is the man really as evil as I've been hearing? And as dangerous?"

"Damn right he is. Both Al and myself was tryin' to spy on him, then Al up and decides that he's sneakin' into the castle. Bold move, that, but I followed, and we saw what we described to you earlier. Deviltry, that's what goes on up there. Can't even rightly describe the sounds comin' outta that poor woman, and I swear she clawed her way to the ceiling like it was nothin'. That was the first Al had seen of Abendroth's evil, but once was enough. He wields power only God should have, and abuses it, what's more. The man needs killin'."

Polishing off his glass of rye, Finnbar poured himself another measure. From his waistcoat pocket he extracted a small bag of opium, which he uncorked and sprinkled liberally into his drink. He held it out to Marcel, who took it and followed suit.

"S'been a coon's age since last I had this stuff."

"From time to time I indulge. Helps me write, truth be told, but 'tis not a good thing to get in the habit of doing regularly." He took a reflective sip. "So what's the game plan for tomorrow, then? March up to Abendroth's castle, guns blazing?"

"Mayhap. We gotta talk it over with Al tomorrow, though. He's a big deal in New York law enforcement; he might have a strategy in mind."

Finnbar used his finger to spin the whiskey around in his glass, keen eyes narrowing slightly as he stared at the whirling contents. "Does it strike you as odd that he took the job to come out here and fetch Deas?"

"Nope. From what Deas said, his mother is worried 'bout him. I guess Al does private detective work on top of bein' a patrolman."

"But how does a police captain in a busy place like New York up and leave for weeks for the sake of a side job? And did you hear him say earlier that he had too much blood on his hands? Something's up with him, you mark my words."

"Well," said Marcel after a moment, "if there is then it's his business, not ours."

"Perhaps you're right. Hey, have you noticed that group in the corner there huddled all secretive like, reading something?"

Marcel did not even have to turn and look. "That's a group lookin' over the books and pamphlets on animal magnetism that Abendroth's followers distribute. He keeps spreadin' that poison around, hoping to spur interest in the topic. First it was just the upper class what was seen doin' that, but now it seems some middle class folks is getting' involved. He's spreadin' his influence, but for what end I can't say. He mentioned something about controllin' politicians last night, but that slave woman went all possessed like and we was made before we could hear more. Don't matter, though- the man dies regardless. You sure you still want in? I seen things at his manor that I can't rightly explain, and from what Al saw of his routine performance, controlling people is none too hard for him. We don't know the extent of his power. Stoppin' him could be very grim business."

The Irishman looked the trapper squarely in the eye. "Listen, I wasn't born in the woods to be scared by an owl, as you frontier types might say. I am not merely thrill-seeking by helping you. A sense of right and wrong, of good and evil, was instilled in me since youth. It is the duty of good people to obstruct evil designs, is it not? The man is powerful and malevolent—I have heard it from several good sources now. If his demise prevents the torture and death of innocent people, then give me the ax and set his head on a block, I'll do the deed meself."

And given the stony look in his dark green eyes, Marcel did not doubt him.

All around them men and women went about their nightly business, boasting, drinking, and gambling, unencumbered by thoughts of such magnitude. The two men lapsed into a weighty silence, each pondering what horrors might await them tomorrow in the manor of Count Abendroth.

Chapter 21

Alvord rose with the dawn after a fitful night's sleep No position could comfortably accommodate all of his injuries, so every hour he had awoken to gingerly adjust and pray for a close to a seemingly endless night.

An unpleasant dryness clung to his mouth, a discomfort he ascribed to his excessive indulgence in gin and beer last night. He took down several glasses of water to combat it before hobbling over to his wardrobe.

After dressing himself with much difficulty, Alvord limped painfully down the stairs. He cursed himself as ten kinds of a fool for failing to detect his assailants before it had been too late. He should have been more alert, should have scanned the area thoroughly before moving through it... ah, no matter now. The damage was done and now his only recourse was the unthinkable—asking the mesmerizer, a man he had personally witnessed committing devilish acts, for help.

But alas, he could not carry out his plans to bring down the man in his present condition, particularly if he and Volkmar were to go head to head. And to sit around waiting for his injuries to knit themselves up would take weeks and could not be entertained as a serious method of dealing with this dilemma.

As he sat at a table in the hotel's dining hall, stolidly working through a bowl of porridge, he noticed people sneaking concerned glances at him. It was no wonder, really—he looked a proper mess. None of them inquired as to the nature of his injuries, but he could almost hear the cogs working as they concocted narratives of their own.

The porridge proved to be a wholly unedifying meal, but soft food was all his swollen jaw could manage. Grabbing a piece of pineapple from the buffet on his way out, Alvord headed for the front door with unsteady steps. A cane would be of use, but he did not have one and, if Abendroth could heal him, would hopefully not need one.

His concern was great. The idea of letting the mesmerizer exert his supernatural influence over him made his skin crawl. Yet he also resigned to the fact that he had little choice. Abendroth needed to be dealt with before he and Deas departed for New York, and he knew of no other way to accomplish that other than allowing the man to heal him. If he was willing to, of course.

But just what might he be subjecting himself to? If Abendroth worked his magic and he slipped in a trancelike state, would he have any control over what he did? Would the mesmerizer be able to read his thoughts, thus uncovering the plot to destroy him?

Reflecting on the rumors concerning the rapidly filling madhouse, he was unable to suppress a shudder. He would be treading in turbulent waters; he wondered what sort of mental defenses he might be able to muster should Abendroth attempt to exploit his weakened state.

Leaning against the hotel for support, Alvord waited for a carriage to flag down. Several passed by and he made no move. Then a small black carriage rattled towards him, borne swiftly along by a long-legged whiskey roan.

Alvord stepped out into the street, waving his hand at the driver. This was the vehicle he had been waiting for, a phaeton. Of the many carriages used for transportation, the phaeton took the biscuit when it came to speed. Most carriage-related accidents could be traced to some fool racing a phaeton down a busy street, unmindful of the fact that the fast, narrow carriages were prone to flipping. Yet it was not speed that Alvord had in mind; given his condition slow travel would be the most sensible means.

Phaeton builders employed a clever design of spring suspension generally found in mail carriages, one that absorbed the jarring impact of uneven roads to make for a more comfortable ride. So if he demanded that the driver take it slow, the suspension would negate the usual bone-jarring bumps that accompanied coach rides.

"Hop on in, suh," said the driver, a grinning middle-aged black man dressed in tasteful clothing.

Alvord was incapable of hopping anywhere, and painfully clambered on up to sit next to the driver stiffly.

"Lord above, you alright right there?"

"Fine, thanks."

"If'n you say so. This here is the fastest carriage to be found in the River Queen, can get you anywhere in the city fast as Mercury himself."

For a Southern Negro the man's English was surprisingly good, containing little of the slang and dialect that riddled the speech of most other blacks in St. Louis.

"Of that I have no doubt. She seems a fine, swift vehicle, as yon horse seems of fine pedigree. Both please the eye, too. But 'tis not speed that I seek, it is comfort. As you noted, my physical condition is none too good at present and I require slow travel."

The driver frowned. "Suh, this here vehicle is intended for *speed*. I'd be losin' money..."

"I will pay three times the normal fare."

The man considered for a moment. "Four."

"Three."

"Done," exclaimed the man happily. "And we takes it nice and slow. Now where to?"

"The manor of Count Abendroth on the western fringe of town."

Alvord saw the distaste in the fellow's eyes and mouth, but he urged his horse into moving nevertheless and took it slow down Fourth Street.

Even with the spring suspension, the ride proved to be an exercise in pure torment. Around Alvord's ribs a knifing pain set in, driven ever deeper by each bump in the road. His head ached after a while as well, but he did all he could to disguise his discomfort.

The driver, noticing the hard-set jaw and ashen face of his passenger, slowed his pace to a crawl.

By this point they were west of the main city, in The Common. Goats and cattle grazed placidly, and on occasion deer could be seen along the forest's edge. Passenger pigeons flew overhead in flocks numbering in the thousands. As Alvord watched a shotgun sounded and dropped four of the tightly bunched birds.

"I hope it ain't prying, suh, but I must inquire as to why

you are going to see this man."

"It is prying, actually, but that's alright. I go to be healed. Certain business I must attend to requires my being at full strength, so it is my hope that Abendroth will use his powers to restore my health."

The Negro maintained his silence awhile, watching with pursed lips as his strapping horse plod along at a nag's pace. When he did speak his words were measured.

"You know what goes on up there in the witching hours of the night?"

"No," replied Alvord, feigning ignorance, "what goes on?"

Staring at some point on the horizon, the driver spoke. "Some say he's the Devil, others say he's just a devilish man with gifts that no man should have. Word is that he's using his powers in wicked ways, somehow driving people to madness. To what end I can't say, but I'm told slaves is particularly fearful of the place. Folks hear noises coming from his manor at night that ain't of this earth. Madhouse is getting mighty crowded too, filled to the brim with crazies just a'sittin' there drooling when they ain't screamin'."

"Why have none stood against him, if such transgressions can be traced to him? Why has the law failed to intervene?"

"Some evil is best left alone, suh, and given a wide berth. I lived in New Orleans for a spell, where they got the voodoo magic. It can be dark, dangerous stuff, but it ain't nothing compared to this here mesmerism. The man is powerful in the manner of angels and demons. And if rumor is to be believed, the Sheriff is allied with Abendroth and never looks into any of the accusations made against him. There are whispers too; some say he's building an army to serve him. Now I ain't the superstitious type, but I do my best to steer clear of this place."

The driver reached into his shirt pocket, revealing a small cloth bundle. "This here is a voodoo charm said to ward off evil. Between that," he grabbed the chain and cross around his neck, "and this, I figure I got me protection enough. That bastard won't have *my* soul."

"Not superstitious, eh?"

"Call it what you will. All I know is that those who hang around him have grown strange, and those he's driven mad suffer a fate worse'n death. I'll take all the protection I can get, superstitious or otherwise."

Silence presided over the remainder of the trip. As the phaeton slowly wound its way through the undulating hills that encircled Abendroth's manor, a wave of anxiety washed over Alvord. Danger lurked beyond those lofty stone walls, but he needed healing fast and knew of no other way to obtain it.

The carriage came to a creaking halt in front of the manor. Dull, formless clouds of steel gray hung low in the sky, enveloping the tops of the small mountains in the distance. A sickly humidity clung to the air, but thankfully the temperature was bearable and a light wind blew at intervals. Body screaming with pain, Alvord gingerly lowered himself off the carriage.

"I shouldn't be any more than two hours, and if I am to be longer I will notify you. Stay here and you will be handsomely rewarded. I believe Abendroth keeps a small stable around back, you could water your horse there if necessary."

The Negro cocked an amused eyebrow. "Half up front or no deal."

He handed the man some coins. "I give this to you in good faith. Leave me and I *will* track you down. On that you can rest assured."

"And here I was thinking that I come off as a nice, honest fella."

"You do. But don't make me regret doing this. For you sake."

"I'll be here awaiting your return, suh."

Alvord turned and stared at the imposing stone structure.

Exhaling loudly, he pondered the prudence of his decision. For this would either be a brilliant instance of using an enemy's own strength against him, or the very height of folly.

Time would soon tell.

Limping up to the door, Alvord tapped the knocker several times. As he waited, he let loose with a coughing fit that left a trickle of blood running down the corner of his mouth. The door began opening, so he hastily wiped it away and stood tall.

"Good morning, sir," said a man with a shaggy, graying neck-beard. His features betrayed no surprise or even interest at Alvord's frightful appearance.

"Morning. I am Alvord Rawn, friend to the painter Charles Deas. Two nights past Count Abendroth entreated me to stop by for a visit."

"A friend of Master Charles, eh? Very well," the fellow droned, and beckoned Alvord inside.

The hallways danced with the shadows cast by flickering torch flames. Alvord groaned inwardly as the servant mounted a broad staircase, but stubbornly began the ascent. A red haze marked the outer fringes of his vision, intensifying to the point where he had to lean against the cool stone of the wall for a brief moment after finishing the climb.

They entered a hallway, at the end of which lay the room he and Marcel had leapt into from the tree. The servant did not tarry here, though, instead turning into an even longer corridor. Here the walls were tastefully lavished with all manner of tapestries, suits of armor, and Classical sculptures.

The faint sound of voices emanated from a nearby room, which the servant led the way into. Inside a most peculiar sight met Alvord's eyes.

Three people sat around a large wooden tub, out of which protruded a number of iron rods. Each person clasped a rod, sitting with their eyes closed and looks of utmost serenity upon their faces. One of them, Alvord realized with a start, was a woman whose countenance was marred by what appeared to be smallpox. He took a few hasty steps back.

The servant stood still and bowed his head worshipfully. Other people stood off to the side, all assuming similar postures.

A sudden movement caught Alvord's eye. Count Gregory Abendroth strode phantom-like from the shadows towards the trio around the odd tub. Standing before the tallest of the iron rods that stuck out from the tub, he gave a nod to two nearby men, who hurried forward to pour buckets of water into the tub.

Probably magnetized water, thought Alvord, recalling the events of two nights ago.

That accomplished, the mesmerizer grasped the rod with both hands. Eyes closed, he began deepening his breaths. A crease appeared on his brow that grew with the passage of time. Several minutes in, the patients began leaning over, as if asleep. Nothing happened for a few more minutes.

Then the state of the patients changed quite abruptly, whereby writhing and moaning came to replace their listlessness. All of them retained their death-grips on the metal rods, though they thrashed around most violently. A tingling feeling of some unseen energy filled the room as Alvord stared fixedly at Abendroth, whose slim, wan face seemed to glow in the dim lighting. The water began bubbling noisily, though no steam rose from the tub. In one voice the patients began wailing with a sound like some Hell-choir hitting high notes. Alvord, watching wide-eyed, felt a great pulse in the air, a wave of power that passed through him before diminishing. Soon enough the patients relaxed.

One by one they came to, panting, sweating, and looking around confusedly. Several of the onlookers rushed over, eagerly looking over the patients.

"Stay back," the mesmerizer ordered imperiously.

He allowed them a few moments to recuperate before leaning close to each patient, inspecting them.

"Mark, your gout symptoms?"

"I feel... salubrious. No aching or swelling to speak of."

"Good, good. And Nathaniel, what of your dropsy?"

The man he addressed pulled up his pant leg and firmly pressed a finger against his leg. "Amazing! No imprint, no discoloration or pain! I'll be damned, but I'm cured!"

He vigorously shook his healer's hand. "Truly, you are a worker of miracles."

Abendroth clapped him on the shoulder. "And that brings us to you, Margaret. I see no pustules- how do you feel?"

After examining her arms and feeling her face and neck, she began weeping joyously into her skirt. "For the first time in days, I am not crippled by pain! My clothing no longer sticks to the sores! My skin does not crack and ooze! Thank you, bless you!"

Abendroth received an affectionate embrace from his patient, whom he gently patted on the head. A small but rather genuine smile lingered upon his lips.

People began getting ready to depart, shaking hands with Abendroth and thanking him with due sincerity.

Alvord stood rooted to the spot, thunderstruck. It was one thing to hear stories of miracles, but observing one firsthand was another thing altogether. This man might be evil, but his capacity to do good in the world was enormous. He had, beyond all sane conjecture, cured people of debilitating diseases through his mesmeric powers. Even he, a man of faith, conceded that mere faith healing could not accomplish the miracle of Christ-like power he had just witnessed. Truly, it was a wonder that defied all science and logic, and it was a shame that the man chose to horribly abuse the gift God had granted him.

But it still stood that he did, so for that he would die. Too many stories of the man's maleficence were in circulation to discount. If that fellow in the tavern last night was to be believed, the mesmerizer was attempting here what he had in England; that was, gaining a following and expanding his influence. He had to be stopped, and soon.

"Sir," wheezed the servant, "an Alvord Rawn is here to see you."

Abendroth turned that arresting stare upon Alvord, his bright green eyes snakelike in their focus. "Mr. Rawn! A pleasant surprise."

"Count Abendroth." greeted Alvord. "We spoke two nights back. I was with my good friend Charles Deas and you issued an invitation, that I might come to learn more about animal magnetism."

The Count looked over his unsightly face with concern. "I say! Are you alright, Mr. Rawn? What has happened to you?"

"A brawl with some ruffians. It appears worse than it actually is, trust me. I must remark, that was a most incredible thing you just accomplished. Are such healings routine for one with your power?"

A broad smile crept across the mesmerizer's face. "Well, healing *is* the most common application of animal magnetism, but those three healings there were more difficult than usual. Three patients were simultaneously healed whose ailments required varying degrees of power flow."

"You must explain to me exactly how it works. Modern science must be tearing its hair out over the miracles you perform, am I right?"

"In due time, Mr. Rawn, in due time. But as for modern science, you are quite right. In my day I have been labeled an occultist, a demon, and a charlatan by the scientific world. That last one stung, but I got over it quickly enough."

Alvord chuckled as if appreciatively, while suppressing a strong urge to cave in the bastard's skull here and now.

"What say you a stroll around my grounds? If your condition allows, that is. It looks like the rain will hold off for a time."

A stroll was on the very bottom of his priority list, but he realized that if he was able to endure it, scouting out the surrounding land could come in handy for tonight's attack on the manor. He had in mind some diversionary tactics that would draw most of Abendroth's servants out of the manor, leaving the mesmerizer vulnerable to attack.

"A walk would be fine. I could do with a stretch of the legs."

"Splendid." Abendroth led the way into the hall, signaling for his assistants to clean up the room.

"Just a minute," requested a gruff, commanding voice.

A rawboned man of average height but exceptional build stalked their way. Alvord immediately noticed the burnished copper badge pinned to his vest and the authoritative swagger in his step. A pistol handle could be glimpsed in his waistband as he moved, and a sizable sheath knife was strapped to his left leg. This was, no doubt, Sheriff Bogardus.

"Yes, Andrew?"

"I need a minute with your guest here."

Abendroth frowned. "You two know each other?"

The man snorted nastily, a scar on his stubbly cheek deepening as he did so. "A fight occurred yesterday on Market Street that involved some very prominent members of our community. Two of 'em are dead, some others are badly wounded. One feller's nose was head-butted almost into his brain meat."

"They call it a Liverpool Kiss across the pond," Alvord offered conversationally.

The man's sneer deepened. "Witnesses said a big man with dark hair and a red beard started it all. Judging from the description and his battered appearance, I'd say there's a damn good chance it was this feller right here."

Alvord bristled, and forgetting his awful injuries stepped squarely in front of the stocky man. "And may I be so bold as to ask who levels this accusation?"

He pointed to his badge. "Sheriff Andrew Bogardus."

"And as a sheriff, a man of the law, you honestly believe that a single man would dare accost twelve, half of whom just happened to be toting clubs? Seems to be a stretch, wouldn't you agree?"

Bogardus's eyes narrowed. "Just who the hell do you think yer talkin' to?"

"I might ask the same of you."

The man wasn't afraid of Alvord's size; he had to give him that.

"From where I stand, I see a big arrogant feller that started a fight, got beat up, then had some friends bail 'is worthless ass out at the last minute."

"If you truly believe that then you defile the badge you wear."

The sheriff's hand strayed towards his knife. Alvord mentally rehearsed the left hook that would dislocate his jaw.

"Yer guilty of murder. I say yer coming with me," the sheriff sibilantly hissed.

"As a fellow lawmen of superior station I very much disagree, and order you to stand down."

Abendroth, meanwhile, watched the proceedings with obvious amusement, even chuckling quietly from time to time.

Bogardus looked dumbfounded. "Fellow lawmen? *What*?"

Reaching into the pocket of his waistcoat, Alvord withdrew one of his old badges. His official badge he had left with Matsell, but several forgeries he had had made up remained.

"I am Captain Alvord Rawn of the Municipal Police Department of New York."

Slack-jawed, Bogardus stared at the badge.

"But see, I have witness testimonies-"

"That aren't worth shit. I myself have several witnesses who will happily verify my story at the drop of a hat. I was waylaid by that cape-wearing blackguard and his friends. Two companions of mine came to my aid just as your upstanding citizens were getting ready to lynch me. So are you still prepared to take the word of lying dogs, or will you listen to a fellow man of the badge?"

"But... but wait, what's a police captain from New York doin' here in St. Louis? Yer outside yer jurisdiction."

"Would be, were it not for the fact that I have been sent on a special mission by the Department."

"And just what mission might that be?" the sheriff demanded obdurately.

"Here are the papers. Read it yourself." He furnished the false documents he had drawn up before departing.

As he watched Bogardus scrutinizing them, Alvord could tell that the man hoped to find some inconsistencies. But he wouldn't, as there were none. The letters had been crafted too carefully.

He also possessed imagined records containing travel information and the projected costs of the journey. After looking these over as well, Bogardus relented.

"Well, I guess all this checks out."

As if you could tell if it didn't. "Indeed. I will be on my merry way then, and look forward to hearing of the charges those men will face for attacking and planning to lynch me. Soon."

He received a bitter glare for his words, but he merely chuckled at the man.

Abendroth clapped his hands together. "So, I believe that concludes introductions. Andrew, take care. And contact me straight away should your brother's dropsy return."

"You'll have to forgive him," he whispered as they walked away, "he takes his job quite seriously and is suspicious of outsiders. It took me awhile to get in his good graces myself, but in the end I worked my magic."

I'll bet.

A repetitive clanging, familiar to Alvord's ears, could be heard down the hall. As they passed the room the noise issued from, the open door revealed Volkmar, lightly dressed and dueling with another man.

The Swiss Walloon flashed brightly in his hand as he wielded it effortlessly. His attacks were sudden; his ripostes and parries deft, leaving few exploitable holes in his defense. Alvord took in as many details as he could, for an understanding of the man's fighting style could be useful if they came to face each other.

With a clash of hilts, the Prussian performed a clever disarming move that sent his opponent's saber flying into a corner of the room. Both men stepped back and bowed stiffly.

"Are you an admirer of swordplay, Mr. Rawn?" Abendroth had stopped alongside Alvord, who had ceased walking without realizing it.

"Quite. I am also a practitioner."

"Have you met Otto Volkmar, my bodyguard?"

"Actually, we drank together just yesterday."

"Is that so?"

"It is, as is the fact that shortly after we hoisted steins he failed to back me when I was assaulted by those men Bogardus mentioned."

The mesmerizer clucked disapprovingly. "Otto! Come hither!"

Volkmar removed his leather gloves and walked towards them, looking Alvord over with a smirk on his lips.

"Did you drink with Mr. Rawn here yesterday and then fail to aid him during a fight? That is not in keeping with your character, Otto."

The Prussian gave no notice to his master's chiding. "You gave a good account of yourself yesterday, Herr Rawn."

"Why thank you. And thanks for the help."

"Come now. You know I needed to see what manner of man you are. And there is no better way to determine that than to watch a man during a fight, particularly a fight for his life. Those two men who helped you intervened before I could myself."

"Coward."

The word was spoken plainly but had the desired effect. Volkmar's face tensed up and flushed, his bulging jaw muscles flexing and unflexing.

Abendroth stepped in between then, his form absurdly petite and frail amidst the two hulking men.

"Easy, gentlemen. The tension is palpable, and for one as sensitive to energy levels as myself that's quite literal. Trust me, the very air crackles with the force of your mutual dislike."

"Very well. Why has he come?"

"I am giving him a tour of the grounds and educating him on some of the finer points of mesmerism."

The bodyguard locked eyes with Alvord. "Yes, he has quite an interest in the topic, though I have a *sneaking* suspicion that he might want more information than you are willing to provide."

Sneaking? *Oh shit.* In the torment of his pain and his desperation to be well, he had overlooked the fact that Volkmar knew him to be one of the men who had snuck into the manor. Did Abendroth already know that? Or had the Prussian, in his odd way, decided not to tell his master about seeing Alvord in the manor two nights back?

"Peace, peace, Otto. You needn't be a churl. Civility costs nothing, after all. We will be out on the grounds if you need me."

"Perhaps I should accompany."

"Not necessary. Carry on."

They continued on their way, leaving the Prussian behind.

"Are you sure you are alright to take a jaunt? You look a right old mess, I fear."

"Yes, let's go. I am eager to see your grounds and hear more of your unique gift."

So they walked down a flight of stairs and out the door, and through the red mists of pain Alvord could have sworn he detected a brief but unsettling glint in the eyes of the mesmerizer.

Chapter 22

The clouds had broken, and although the occasional peal of thunder could be heard in the far-off distance it seemed that good weather would prevail for at least a while.

Alvord did his best to keep pace with Abendroth, whose lapse into thoughtful silence was accompanied by an unwelcome increase in walking pace.

Suddenly noticing that his guest lagged behind, Abendroth shortened his stride.

"Forgive me. I am easily lost in thought. So, twelve men, eh? I'm no fighter, but even I can surmise that it must've been a rather frenzied affair."

"That it was."

"Yet you managed to kill some and injure many. Your fighting skills must be first-rate, your great size aside."

"Perhaps, but sometimes the race is not to the swift, nor the battle to the strong. I lost; they would have killed me had not two friends of mine shown up with impeccable timing."

Examining him closely, the mesmerizer continued his line of inquiry. "You killed two men but do not seem distraught. Death is something you are accustomed to?"

"Somewhat," said Alvord quietly, recalling the many men who had fallen by his hand. Yet what had started with his sparing of the highwaymen during the carriage hold-up had extended to his show of mercy yesterday. And those bastards had deserved death, too. Was he perhaps a changed man? Or at least changing?

"But I only killed one myself. After I had been beaten down my friends came to my aid. One of my assailants ran for it at that point. Your bodyguard demolished him as he ran."

"Otto failed to mention that. But I don't doubt it. His strength is second to none, and his bulk belies his quickness.

Fighting is in his blood, too. His grandfather was one of King Friedrich Wilhelm's Potsdam Giants. From what I'm told he was a ferocious warrior."

Surmounting a tall hill, they faced north, where the prairie merged with woodlands a half-mile away. Hawks circled lazily overhead, and above them turkey vultures hung motionless in the air. Alvord scanned the land around them, making note of strategically important locations.

"I mean not to pry, but this land and the manor—they must have cost a pretty penny."

"Oh, it's no Schönbrunn Palace, but it is a fine home, and it did cost me. But fortunately, I had a benevolent uncle who bequeathed to me a considerable fortune. My parents were also quite wealthy. A number of well-informed investments bolstered my financial position and now... now I make a small profit from my demonstrations and healings, and that is enough for me."

"So was your father the Count that you inherited the title from?"

"I am not a Count, actually, but let's keep that between us."

Having suspected as much all along, Alvord was nevertheless surprised that Abendroth would freely offer that information.

"So... you are a self-styled Count, then?"

"I suppose so," he confessed with a carefree chuckle. "But it sounds good, does it not?"

"I'll grant you that," Alvord admitted. "So no one else knows?"

"No one has had the nerve to ask, frankly."

Turning west, Abendroth began a slow descent along a path leading towards an agreeable, park-like area of short grass and widely spaced trees. A broad stream gurgled past the area, attracting a number of bitterns and herons.

Abendroth looked up into the lofty canopy and sighed. "I love this land, I am surrounded by beauty, but alas, this is my place of exile."

"Exile?" He already knew that Abendroth had been forced to leave Europe, but was interested in hearing it from the horse's mouth.

"Much like my master, I chose to turn my back on the

scientific world, instead opting to do some good in a world gone to hell. His place of exile was Meersburg, near Lake Constance in the German Alps. It is a lonely land, full of fog and vast, trackless stretches of mountain terrain. Over the whole place there hangs a feeling of detachment, as if the rest of the world lies on the other side of a veil. Indeed, when in 1811 the savants at the Academy of Science in Berlin met to unravel the mysteries surrounding Mesmer's own doctrine, he stayed put, content with the crisp mountain air and crystalline lakes. He would heal the sick within his community and any who traveled to his home to be healed, but he was through trying to prove mesmerism to a bunch of blinkered empiricists."

"That was where you were schooled in the art of mesmerism, correct? Mesmer himself taught you?"

His green eyes grew misty and Alvord could tell he recalled bygone days. "I was young then, and desperate for answers. Since my early youth I had been capable of things that defied all logical explanation. First, my gift manifested itself in horrific nightmares during which I levitated and thrashed about with the strength of many men, whilst speaking in tongues unknown to me. My parents feared for my sanity, for I grew more morbid and introverted with the passing of years.

"Then came the day when a servant of ours sustained a bad injury to his leg, and I was the first to find him. Some part of me simply knew what to do. By laying my hands on him and focusing, I was able to completely alleviate his pain. I requested that he kept it quiet, but it is not in the nature of man to remain silent on such matters. Needless to say, people heard and were shocked and awed, rightly so I guess. Yet I grew troubled, uncertain of what this newfound power meant for me. Had God granted me this power? Or was it merely some innate force that I had awoken through unknown means? Whatever the case, it was a heady experience that left me pondering my destiny. So one day I decided to find the man whose awesome powers of healing were still spoken of despite his absence from society. I arrived at Lake Constance tired, hungry, but finally in the presence of the great Mesmer himself."

Having read the material on mesmerism provided by Mrs. Deas, Alvord found himself able to converse on the topic proficiently enough.

"Why Mesmer himself, though? Animal magnetism was

flourishing in late eighteenth and early nineteenth-century Europe. Aside from Mesmer a number of other noted magnetizers could be found, shocking the upper classes with their talents. Why not go to them instead of trekking through mountains to find Mesmer?"

"You are right, Mr Rawn. In fact, by the time I began my journey into the realm of mesmerism, it was no longer Mesmer's doctrine that held sway. Marquis de Puysegur, the most capable of his early disciples, perverted our master's doctrine, asserting that mesmerism worked on psychological levels rather than physical. For him, the power of suggestion and the discovery of the somnambulic state marked the acme of mesmerism."

Here a very unpleasant look contorted Abendroth's pale face as he stared into the distance.

"*The fool.* The power of suggestion is but a scratch on the surface of mesmeric potential. Yet this ideology was deemed acceptable by mainstream science, and it came to be filed into the stock of acknowledged scientific ideas. Here in America, it is Puysegur's doctrine rather than Mesmer's that is thought of when people speak of mesmerism. But as something of a purist, I wished to be instructed in the art by one man—the pioneer in the field."

Alvord eased himself down onto a stone bench, grimacing all the while but forcing himself to speak. "So men we've seen here in America like Charles Poyen and Robert Collyer—they employ Puysegur's brand of mesmerism?"

Abendroth gave an appreciative nod, obviously surprised and pleased at Alvord's knowledge. "Exactly! But Poyen cannot be considered a true magnetizer, for although he could tap into the cosmic fluid to a limited extent, so self-absorbed and insane was he that he had under a fifty-percent success rate in his efforts at inducing the mesmeric state. He was tampering with powers that he could not fully grasp. It seems that soon after crossing the pond, Puysegur's mesmerism became even more warped, rendered so by the American zeal for religion. Both Poyen and Collyer spoke of an impending utopia ushered in by animal magnetism. This appealed to American audiences who were bearing witness to a glut of religious revivals. Unfortunately, many of their patients were driven insane through improper magnetism."

Alvord's eyes narrowed. "So insanity can be a by-product of improper mesmerism?"

"Yes. Marquis de Lafayette tried to introduce proper magnetism to the United States during and after the Revolution. An accomplished practitioner himself, he wished to share Mesmer's secret with Washington and the intellects of America, but ran into a wall. When he preached mesmerism at the American Philosophical Society in Philadelphia, his doctrine was found offensive to American sensibilities. The assembled men asked how an imponderable fluid passing through objects could serve to influence and move them. No matter how eloquent and patient Lafayette's explanations, the American intellects could not move beyond that question. Later, both Franklin and Jefferson stood in staunch opposition to what they considered an odious occult practice."

Sudden movement in the nearby wood line caught Alvord's attention. A deer, a small doe, trotted out of the forest before it noticed the two men and came to an abrupt halt. It stared unblinkingly at the mesmerizer as it twitched its ears at harrying insects. Those queer green eyes returned its gaze. To Alvord's wonder, the animal started loping towards Abendroth, who chuckled and reached out to pat the beast on the head. Licking his hand, it gazed up at him with what appeared to be adoration. As Alvord watched, nonplussed, a group of small birds began flying wide circles above the man's head.

"Am I to interpret this as animal magnetism at its most literal?"

"My master attracted animals as well," replied Abendroth with a grin, "and in his later days always had a small flock of birds following him around. Foxes and stoats were also quite taken with him. They sensed his power, as these beasts do mine."

"Can you bend them unto your will?"

"Power exerted foolishly is power wasted, Mr. Rawn."

The deer looked Alvord squarely in the face and fled a moment later.

"What exactly was Mesmer's doctrine?"

"To begin, you must understand that the German race has spawned many a mystic. It is the native soil of Dr. Faust and the Rosicrucians; in the dustier pages of German history can be traced a long tradition of occult mysticism. Yet Mesmer considered himself a scientist, despite the obvious occult nature of his discovery. He tried to convince the German aristocracy and scientific community of the scientific validity of animal magnetism. Naturally, his earnest lectures were met with nothing but scorn and suspicion, for the preternatural character of his power was obvious to a people whose relationship with the occult was an intimate one."

"With a name like Abendroth, you yourself must have German blood, London accent notwithstanding."

"Yes. My father was Hanoverian, but moved to London after marrying my mother, an Englishwoman. My schooling took place all over Europe, particularly Germany, though I've always considered myself an Englishman."

He sat down next to Alvord and leaned forward, resting his frail, bony chin on his steepled fingers. "Mesmer's early doctrine reflected his schooling in medicine, whilst fusing it with his interest in philosophy and cosmology. Descartes's idea that medicine could be cast into an exact science by melding cosmological laws with the bodily processes intrigued him greatly. His dissertation bore the title *De Planetarum influxu in Corpus Humanun*, or *The Influence of the Planets on the Human Body*. In it he theorized that a universal fluid, invisible to human eyes, flowed throughout the cosmos. All-pervasive, it penetrated human bodies. Illness he considered nothing more than the imbalance that results from this fluid flowing too forcefully or too weakly through the body. So basically, when animal magnetism ceases to flow properly, all manner of physiological disorders can wrack the human body. Early on Mesmer employed magnets to concentrate this force in patients, to control its ebb and flow, but soon realized that the true power stemmed from within himself."

"What of the stars?" asked Alvord.

"Oh, their tidal effects on the cosmic fluid are great, and those of us who can channel animal magnetism learn to use this knowledge to our advantage. Certain nights are better than others; there are times when the interstellar harmony is so flawless that magnetism is achieved with scant effort. Thus armed, Mesmer grew determined to show the world of science the miracle of his discovery. But he was wrong to try and define it in terms of logic and scientific exactitude, having confided as much to me later in life.

"So he did his best to share his miracle with the scientific world, receiving only skepticism if he was lucky, open derision were he not. The French Academy of Sciences scoffed even when he cured an asthmatic before their very eyes. The excuses surrounding their careless dismissal of him were legion. Few scientists were willing to back him if they did believe him, so fearful of reproach were they. Most men are naught but sheep, as I am sure you know, and move only with the confined flow of the flock."

He paused abruptly. "If I am boring you with this, please alert me to the fact. My capacity for rambling is without limitation."

"Oh no, please continue. And, by the by, I am with you on the sheep metaphor." It was odd, but Alvord actually experienced less pain while the mesmerizer relayed to him Mesmer's theory. His silken voice had a soothing lilt to it; as he spoke it almost seemed as if he was radiating healing rays. Considering what he had just witnessed back up in the manor, it seemed quite possible.

"Very well, then. So while vainly trying to convince science of the legitimacy of his findings, Mesmer healed the sick of Europe, catering mostly to the aristocracy but attending lower class folk as well. He cured Maria Theresia Paradis, the godchild of the Empress, of blindness. But before he could finish his sessions with her, her parents grew suspicious of his motives, wrongfully so, eventually ordering him away. She relapsed shortly thereafter, which Mesmer's critics gleefully noted. This 'failure' caused his mentors at the University of Vienna to disown him, ultimately leading to his departure from that city. He continued to heal, however, and his power grew with time and practice. He perfected the baquet, that large wooden tub you saw me use earlier, allowing him to heal multiple patients. No other mesmerizer could boast of such an accomplishment until he instructed me towards the end of his life. My master healed the blind, the paralyzed, the palsied and hysterical. And still science and medicine dismissed him out of hand.

"Central to Mesmer's theory was the role of the mesmeric trance. This he could induce by touch or merely by pointing at a person who was experiencing imbalance. It is this state that has become the focus of my own progression through the realm of mesmerism. This state lingers between sleep and wakefulness, and it is while patients are in this state that I work my magic. Something deeper that our typical consciousness comes into play and it took my master years to figure out what.

"For only later in life did Mesmer finally come to accept that what he tapped into was nothing that science would ever accept or properly describe. He realized that it was pervasive cosmic power that he dealt with rather than a fluid that could be accurately quantified; something that science would never be able to wrap its inflexible head around. For when the outer senses go into abeyance, a sixth sense takes the reins and produces the wonders you witnessed two nights past. Not until 1799 did he develop a new doctrine that tried to encapsulate his new ideas. He admitted that strange, dormant powers could be awoken through mesmerism, but this troubled him. Trances, prophecy, mental telepathy, clairvoyance, precognition, the transference of thoughts—such things are the stuff of the occult. These were concepts that he was loathe to associate with his new doctrine but he had no choice, for as he grew more powerful these occurrences became commonplace. Before 1799 he wished to be seen as a physician and scientist, but he encountered a problem when he could no longer ascertain where mainstream science left off and occult science took over. After that time he cast empiricism aside and immersed himself in the occult, leaving Paris in 1802 to seek revelation near his old home by Lake Constance."

"Can you activate such powers within yourself?"

"Not since I learned to channel the cosmic fluid properly. Gone are my nightmares and instances of levitation. While working with extremely ill patients I get snatches of prophecy sometimes; once in a while I can read thoughts or glimpse events of the past, but those are exceedingly rare occurrences."

Alvord hoped they were, particularly the mind-reading component. "So, Mesmer had withdrawn from society when you began searching for answers concerning your own gifts?"

"I came into contact with what remained of his following before I sought him out. This was in the early years of the century, and by this time his followers had already allowed petty disputes to grow into divisions, as followers are wont to do when their leader abandons them. What resulted was a proliferation of divergent articulations regarding the nature of animal magnetism. The Fluidist Mesmerists were original doctrine followers, those who maintained that the mesmeric trance could be explained by the cosmic fluid, or animal magnetism. The Animist Mesmerists insisted that spiritualism lay at the heart of mesmerism, but soon their faction splintered into smaller clusters of men with conflicting ideas. Mesmer, meanwhile, had actually incorporated elements of both theories into his later ideology, caring little what others would say. He was an egotistical one, my master, believing that he alone grasped the secrets of animal magnetism and believed that only he could properly dispense the knowledge. When I finally tracked him down he deemed me a worthy recipient of the knowledge and the rest, you might say, is history."

"Was this force known to the ancients?"

He was rewarded with another surprised look. "How probing are your questions! Well, I suppose it behooves a policeman to develop a methodical mode of inquiry. Yes, is the answer to your question. To a certain extent. The Oracle of Delphi was able to bring herself into a mesmeric trance of sorts, merging her subconscious state with that of the cosmic fluid by dint of volcanic vapors. The violent seizures it produced and the gift of prophecy she became famous for points to an affinity with animal magnetism. Similarly, the Cumaean Sibyl used volcanic vapors to induce a state of unity with animal magnetism. She too would speak in tongues with voices not her own, often prophetically. The Seer at the Oracle of Ammon at the oasis of Siwa was perhaps the most impressive example of ancient mesmerism. This oracle relied solely on self-hypnosis to achieve a state of unity with the cosmic fluid, without the use of drugs or vapors.

"And then there are the stories of Druid priests wielding elemental powers and Indian shamans inducing sleep or violent fits with a single touch. Further along history's path, we find that outlandish genius Paracelsus using magnets to concentrate the 'animal fluid' in his patients, healing them from a variety of ailments. It was also said that he could cause people to have specific dreams, also through the use of magnets. But it was not until Mesmer shocked the enlightened world with his findings and abilities that mesmerism reached full flower."

Alvord stared at the remarkable individual before him, fervently wishing that Abendroth was not the twisted, mad scientist of a man that he knew him to be.

A cold breeze accompanied the progress of the encroaching clouds, which swallowed up the azure sky around them. Gray, wispy veils of rain hung low over the hills; it would not be long before they enveloped the land around the manor.

"I take it by your pensive expression that you have either a statement to make or a question to ask of me."

"Yes. I must come clean. I have come for two reasons. My interest in your gift is genuine, and I am thankful of your invitation and detailed history of it. But as of yesterday I had another motive. The beating I took left me nursing a multitude of injuries, some of them internal, I can tell. And what's more, my condition is deteriorating. Simply put, I am in sore straits. I need to travel back to New York with Charles, and am in no shape to do so. Is it in your power to heal me? If so, are you willing to?"

With a solemn expression, Abendroth nodded slowly. "It is in my capacity to heal your injuries. Mesmer dismissed physical injuries as being beyond the power of animal magnetism, but I happen to know otherwise. It is extremely taxing, however, so I will require a bit more time before I can properly knit you up."

"How much will it cost?"

The mesmerizer turned that unsettling stare on him. Alvord averted his eyes involuntarily, lest the man see right through his facade. "Nothing, so long as you are willing to join my ranks, Mr. Rawn. You radiate an uncommonly powerful aura; your potential is great, beyond your most fanciful imaginings. I see it in your eyes, though you strive desperately to keep them free of expression. Yet they are the gateway to the soul, and I can see plainly that yours hungers for the wisdom that I and I alone can impart."

Here Abendroth stood and began pacing back and forth, a look of unconstrained madness emerging in his eyes. "What I offer is no gaudy séance, no parlor-room frivolity. No—such lowbrow delights are not to be found in *my* manor. To the narrow-minded elite of the intellectual world, my power was too much. It defied their supposedly ironclad logic; it could not be quantified or reproduced through experimentation. They feared what I was capable of and relegated me to the tattered fringes of scientific respectability."

His narrow chest strained at his black waistcoat as his breathing quickened along with the intensity of the speech.

"Fear of the unknown haunts modern society, Alvord, and it haunts science most of all. What science cannot explain it blindly and rabidly attacks, yet also fears with every fiber of its bitter, coltish form."

For the first time Alvord saw Abendroth's urbane self-possession crumbling. But he also felt the coursing waves of power that radiated from the small, pallid-faced man before him. How incredible it was that one so physically pathetic wielded astounding, untold powers.

"Let science vainly try to explain the workings of our world. Let the followers of Linnaeus try to classify all life. Let Humboldt attempt to unravel the mysteries of geology and the natural world. But *always* there will remain that which is unexplainable, that which defies all efforts at definition and formal description. And mesmerism is just that; despite its ridicule, science really stands mute in the face of my power."

"So join me, then." Abendroth posed it as more of a question than a request.

Face immobile, Alvord lied most convincingly. "As soon as I get Charles back to New York, as I have promised I would, I will return. Nothing awaits me back there and the promise of such power is too much to walk away from. Heal me, allow me to see Charles back safely, and I will return. I give you my word."

Abendroth cast a calculating look over him, and iron-gray eyes met ones of brightest emerald as Alvord returned the stare. The clouds gloomily circled overhead, leaving only a small porthole of blue sky directly above them.

"Your job?"

"I can quit, as I have enough money for now."

"I trust you," the mesmerizer said at length. "But for your sake I hope that you are not lying to me. The consequences would be most tragic."

"Threaten me again and the deal is off."

A dark look passed over Abendroth's face, but was soon replaced by approval. "I admire a man who gets riled at a threat. Alright, Mr. Rawn, I apologize. But I still expect you to honor our deal."

"Very well. How much longer until you can heal me?"

"Shortly. In the meantime, I suggest we move inside, for the rain is fast approaching. In my spare time I am an avid admirer and collector of art; care to see my collection?"

Chapter 23

Inside of Deas's studio Marcel stood rooted in place, transfixed by two of the artist's paintings.

The roiling action in *The Death Struggle* appealed to him immensely, yet the mood of gnawing expectancy seen in *Long Jakes* certainly had its allure. Having led the rugged life of the mountain man for most of his time on earth, he was struck by the vivid detail that had been given to every aspect of the paintings. The saddles, the clothing, the war paint, the weapons and equipment, the land—Deas obviously paid painstaking attention to such things. Looking at *The Death Struggle* Marcel could almost feel the tensed muscles of the panicked horse beneath him, hear the creak of leather and the frantic clatter of hooves upon rock, smell the musky odor of the attacking red man. He recalled the feeling that comes over a body when Death's rancid breath spills hot upon your neck, when your heart jumps into your throat and your body cringes in pessimistic anticipation of the next bullet, the next arrow meant for you.

Moisture built up in the corners of his dark eyes as his broad chest swelled with pride, straining at his red calico shirt. He had lived this; the themes of these paintings had been constant themes in the drama of his own existence. That was his life, right there on the canvas, his land too, and *damn*, but he wouldn't have it any other way.

Finnbar and Deas, meanwhile, were engaged in energetic discourse regarding the future of American and European art.

"But you must admit," Finnbar was saying, "Europe has been and always will be on the cutting edge of artistic development. Everything will continue to be judged against the fabric of European art. Come now, lad, even the best and most original of American artists take a trip across the pond to study the Old Masters. The States have yet to produce the kind of enduring artists that change the face of art. 'Tis a right old shame, but a fact nonetheless."

"So what do you call Thomas Cole? Or Gilbert Stuart? Or Benjamin West, John Singleton Copley?"

"A talented bunch, all of whom journeyed to Europe to study Old World paintings and techniques, which subsequently influenced their style."

"I don't think you are fully grasping my point," Deas retorted mildly, sipping a cup of tea. "We Americans should not seek to outdo European art by attempting to mimic it. I am of the opinion that American artists need to sever some of the ties we have with European art. Not all, mind, but some. In depicting our glorious landscape we can make the ascent to a new understanding of the Romantic and Sublime, as is witnessed in Cole's work. Likewise in our genre scenes we should forgo European convention and strive to depict the manful acts that make our country so unique. We should paint in a manner untrammeled by the brushes of others. From mountain men and voyageurs to explorers and frontier soldiers— we have in our own backyard what Europeans can find only in faraway lands. The frontier painter Alfred Jacob Miller understood that. This country was founded by a bold and enterprising race, and our march into history has been and will continue to be made on the backs of the intrepid. There is something unique about our republic, which our art is just starting to reflect. Nationalism will be the vehicle by which modern American art is transmuted into something immortal."

The Irishman considered this with pursed lips. "And this new brand of art will, in your opinion, surpass European art?"

"It will be magnificent and enthralling beyond anything Europe can offer. If it does not surpass it, it will at the very least equal European art."

"Ah, who's to say, really?" Finnbar conceded, running fingers through his upswept hair. "For aught I know, the next Caravaggio might be born in America tomorrow. Now, how's about another dram of that tea? My body is in dire need of liquids. I was pretty well over the bay last night, as my cramping gut keeps reminding me."

Deas rose to fetch the pot, pausing to look out the west window of his studio.

"Storm's coming," he mentioned offhandedly.

"Hey Marcel. Marcel... *Marcel?*" Finnbar got up and walked over to the engrossed trapper. Waving a hand in front of his face, he finally succeeded in stirring Marcel from his reverie.

"What?"

"You alright there, lad?"

"Just lookin' at these paintin's."

Finnbar chortled merrily. "I believe the proper term would be gaping. Like what you see?"

"Yep. This ain't what I figgered art to be. This here is... robust, vigorous."

"Keep that up and you might have a career as an art critic," joked Deas, handing Finnbar a steaming cup of tea.

"I like what you did with the white horse. It's like he's jumpin' out at you."

"That's called foreshortening. Adds to the dramatic effect."

"Yer a damn fine artist, son."

Deas grinned sheepishly. "Thanks. It is my hope that my work will be found pleasing not only to art critics, but to the wider American audience as well. The fact that you, one who belongs to the breed that forms America's marrow, approve of my work is of great importance to me."

"You like the frontier, huh?"

"I revere and relish it."

"Think it'll last much longer?"

Deas replied with ready response. "Wilderness will endure, there will always be places that most would not dare visit. So yes, although much land will be settled, we who fly in wilder skeins will always find our secluded haunts."

"Quite the wardrobe you've got, Charles," remarked Finnbar, peeking into a nearby closet. "You and Marcel would make a quite a pair."

"Are you generally so nosy?"

"Of course. Aside from my natural inquisitiveness, as a writer it behooves me to pry and snoop around. That's how you uncover interesting subject matter, doncha know."

Inside the closet were several buckskin outfits, wide-brimmed hats, calico shirts like the one Marcel wore, and various implements and weapons.

"You wear this stuff?"

"Yes Marcel, when I am afield. Some say it's eccentric, but I favor the look."

"Well ye've got fine taste, then."

Having already grown bored of the closet's contents, Finnbar peered at a small painting of Sioux Indians playing lacrosse, and laughed.

"Rough pastime, by the looks of it. Reminds me of hurling."

"That's lacrosse, Finn. 'Little Brother of War' is what the Indians call it. Savage game, injuries aplenty, but it is a rather civil substitute for war."

The Irishman frowned. "They play a game instead of fighting it out? How's that work?"

"Work's well," Marcel assured him. "No death on either side, generally speakin', and you still got a winner and a loser. Plus, competition often forms bonds between men. Sometimes those you play become yer allies outta mutual respect. Why lose men in a war when you can beat the almighty hell outta each other on the field and still resolve the problem?"

"I think I see what you're saying."

The men sat down in the largest room of the studio, multiple canvases gracing each wall. A cold wind swept into the room, scattering a pile of papers and prints.

Deas closed the window and let out a whistle. "Look at those clouds. I do believe we are in for a proper downpour."

Marcel shook his head. "Nah. It'll rain, sure, but it's likely to be light."

"And on what do you base that assumption?" Finnbar inquired.

"Low-hangin' clouds that're light to medium gray in color, pushed by a fast westerly wind; trust me, might rain for a spell, but it'll be light and probably quick if that wind keeps up."

Finnbar quickly scribbled down this bit of forecasting information in his leather notebook.

"Good to know, good to know."

Deas sat down and took a deep breath. "Alright gents, while I have you here, I just... well, here it is. Alvord is a fool, a courageous fool but a fool nonetheless if he thinks he can take out Abendroth. And you along with him. You've got an icicle's chance in hell of defeating him, and you would do well to talk

Alvord out of it. At least try, *please*. I have seen firsthand what that man is capable of; it is not just bodily harm you risk, it's... you would be better off dead, really."

Finnbar chuckled merrily. "A zero percent chance of success and a fate worse than death. Real encouraging, eh Marcel?"

"Do not make a mockery of this situation. Using his powers, Abendroth can summon an army to his side instantly. And I'm not talking about Volkmar and his other servants, although he's got them at his disposal too. The tortured souls that have been filling the cells of the madhouse are so much putty in his hands. They are devoid of will and—"

"Hold it," Marcel ordered gruffly. "'Devoid of will?' How's that? What's he done to make 'em like that?"

The face of the painter grew wan and pained. "Experimentation. The men you saw with him that night were there for instruction. Abendroth has been schooling them in the art of mesmerism for several months now. The problem is that early on most of his disciples were woefully inadequate. Their training resulted in dozens of accidents involving the slaves or prisoners they practiced on. Improper magnetism can cause massive damage to the brain, and in rare cases something happens with the soul, at least that's how Abendroth explains it... it leaves the body, passes on..."

"And you stood idly by while he did this?" snarled Finnbar, disgust contorting his usually pleasant face. "I figured you for a likely lad, but this—this is cowardice *ad nauseum*."

"I am no hero," responded Deas calmly. "There was no one willing to stand against the man until you three lunatics came to town. I was blinded by the promise of personal gain, seduced by the occult. So yes, I am not proud of it, but I stood by while he destroyed the minds of those slaves... he did the same to some white criminals too."

"And you wonder why we're takin' this bastard down?" added Marcel. "The man's evil and apparently the law in these parts couldn't give a damn. So it's up to us, who are savvy to the madness goin' on up in his manor, to stop him. Otherwise, who knows what he'll seek to do?"

"I do."

Finnbar and Marcel exchanged troubled glances.

"And what might that be?" asked Finnbar.

Deas stared out the window, looking distant. "Control. And not just in a mesmeric sense. Politically. Those men, the social elite of St. Louis, will soon be sent forth to use their newfound power to influence certain politicians. Abendroth wants control of this part of Missouri, but seeks to do it in a most clandestine manner. He himself will be the puppet master, sending out his followers to do the dirty work while he manipulates things from a lofty perch. He is essentially staging a coup of the state government. Should his devotees prove powerful enough, it will no doubt succeed."

"And what sorta role would you be playin' in all this? He certainly took a liking to you. He also said you and he were going to have a private session that night."

Here Marcel paused abruptly, giving Deas an odd look. "You ain't one o' them sodomites, are you boy?"

"Judas Priest, man! Of course not. I was to be his personal artist. Soon after his arrival he began showing up at exhibitions and, much taken with my work, offered his gift as a means by which to reach new artistic heights."

"Let me get this straight," asked Finnbar, frowning, "he uses this 'animal magnetism' to influence your art? How? I know he can heal and control people, sort of make sense I guess, but how would that affect your painting? Unless he personally manipulated you?"

"I do not wish to speak of it," Deas answered shortly, glancing sidelong at the red door. "I am no longer his artist and am doing my best to forget my involvement with him."

"What else do you know, then? Anything that could be of use when we go up against him?"

"There is another realm he talks about, a place he can access using his powers. The place is apparently full of dark, ancient powers, and he mentally crippled those people so that he could unite their bodies with whatever lurks beyond the veil separating the two worlds. Whatever it is they become, he can control them. This is not standard mesmeric control, which is frightening enough—this is something new and unspeakably evil."

"I've heard a sight too much about how powerful he his. What're his weaknesses?"

"Marcel, he doesn't have any," Deas answered hopelessly. "He is highly intelligent, surrounds himself with wealthy, influential people, seems able to detect lies, and can control people with a single touch. Whereas other mesmerizers control only the sick or willing subjects, his power far exceeds that of most. The only thing you've got going for you is the element of surprise. Were I you, I would shoot the bastard from as far away as possible, but even that will be tough as he rarely leaves his manor. And Volkmar—there's another man to avoid. His combination of freakish strength and fighting skill make him an extremely formidable man. I doubt even Alvord could stand against him."

"Well, I reckon we'll talk it over with Al and draw up a plan. There'll be a way, trust me."

"So you're still set on this?"

"Have I mentioned that your lack of confidence in us is rather irritating?"

"You go to your deaths!" Deas regarded Finnbar with frustration. "When your plan goes to hell, as it inevitably will, remember my unheeded warning."

His words were met by awkward silence.

A gunshot rang out from down on the street, followed by hearty laughter.

Finnbar gave a snort. "Hell, 'tis not even noontime. I guess they kick off the festivities early in these parts. I approve."

"Listen," Deas implored them, "go out there and enjoy yourselves at the celebration tonight. There will be feasting, drinking, gambling, games, fireworks, women—just immerse yourselves in pleasure seeking and forget this nonsense."

"Can't." Marcel rose swiftly from his chair and headed for the door.

"Why not? My God, I just don't understand it! What motivation do you have? Neither of you have anything to do with this!"

Finnbar sighed. "I'd explain it, me boyo, if I thought that there was any chance of your understanding it."

Marcel stopped at the door and spun around. "Son, yer right. We ain't involved in this like you was. Which leads me to ask—why won't you help? You know what that man's capable of, know the evil surroundin' his actions—we could use another man, 'specially one who knows the mesmerizer's habits and personality. So instead of offerin' us words of caution, why don't you buck up and join us?"

Deas clenched his jaw and stared at the floorboards. "I cannot."

"Can't, or won't?"

"Won't, Marcel. The burnt child dreads the fire. I... I am sorry, and I quite understand if you don't want anything to do with me anymore, but too easily can he exert control over me. I will not walk blithely into the antechamber of death. Best of luck, gentlemen."

Marcel left without another word. Finnbar hesitated, casting a searching glance over Deas before slowly leaving the room.

For a long time after they left, Deas sat staring at *The Prairie Fire*, face unreadable.

The streets grew more raucous and crowded as the hours passed. Games were played by children and adults alike, music filled every corner of Market Street; even the brief rain showers did not impede their designs. People ate and drank, talked and laughed, merrily unaware of the monumental task that awaited three men later that night.

Finnbar and Marcel retired to their respective lodgings and spent a long time lying upon their beds, pondering the consequences that might result from their actions. At times doubt plagued their minds, knots formed in their guts. Much could go wrong, more perhaps than they were capable of comprehending. Physical harm was one thing, but a man who could damage or manipulate the soul?

Both were hardened in the ways of pain and violence, Marcel to a greater extent, yet never before had either tangled with occult power. Deas's desperate warnings were based on firsthand experience with Abendroth's power. Could he be right? Would Abendroth prove to be an invincible foe?

In the end, nerve won out. Perhaps it was arrogance, perhaps a grim determination to not seem a coward. Whatever the case, both men determined that Abendroth had to die, and theirs would be the hands that did it. Each reasoned that they had two other solid fellows on their side, not to mention the element of surprise. So really, they assured themselves, the decision to carry out their plan was a natural one.

And upon such decision are the fates of men decided.

Chapter 24

"**Why** the emphasis on the underworld?" Alvord wanted to know.

His host poured himself a large cup of water from a pewter pitcher. "I tell you, mesmerizing certainly dehydrates a body. But to answer your question, I find imagery of Hell to be captivating in the extreme. When I think of art, this is what I imagine, what I crave."

"A morbid preoccupation."

"You never find yourself wondering what Satan's realm might be like?"

"No, and I hope never to find out."

They stood in Abendroth's brightly lit gallery on the second floor, regarding the twenty or so paintings that hung there. As every last one of the paintings was filled with hellish imagery, Alvord was strongly reminded of Deas's secret room. And an odious comparison it was.

The mesmerizer stalked slowly about the room, hands clasped behind his back and features smugly arranged.

"Doesn't it strike you as odd, how some artists become obsessed with the grandeur of mountain ranges or the intimacy of enchanted woodlands, others with historical subjects or the subtleties of human interaction, but a few, a quirky few, fill their canvases with the awesome ruin of the Apocalypse, or the ghastly torments of Hell? John Martin, Francis Danby; artists like these are the chosen few who, for whatever reason, possess insight sufficient enough to grasp the horrific realities of Pandemonium. I aided these men in creating some of their more, ah, *lurid* paintings, but unfortunately both balked when I offered them a place in my fold."

Alvord inspected a painting that depicted some dark recess of Hell, filled to bursting with flames and molten rock, demons and tortured souls. He read the name of the artist on the lower right-hand corner and quietly sighed.

"Yet you also favor Charles's work?" he asked, nodding at the painting.

"Yes," replied the mesmerizer, eyes wide and blazing with intensity. "When gazing upon Charles's work I feel that I am beholding the most accurately delineated portrayals of Perdition. But it goes beyond supposed accuracy, too. The hellish subject matter he chooses, the delicate nuances of texture and light; it is such facets of his style that really drew me to his paintings. The work he does for me is a poetic fusion of earthly and hellish realms, as he calls it, an integration wherein Sublime and Romantic painting principles are subsumed under the broader scope of the hellscape. Charles is a painter who can present a theme with consummate skill; I doubt that you could find his like anywhere else on earth. Never before have I encountered a person who grasped so quickly the fact that anyone can use animal magnetism to enhance their lives. So finely attuned to the cosmic fluid is he that if the stars are right, he does not even require my guidance to tap into its power. It is also nice to possess his original works, for many of the Martin's and Danby's I possess are copies made for me by the artists. In Charles's work I can observe and enjoy true originality."

The two moved on to the next wall of paintings. Located between John Martin's fiery hellscape *Pandemonium* and Francis Danby's apocalyptic *Opening of the Sixth Seal* hung a half-finished work that Alvord could tell was Deas by the coloration and detail.

"What have we here?" he asked of Abendroth.

"Ah yes. This is one of Charles's more recent projects. A pity he will be leaving on the morrow; I had such high hopes for this work."

"Perhaps he will come back," Alvord lied, "for he does not much care for New York."

He had been standing for too long, moving around too much. The pain began to intensify to nearly unbearable levels.

"I can only hope. He has come so very far, and his artistic maturity lies just around the next bend. You see, art is my true passion. One day I hope to serve as a mentor to young American artists who are willing to take this country's art in a new direction, the direction that Charles's is currently exploring. For while some American landscapes display a glimmering of what is to come—"

Alvord heard his words but they were indistinct, like the mesmerizer yelled them from the opposite side of a valley. The world quite suddenly grew dark and blurry as an intense ringing shut out all other nose.

"Mr. Rawn? *Mr. Rawn!*"

Abendroth grabbed him as he started going down, displaying incredible strength for one so frail looking.

"Alright. Let's get you to a chair, shall we?"

All Alvord remembered of the next few moments was half-walking, half-falling as Abendroth guided him into a nearby room. Then he was in a chair, pain slashing away at his body, vision swimming crazily.

"Here, drink this."

He had been hoping for whiskey, but it was water that Abendroth held to his black, scabbed-over lips.

"This is magnetized water; it will aid my efforts at healing you. Now, I need you to breathe easily and relax your mind and body. I know you are aflame with pain, but try."

Alvord did as Abendroth bid him do, soon getting control over his breathing. Yet just as he had achieved this, another wave of nauseating pain swept over him.

As he doubled over, he gasped, "Quickly!"

"Your hands!" Abendroth requested urgently.

Extending his arms, Alvord fought to stifle a coughing fit. The mesmerizer seized both his hands and a second later a miraculous calm came over him.

The pain eased, becoming quite manageable, before vanishing altogether.

"Now, Alvord," intoned Abendroth from somewhere very far away, "I have eased the pain, but in order to heal you I must first induce what is known as the crisis. I am able to heal injuries such as yours through mesmerism, but first what must occur is the flooding of your system with animal magnetism and an accompanying intensification of your pain. This could last up to thirty seconds. After that the healing process begins, which will be painless. Are you ready?"

"Yes," he said, and was surprised at how calm and faraway his own voice sounded.

Then came pain the likes of which he had never known. He relived each blow, each punch and kick and club stroke, but the attendant pain far exceeded that which he had felt during his ignominious beating.

No scream escaped his lips, though one longed to do so. He could hear himself grunting loudly against the pain, jaws clenched and eyes clamped shut. A dazzling light could be seen even through his closed lids, so slowly he opened his eyes to find out what it might be.

The head and hands of the mesmerizer shone with a brilliant, pure white light. The rest of his body remained dark, but as he watched his body and the room around him was consumed by the stunning light emanating from his hands and head.

Alvord looked down and saw that his body glowed as well. It qualified as the strangest experience of his life.

Muffled cracking sounds met his ears, and he actually felt his ribs and nose being mended. His pain began to diminish, replaced by a pleasant warmth, as if he had quaffed some quality claret.

Many minutes ticked by before Abendroth let go of his hands and stepped back. The blinding light instantly disappeared, leaving Alvord to wonder if he had been hallucinating from the pain.

The mesmerizer, though drained-looking, seemed pleased as he admired his own handiwork. "And the verdict is...?"

Alvord lifted his hands out in front of him, hands that had been bruised and swollen. They were without blemish, aside from old scars.

He stood and slowly rotated his torso, waiting for his ribs to scream in protest. No pain met his actions, so he shook his head back and forth quickly. No splitting headache.

The room contained a looking glass, which he hastened over to. His nose was straight and thin again, his cheek and forehead free from bruises and cuts. Slowly he ran his hands through his dark hair, checking for bumps and crusted-over lacerations. Nothing.

He was cured. The mesmerizer had knitted every one of his wounds. Rolling his shoulders and tensing his muscles, he came to realize that he was better than cured. Power coursed through him; he felt strong and more limber than he ever had.

"I must apologize for my initial skepticism, Count Abendroth."

"No worries. Skepticism is a natural human response to phenomena it cannot explain."

Something in Abendroth's tone did not agree with him. There was a faintly mocking quality to his voice that had Alvord's guard up. Had his plan backfired on him? Had Volkmar already told Abendroth about seeing him in the manor that night?

He maintained a calm demeanor and kept talking. "I cannot possibly express my gratitude enough. You performed a miracle today, one that others will hear of."

"You'll have me blushing, Mr. Rawn!" laughed Abendroth. "So then, now that you are in proper condition you can escort Charles home. After that I shall expect your prompt return. And do try to talk Charles into coming back after his business is concluded, will you?"

"I will do just that. Again, I am indebted to you." He turned to leave.

"Oh, and Mr. Rawn?"

Something about the mesmerizer's overtly casual tone triggered Alvord's police instincts, alerting him to the fact that he had been made. When he turned it was with blazing speed, Colt drawn.

But Abendroth's hand was already outstretched, and Alvord felt himself freeze in place. No matter how hard he fought he could not shift himself into moving, could not move a muscle for that matter. He could breath, barely, but could not speak. Then an invisible hand clamped onto his wrist, tightening its hold until the Colt clattered harmlessly to the floor.

"So," said Abendroth, smiling hugely. "When I was healing you, guess what information I dredged up?"

Straining against the force that held him in place, Alvord managed to take two steps forward, nearly passing out from the effort. Everything seemed so far away, he could barely gather his thoughts...

Abendroth frowned deeply, but closed his eyes and grimaced, preventing Alvord from moving any further.

"I lied, Mr. Rawn. When healing patients I am often able to sense their most pressing thoughts and passions. Nothing too detailed, just a general outline, really. Now I know your mind, and it is mine. So you had your heart set on killing me, eh? And here I was laboring under the misapprehension that I had in you a valuable ally. Oh well. Bold as brass, aren't you? Most unusual too, I must admit, as you had nothing to do with either myself or my plans until quite recently. And even when you dug deeper, uncovering the more unsavory applications of my power, it was still really no concern of yours. You could have left here tomorrow and lived your life untroubled by me and my little scheme.

"But no, perhaps you couldn't have," Abendroth mused, circling Alvord's immobile form. "You had need of my healing. But even barring that, you couldn't have left, for you consider yourself greater than others and therefore obligated to intervene on their behalf in situations like this. Even when your intervention would be downright suicidal, as it was in this instance. Your sense of justice overrides your survival instinct, doesn't it? How very curious! I do believe that I miscalculated when I thought you would be a welcome addition to my fold, Mr. Rawn. For while you would have been a powerful practitioner of mesmerism and a valuable ally, your conscience would not have allowed you to throw in your lot with one as 'immoral' as myself. You would call me evil, no doubt, were you able to speak now. Not true. I merely seek peace, wealth, and a healthy dose of power, as do all men. And if I happen to use slaves and politics as a means to that end- so what? Other men do so all the time.

"Well, no need to explain myself now. Dead men tell no tales. I've got something special planned for you. Do you recall that point in my demonstration the other night where that woman began reading minds, spouting out crazed prophesies of dark things to come? She did so because I mentally led her into a place where such powers float in the very air. Between the darkness of Earth and Hell there lies another realm, Mr. Rawn. A world of phantoms and forgotten memories. Through self-hypnosis I can visit that dolorous place, where ancient entities long gone from this world still seethe with fantastic might. Terrible things inhabit that place, things I try not to think about, frankly. And today, Mr. Rawn, you have the singularly unique opportunity to meet some of the denizens of that shadowy realm."

Straining with everything he had, Alvord made one last colossal effort to break free from the mesmerizer's hold.

Nothing.

He had been in some bad situations before, some in which he thought he might die, but never before had he *known* that he was going to die.

Or suffer a fate worse than death.

The world grew dark, as it had before. He saw the brilliant light burst out of the mesmerizer's hand, saw as it struck him in the chest. His body tensed, then relaxed, and he crumpled to the floor.

When he awoke he was standing once again and Abendroth stood nearby, smiling at him.

"Awake at last, are we?"

Alvord stood before him, face inexpressive. His powerful shoulders slumped and he swayed slightly.

Something was very, very wrong—he felt empty, totally hollow. Like he would never again know happiness. He found himself not caring what Abendroth had just done to him, or what might await him in the future. The world was bland, colorless, and utterly uninviting.

And worse yet, he felt like something watched him from the shadows of the room, something menacing and unseen. Yet fear did not accurately describe what he felt; resignation was more like it.

With a smirk, Abendroth issued an order. "Go home, Mr. Rawn. You are about to embark on a voyage of self-discovery. I wish you the very best of luck, though I doubt that will count for much."

Alvord, hardly aware of what he did, turned and began staggering towards the door.

"Oh, and pick up the revolver on your way out. You'll be needing that. Trust me."

Chapter 25

Gregory Abendroth chuckled heartily as he watched Alvord stumble away.

There went a dangerous fellow and no mistake. Aside from his physical prowess and bold character, the man exuded an aura the likes of which he had rarely encountered. This was not your average man nor enemy.

But even for him there existed no hope of recovery, Abendroth assured himself, as he had exerted his power upon him to its fullest and most malevolent extent. What he performed was no mere infusion of animal magnetism; it was a spiritual piercing of the obfuscating veil that hung between two worlds, and the subsequent unleashing of malignant, otherworldly beings upon the man who had plotted to kill him.

It had come as a shock, that uncovered nugget of information. Abendroth wondered how close to death he had come.

Death was something he rarely considered. Though he was sixty, he looked closer to forty and felt thirty. His knowledge of and affinity with animal magnetism kept him young, he knew, and might even be the key to immortality.

Yet had Alvord not been attacked yesterday and consequently forced to seek him out for the purpose of healing, what might have transpired?

Ah. Such things were better left unexamined. He was alive and well now. And with this new (and quite unexpected) enemy already taken care of, little stood between him and the control of this region of Missouri.

"You should have let me kill him," insisted Volkmar, his huge form emerging from the shadows.

"Well Otto, if he survives, which is unlikely, you shall have an opportunity."

"What are his chances?"

Abendroth chuckled delightedly. "Slim to none. You see, one useful aspect of mesmerism is the power of posthypnotic suggestion. So all I had to do was steer him close enough to the shadow realm and urge his subconscious self to stay there. Soon enough he will fall prey to the unpleasant... *things* that dwell in that place, and they will quickly seek out the dankest, gloomiest recesses of his mind. What follows is an overwhelming intensification of his most morbid thoughts and fears; he will plunge into deepest melancholia and seek a way out, any way out of this life. In theory at least. And frankly, this theory does not disappoint."

"So he is possessed?"

"No. Merely... *exposed*."

Volkmar knew well what happened to people when subjected to those infernal powers.

"I see," he muttered unhappily.

"By the by, Otto, why did you fail to inform me that you suspected Alvord to be one of the men who snuck into this manor the other night?" He was not mad, merely curious.

"I was going to take care of him myself, and did not want to burden you with it. It seemed to me you had enough to worry about these next few days. How do you know about that?"

"It was revealed to me as I healed him. That was one of his most pressing concerns. You know, I was suspicious of that fellow from the first, for I simply *knew* he had come to take Charles back East. Yet after speaking with him this morning I felt so sure that he would join us, his interest struck me as so genuine... he is cunning, and disguised well his hatred of me. A specious fellow, that one. Odd, too. He despises most of mankind with an intensity I've rarely seen equaled, yet at the same time feels obligated to act in its defense. Most peculiar..."

"Should he survive," said Volkmar soberly as his fingers tapped a beat on his sword's pommel, "he is mine. It must be me who faces him."

His employer cocked his head to the side, amused. "And why is that?"

"I need to see who the better man is."

Abendroth rolled his eyes hopelessly. "I declare, I shall never understand this code of honor you comport yourself in accordance with. But fine, should he survive, he's yours. Do you think you can best him?"

"Of course. But he might surprise me."

"Hmm. Alright then. I am going to catch a swift forty winks. It has been a most taxing afternoon. Kindly see that I am woken in two hours; there is much work to be done tonight, old friend."

Within the confines of his large but rather Spartan room, Gregory Abendroth prepared himself for sleep. This was not a task that he could go about as most people did, as it required great concentration and an unconscious exercise of will even as he slumbered.

In truth, it could not rightly be termed sleep. A slumberous torpor was more like it, sufficient to restore his energy but hardly as satisfying as actual sleep. Actual sleep had eluded him for years now.

But alas, he had to keep his wits about him and his guard up, for it was during moments of sleep that *they* came for him.

When Abendroth first discovered that he could enter upon that other world, the shadow realm as he'd dubbed it, he had no inkling as to the dangers he exposed himself to. The initial discovery was mind-blowing; he had been caught up in the arrogance that often accompanies major breakthroughs. He could spiritually access the place and even impose his will upon many of the beings there. In fact, with some practice he could even transfer their essence into human hosts, although that often produced volatile results. These beings, for all their power, were subject to his will; *he*, a mere man. Intoxicated with his newfound power, he blithely overlooked the possible dangers.

For as he pierced the veil, so too did the denizens of that realm. It was as if in chancing upon their world, he had inadvertently opened up a rift between the land of those puissant creatures and his own.

The ominous feeling of being watched began plaguing him after each visit to the shadow realm. This baffled him initially, but soon enough he came to the startling realization that its inhabitants were stalking him in this world. At first their presence was nearly imperceptible, but eventually they grew in strength to the point where Abendroth could actually see them, as one might perceive the faintest of shadows. They were not always present, but hung around often enough for it to be both worrisome and frustrating. During several efforts to seal the rift he had exerted his powers to their fullest, but to no avail.

In his fervid quest for power and heightened awareness he had swung wide a door that could not be closed.

While awake he need not worry about them, for he was strong enough to overcome them should they harry him. Sleep, however, left his mind quite vulnerable, a revelation that had nearly ended him. Just in time had he awoken one night to find those things poised to... well, he wasn't quite sure what they were about to do. It couldn't be good, for he'd felt the ominous cloud of their evil settling over him, had heard the seductive whispers that urged him to embrace them.

But as long as he remained vigilant, Gregory Abendroth felt confident that he could keep his odious stalkers at bay. As he lay upon his bed, he went through the defensive routine that he employed each time he dozed.

First, he slowed his breathing until his chest rose and fell in a perfect, unbroken rhythm and his nose whistled slightly with each lungful of air.

He focused on relaxing, on sinking deeper and deeper into his mind, detaching himself from his body and all earthly stimuli.

This only took around a minute. He was, after all, an old hand at this.

Next he summoned animal magnetism to him and he felt its familiar jolt, though he was only vaguely aware of the sensation. Molding it as an artist molds clay, he wrapped a protective cocoon of it around himself, impervious and absolute.

This was his only defense but it was a sound one.

As he began drifting into an uneasy sleep, his half-closed eyes detected them, those shadowy things that flitted around the room like restless birds. They encircled him; he could feel them probing his enveloping blanket of pure power, seeking any exploitable gap or weakness. They found none.

They were powerful, so very powerful in an ancient way, yet his own power was sufficient to hold them back. The barest hint of a smile appeared in one corner of his mouth as he sensed their mounting frustration.

These beings possessed inhuman power, so he, a man able to best them, must be more than a man, right? Perhaps in him there sparked a glimmering of what man had once been capable of, or maybe he, Count Gregory Abendroth, was at the forefront of man's next great march into progress.

With a surge of focus, he flung the amorphous specters away from him, as something of a chuckle sounded in his throat.

As fearsome as these creatures were, they were nothing, *nothing*, compared to the most ancient and powerful madness that haunted that other world. Something altogether more infernal and calculated than the frothing chaos of the lesser shadow beings.

The Dweller on the Threshold was what author Edward Bulwer-Lytton had referred to it as in his occult novel *Zanoni* of 1842. It was an entity that lurked just beyond the veil separating the physical world from the spiritual one. A tortured being comprised purely of primordial malice and scorn, something that above all else longed to attach itself to a human so as to corrupt, distort, and ultimately destroy. The first time Abendroth encountered one of them it had nearly done just that to him; only by a last minute strengthening of his defenses had he been able to overcome the demoniac presence that sought to seize control of his very soul.

Somehow he had managed to force it back into its own world, where it had not tried to escape from since. Perhaps it was biding its time. He could sense the Dwellers from a long way off, could feel their surging aura even among all the interference of the shadow realm. During his forays into that world he was always careful to withdraw if he sensed one of them, lest they attack or follow him out. But they seemed content to hang back; maybe they respected his power?

Yet even as the thought passed through his mind he could not quite bring himself to believe it.

Ah—enough worrying about that. Alvord now grappled with the other shadow beings, which could do him no harm. Never before had anyone survived an encounter with those nightmares. By nightfall the deed would be done.

The flickering phantoms reassembled around him; ravening, baneful, and above all else, unrelenting.

Although ensconced deep within the cavernous recesses of his own twisted mind, Abendroth curled his lips into a wicked smile.

Rawn stood not an icicle's chance in Hell.

Chapter 26

Alvord passed through the world as if in a dream. Nothing he observed or felt bore the mark of reality. The grass, the trees, the sky; none held their usual rich hues, appearing to him instead as dreary and utterly lackluster.

Sweltering temperatures had followed hard on the heels of the brief rain showers. The heat could be seen in the distance, an obscuring, shimmering haze.

Apathetically he sat in the seat of the phaeton, taking in his surroundings with no real interest. After a while his head lolled back and over to the side as he stared at the swiftly migrating clouds overhead.

The driver, meanwhile, was not yet over the shock of seeing Alvord completely healed. He could not make out a single bruise or cut on the face that had been marred with both just two hours ago. His passenger gave hollow, disorganized responses to the few questions he posed and appeared completely preoccupied. The man's listlessness was downright disturbing, and he wondered what evil might have been visited upon him during his time with the mesmerizer.

Unaware of the driver's concern, Alvord let his eyes rove and his mind wander. At intervals shadowy forms appeared in the fields and woods, and he knew, as if instinctively, that they were things indescribably tainted. It was as if a curtain had been lifted to reveal another world that somehow existed within the confines of this one. Neither fear nor loathing reared up from the stagnant pool of his emotions, though deep down he knew he should have felt *something*, surprise at the very least.

But he simply didn't.

When the carriage rolled past a sprawling field of wheat, he saw those nameless horrors marshaled out there in serried ranks, an army awaiting an order.

Forms without fixed shape floated in the cheerless skies above, some close by but others soaring far overhead like ragged vultures. Colors Alvord had never known to exist dappled the sky at times like an expansive rainbow, contributing to the peculiar nature of his experience.

From time to time faint, sibilant voices whispered into his ear in a strange tongue. Although he could not understand them, he felt the power and seduction of each alien word.

He recalled his days of opium addiction, those few weeks of utter euphoria and peace. The way he now felt was akin to the effects of opium, yet the elation and tranquility that the white powder induced was not to be found. His head buzzed and his body felt warm and light, but an underlying emptiness dominated these sensations.

The carriage rattled into the outer fringes of town, the driver urging his horse on to greater speeds. The deranged look upon the face of his passenger frightened him; the sooner he rid himself of this man the better. That lost look in his pale gray eyes was unlike anything he had ever seen.

So distracted was he that he ended up on Choteau Street rather than Market.

"Suh? I have to stop here. Ah, urgent business, you know. Please get out."

"Right."

He stepped down. Having already paid the man, he turned away and began to walk. The road beneath him was poorly paved and littered with trash and animal feces.

The sound of toil assaulted his ears. To the immediate south lay two iron foundries and a sugar refinery, while to the north a number of sawmills sat clustered around Choteau's Pond. The clamor produced by these industries was truly incredible.

Before him lay crowded streets full of yelling men, distracted women, scurrying children, and bellowing beasts of burden. People's voices ran together; the Southern, Irish, and German accents creating a whirlwind of sound that buzzed hornet-like around Alvord's head.

Turning north onto Fourth Street, he passed clerks offices and butchers, law practices and dry goods stores. Men he would describe as popinjays and coxcombs sauntered out of haberdasheries and barbershops, chatting loudly and maintaining expressions of superiority.

A sneer formed upon his lips. The world was a thing utterly hateful to him. He had been lying to himself for some time now, assuring himself that since the loss of his family there was still some purpose for him to fulfill in a world gone to hell. A world full of covetous, lustful, arrogant people leading unexamined, earthbound existences to which he simply could not relate. It had been a well-executed lie, but a lie nonetheless.

People—how perfectly execrable.

Not all of them, insisted a quiet voice in his head, *think of Marcel and Finnbar, ready to die by your side this night.*

Weak, he countered fiercely. *Whoremongers of French and Irish descent—inferior by blood alone, predilections not even taken into account.*

Folks scurried about like so many rodents, hardly aware of their surroundings. They bumped into him now and again but he hardly noticed, so consumed was he with his own thoughts.

Whatever Abendroth had done to him had opened his eyes to the fact that he hated this hollow life of his. Surrounded by inferior beings and with a recent history drenched in loss, it was surprising that he had lasted this long.

With a slight start he realized that the shadows stalked him as he went, sometimes flitting among the roiling crowd, other times appearing in windows or on rooftops.

He knew not what they were or why they'd come. Perhaps they were messengers sent to open his mind to the abhorrent truth about mankind. He did not mind them, but wished he knew their exact purpose.

A resonant female voice hailed him.

"Mr. Rawn?"

Valda stood in front of him, carrying a basket full of various foodstuffs. Her flaxen hair ran down her neck in two thick braids.

"Good to see you again, Mr. Rawn!"

"Yes. Hello Valda."

His bland tone surprised her. Upon closer inspection she realized that Alvord bore none of the wounds he had received yesterday during that fight. She also noticed the unfocused look in his eyes and found it most unsettling.

"Vhat happened to ze cuts and bruises on your face?

How is it ze are gone?"

"Oh, that. Well yes, I am healed."

He offered no further explanation, but he gazed into her eyes for a moment. A powerful wave of fear passed through her.

Valda took an involuntary step back. "Are you alright, Mr. Rawn?"

A shadow being appeared behind her and Alvord stared at it.

"Fine, yes. Thanks. I just need to go think, that's all. Good day."

As he swept passed her, she turned to watch him disappear amidst the crowd.

Alvord stood inside the entrance hall of the Planter's Hotel, staring fixedly at the complex parquetry of the floor. He discovered that the patterns shifted around if he stared hard enough at them.

The Kentish desk clerk walked over and greeted him jovially.

"Ah, hello sir! I see you have survived the heat, then! You are just in time for an early potluck dinner being held in the dining hall. We also have a prodigious selection of..." His voice trailed off as Alvord walked right by him, heading for the staircase.

After a slow ascent up the stairs, Alvord walked out onto his balcony.

Boats swarmed over the Mississippi, as usual. The sun shone hot in the sky and people came and went, few leaving their mark upon the place. Watching them from this lofty vantage strengthened his sense of detachment.

From his perch he could see whores hanging around the entrances to bawdy houses, drunken men stumbling out of dram shops, and some slaves stooping under the weight of heavy loads.

He clenched his fists and scowled. What an opprobrious testament to human frailty.

An initial tightening of muscles graduated to sharp pain in the vicinity of his heart, a pain deepened by his subsequent sigh.

Life seemed so empty, so devoid of purpose...

He staggered over to his bed and collapsed upon it. The

room was warm and soon sweat beaded on his face.

Dark, ugly thoughts consumed his mind as he stared up at the richly tiled ceiling. Hours passed and the sun slunk low in the sky.

This might be Hell, he thought to himself. *The people I am forced to call my fellow man, am forced to share this earth with, render life a veritable Hell.*

Throughout his thirty-six years, misanthropy would occasionally take hold of him, and now he felt that hatred afresh as it descended, talons outstretched.

In the past a hammering rage would have set in but now resignation swept over him, in concert with a calm resolution.

For now he knew the way out.

Death. It was his only realistic avenue of escape from this indigestible emptiness.

Immediately the God-fearer within him bellowed in frightened protest, but this new, resigned attitude of his quickly overrode the objection.

Death. What a glorious simplification of things. Heaven or Hell. Paradise or Pandemonium. Cut and dried.

Self-negation. Yes. It was the only way out of the monotonous farce he'd dared to call a life. For what was life without hope?

He might even see his family again, if he was lucky. Could removing himself from a world gone awry really entail punishment? God would surely forgive him; he looked down on this earth each day and saw the marked paucity of decent people, did he not? Surely God shared in his disgust?

Recalling a line from Milton's *Paradise Lost*, he began muttering disjointedly.

"So farewell hope, and with hope farewell fear..."

With an eerie smile, he dragged the Colt from his belt.

Part Three

"You get to delving... delving deep... well, there's no telling what you'll bring up.

Louis L'Amour
The Californios

Chapter 27

*T*he crowd at the Bavari Inn swelled to capacity at five o'clock. Germans formed the bulk of those present, but a handful of Americans and Irishmen rubbed elbows with them up at the bar. The tables were all full of feasting, chattering people, with the aroma of first-rate German cooking being enough to draw saliva from even the most hardened connoisseur's mouth.

By the bar an Irishman tried to "walk the chalk," a task at which he struggled mightily. An age-old sobriety test among sailors, walking the chalk had become a popular form of amusement and gambling in frontier taverns and saloons.

As Finnbar watched, his countryman teetered to his left, nearly falling, then overcompensated and went crashing down, vomiting beer and knockwurst onto the polished floor. Raucous laughter mingled with the hostile epitaphs of those who had lost money on the bet. Finnbar chuckled himself, shaking his head.

Rudolph walked over, calmly dragged the bedraggled man up by his collar, and hurled him out the door. He dispersed the group of onlookers and gamblers with a few thunderous orders before returning to his place behind the bar. Pulling on his watch fob, Finnbar checked the time and sighed.

"An hour late. Does Alvord strike you as the type to show up an hour late?"

Marcel scratched his beard reflectively. "No. I'd say Al's the punctual sort. Somethin's up."

"To arms, then?"

"Think so."

Scanning the room, Marcel shook his shaggy head.

"Something's up," he said again, "got me a feeling in my gut. Let's go."

Finnbar drained his stein of its last frothy dregs of Spaten. "Good. I'm tired of eavesdropping on the conversations around us—dry shite if ever there was."

"And why exactly are you eavesdropping on other people's discussions?"

"It becomes a writer to understand the ebbs and flows of human interaction, Marcel. See, in order to connect with one's potential audience, one must strive not only for originality but for authenticity as well, and to ensure this one should—"

"Alright, alright. Don't go gettin' verbose on me."

"A favorite word of mine, it so happens."

"Oh! You two! I vas hoping I vould find you here tonight!"

Valda approached them swiftly from across the bar. Finnbar immediately discerned the worry that creased her eyes and mouth.

"Something the matter, m'darlin'?"

"Ja. Very much the matter. I saw Mr. Rawn earlier today, and there is somesing wrong vith him."

"How so?"

"Vell, I saw him in the street, and he barely recognized me. Vhen he looked at me it vas like he looked right through. He spoke slowly in a strange voice, an empty voice..."

Marcel frowned. "You say he was outta his head, eh? You sure he wasn't on the drink?"

"No, no," she assured him distractedly, "it vas different. He kept looking around like somesing stalked him, and the blacks of his eyes vere massive. He gave short answers to my qvestions and just looked... *haunted*, I think is the vord."

"Was there anything else?" Finnbar inquired.

"Oh yes! Vhy did I not mention it? His face vas free from bruises and cuts, he said he had been healed. I just don't understand how zat could be, and he vould not explain."

Finnbar and Marcel exchanged grave looks.

"Did he say where he was headed?"

"No, Mr. Fagan. He just said he needed to think. I am very worried."

"He's stayin' up at the Planter's Hotel, ain't he?" Marcel asked of Finnbar.

"Yes. We'd better head over that way, maybe check his room. Thanks, Valda. We'll be in touch, lass."

"Is there somesing else what I could do to help?" Her face was resolutely set, a shadow of her father's fearsome countenance showing in her own.

"Nah, reckon you've played yer part, girl. Just have some drinks waitin' fer us when we get back tonight. We got some business to attend to and will be workin' up a powerful thirst."

Shaking his head at the mountain man's glaring lack of decorum, Finnbar thanked Valda again before following him out the door.

The sounds of revelry met their ears as they stepped out onto Fourth Street. The brief showers had dampened the roads but not spirits. The celebration of St. Louis's eighty-third anniversary went on unabated.

The main roads were clogged with pedestrians and equestrians alike, and among them marched instrumental bands and singers. Pushcarts laden with fruit, vegetables, and bread could be found just about anywhere. On some streets pigs and beef briskets roasted over open fires.

Groups of men sat on upturned barrels, sawing vigorously on fiddles and setting many sets of feet to dancing. Numerous cockfights were underway, the urgings and oaths of onlookers adding to the ruckus.

Guns were being discharged into the air in sheer exuberance, adding a wild aspect to an already rowdy situation. All manner of people, from factory workers and merchants to farmers and physicians shared the streets as they expressed their pride in St. Louis, The River Queen.

Incongruously enough, in the midst of all the noise and raucous merriment, a temperance march was underway. Poorly received by the majority of those present, they handed out pamphlets and sang ballads about the dangers of inebriety in the face of ridicule and threats. That took some guts.

So massive was the celebration that dragoons had been dispatched to roam the streets in the event that the spirit of celebration grew too intense. Of course, some of them accepted free drinks from civilians and were getting a bit boisterous themselves.

Marcel asked, "You armed, Irishman, or should we stop over at my boardinghouse first? I've got weapons aplenty."

"I've got an eight-inch dagger and a surplus of wit at my immediate disposal. What more could I possibly need?"

Marcel had himself a long laugh at that. "Impressive munitions, I'd wager, but I still think a couple pistols'll give us the edge we need. We'll stop by my room real quick-like. So, regardin' Alvord, are you thinkin' what I am?"

"If you're thinking that the madman went to Abendroth for healing, then yes."

"I knew he was hurt worse'n what he let on. Imagine that, goin' to Abendroth's fer healin' on the day we planned to kill him. That feller's got some dash-fire in 'im. Sounds like he got healin', but somethin' else happened along the way. You think the mesmerizer can read minds?"

Finnbar shrugged. "You know his powers better than I. It seems likely, if he cast some sort of spell on Alvord. What other reason would he have to hurt him?"

"Well, Alvord is bringin' Deas back to New York, and Abendroth seems to fancy his work. Could be that he didn't want Deas leavin' St. Louis, and figgered that killin' Alvord would be the best way to prevent it. But I guess he didn't kill him, just messed with his mind or somethin'..."

As they walked for a while in silence Finnbar came to detect a subtle change in Marcel's stride. He moved more slowly and with calculated steps, eyes darting from side to side all the while. Finnbar slowed down too, casually following Marcel's sidelong glances.

To their right, by a smoke-belching blacksmith's shop, stood a stout man with a badge on his chest next to a fop whose face was a bruised and scabbed mess.

"We in trouble?" he casually asked of Marcel.

"Think so. That's Sherriff Bogardus with one of those fellers we whupped on yesterday."

"Shall we run for it, then?"

"Yep. If we get separated, we'll meet up over by the—"

"Hold it!" ordered a stern voice ahead of them.

A thin, balding man stared at them with narrowed eyes, pointing a shotgun their way.

They stopped in their tracks. Shotguns often have that effect on folks.

People walked and rode horses all around them, but something about the man's tone implied he had no problem taking a shot at them, bystanders be damned.

The balding fellow kept the gun trained on them while Bogardus stomped his way over.

"So, you boys out huntin' more trouble?"

Finnbar's gold tooth gleamed in the sunlight.

"Are ye startin'?"

"Shut yer spud-eating bone-box, Irishman. I'm Sherriff Bogardus, and several prominent members of this community have identified you as men who took part in an attack on them yesterday that left two of them dead. Needless to say, I've got a fair amount of questions for you to answer. You two are comin' with me."

"Listen," began Marcel gruffly, but Bogardus cut him off.

"No, *you* listen, trapper. I'm the law in this city and I say that I'm takin' the both of you in for questioning. Give me any more lip and my friend'll give you both barrels. Think me a liar-call my bluff."

"Is this lawful?"

Bogardus grinned nastily. "It is if I deem it so, Irishman."

"Well this is rather inauspicious," Finnbar commented.

"Yeah, but they kinda got us by the short hairs here," replied Marcel as the sheriff broke out his cuffs.

Chapter 28

Far beyond the main fray of revelry, in the dark and moldering old French section of St. Louis, Count Gregory Abendroth strode briskly along with Volkmar at his side. The sounds of jubilee reached fever pitch along the main roads, but here it seemed that a dense cloud of gloom shrouded the night air, keeping at bay any joy the outside world might offer.

The streets here were constricted, crooked, and poorly paved. Houses of a vaguely French style slumped with age, some looking to be in danger of imminent collapse. Others were already so ramshackle that they could only be entered from below with a ladder, the lower floor having caved in.

"What a dreadful eyesore," Abendroth complained loudly as he looked around. "One would venture to think that the French, with their ostentatious love of gaudiness, would be inclined to keep tidier homes than this."

His thin nose crinkled as he skirted a crater in the road that contained a dead horse.

"How perfectly revolting. Are there no sanitary standards for this city? They would not abide such filth in Berlin, now would they Otto? I say, one can almost see the miasmic vapors rising from this putrefying district..."

Volkmar nodded and grunted at intervals, wholly unconcerned with his master's musings. Instead he watched the shadows for movement, for already once tonight a roving gang of thugs had tried to rob them. Their efforts had, of course, been met with utmost brutality from Volkmar, whose bloodstained saber and clothing told of the gang's grisly fate. Those were the only people they had encountered while in the heart of the French district, though occasionally the distant sounds of fights or wailing babies could be heard.

"The problem," his master continued, carefully stepping

over a towering pile of ox crap, "is that the French never made the most of this promising location. Surrounded by fertile ground, they rarely put plow to earth. Encircled by forests of mighty timber, they never really bothered to log. Instead they were content to live off the river and reap the rewards of the trapping industry. Understandably, this bred a remarkably slothful race of people. Yet when the fur trade sagged following the Panic of '37, these loafers were forced to confront life in a more productive way. At this they failed miserably—the decrepitude you now behold is the end result of a decade spent skirting honest toil. Not until the arrival of Anglo-Saxon blood and later that of Germans and Irishmen did this city truly begin to prosper again. Actually, this place has taken on something of a New England character, a drastic departure from the indolence of the French and the key to economic prosperity. Farming, logging, manufacturing—those are the industries that made this city what it is today, a burgeoning power on the threshold of illimitable wilderness, situated on the banks of America's mightiest river. What a place to carve out an empire, I tell you, Otto..."

Volkmar unbuttoned his blue greatcoat. Though the night was cold for this time of year, they had been walking for nearly an hour, as Abendroth had insisted on walking rather than taking a carriage. Not that Volkmar minded—there was nothing wrong with a healthy stretch of the legs.

They turned onto Cherry Street, where a long, two-story building made of dark stone took up a considerable portion of the nearest block. It was the city's madhouse. As they stood staring at it a hideous, strangled scream issued from its tiny windows.

Abendroth clapped his hands together. "Ah yes, here we are..."

A pack of rats had congregated at his feet, and noticing this he recoiled and sent them scattering with a wave of his arm. Volkmar felt the brief surge of power that made the hair of his neck stand rigid in its aftermath.

"Filthy creatures, but to be expected in such a hellhole, I suppose."

A large wooden door of solid construction served as the sole entrance to the madhouse. Abendroth firmly rapped on its knocker three times.

Heavy footfalls could be heard a ways off, taking some time to get to the door. When the door finally creaked open, a short, thickset man with a shining bald head stood on the other side.

"My good man," Abendroth began in fluent French, "I am Count Abendroth. I was hoping to take a look at some of your more recent charges."

The attendant's eyes shifted from him to Volkmar and back again, bearing upon his face an expression of utmost alertness.

He bade them enter, however, turning to lead them up a flight of crumbling stairs. Torches lit the way, revealing filthy floors and walls dripping with the water of recent rain.

"So, no pleasure-seeking for you tonight?"

"No, Master Abendroth. Someone must stay behind with the mad."

"Lucky you."

After passing through a long hallway, they came to a dimly lit, circular room containing a large wooden desk and numerous sets of manacles piled atop each other.

A metal door stood on the other side of the room. The bald man walked towards it, sorting through the keys on the ring attached to his belt.

More screams rang out, reverberating off the walls in a most dreadful manner.

"You really wish to see them? It is not pretty in there," the attendant said in English, hand poised to pull open the door.

"Oh yes. As you might know, I am a healer. It may very well be that I can help these people."

The man's lips tightened before he spoke. "From what I've heard, you are the very reason these slaves came to be here."

The mesmerizer smirked most eerily. "Can't believe all that we hear, now can we? Trust me, I seek only to aid them."

The bald man led them down a wide hallway studded with thirty iron doors. Torturous bellows and shrieks met their ears, while a fetid smell assaulted their nostrils; that of decay, fecal matter, and unwashed bodies.

"What are their symptoms?"

Peering through the peephole the attendant answered.

"Varies depending on the day. Sometimes they just sit there listlessly, muttering to themselves in odd tongues, others rant and rave about things coming for them, horrible things... and then some seem okay for hours at a time, only to start throwing themselves at the door and scratching at the walls like animals, like some are doing now. The queer thing is, all of them are slaves or white criminals, and they all exhibit each of the symptoms I just described. It's like a cycle, you know? Some days, when they all act in unison, it begins with them sitting there like dead folk. Then they scream and cry, then they try to escape. Over and over, like some endless circle of Hell. I'm no physician, but I've been here for many years. Never seen aught that compares."

"I see. So each one you have here is similarly afflicted?"

"No, we got twenty-two that were here long before this... *epidemic*, I want to call it. They're just your everyday brand of crazy, not like the rest we got here."

Volkmar peered into one of the cells. A skinny, filthy white woman sat limply on a cot, staring listless at the floor. She muttered sibilant words, her lips the only part of her that moved. As he kept watching, her head slowly turned towards him. When the torchlight from the hall illuminated her eyes, Volkmar stepped back abruptly in spite of himself.

For those were the eyes of a being already in Hell.

"So what do you think you can do for them?" the attendant inquired up ahead, where he and Abendroth observed a frantically struggling black man.

"Alas, it seems as though their minds are rightly fried. It is doubtful whether any power on this earth could restore their sanity. But what I can do is offer them a life of industrious servitude."

"Come again?"

"Servitude. I can assuage their unutterable anguish and put them to work. They can serve me, rather than rot in this unwholesome madhouse."

Round face contorting with perplexity and displeasure, the attendant stared at him.

"You've done enough to these shattered souls. I cannot, *will not* let you do this. Enough evil has befallen them at your hands."

He squared off on them resolutely. Fear appeared amidst

the determination on his face, particularly when he looked Volkmar's way, but he tensed his body in preparation for the approaching fight.

"If you want them, you'll have to—"

"Try and stop us if you wish," Abendroth checked him brusquely, "but I know you've heard of my power. And should that fail, which it won't, Otto here would be glad to offer aggression that is more... immediately tangible."

The man bowed his bald pate and sighed with what seemed to be reluctant acquiescence. Abendroth's smile widened, and he made to walk past the attendant.

The man exploded into action, landing a solid blow to Abendroth's delicate nose before hurling himself at Volkmar. Such was the speed of his attack that he actually managed to land two decent punches to the surprised Prussian's face. These punches, while hard, were hardly enough to put down the likes of Volkmar, who in an instant had recovered.

Side-stepping the next wild punch, he sent the heel of his right hand crashing into the attendant's chin, putting his lights out instantly.

Volkmar stood over the man, looking down at him thoughtfully.

"A bold one," he said quietly.

"Dispatch the benighted fool, Otto," sneered the mesmerizer from the floor, as he tried to stem the flow of blood from his swelling nose.

"No."

"*What?* That's an order, Otto, this is what I pay you for, I'll remind you."

Coldly and steadily did Volkmar hold that hypnotic gaze.

"You pay me to protect you. And pay me well. Have I ever failed at that? I am here to ensure your safety, not kill brave men on your whimsy."

Nodding, Abendroth grinned, teeth tinged red with blood. "Alright, alright. Fair enough. But do this too often and you hazard my displeasure. Disobedience is an unseemly habit to get into and you would do well to remember that, or else—"

"Or else what? You'll work your magic on me? Remember, that doesn't have the desired effect on me. No one is better at this job than I, so let me do that job, and don't ask dark deeds of me unless they directly correspond to your safety.

The man is unconscious; I shall tie him up presently. He is no longer a threat. True, he will run and tell Bogardus after he is found, but nothing will come of it, as Bogardus is in league with us."

The mesmerizer accepted his bodyguard's proffered hand and was quickly dragged up from the cold stone floor.

"Well then," he said briskly, wiping dirt from his single-breasted black frock coat, "right to it, then. Otto, kindly open the cells. Except for those last twenty-two on the end. Those contain the other crazies. They are of no interest to me, at least not tonight."

"Why is that? You could control them easily enough."

"True, but it will be far easier to control those stupefied by improper magnetism. I need to control them *en masse*, and doing so is easier when there is no resistance at all. Were I to mesmerize the others, one of them could conceivably offer resistance, which could lead to my losing control of the whole lot. Those already damaged by magnetism offer no resistance and are therefore a perfect army. Hollow shells. As you well know, a good soldier never questions orders, right?"

Volkmar's jaw clenched tightly at that mocking tone. Without a word he moved to open the doors, noting that the frenzied screams and banging had ceased. After unlocking all but those at the end of the hall, he went back and stood at his master's side.

Abendroth bowed his head and frowned deeply; Volkmar felt the energy welling up around him. When the mesmerizer suddenly raised his hands in front of him, Volkmar's golden hair stood on end as he sensed its distribution throughout the hallway.

Abendroth moved his hands in strange patterns for a while before speaking again. "Alright then troops, up and at 'em!"

The occupants of the cells marched out in unison, turning sharply on their heels to face Abendroth. Volkmar's hand involuntarily strayed towards his sword's hilt. Looking at the closest slave, a handsome mulatto, he saw that her pupil's had dilated almost completely, reducing the brown of the iris to a thin ring.

The twenty people before them were mostly blacks or mulattos, but three whites stood out among them, including one man nearly as tall as Volkmar.

"The three whites. How did they come to be here? Is not white slavery illegal?"

"Two are lowly criminals, but one was actually a white slave. Don't ask me how that came to pass—I haven't the slightest inkling. Choteau and Lynch offered them up as test subjects. But for all intents and purposes, each one is now a slave."

Abendroth raised his right arm and closed his eyes. "Good, good. Soon I will be able to control them from afar, with only the slightest amount of concentration."

Bringing his fingers together into a fist, his green cat eyes snapped open. "March."

The slaves began marching in place like some motley peasant army.

"Putty in one's hands," Volkmar heard his master mutter. "Forward march! Quick step, now!"

His voice rang with unbridled amusement.

Fresh air blew gently across Volkmar's face, air that he breathed deeply of. It was good to be shot of that dismal chamber of horrors.

His master stood beside him, the slave army forming two ragged lines behind them. "Do you know the definition of the word *advent*, Otto?"

"Not offhand, no."

Abendroth inhaled deeply, looking up at the stars. Some rockets lit up the sky, casting an orange glow over his face. He exhaled, and it trailed off into a gleeful hiss.

"Advent means the coming of something great and momentous. And tonight, as we begin to assemble our army, we bear witness to the advent of a grand new age. Imagine, a land ruled by one who wields god-like powers, one who can offer incontrovertible evidence of his greatness! Who will stand against that? Missouri might well be just a stepping-stone. After we meet with my disciples tonight and send them off to their duties, it might be time to plot anew. If their artifice, which is really *my* artifice, succeeds, then expansion might be in the works. Imagine it! If we can infiltrate Missouri's governmental infrastructure, other states could surely fall to us by the same means. Or we could rule the frontier, Otto! A near empty, resource-rich land to populate and lord over? Why not?"

He paused for a moment, chest heaving exultantly. Volkmar saw the madness fade slowly from his face.

"Ah, but look at me! All agog over prospects not even properly examined. Let's go, shall we? Okay, troops! Quick march, chin up, chest out, never say die!"

Abendroth led the way back to the manor. Volkmar walked behind him, every now and again glancing over his shoulder at the marching slaves. Their shuffling steps were not in unison, but for mesmerized *untermenschen* he supposed it was a start.

They skirted Market Street, where the celebration raged on, sticking instead to side roads where they encountered few people.

Abendroth suddenly stopped, as did his slave army.

"One more stop today, Otto. The most important, I might add. Shall we?"

Charles Deas hummed cheerfully to himself as he gathered up some of the smaller paintings in his studio. Already tonight he had sold a dozen paintings to high-ranking members of St. Louis's aristocracy, and some more to visiting men from other Southern states. At this rate, he'd be going back to New York a rather rich man.

His larger paintings he'd made arrangements for; those would be shipped back to New York, to the American Art Union. He was not ready to part with those just yet, not until he saw how much New Yorker's were willing to dole out for them. Sprawling canvases depicting purely American topics like *The Death Struggle, Long Jakes,* and *The Voyageurs* would surely fetch him a pretty penny.

Some of his smaller paintings had proven very lucrative, which was welcoming knowledge as he looked over his remaining ones. Frontier paintings like *The Indian Guide, Wounded Pawnee, Dragoons Crossing River,* and *A Group of Sioux* were ever popular. Although lately, since he had gained some renown, even his genre paintings were selling, so he anticipated parting with *Walking the Chalk, The Turkey Shoot,* and a number of other smaller pieces this night as well.

He glanced around his studio. Indian artifacts still

covered the walls; he would have to pack them up later tonight in preparation for his departure with Rawn tomorrow. Initially he had been concerned about the man's vow to kill Abendroth, but the more he thought about it the more he realized that Rawn's injuries precluded any attempt to do so. He would come 'round; perhaps in a bit he would visit his "rescuer" over at the Planter's, to talk to him about the whole matter.

Plucking an ornate Fox war club from the nearest wall, he swung it back and forth, feeling the balance and lethality behind every swing.

Ah, how he would miss his life out here. Painting in this studio, surrounded by a city full of fawning admirers. Heading to the frontier each summer to consort with frontiersmen and Indians. That was how to live life.

Even this room he'd sorely miss- it had been his place of refuge, the first place he'd eat a civilized meal and sleep in a real bed after those rugged forays into the woods and wilds.

Hanging the club back on the wall, he sighed loudly.

It would be unwise to ever come back to St. Louis. Abendroth had become obsessed with his art, and he knew that his decision to leave had angered the man. Honestly, he had anticipated more resistance from Abendroth, perhaps an attempt to bribe him to stay, but so far, nothing.

It would be a weight off his chest to put Count Abendroth and his dark powers of animal magnetism behind him. His involvement with the man constituted the darkest chapter of his life, one that he must try hard to forget. He had come so close to drifting into utter darkness, for so long he had experienced this feeling of being taken possession of...

That was behind him now. Except—his hidden store of paintings done under Abendroth's guidance! What should he do with them? He did not know if he had the heart to destroy them, so brilliant and groundbreaking were they. He could try to sell the more mild ones... but even they could elicit suspicion and rumors as to his sanity.

It hit him then. He could have them sent to Abendroth! That would be a nice parting gift—a peace offering, and a fine way to rid himself of those heinous paintings. Yes, that seemed to be a good solution to the problem—

The front door exploded off its hinges in a shower of splinters to reveal Volkmar's hulking form.

Getting over his initial shock with admirable speed, Deas snatched the war club from the wall and with shaking hand held it aloft.

Ducking under the mangled doorframe, the Prussian stalked into the room with a broad smile upon his face. Abendroth stepped out from behind him, and in his wake followed twenty or so slaves and bedraggled whites.

"Evening, Charles."

Panic welled up in Deas's throat. "I still have all the paintings; they are in the room behind that red door. They are yours if you want them."

A sinister smile creased Abendroth's face. "Why settle for the works when one can tap their very source?"

Noticing the almost completely dilated pupils of the slaves, Deas frowned. "They are all mesmerized. Where did you get them?"

"These are the erstwhile occupants of the madhouse. Before they served as test subjects, now they are the first recruits to my new army. Tonight marks the beginning of a new order in this land, an event you have the privilege of bearing witness to."

Deas eyes casually strayed towards a nearby table, where his charged flintlock sat uselessly. He took a short breath and burst into a wild charge towards it, but Volkmar beat him there.

The artist backed away warily in a crouch, club upraised.

Abendroth stood motionless across the room, staring down the artist.

"Come, Charles, we can always do this the hard way. Well, not that it is really all that hard for me, but you get the gist."

Deas set his jaw and squared off on Abendroth. "No. I've grown stronger. I can keep you at bay."

Raising his hand, the mesmerizer smirked. "No, you can't."

At the outskirts of the city they passed a group of children, who paused to wonder at the sight of two well-dressed men (one of them a giant) leading a group of marching slaves away from the city.

The largest of the slaves carried an unconscious Deas over his shoulder.

Volkmar, grown pensive by this time, recalled the old German folktale about the Pied Piper, who first led all the rats out of Hamelin with a magical flute, only to lead all the children away after he was refused his pay. The supernatural tale had always made him uneasy as a child, and as he watched Abendroth humming happily to himself at the head of his mesmerized slave army, some of that boyhood fear returned.

Chapter 29

The cold barrel of the Walker Colt rested lightly against Alvord's temple. One quick squeeze, one tiny application of strength, and he could put this dismal world behind him.

Pulling the hammer back, he took a quick breath and prepared himself for death. But as he did this, doubts began cropping up in the back of his mind. His head pounded something fierce as these seeds of new thoughts took firm root. So challenged by these quiet but persistent uncertainties, his resolution wavered.

Like the raging waters of an unleashed dam, reason flooded his mind, casting aside all thoughts of self-pity and death.

Yes, he reasoned, this world might be hateful and vexatious to him, but at least he knew what to expect here. In seeking an escape from his miseries, he would be plunged into the great unknown. Who knew what awaited him there? A moment ago he had been athirst for any avenue of escape, yet now this world of loneliness and sorrow seemed preferable in comparison to the ambiguity that was the next life.

What was he doing? What on earth had he been thinking? *Suicide*—how had he arrived at this insane conclusion, that self-annihilation was the only cure to his ennui?

It hit him all at once, his visit to Abendroth's and the subsequent spell that had been cast upon him. Somehow that memory had been blocked, like his mind had been too preoccupied with gloom to retrieve it. But it came back to him now and he remembered all.

He pointed the gun away from his head and slowly lowered the hammer. Sitting upright on his bed, the smell of lavender, the lavender he had laid down to keep away vermin, floated into his nostrils. It was a delicate, refreshing scent.

"Most impressive," hissed a disembodied voice from across the room.

His eyes widened with astonishment soon converted to terror. Never had he heard a sound more odious. He sat bolt upright, re-cocking the Colt and aiming it in the direction of the voice.

Nothing filled the sights of the gun, but he knew some unseen horror lurked in the room, some malignant entity whose presence tainted the very air. His mouth grew bone dry. He could hear something on the other side of the room; something that sounded like the unfurling of loathsome coils.

The voice seethed with power when it spoke again. It contained no discernible accent but felt ancient, and dripped with malice and ill-concealed scorn.

"I felt quite sure I would have to intervene to prevent your self-termination, but bravo, you dispersed the cloud of gloom that settled over your life most resolutely."

Alvord became quite aware of how very hot it was as sweat began dripping down his face. He suspected that this thing across the room was one of the shadows he had observed earlier.

"I wish to know what you are and why you've come. How you've come, too." Much to his dismay, he detected a slight, nervous quiver in his voice.

The thing chuckled, a deep, sinister sound. "My, aren't you a cool one? Or so you'd have me believe. But I can hear thine heart racing from here, Alvord Rawn, pumping that delectable blood through your veins at an incredible rate."

"How do you come to know my name?" He received no answer. "Is this a dream?"

"Far from it. Stop peppering me with inane questions and take heed of my words. Thy very future depends on it." The voice surged with authority, and Alvord was obliged to lower the pistol and listen.

"There is no need for introductions beyond the fact that I hail from another realm and am as old as human frailty. As I'm sure you're keenly aware, the mesmerizer did far more than just heal thee today. He opened a rift in the fabric separating our two worlds, unleashing upon thine mind entities spoken of only in the frenzied nightmares of the insane."

"Including you?"

"Including me, foremost among them."

A large shadow took sudden form in the room—tall, slender, and regal. It bore some similarities to the outline of a man, though it was far larger and somehow more substantial. Alvord thought he detected wings folding behind the thing, which kept shifting and bulging like some kind of gaseous cloud. It was darker than the other shadows in the room, darker even than the night sky beyond the window.

The oil lamp on his bed stand flared up suddenly, lending light to the room but further obscuring the specter.

Alvord sat there, shocked beyond measure. Here he was, conversing with some spectral being from another realm. The surreal nature of this situation was not lost on him, but what choice did he have but to sit and listen? He could feel the power radiating from this thing, and was in no hurry to anger it again. He stared intently at its form and waited for it to speak.

"Gregory Abendroth has of late graduated from a minor nuisance to a major threat to the stability of our worlds. He has been entering upon my realm for years now, cleaving open cosmic rifts and influencing the beings that dwell there. The earliest of these visitations were sporadic, involving only the weakest of my kind. But recently these forays have grown increasingly frequent and brazen; the rifts larger and more numerous, the beings influenced more powerful. The fabric of our worlds are not meant to intertwine, and should the rifts the mesmerizer opened persist and continue to widen, the merging of the two would engender cataclysm for both."

Alvord asked what he had been pondering since first laying eyes on Abendroth. "How is it that a mere man is capable of feats of such magnitude?"

"A valid question, I suppose. I freely confess—Abendroth is no *mere* man. He is an exceptional one. Through self-hypnosis he can achieve astral projection, and has journeyed to realms of awareness so terrible that most human beings would recoil at the very thought of them. His power is such that he is able to protect himself against even *myself*—as long as he remains vigilant it is impossible for me to destroy him. And trust me, I am under considerable pressure to do so."

Alvord ruminated over this for a moment. "So he pulled you from your world and unleashed you upon me?"

The shadow snorted derisively. "*Hardly.* While I am

unable to penetrate his mental defenses, the mesmerizer holds no power over me either. I merely slipped undetected through the rift he opened, hiding among the small army of others whom he forced through. They were sent to afflict thee with the overwhelming grief and isolation you just experienced. Normally, I would be inclined to let them see their task to completion. In your case I made an exception."

Alvord sensed a lurking motive, but maintained his silence.

"I am restraining my brethren at present. Were it not for that they would be rallying for another attack on thee. And while you were able to counter their emotional manipulation just now, they will never relent, as they cannot return home without accomplishing the task Abendroth assigned them. You cannot escape it. I therefore propose this—aid me this night, and I call off the ravening hounds. I know it was thy intent to kill the mesmerizer on thine own terms, but at that you failed. Had I not deigned to manifest myself before thee, my kin would have returned to finish what they started. Help me to destroy Abendroth and get thy life back. I myself will depart this festering place and will likewise return my lesser brothers to our world. Refuse, and not only will I allow my brethren to renew their assault on thee, I will join in the amusement. And see, whereas the others are a rather impetuous lot, eager to end you and be on their merry way, I am the patient type. I am inclined to let you linger, denying you the outlet you nearly pursued with that Colt you still clutch so uselessly in your clammy hand. Death would be a mercy, but I will not grant it to you in the form of self-negation. You will live a long life of paralyzing depression, misery without interval. What you experienced earlier was but a mild foretaste of things to come.

"So I ask you- what will it be? Our interests are mutual, are they not? We both want the mesmerizer dead for the sake of restoring harmony. You are driven by a curious sense of duty and justice, I by pragmatic self-preservation, yet our endgame is one in the same. But as thou hast failed, things are now to be done on *my* terms. Be you willing to accept that?"

This thing could be lying to him, but what choice did he have? This seemed to be the only way he could both kill Abendroth and free himself from the mental assaults of the other specters.

"I am."

"*Good.*" Languidly the shadow drifted across the room, eventually settling next to Alvord's bed. He could feel the raw power the thing exuded, heard snatches of disjointed whispers flitting about. A droplet of sweat dripped off his nose, but his voice remained steady.

"So, you really need a mortal to aid you?"

"Would I be here conversing with a lower life form were it otherwise?"

A moment of weighty silence followed.

"Come hither," the entity beckoned imperiously.

Stifling his fear, Alvord leaned in and received his instructions.

"Aye. That I can do," he affirmed afterwards.

"*Deal.* Rise then, Alvord Rawn, and woe betide to Gregory Abendroth this night."

"I have never been a pawn before. I like not the feeling."

The thing chuckled dryly. "Pawn? Come now, you needn't self-deprecate! Thou art the spring that sets the greater machine into motion! Great and momentous things are expected of thee, deeds that most would tremble to contemplate. But I have faith in you."

Alvord looked into what he thought to be the shadow's face. "Just as I have faith in my own ability to resist you should you renege on our deal."

The specter let out a sibilant hiss.

"Careful now. That is barefaced pride, and therein lies damnation."

A rushing sound filled the room. Alvord became acutely aware of the thing's absence, as if with its departure the veil of unreality had been fully lifted. He did not have the luxury of time, or else he would have taken a moment to puzzle over the unadulterated madness that had just transpired.

He tucked the Colt into his belt, put the Elgin Cutlass Pistol in its sheath and tucked it behind his back, and put his knife in its boot scabbard. Reaching behind his pillow, he pulled out his truncheon. Slowly he ran his hand down its length, feeling every dent, every chip on its surface. Many were the foes who had fallen to this club. If luck was on his side a few more would be added to that sum tonight.

From his valise he grabbed a small leather pouch and

rose, ready to leave.

Exiting the room in a hurry, he recalled with a shudder the lines of an old poem.

> *The End must justify the Means:*
> *He only Sins who Ill intends:*
> *Since therefore 'tis to combat Evil;*
> *'Tis lawful to employ the Devil.*

Chapter 30

Jail was an entirely new experience for Finnbar. Marcel, having been incarcerated several times before, knew the drill and sat listlessly on the cell's cot. The Irish writer, however, initially leaned up against the iron bars, eager to take in each detail.

Three hours later he sat next to Marcel, bored out of his bloody skull. Having blunted his powers of observation against the bland surroundings, he slumped over and propped his chin up on his hands.

This was the smallest of St. Louis's jails, and Finnbar was willing to wager that it was the hottest, dingiest, and most poorly ventilated too.

Yet the three windows, small though they were, did not prevent the sounds of celebration to drift into the place. The reverberating sounds of conviviality did not assuage any of the profound boredom that confinement engendered.

Only one watchman remained in the jail, a bored, tired-looking fellow with several days' worth of stubble showing. He took deep pulls from a hip flask whilst he waited for his fellow lawmen to return from a trip down to the waterfront, where fighting had broken out between some whites and free blacks.

Finnbar turned his head to observe the guard again. Judging by his frequent, substantial, yet rather casual gulps, Finnbar had him pegged as an inveterate drunkard.

The watchman's comrades had been gone for a half-hour. Since their departure the rays of sunlight had faded from the room by slow degrees, casting gloomy darkness over the cells.

A dozen or so oil lamps illuminated the jail's dank interior. The flickering interplay of light and shadow would have made a fine study in chiaroscuro, quite fit for the brush of Caravaggio himself.

Three other cells in the room stood empty, while the one closest to Finnbar's and Marcel's held a sleeping black man who muttered disconnectedly to himself as he slept.

Finnbar's fingers tapped out a fast tempo on his knees. Never before had he been caged like this, particularly when something significant was expected of him. There must be a way out; to find it he needed to apply his intellect to this maddening predicament...

Alvord needed their help, desperately perhaps, but who knew how long they would be detained here? He and Marcel hadn't killed anyone—how can you hold a little rough and tumble against a man?

The sullen watchman across the room shifted in his seat, causing the large set of cell keys to jingle on his belt. The germ of an idea took root in Finnbar's mind.

"Finn," Marcel suddenly uttered in the best whisper he could muster, "we aren't getting out of here anytime soon, and Al needs us."

"Any ideas?"

"Yeah," said Marcel slowly, watching the man take down some more rotgut. "You any hand at insultin' people? Figger you can get him riled?"

Finnbar grinned slyly. "You want riled, or vengeful in the Biblical sense of the word?"

"Have at, Irishman. Try and lure him close, so's we can grab him and blow this calaboose. He's only got that club, the others took all the guns with them, so it should be easy to get him within proper distance."

The watchman heard noise issuing from their cell and snarled at them.

"You two talking in there?"

"Why, yes." Finnbar replied cheerfully. Twice already he'd been informed that his tongue would be slowly cut from his mouth if he didn't keep it shut.

"Well, stow it. What do two scoundrels destined for a short drop and a sharp jerk have to talk about, anyway?"

The Irishman's dark green eyes narrowed with delight. "Your revolting mother, as it happens, you despicable arse-bandit."

The man's jaw dropped. "What did you just say, you worthless Irish dog? *What'd* you just say to me?"

Finnbar thickened his usually mild brogue, which made his insults sound all the more mocking.

"Oh, hard of hearing, are we? I said we were just talking about your putrescent mother, and trust me, she's proven to be an enduring topic of conversation. No surprises there, really—'tis not often one comes across so heinous a specimen as she."

Clenching his jaw and fists, the guard stood staring at Finnbar with a disconcerting inferno blazing in his unfocused eyes.

"I tell you now, she'd make a blind man praise God above for his sightlessness. Poor lass, not even the tide'd take her out..."

The man clumsily grabbed a nearby cudgel as Finnbar stuck his laughing face through the bars.

"Now me, I'm more the practical sort. I'm actually of the opinion that while she's no show pony, your mother would still do for a ride around the house, if ye catch me drift... say lad, ye seem to take after her yourself, if I might say. Got a face on ye like a well-slapped backside, ye bloody gobshite ye..."

The man charged with a strangled yell, club upraised.

Finnbar timed his drunken swing perfectly, stepping out of the way at the last moment, so when the club found only air the man fell forward with the momentum of his move.

In a flash Marcel had pulled his arm through the cell's bars. Twisting it, he stomped down hard and dislocated the elbow with a loud crunch.

As he did this Finnbar grabbed the watchman by the back of the head and smashed it into the bars. The man collapsed in a heap before them, and Finnbar quickly bent down to retrieve the cell keys.

"Nasty temper you've got there," he tutted the man's supine form as he unlocked their cell.

Marcel stepped over the man, chuckling. "Ho ho! You sure got that feller's bristles up! Good thing he went fer the club!"

Finnbar looked at him in surprise. "Come again?"

"Well, there was a chance he'd go fer the guns."

"Guns? I thought you said they took them all when they went to stop that fighting. You said he only had that club."

"Nah. They didn't take all of 'em, but you didn't need to know that. They took all the Colts, but left a couple 'o flintlock pistols an' a shotgun over in that chest there."

Looking over at the chest, Finnbar smiled roguishly. "I think I know how we can make our stay here worthwhile."

Marcel chuckled knowingly. "Stealin', eh? Serves the bastard's right. Let's do it."

The occupant of the other cell, now quite awake, grabbed the bars of his cell and spoke.

"Suhs? Good suhs? That was some kind of brilliant! How's about a little help for a fellow victim of circumstance?"

Marcel walked over to the man, motioning Finnbar over towards the guns.

"What's the crime, pilgrim?"

The Negro, an older man with graying hair and several scars on his face, spoke fiercely. "I didn't git outta some Louisiana plantation owner's way fast enough. He claimed I tried attackin' him."

"Seriously?"

The man shrugged, smirking good-humoredly. "Nah. Stole a small measure o' whiskey when I thought nobody was watchin'. On a night of celebration like this, any white man'd be let off scot-free, but things ain't great for free blacks here in the River Queen, suh."

Marcel nodded understandingly. "No, I don't reckon they are. So you're a free black? South's the wrong place fer you, friend. Although some say the North ain't much better."

He unlocked the cell. "On your way, then. And careful—lotta race fuedin' out there today."

The black man clapped him on the back and whooped loudly. "Don't you worry about that, trapper ol' friend. I ain't no young, hot-blooded nigga'. I'm like an old mossy-horn stag—don't pay no mind to breedin' or fightin', cause I'm too damn concerned with the business of survival."

"Best'o luck," grunted Marcel, and turned to start collecting the possessions the Sheriff had taken off him. The black fellow ran full tilt out the door without a backwards glance, though he did snatch up the watchman's flask without losing a step.

"That darkie could've been a murderer, you know," Finbarr commented offhandedly.

"Nah. Didn't have it in 'is eyes."

Chuckling, Finnbar thrust his knife back into its leg

sheath before checking to make sure the remaining pistols he grabbed were properly charged. He stuck two into his belt before handing Marcel the two that remained and the shotgun.

"Charged and ready to go. Got some ammunition and powder, too."

"Good. Let's get goin', *mon ami*—they could be back any time now."

"What's the plan of attack?"

"We'll see if Al's in his hotel room. If not, we head for Abendroth's."

At a trot they exited that grimy jailhouse, heading for the looming outline of the Planter's Hotel.

The crowds in the streets scarcely noticed the quick movements of the trapper and Irishman. The celebration reached fever pitch, liquor and beer flowed aplenty, and spirits soared.

Alcohol loosened many a tongue, and from countless mouths came rumors and tales of Abendroth's manor. Some folks had seen him and Volkmar taking his army back towards the manor a bit earlier, and speculated aloud as to its meaning. It seemed that the mystique surrounding the mesmerizer had reached an intolerable height; they simply had to speak of him lest he proved to be a dream. Enough pamphlets circulated among them to offer easy consultation on the subject of mesmerism, and by nine o'clock that night no section of the celebration was without enthusiastic talk of Count Abendroth, the mesmerizer.

Chapter 31

Alvord ran at a slow clip towards Abendroth's manor. Already he had left behind the clamor of downtown St. Louis, traveling now by the light of the waxing moon. Some part of him urged his legs on to greater speeds, but he did not allow it. A great drama would unfold tonight, and it would not do to tire himself out before it had begun in earnest.

At times Alvord ran into dense clouds of mosquitoes that descended upon him in truly disgusting numbers, yet he found they were unable to keep up with him for long. The flies were another matter altogether, for they seemed quite capable of keeping pace.

Striding through The Common he encountered a herd of deer, which fled towards the wood line when they saw him, tails held erect like feathery flags of truce.

At what he figured to be the halfway point, he stopped to catch his breath and drank out of a crisply flowing stream, splashing some water onto his head and chest as well. Though the night was cool he sweat a bit from exertion. He wore only his trousers and a thin brown shirt with the sleeves rolled up. It would be an action-packed night and heavy clothing would only hamper him.

Standing straight he shook his head dry like a dog, flexing his neck back and forth. Never had he felt more powerful, more vigorous- Abendroth had restored his health and then some, and foolishly so.

Making sure the Colt and Cutlass pistol were still firmly tucked into his belt he began running again, his mind going over the endless number of scenarios that could play out tonight. Sure, he had a plan, but he knew Fate to be a fickle friend at best. In all likelihood his plan would undergo many alterations once battle had been joined, at which point fluidity would be of paramount importance lest he botch an opportunity due to stubbornness or hesitation.

A figure appeared up ahead, materializing out of the silvery night. It was an Indian wrapped in a long blanket, sporting a stovepipe hat and puffing on a cheroot. Alvord stopped to investigate.

The Indian was an old man whose silver hair gleamed in the dazzling moonlight.

"Good evening, friend," he said in almost perfect English.

"Evening."

An awkward silence stood between them for a spell, so Alvord spoke again.

"Your English is exceptional. How do you come to speak my language so well?"

"I was schooled in the east, during my youth, and I have used English much ever since. It is the dominant language in these parts, after all."

"What are you doing out here, if I might ask?"

"I seek respite from the noise and confusion of town. Here one can walk and think in peace."

"I hear you."

The old man's dark eyes sized Alvord up with one quick sweep. "You move in the manner of one who has great business to carry out this night."

Alvord chuckled. "I suppose you might say that, yes."

The Indian inspected him closely. "Does Death dog your steps?"

"Yes, but tonight he shall have only those I leave strewn in my wake."

The man nodded solemnly. "I see. As my ancestors might have said, your medicine is strong. You have a great confidence about you, which has carried many a warrior through the frothing sea of battle. Good luck this night, sir."

"Thanks, and fare thee well."

He began running again and felt the courage flowing through his veins, knowing that the old Indian's eyes were upon him as he went. He wondered if he should attach some symbolic significance to their meeting, but did not want to get overconfident.

With a start he suddenly realized that he'd missed his four o'clock meeting with Finnbar and Marcel. They would no doubt be concerned. Oh well. Much as he would have liked to include them in tonight's plans, there was no time to go back for them now. Although who knew, perhaps they had already launched an attack of their own?

Inhaling deeply, he let out a wrathful hiss. Chief Matsell had been right about one thing. Back when his family was intact he had been a different man. With a wife and children to fret about he had grown cautious, restrained. When others rely upon you for support you grow wary of consequence, you don't allow for uncontrolled passion to win the day. His old self would have waited, would have linked up with Finnbar and Marcel, but his new self was urged onwards by some inner demon. A demon born of tragic loss and burning hatred. Yes, he had grown into an altogether different, more reckless man, yet recklessness might lend him the very edge he needed to pull off this monumental stunt tonight.

The trees and meadows and hills glided by, the landscape bedazzled by the silver glow of the moon. Yet evil also tainted the night. He could both feel and see that phantom or demon or whatever it was watching him from time to time, its Stygian shadow hovering just above the tree line like a tattered kite.

Alvord lengthened his stride, eager to bring justice raining down upon the mesmerizer.

His plan was outlined, but he kept going over it and its many possible variations.

He prayed, too. He found himself doing a lot of that.

Alvord came to an abrupt halt. Abendroth's manor lay ahead of him, its bulk illuminated by the light of many candles and torches. Additional torches lined the well-trod path leading to the manor. Under their flickering light Alvord stood stock-still to observe the final fifty yards between he and the home of his enemy.

Voices could be heard inside the manner, voices yelling warnings and issuing orders. Being spotted was all part of his plan, so this did not bother him. What lay between he and the manor did, however.

Ten figures stood blocking his way. They too stood still, their heads all turned in his direction.

Dressed as they were in tatters, Alvord reasoned that

they were not hired bodyguards, as Volkmar was. The light of the torches told him that they were all Negroes that bore the appearance of slaves (or was that a white woman among them?).

The nearest one began shambling towards him quite quickly. By its irregular, jerky movements he realized that these slaves must be mesmerized. Human beings did not move like that. In the split second before he launched his attack, Alvord glanced up at the manor. Silhouetted against a window was a slim figure with its hands folded in front of it. He could not be sure, but felt that this was Abendroth, controlling his army from afar.

Alvord held his position until the slave, a short female, was nearly on top of him. He spun to the side at the last moment, neatly clipping the back of her head with his truncheon. The copper tip cracked her skull with a loud report, but to his profound amazement she rose immediately and came back at him. With twin strokes he shattered both her knees before bringing all his weight into a downward chop that finished what his first blow had started. Her skull exploded in a spray of fragmented bone and brains, and her body slunk over to the side.

These were innocent people under the control of an evil bastard, but alas he had no choice. Their death or at least incapacitation was an absolute necessity. And it seemed that under Abendroth's influence they were far tougher than human beings should be. So death it had to be.

As three more came at him, he side-skipped to close the distance. The one in the middle stood slightly in front of the others; this one Alvord gave a downward swing with all his weight and momentum behind it. Immediately upon landing this killing blow, he threw himself into a fast sideways roll that brought him just behind the slave on his right. Drawing the Cutlass pistol, he used its knife to slice into the hamstring of his foe. The blade found bone beneath the muscle, bringing the slave to one knee. Two sledgehammer blows to the head put it down permanently. The other slave charged in and powerfully crashed into Alvord, sending him flying. Arms outstretched it advanced, and rising Alvord slashed and clubbed its hands aside before landing a sweeping shot to the man's temple. He stumbled backwards, allowing Alvord to sink the blade of his pistol into his heart. Another well-aimed blow to the temple proved fatal.

Turning towards the rest, he took careful aim in the yellow torchlight and discharged the pistol into the head of the nearest one. The .54 caliber ball exited the back of its skull with a sickening crunch, and it staggered a moment before crumpling.

Alvord tucked the smoking pistol back into its scabbard before bending down to pull out his knife from his boot sheath.

The remaining slaves bunched together in preparation for their attack on him. He rushed to meet them at a dead sprint, a grim smile playing about his lips.

Afterwards Alvord stood amidst the mangled carcasses of the fallen, chest heaving. Taking a moment to reload the bloodstained Cutlass pistol, he stared up at the manor. Abendroth remained by the window, peering back at him.

Alvord slunk into the shadows beyond the glow of the torches that lined the path. Clouds obscured the light of the moon, so it would be hard for them to find him in the dark. From here he would wait for Abendroth's other servants to be ordered after him. When they came, he would climb the oak growing close to the south wall and enter the manor from the window. Even if Abendroth had posted sentries there since his last break-in, enough servants should be sent outside to limit their numbers. He could kill them with the Colt from the tree before jumping through the window to confront the mesmerizer.

Two massive, powerful arms suddenly wrapped around his chest, pinning his arms to his sides. Before he could begin struggling, a cloth was roughly thrust over his mouth and nose. A penetrating, overpowering smell wreaked havoc on his nose and tongue, and he plummeted into blackness.

Alvord came to as he was being dragged into a spacious room. He immediately began struggling with all he had but three strong men held him and he succeeded only in getting smashed into a table. For a moment during the struggle Alvord's hands fiddled with something above a pitcher of water, but no one took notice.

He was patted down and his knife was taken from him, his leather pouch too. Already he had been relieved of his guns and truncheon. His hands were unbound but he was still quite weak and disoriented, his futile struggling having left him with a relentless, pounding headache. Before he knew it he was made to sit in a chair, which he was tightly bound to with a length of rope.

"Quite the performance out there, Mr. Rawn. Although I believe you got lucky with that headshot. I did not think that I'd have to use up so many of my mesmerized slaves in battle quite so soon, but that was a nice test run at least. You've reduced my army significantly, but there are always more slaves where they came from. One good aspect of an otherwise baneful institution."

Abendroth stood over him, leering triumphantly.

"Pity you weren't out there, Gregory," said Alvord, "you could have joined the fray."

"Not my style," Abendroth retorted primly, face showing faint signs of anger at the use of his first name. "Brawling like a brute is something I hire people to do for me. Right, Otto?"

"Mmm," muttered his bodyguard as he looked over the Elgin Cutlass pistol with evident interest. Alvord's other weapons were also spread out on a table.

Vision clearing, Alvord saw ten more slaves forming a half-circle around them, beyond which Abendroth's other servants stood watching. Abendroth grabbed a chair and sat in front of Alvord, who frigidly met his magnetic gaze.

"How is it that you came to know my first name? I have told it to none in St. Louis."

"Funny thing, actually. I bumped into a mysterious bloke from London who was all too familiar with your mode of power seeking. He knew your routine as well as your recent history. You know, I have never been made to flee a country like a craven dog, Gregory- you must tell me what it's like."

Face growing flushed with indignation, Abendroth hissed his words. "You have no idea what it was like for me to face a legion of puffed-up secret societies, all of which were hopelessly jealous of my power and all of which eventually sought my ruin. Ah, signs of the times, I suppose. Neither my powers nor Otto's physical prowess were enough to silence my vociferous enemies across the pond, and yes, eventually we were forced to beat a hasty retreat to America."

"A tad undignified, I daresay. By the way, nice nose there. An interesting night, has it been?"

The mesmerizer's face twitched in a manner most unpleasant, and for a moment Alvord thought he was going to attack. But he didn't, instead rising quickly from his seat.

Abendroth's empty chair was placed next to him, but for the moment remained unoccupied.

"Tristan," he spoke to the man who had been dueling with Volkmar yesterday, "kindly retrieve our other guest and his latest work. It is time for him to finish it."

Looking back at Alvord, Abendroth chuckled darkly. "It was ether, in case you are wondering. Otto stole upon you and knocked you out with an ether-soaked rag. Great for rendering unwanted company unconscious, among other things. Although honestly, I am glad you are here, Mr. Rawn. Now you get to see my greatest passion in action, as soon as my other guest is brought in. And then Otto can cut you to ribbons, which should put an end to his recent moodiness. I tell you, he has spoken of little else since first clapping eyes on you, becoming most dismayed upon learning that you had fallen prey to the darkest of my powers. But against all odds you pulled through; now his wish shall be granted. By the by, how did you manage to survive?"

Abendroth's casual tone could not quite mask his obvious wonder.

"An application of will," Alvord replied, recalling words he had once heard spoken by Abendroth. Turning his head towards Volkmar, he added, "I must say, Otto, that was a lowly thing you did out there with the ether. Cowardly. Do you doubt your ability to put me down without the use of chemicals?"

The Prussian clenched his massive jaw. "Soon, Rawn."

"Soon enough. But now Gregory, should I manage to lay low your hired dog here, what then?"

"I harbor grave doubts as to your ability to kill Otto. Most men of his stature have been in few fights, as most men fear size alone. But Otto has had many fights, fights to the death, too, and is the most formidable man I have ever encountered. You're good, Mr. Rawn, but so is he and when two men are equally skilled the bigger man tends to win."

"We'll see."

Abendroth's eyes narrowed. "So we shall."

The sounds of fierce struggle could be heard down the hall, and Deas burst through the door, restrained by two servants. As Alvord watched, he managed to free a hand and punch one of the servants squarely in the mouth. The man went down, swearing a blue stream. More servants piled onto Deas, who soon found himself bound to the chair next to Alvord.

"Looks like your plan isn't going so well, huh?" Deas flashed Alvord a crooked grin that did not quite mask his fear.

Alvord sighed ruefully. "No Charles, I fear it is not. How long has he kept you here?"

He desperately hoped that the artist would not make mention of Finnbar or Marcel, for if those two were planning on launching an attack of their own, the element of surprise would be of great use. Indeed, it might prove to be the only hope for himself and Deas.

"Only for an hour or so. He captured me in my studio. Any ideas for escape?" It was black comedy, but better that than panic.

"I'm working on it."

"He tried to resist, Mr. Rawn," Abendroth interrupted gleefully, "but found himself unequal to the task. Now Charles, did you honestly think I would let you leave after all this time, after the degree of interest I have shown in your artistic development? It would have been a grand life, that of my personal artist, but now I fear that is impossible. You have grown somewhat refractory, and the only way you will remain my painter is if I keep you mesmerized more often than not. And that's no fun for anyone, really."

"Try to get inside my head again and I will tear you apart from the inside out, Abendroth. So help me God I will kill you."

The mesmerizer laughed heartily, his servants joining in. His voice, that voice that was both soft and everywhere at once, was heavily laced with good humor.

"Oh, that's a rippin' good joke, m'boy. The rosiest of delusions! You are my inferior. No man in the history of the world has wielded power such as I. Not even the great Mesmer was able to penetrate the realms of consciousness that I have. And you think that you, a spoiled little artist of nervous temperament, could bring me down? *Pathetic.*

"Charles," he continued, "I honestly understand why you dislike me. I exposed you to innocence-staining evil. But Mr. Rawn, I must confess my bafflement at your ingrained hatred of me. What I do here is simply none of your concern, yet you chose to make it such. And all for the sake of a humanity that you fervently despise? Why? To what end? Now you are a dead man, and for what precisely? I just don't get it."

Alvord peered long and hard into those brilliant, wicked green eyes.

"To show you that no matter where you go, no matter how powerful you might grow, good men will still stand against you; dying if they must, but standing nonetheless."

"Ah," the mesmerizer relied with a sneer, "so you're a modern day paladin, Mr. Rawn? A knight errant?"

"That's the long and short of it, yes. But what really galls me, what really drove me to this, is the inarguable fact that you're a two-bit showman and you flatter yourself with the fabricated title of Count."

He received a slap in the face for that, but Abendroth failed to move Alvord's head in the slightest.

Alvord laughed loudly in reply. "What a bitch! What a frail, effete, craven bitch!"

Deas guffawed loudly and nervously, and Alvord could have sworn that he saw Volkmar hastily stifling laughter.

"Alright," said the mesmerizer, leering unpleasantly, "Enough of that. To business. Before my disciples arrive I need a little project of mine wrapped up. Charles, you owe me something. It is high time that you finish the work you were prepared to leave uncompleted."

Alvord saw the terror flood the painter's dark eyes; saw it etched into every line of his young face.

"*No.* Please, Abendroth, I beg of you. *Don't.*"

With the mesmerizer focused on Deas, Alvord struggled with his bindings, but the knots were expertly tied and his efforts met with little success. Had his legs been free he would have stood and tried jumping in an effort to dash the chair to pieces, but unfortunately his legs were tightly bound as well.

"I can do it without your help," Deas pleaded, "just untie me and let me show you. Let me have one shot at it!"

"No," Abendroth said with finality, extending his right arm. "You cannot accomplish what I need you to unaided."

"Alvord, help me! *For the love of Christ help me!*" shrieked Deas wildly, fighting with all his might against the ropes that bound him.

Alvord had no idea what to say. Words failed him entirely. Rarely had he seen someone in such a state of panic, and never had he been so utterly incapable of aiding someone who requested his help.

He forced words out of his mouth, not knowing what they might be.

"Organize your mind and fight it, Charles!" he ordered sternly. Deas did indeed seem to try in the instant before Abendroth summoned his power.

The surge of energy from the mesmerizer's outstretched hand ruffled Alvord's hair as it passed him. He could feel those alternating waves of hot and cold sweep by his face.

Deas roared with effort, screwing his face up in concentration. But with discouraging speed his face grew blank, and soon he slumped over in his chair.

Abendroth, hand still directed towards Deas, gradually turned his head towards Alvord.

"Do you know what Charles Deas was like before I began treating him? He was one small step removed from a madman, suffering from intense melancholia and constantly fretting over human weakness. Utterly disenchanted with a world he did not understand, he sought solace in destructive behavior. Drowning his sorrows in cheap beer and absinthe, his artwork suffered accordingly. Self-annihilation awaited him just 'round the bend, and seeing this and the waste of talent that would result from it, I intervened and saved his life. His melancholia is no more; his artwork is receiving national recognition. Now one little letter from his chunnering mother and who knows how many threats from you, and he's up and leaving? I think not."

"You know of his mother's concern?"

"Please. His mind in an open book to me."

"Charles," Alvord said loudly, "Charles, can you hear me?"

"He cannot. He can hear only my voice now, but soon he will hear the voice of another. For he is going to encounter one of the beings that live in the realm your own subconscious visited just earlier today. Should be pleasant, no?"

"You subject him to demonic possession for the sake of

art?"

Abendroth stroked his chin pensively. "Yes, I believe the term fits. I make void his mind and place the essence of one of the shadow dwellers inside of it. A weak one that I can control easily enough. But hell, was it not Voltaire himself that said you need the devil in you to succeed in the arts? I myself am inclined to interpret that quite literally."

Letting out a snort of derision, Alvord shook his head hopelessly. "From the arrogance of fools, Good Lord, deliver us!"

"Say what, now?"

"Hell's bells, Gregory, do you really think this won't come back to haunt you? That one day you'll slip up and come to a sticky end? That one day there shan't be the Devil to pay? Those dark beings must be thirsting for your blood."

"My soul, I think," the mesmerizer said slowly.

The knowledge that those beings in fact did and were on his side bolstered Alvord against the growing panic he felt. He was tied up and at the mercy of his enemies, but he had supernatural beings on his side. They would not let him die, would they? A deal was a deal, right?

Directing his gaze once more on Deas, Abendroth ordered him untied. Slowly, he directed him to rise.

"You see his eyes, Alvord? They are red, as are the eyes of these slaves. The ones you cut down out front were simply mesmerized, mere puppets that I could have some fun with. I controlled them as one controls a marionette. But I am no longer messing around. It took much time and focus, but I have placed a shadow dweller in each of these slaves here—weak ones, but preternatural beings nonetheless. They are under my control and take orders from me and me alone. They are not quite so easy to direct and require more concentration on my part, but are far more dangerous than the feeble cannon fodder you so adroitly mangled outside."

Alvord looked, and to his amazement saw that Deas's eyes did in fact glow blood red. Gazing around the room, he found each of Abendroth's slaves with the same ominous red eyes. It was the eeriest thing he had ever beheld.

"That is not what you did to me, though?"

"No, no, all I did was take your subconscious and direct it towards the shadow realm. Once there, you were, I assume, assailed by horrible, dismal thoughts generated by the beings that dwell there. How they love to destroy; most people would have been driven mad, driven to suicide, once under their malign power for a while. Although your body walked through the real world, your mind was stuck in theirs. Yet you were not possessed; possession by and awareness of something are two very different things. Somehow, it seems, you broke through the wall confining your mind to their world and passed through the void to return to our own. In order for me to place one of the shadow dwellers in your body, your willpower would have to be weak, like Deas's, or your mind would have to have been destroyed through improper magnetism, like these slaves here. It is the most advanced, most difficult, and most dangerous feat that I can perform through animal magnetism."

A canvas roughly fifty by seventy inches was brought before Abendroth, who directed the servant to hang it on the wall. He then ordered everyone back, giving Deas plenty of space.

Deas stood limply before him, those red eyes boring relentlessly into Abendroth.

"Get to it, then," he ordered forcefully, and Deas, or the thing inside him, obeyed.

He walked calmly towards the painting. More torches were lit, and now Alvord could make out the other works on the wall. They were the ones from Deas's secret room behind the red door, works made even more ghastly by this setting. The unfinished canvas Deas moved towards was the one Alvord had seen earlier today in Abendroth's gallery, the one depicting a mighty demon seated on a throne, surrounded by devilish little imps, mutilated corpses, and soaring flames.

A cart laden with paint tubes, brushes, painter's knives, and palettes was brought over by the servant Tristan, who backed away from Deas quite quickly.

"Paint," ordered Abendroth, and the thing inside Deas obeyed.

Its movements began with such speed that Alvord gasped in disbelief. Deas's hands moved in a blur, and the canvas grew fuller with the passing of each moment. No human being could paint that fast, could *move* that fast.

"My God," Alvord breathed.

His thoughts strayed to Niccolo Paganini, the Italian violinist whose preternatural virtuosity was rumored to be the result of an unholy pact with a demon. After watching the thing before him paint with such speed, he did not doubt the veracity of that tale.

At one point Abendroth strayed close to the thing as it painted, leaning in to inspect it.

"A bit heavy on the impasto, wouldn't you say?"

Deas's head snapped in his direction in a blur, his bared teeth resting mere inches from the mesmerizer's face. The red eyes glared menacingly but Abendroth held his ground, smirking.

"I don't recall telling you to take a break. Learn to accept some constructive criticism."

The being let out a demonic, stentorian roar that hurt Alvord's ears, but resumed painting nevertheless.

Deas's face and clothes became splattered with paint, but still on he worked, frenziedly.

Abendroth stood behind him, hands clasped behind this back.

"I could really go for a mint julep right now," he muttered to no one in particular.

Watching Deas paint with inhuman speed as the mesmerizer watched with manifest joy, Alvord struggled against the ropes binding him and prayed for deliverance from this hellish nightmare.

Chapter 32

"I'd say he went that way," said Finnbar, pointing towards the manor as he observed the trail of demolished bodies.

Marcel snorted. "Sharp, are you?"

"You'd better believe it."

Their stolen mounts shied away from the smell of blood, so the two men swung down from their saddles and sent the horses back towards St. Louis with a slap to the rump.

Before heading to the manor they had talked their way into the Planter's Hotel, where they discovered Alvord's unoccupied room. Fearing the worst, they asked around the hotel about Alvord, and were heartened when the desk clerk informed them that he'd seen Alvord leave earlier in the night, belt full of guns.

If Abendroth had tampered with his mind or cast some spell over him, it seemed that it had worn off and Alvord had decided to exact revenge. Judging by the carcasses littering the ground, he was off to a good start.

The mountain man was looking at Finnbar oddly. "You ain't cast in the common mold, are you Irishman?"

"What makes you say that?"

"Figgerin' on how we're about to put our lives on the line fightin' the darkest of sorcery, I'd expect some unease or nervous silence or somethin'. Not humor."

"Oh, 'tis but a charade to help me cope," he joked. "I'm an emotional wreck inside, trust me. By the way, what does this Abendroth look like?"

"Average height, royal sorta bearing, a thin, pale face. But it's the eyes that'll signal to you it's him. They're like cat eyes, glowing green as emeralds."

"Got it."

They drifted into the shadows, eyes fixed on the windows of the manor. No guards or lookouts could be seen through the windows, but they took no chances in being spotted. Moving at a lope, Marcel led Finnbar towards the large oak that grew near the south wall, their footfalls muffled by grass still wet from the earlier rain showers.

A horrible roar filled the night air, causing both men to stop in their tracks and wince.

"What the bloody hell?" breathed Finnbar in disbelief.

"Told you, boy. Things that ain't of this earth await us in there. You ready?"

The Irishmen took a deep breath, composed himself, and grinned rakishly. "Born. Shall we?"

Deas continued painting at a preternatural rate of speed. Soon now the work would reach completion.

"You know," said Abendroth reflectively, "there was a time when we had to chain Charles's legs to the floor as he painted. Such was the fury of the wraiths inside him that he was totally unmanageable. I have since become better at controlling them, but about a month ago I slipped up and Charles, at this point no longer being bound anymore, jumped through a two-story window and fled into the night woods."

Alvord shook his head. "And he willingly subjected himself to this?"

"With a smile stamped across his handsome face. He was hesitant at first, understandably so, but once he saw what other artists had achieved under the influence of the shadow dwellers, he decided to dabble in it himself. Pleased with the results, he persisted. Eventually his work outside our sessions here markedly improved, as if some residual vision remained fixed in his mind even after I removed the demon from it. He has me to thank for his financial success and national recognition, truth be told."

"How long has this been going on?"

"The better part of two years."

"So is it Charles or the demon who does all the work?"

The mesmerizer looked at him carefully. "A deep question, Mr. Rawn. The answer is that the thing uses the artist's physical capabilities to communicate visions of Hell. The shadow dwellers have seen it, have experienced it, and each one I place into Charles depicts the same theme without fail, although individual paintings are subject to great variance. So essentially, the artist is the vessel; the demon, the visionary."

"So the shadow realm you enter upon is Hell itself?"

"No, it is not. But the beings there have singular knowledge of the place."

"And you knew to do all of this... how?"

"Years of careful experimentation."

Alvord regarded him solemnly. "What is your endgame?"

"Oh, so you didn't get quite that far?"

"Would I be asking if I had? Tell me."

"Political control of Missouri," Abendroth responded without hesitation. "Perhaps a goodly chunk of the frontier, too. Having accumulated my fortune I will then live in bliss, surrounded by my paintings and healing those who seek it."

"So those men you are training—they will be your pawns? Are they really ready for that?"

"Most of them are, though I'll allow that a few need to refine their technique a bit. They will use their newfound powers of animal magnetism to influence political policies. They are all friends of politicians and can be assured physical contact with them. Some of my protégés will themselves secure seats within the state government, while others will simply be the devils whispering into the ears of the weak-willed. In that instance the power of post-hypnotic suggestion will be our appointed means of achieving our goals, for even after coming out of the mesmeric trance, men can be made to respond to orders that were given while they were in the mesmeric state. Soon enough state policies will be controlled by my men; we will have a hand in most decisions that are being made."

"How is this going to make you a rich man?"

"I cut a deal with my disciples. In exchange for my tutoring them in the art of mesmerism, they each had to give me a substantial portion of their shares in local real estate. That is how *they* became rich, you see. Back in 1803, when the United States first acquired St. Louis, there was no public land for sale, none of the cheap federal lands that made settlement so easy in other regions. Instead, real estate was hopelessly mired in conflicting claims of private land ownership. It turned out that right before the finalization of the Louisiana Purchase, the French had doled out land grants to the wealthiest and most influential men in town. Chouteau, Lambeaume,

Soulard—all are names of great importance in this city, all can trace their status to the land grabs of 1803. To this day people are forced to purchase private land directly from owners, who sell acreage only at a premium rate. I now own a vast amount of the available real estate in St. Louis; already I have seen enormous profit.

"Not only is the land expensive, but one must also take into account the scarcity of building supplies. Do you realize that there is not one substantial pine forest within fifty miles of this city? Not one. Most of our lumber comes down from the Wisconsin Territory. So there you have it. I let the peons pursue political careers, thus ensuring myself peace and protection, while I lead a quiet life. Unless, of course, I choose to set my sights on the control of the frontier... that would necessitate my engaging in a more active role."

"And if they turn on you?"

"They won't," Abendroth assured him. "My disciples fear me as they have never known fear before."

He walked over to the table and poured himself a cup of water from the pitcher.

Draining the silver cup, he smacked his lips and got another cupful.

Alvord's eyes narrowed and his lips curled upward imperceptibly, but no one noticed.

Glancing at the painting, Alvord watched as Deas's head twitched left, right, and upwards at a speed that was hard to follow. He feared for the wellbeing of his body. Too much more of that and tendons would stretch to snapping, bones would surely break...

Redirecting his gaze at Abendroth, he saw that the slaves had formed a gauntlet. As the painting neared completion their heads, like Deas's, began rolling in all directions with frightening quickness. The mesmerizer stood before them, entranced by the unholy joint venture between Deas and the demon.

"I have seen this before," Alvord said quietly.

"What was that?" Abendroth asked distractedly.

"I said that I have seen this before, in a dream."

The mesmerizer stared at him carefully. "Really? A veridical dream, eh? The power of premonition is a useful one. Pity you failed to heed the warning."

"You'll notice I didn't say how it ended."

"*You'll* notice you didn't say how it began."

"I was stuck in a labyrinth, chased by some sinister manifestation of my conscience. After escaping I walked across a desolate plain until I reached a broad and muddy river. Traveling along its banks I saw a temple atop a hill, a temple in which acolytes were being controlled by a pervasive force that filled the place. They were arranged as your slaves are right now. A painting hung beyond a billowing veil, a portrait, and... now that I think about it... I see it clearly, now... all is falling into place, Gregory..."

Alvord could tell the mesmerizer did his best to appear unruffled, but something about his words had definitely gotten to the man. As well it may—the events of this night had been ordained by Fate, all *was* falling into place...

Face more wan than usual, Abendroth attempted a chuckle. "Death will have to wait, I'm afraid. My painting is done and I need to examine it."

The demon inside Deas slowly stepped away from the canvas, head bowed.

"*Exquisite*," breathed Abendroth. "Revelatory. Perhaps my finest yet. Let us see what the title is—ah, *Lucifer Enthroned*. So that's what the chap looks like, then? I rather like the head trod underfoot—a fitting emblem of human mortality and insignificance. I have always favored the *memento mori* motif. I declare! This is magnificent beyond my wildest hopes! And totally unbound by the trenchant strictures of contemporary artistic ideals. Total, refreshing divorcement from prevailing standards, and brilliantly so!"

The painting showed an immense, armored angel seated upon a blood-spattered throne, one foot resting on a severed human head. In one hand he held a massive spear, in the other a spike-tipped whip. His face was long, rectangular, and bony, with sharply defined cheekbones. Brimstone flared up in a solid wall behind him, while little devilish imps tortured human souls before him on the stairs leading up to the throne. But it was the eyes, those yellow, piercing eyes of Satan that really captivated the viewer.

Alvord looked away from the hideous painting, disturbed by what he beheld. "Enjoy it while you can, Gregory."

"Quiet, Mr. Rawn."

"I'm serious. You are not long for this world. Your death rattle will echo through these halls soon enough."

"Right. And you, bound to a bloody chair, are going to accomplish that... how? And if not you, then what other man for the job?"

A deep, resonant chuckle sounded from Alvord's throat. "I am not, in all likelihood, going to accomplish it. But alas, I am not the only one who wants you dead. Those I cut a deal with are not fond of me, detest my kind in fact, but we bonded over the matter of your downfall."

"Kindly get to your point, Rawn," Abendroth snapped with curt impatience.

"I cut a deal with the very ones you loosed upon me, Gregory, and soon your inmost fears will be realized. My associates will feast upon that withered soul of yours. Simply put, your doom has been pronounced."

A spasm of fear wracked the normally composed face of the mesmerizer.

"You rave, man."

Alvord cocked his brow. "Really? We'll see soon enough. Because the opium I managed to spill into that pitcher of water should be kicking in right about now."

"*What?*"

"I said I laced your water with opium. Even if it's not enough to put your head adrift among the clouds, it will break your powers of concentration. I acquired that stuff from a New York Chinamen with a far-ranging reputation for dispensing quality product. So I ask you now—how are you feeling, Gregory?"

Alvord knew he risked being killed where he sat, but also realized that Volkmar desperately wanted a piece of him and might well prevent his master from dispatching him before he was given the chance to indulge that fancy.

Sweat broke out on Abendroth's pale face and he kept swallowing loudly. "I thought I tasted something unusual in that water..."

"Well that's because you did, Greg."

"Shut up!"

Volkmar picked up Alvord's leather pouch and opened it. A yellow-white powder spilled out, which he put a finger to and tasted.

"Opium," he pronounced gravely.

Regarding Alvord carefully, Abendroth asked, "Was this your plan from the get go? To be captured so as to spill opium into a water pitcher that I might drink from?"

"No, but one flows with the stream of Fate."

Deas's body, meanwhile, began shaking violently. Hideous shrieks tore from his throat, sounds so dreadful and otherworldly that one of the servants bent over and emptied his stomach's contents onto the floor. The others clapped their hands to their ears in an effort to shut out the sound. Alvord shut his eyes and turned his head away from Deas; never had he heard such a sound, a powerful blast of elemental torment.

Abendroth raised his hand, closing his eyes as he strove to control the demon inside the painter.

"Careful now," Alvord whispered tauntingly during an interval in the screaming.

"*Shut up*! Otto, seize Deas! Tristan, fetch some magnetized water. Percy, get me a wand from the room at the end of the hall!" He had to yell to be heard over the wild screams that renewed in even greater volume.

The servants sped off to do his bidding.

"Otto, restrain him!"

The bodyguard moved in to do so, but as he neared the flailing body of the painter it began clawing its way up the wall, as had happened with the slave several nights back. Alvord could barely recognize the artist; Deas's face was creased and twisted in a manner most inhuman. Foaming at the mouth, it hissed and roared at all present, red eyes blazing like molten metal. The thing made a terrific leap and latched onto the ceiling twenty feet overhead. Words poured out of Deas's mouth that sounded like Latin.

Volkmar snatched Alvord's truncheon from the table and flung it at Deas, striking him in the chest. His body seemed to lose its suction to the ceiling and he fell hard to the ground.

As soon as he hit, however, Deas rose to his knees and, head thrown back, exhaled as though he were expelling every bit of breath he had.

The servants arrived with their prescribed items.

Abendroth dipped the wand into the water before pointing it at Deas.

"Go pour the water down his gullet! Quickly now!"

Alvord strained against his ropes, desperately trying to loosen the knots. If he could get even one hand free...

All of a sudden the same lurking presence Alvord had felt two nights back during Abendroth's demonstration returned full force. He could feel it circulating around the room like a stray wind, accompanied by the hollow roar that seemed to have its origin some miles away.

Tied up like he was, Alvord felt even more vulnerable as the thing passed by him unseen. Was this the entity he had dealt with earlier?

Abendroth seemed to take no notice. Directing the wand at Deas's head he advanced, his servants half a step behind.

To Alvord's surprise Deas came up fast, sending a stiff right hook into the mesmerizer's face. From the sound alone Alvord could tell it was a fine shot, and it floored Abendroth immediately. Alvord noticed that Deas's eyes no longer shone red.

Deas lashed out at the closest servant and sent him reeling. But as he grappled with the next one, Volkmar descended upon him. Grapping the painter by the shirt collar, he effortlessly flung him against the wall. After taking a moment to get back up Deas moved in to attack him, but the giant Prussian merely backhanded him across the face. Though made with an open hand, the blow connected with a sound like a small caliber gun and sent Deas spinning and eventually crashing to the floor. Gamely he began rising, but suddenly grabbed his head and went down again. Writhing in agony, he let out one last scream before going quite limp.

Alvord feared that Deas's mind had snapped under the strain of possession, but was glad that he had exorcised his own demon—it was proof that Abendroth was indeed weakening.

Abendroth, punched twice in one day, got up cursing most eloquently.

"Seize him!" he snarled, raising his hand towards the corner of the room where the dark presence could be felt. Alvord felt the sudden pulse of energy that the mesmerizer sent at it. A moment later the thing no longer filled the room with its tainted presence.

Volkmar and two other servants moved in to grab hold of Deas, but then the door to the room was flung open and

Finnbar and Marcel dashed in, guns blazing.

Relief flooded his chest, even though he knew they were only two men against over twenty. But they did not hesitate and showed no signs of fear, and that, Alvord knew, took a certain kind of person. The kind of person to place great faith in.

The Irishman fired a flintlock point-blank into a servant's head before snatching a torch from the wall and braining another man with it.

Marcel let loose with a shotgun that blew a hole out the back of a shocked servant. He then drew a brace of pistols and fired both at once. Before the men he shot even hit the ground, his knife was out.

The remaining servants charged them, but the slaves took no notice of the action. Alvord reasoned that Abendroth had yet to give them an order. Either that or he was unable to muster enough power.

He hoped it was the latter.

Being tied to a chair while a battle raged just feet away was the most unbearable, helpless feeling he had ever experienced. Enemies attacked his two friends and he could do absolutely nothing about it.

Finnbar fired his second pistol, dropping another servant. Their numbers dwindling, the servants hesitated.

Alvord watched as Volkmar calmly but quickly grabbed Abendroth by the shoulders. He opened the door leading to an adjacent room and made to push his master inside, but before he could Marcel threw one of his empty guns, striking Abendroth squarely in the back. The mesmerizer gasped loudly but carried on. Volkmar too entered the next room and closed the door behind him.

The servants were unarmed aside from one man who had snatched up Alvord's confiscated knife. This man engaged Marcel in a wild knife fight, but the mountain man's blade moved faster than the eye could follow. It was not long before the servant slumped to the ground, the fingers of his knife hand reduced to stumps and his slashed throat rendering his screams little more than hoarse moans.

Also armed with a knife, Finnbar engaged a group of unarmed servants who tripped over each other in their haste to get out of his way. Their retreat brought them to the opposite side of the room, buying Finnbar enough time to cut Alvord loose.

"You alright?" he asked of Alvord.

"Fine," he answered, glad to be free once more.

Bursting from the chair Alvord joined his friends as they charged the remaining servants who clustered together at the back of the room.

At first he thought they might surrender, but at the last moment they came out to meet them with a shout, some wielding torches.

Alvord dodged a wildly-thrown chair and, swinging accurately and with pent-up anger, knocked two servants unconscious in the blink of an eye. He took a moment to stomp both men's throats, and they twitched and gasped spasmodically when he did. A savage thing to do, but there was no time to take prisoners in this all-or-nothing fight.

Marcel and Finnbar cut the rest to ribbons, though they took some punishment doing it. They were brave, these minions of Abendroth's, and all fought to the last gasp but one, who died begging for mercy. The last man standing was the one named Tristan, who snatched a torch from the wall behind him and flailed it at Finnbar's face. The Irishman ducked the flaming torch that singed his hair, but received a vicious kick to the face as he did. Tristan aimed an overhand shot at his head, bellowing loudly. Finnbar spun to the side, avoiding the torch, and sunk his knife into his enemies' liver. The man shrieked and ferociously head-butted Finnbar, who staggered backwards, knife still lodged in his opponent. Luckily the head-butt hit his cheek and not his nose or mouth, and he recovered quickly.

Tristan made as if to rip the knife out, but before he could Marcel hurled his own with evident expertise. The knife found his throat; he collapsed and spent his last moments gagging on his blood.

Marcel yanked both blades out and handed Finnbar his.

"Fierce bastard, that one. You good?"

"Peachy," Finnbar replied, wiping blood form the nasty cut the head-butt had opened on his cheek.

"Quickly," urged Alvord. "The slaves. Kill all of them—they are demonically possessed and controlled by Abendroth."

Marcel immediately moved in to oblige him, but Finnbar held back.

"Demonically possessed? But they're just standing there. Maybe he can't control them—do we really have to kill them all?"

"Look at their eyes. I don't expect you to understand but there are supernatural beings trapped inside of them. I don't like it either, but we haven't a choice. They will be absolutely deadly if unleashed upon us. It is a necessary evil."

He grabbed his Colt and Cutlass pistol. Three slaves he shot in the head with the revolver but his fourth was a misfire. Swearing bitterly, he realized too late that he should have left himself more rounds. Colts were known to misfire and he still had Volkmar and Abendroth to deal with.

He therefore kept his Cutlass pistol loaded and used his truncheon to dispatch the other slaves. He aimed his swings at the back of their heads, were the spinal cord met the skull. As each one fell, they let loose with that loud exhalation that Deas had made when the demon left his body.

Finnbar and Marcel used their knives to systematically kill theirs.

"This just doesn't feel right," muttered the Irishman. He raised his knife to stab the next slave in the heart, but was suddenly grabbed from behind and sent flying across the room.

Two slaves remained; it seemed that at last Abendroth was able to order them to fight. One was the tall white criminal, while the other was a black slave—shorter, but equally broad. Both now stared at their assailants with evil eyes, baring their teeth.

Alvord instinctively raised his Colt and shot. One round missed but the other round found the white slave's stomach. The thing inside him merely snarled tauntingly. Taking careful aim Alvord hurled his now-useless pistol, which the man deftly caught.

"Al!" Marcel shouted, backing up, "Go fer Abendroth. We'll take these!"

"Right!" Alvord replied, tossing Marcel his truncheon. "Just know that Deas is over there—check that he's alright before you come after me."

And he raced into the next room.

Marcel helped Finnbar up and they turned to face their foes. Both slaves dwarfed them, standing taller and significantly broader. Their red eyes glowed like hellfire, and twisted smiles warped their faces. With raspy hisses, they advanced unhurriedly.

"Shit," Finnbar and Marcel said in unison, and charged.

Alvord flew into the next room, a long one with a high ceiling and many sculptures and tapestries lining its walls. The first thing he noticed was Abendroth slipping through a door on the other side of the room.

"*Damn!*" Had he been just a bit quicker...

But there was no time to worry about that, for Otto Volkmar strode purposefully towards him holding two swords.

Honor. It was a quality that Alvord respected in friend and foe alike, and much as he hated to admit it, Otto Volkmar had it in spades. It would have been far easier to shoot the colossus before him and be done with it, smarter too, but what was he if not honorable?

So he placed his Cutlass pistol on a nearby table and walked out to meet his enemy.

In his right hand Volkmar held an unsheathed blade, which shone brightly in the torchlight. In his left he carried a sword of similar size still hidden in its iron scabbard. Smiling broadly, he tossed that one to Alvord.

Alvord caught it by its haft and, spinning swiftly, launched the metal scabbard at Volkmar's face with a sweep of his arm and a rasp of metal on metal.

The Prussian skillfully deflected it, but just barely in time. Both men crow-hopped to close the distance, meeting with a roar and an almighty clash of steel.

Never, not even in the frenzy of war, had Finnbar thought himself a dead man. But now, as the life ebbed out of him, he was forced to consider the possibility.

The Negro had him pinned to the table and was slowly choking the life out of him. Already the Irishman's face was bruised and bleeding from multiple punches, and his ribs stung from a vicious kick. The demon inside him lent the slave incredible strength; not helping matters was the fact that he seemed impervious to pain. Several times Finnbar had landed his best shots to the man's button and slashed and hacked deeply with his knife, but to no avail.

Gasping horribly, he managed to bring his legs up and push the man back a bit, taking some of the pressure off his throat. But the slave still had him, and Finnbar's legs were fast tiring.

His straight-edged knife was lodged in the man's sternum up to its crossguard, but apparently that wasn't enough. He used his feet to kick the handle of his knife left and right, widening the already gaping wound. The thing bared its teeth, dripping saliva onto his face.

Suddenly and quite unexpectedly it reared back, roaring in fury.

It turned and Finnbar saw that Marcel had used a torch to set its ragged clothing on fire. It bellowed with rage and advanced on Marcel, whose hands were suddenly full dodging the flurry of sweeping punches his adversary rained down on him.

The Negro grabbed the burly trapper and hurled him across the room like a ragdoll. Both slaves then advanced on him, and Marcel, nursing his ribs, was slow in rising.

Finnbar picked up Alvord's truncheon and raced towards them. The massive white slave was dealt a devastating shot to the skull with it. As the other slave turned on him, he reached out and tore his knife free from its chest. Marcel brought the Negro crashing down with a clever leg sweep and followed it up by thrusting his bowie knife into the hollow of the slave's throat. He had to be careful, as some of the slave's clothing was still aflame. It spewed forth a torrent of blood but still managed to lash out with a punch that landed on the trapper's chin.

Marcel felt his legs give out beneath him but caught himself just in time.

Finnbar struck the white man again on the crown with the truncheon, then rammed a shoulder into him that sent him staggering away.

He turned to help Marcel, and together they stabbed and bludgeoned until the black slave's head was pulped, attached only by the spinal cord and a few tendons.

Bleeding profusely from the face and limping slightly, Marcel moved in and slammed his blade through the man's eye socket. His body twitched in a paroxysm of death as the shadow dweller left his body, and then he lay still.

"That should fix 'im," panted Marcel. "Go fer the head'n the spine, seems to be the only way put 'em down."

Finnbar made as if to reply but both men were snatched up from behind by their collars and swung aloft. Turning their heads, they stared into the maniacal face of the remaining slave. The wraith within him howled insanely and threw both men backwards into the wall.

They fell hard, taking more than a moment to recover.

Finnbar looked up and saw the giant leering at them, its partially crushed skull cocked to the side.

"These things are devils to take down!"

"Yep, this ain't gonna be pleasant," Marcel commented.

For all the years of fencing and sword training Alvord had done, nothing could have prepared him for this. The fight between he and Volkmar was conducted with deftness and speed that left little room for either error or excessive planning. It was attack, defend, survive; life reduced to three basic principles as the men engaged in a vicious *danse macabre*.

No initial feints or probing thrusts were made. They did not perform the preliminary circling that combatants often engage in as they search for weakness and gaps to exploit.

They had clashed decisively and in the early stages of their fight all was fury and raw power.

For the first twenty seconds of their duel, each man sought to overpower the other, resorting to heavy, all-or-nothing blows. Yet none of these found flesh, meeting instead only the polished steel of the other's sword or thin air. The sounds of their mighty clashes and the hiss of sword edge on sword edge resounded throughout the room.

Massive overhand and underhand swings were met with desperate ripostes and lightning counter attacks, and at the end of that first flurry of action they had locked hilts. They stood at a standstill for a while, each pushing with all the strength he could muster but neither quite gaining the upper hand. But Volkmar, being taller, had more leverage and in the end shoved with incredible force, sending Alvord stumbling backwards.

This was swordplay at its most dangerous—neither man was armored in any way, clad as they were in trousers and thin shirts, while the 15th century hand-and-a-half swords they brandished were capable of lobbing off a limb or head with a single stroke.

They broke for a moment to snatch a few breaths before charging in again. Both men eagerly sought the role of the aggressor, but so well matched were they that the ebb and flow of the fight had them regularly switching from offense to defense.

Volkmar vacillated much between a two-handed and one-handed grip, and seemed fond of taking misleading steps to draw Alvord off guard. His height gave Alvord fits, for he was not experienced with dueling taller men. That sword point was always in Alvord's face, disrupting his guard. To counter it meant expending more energy than his opponent, for to move a sword upward was far more taxing than bringing it down.

Feinting high, Volkmar swept his blade down low, seeking Alvord's right knee. Alvord hopped back and lifted his leg just in time to avoid the blow, but the Prussian lashed out with a backhanded fist, knocking him off balance. He stepped in quickly to capitalize on this opportunity, but was met with several high-low slicing combinations so swift that he had no choice but to retreat.

Circling for a moment, they finally settled down and looked for any weakness the other might offer. Finding none, they met with identical overhand hacks. The tremendous reverberations sent through the steel hurt Alvord's hands, but he recovered just in time to perform a spinning duck to avoid his opponent's next slash. As he spun he whipped his sword around and fully extended his arm to add distance to his slice.

A thin red stain appeared on Volkmar's white shirt just below his naval. Alvord knew it was but a flesh wound. And a man with Volkmar's size and power would take many a flesh wound to weaken.

Alvord parried two high, chopping strikes, on the second one using his crossguard to shove Volkmar's blade aside. Bringing his sword around he opened another shallow cut along the Prussian's right side. His sword ended up deflecting off a rib as it cut, but he quickly regained control of it and backed off.

Ha! The Prussian might boast enormous size and immense strength, and his bulk might belie his quickness, but here he was getting the best of the man. Emboldened by his two small victories, Alvord faked a low thrust and sought to drive the point of his sword upwards through his adversary's throat. To his surprise, before his feint was even completed a painful pressure occurred on the inside of his left thigh. This was followed by an icy sensation that quickly yielded to a fiery burning. He knew he'd been cut badly and stumbled backwards, away from Volkmar's questing blade.

Suddenly he was on the defensive and frantically so. Volkmar drove him relentlessly backwards, cold fury consuming his face. As best he could, Alvord parried the hammering strikes that sent waves of pain through the length of his arms. His very bones ached from the blunt force. Several times he succeeded in turning Volkmar's blade, but too off balance was he to make anything happen.

Volkmar threw an unanticipated kick behind a canting slash, driving his heel into the cut on Alvord's leg. Sword not poised to strike, Volkmar delivered a left hook to Alvord's face before lunging back to avoid his enemy's flailing blade.

Alvord gritted his teeth against the searing pain. He had been maimed, but he could not go berserk and simply try to out-violence this adversary in a state of blind rage. This would require calculation and better yet, speed.

Time to up the tempo.

Shouting with pain and anger, Alvord parried another high strike and beat Volkmar's blade down with a successive chop. The force of it bent Volkmar's body sideways, but he immediately turned it into a quick, rising spin.

In a moment of intuition Alvord anticipated that exact move, dropping to one knee and thrusting his sword. His enemy's weapon hummed through the air just above his head.

He heard the gasp and felt his sword find flesh. The first few inches of his blade were lodged in Volkmar's abdomen. He went to drive it home but, moving like greased lighting, Volkmar kicked the crossguard of the sword and dislodged it. He then slashed sideways, before being forced to snap his head to the side to avoid an oncoming counter-thrust.

They broke, but advanced again after gulping some air.

One-handed, Alvord brought his sword up and around for a low swing but found nothing, as Volkmar had stepped back. He was slow in recovering his blade, and Volkmar grabbed his sword arm and ran his blade across Alvord's right triceps. It bit but not too deeply, for the sword blades, while sharp, were not nearly so keen as good quality knives.

Yet he knew the injury would soon render his right arm nearly useless in terms of wielding a sword, so he determined to either end this now or try and make this a battle of fists.

Dropping his weapon into his left hand Alvord took the sword's pommel and smashed it into Volkmar's face, targeting an eye but striking his forehead instead.

Volkmar immediately staggered back and then stood still, his eyes and flaring nostrils the only parts of him that moved. Alvord stopped as well, unsure of how to proceed. He did not want to lunge blithely into some trap.

Suddenly his enemy struck like a coiled viper. Before Alvord could move to block, Volkmar's sword cut into the flesh just below his left ear. It was a fast thrust that had been made, and only the very edge of the blade caught him, but *God* did hurt!

"A nice *Schmisse* for you," the Prussian sneered between breaths.

Alvord happened to know that word to mean "honor wound" but did not have enough breath to say so. Volkmar also panted heavily, moving more sluggishly than before.

His next attack was a high thrust, and Alvord decided to take a chance and attempt a disarming move he had learned from the *Fechbuchs* his old German sword instructor had owned.

Sidestepping the thrust, he locked crossguards with Volkmar and lashed out with a kick that connected with the man's groin. His grip faltered, and Alvord pulled his sword away from him with a twist of the wrist. The crossguards remained locked and Volkmar's weapon was promptly dragged from his hands.

Unfortunately, this move not only threw the Prussian's sword behind Alvord, but so sweaty were Alvord's palms that his own sword went flying as well.

Cursing bitterly in German the Prussian brought his fists up and they doggedly renewed their fight.

By this time Alvord's right triceps had tightened up considerably due to his wound. Though he raised it along with his left he knew he would not be relying on his dominant hand. This lent complication to an already unusual situation for him;

generally he fought as the taller man, making use of his superior height and reach. But Volkmar had about five inches on him and proportionately longer arms, meaning that Alvord would have to adjust his style accordingly.

He baited Volkmar into throwing first. After skillfully batting the punch down with an open hand he lunged in with a left hook that thudded into Volkmar's blocky jaw. He would have figured that punch to contain enough force to knock any man out, yet the giant Prussian merely stumbled back a few steps, shook his mighty head clear, and waded back in.

He landed two fast, straight punches that snapped Alvord's head back, but Alvord was able to counter with a jab-hook combination that opened a sizable cut under the bodyguard's eye.

Barely reacting to the punches, Volkmar feinted a right and swiftly went in for a takedown. Alvord sprawled without a moment to spare, slamming his hands into his enemy's shoulders to stop his momentum before snapping the man's head back with a short but cracking left uppercut. This he following up with a kick, but his foot missed by a small margin as the Prussian reared back.

Volkmar quickly took notice of Alvord's disinclination to use his right hand and began circling fast to Alvord's right, making it nearly impossible from him to land a solid jab or hook.

With an expeditious half-spin Alvord attempted a backhand with his good arm, but Volkmar caught it with ease, kneed him in the back, and hurled him to the floor. He rushed in to land a kick but Alvord rolled and rose so quickly that he checked himself.

With a sardonic smile Volkmar began circling right again.

Alvord decided to simply deal with the pain and unleashed a totally unexpected right off a feinted left, which broke the Prussian's nose. Although fiery pain lashed at his wound, Alvord knew that he needed to make the most of this opening. His subsequent uppercut again snapped Volkmar's head back and a flurry of high-low jabs and hooks had him giving ground. His body shots thudded into the Prussian's thick abdomen, and he could tell that only a perfectly placed punch to the ribs would hurt the hulking man to the body. Twin rivers of blood poured down Volkmar's face; he had to keep spitting to keep the crimson liquid out of his mouth.

In a blind rage Volkmar unleashed a number of wild punches, throwing with all of his two hundred and eighty pounds.

Most of these Alvord either blocked or slipped, and he was even able to counter here and there, but some were driven home. And hard. He caught two on the ribs and actually felt his bones bend inward with the force. The next punch landed on his temple and quite suddenly Volkmar was on top of him with his hands around his throat.

But the Prussian had not yet brought his elbows together as he applied pressure. Before he could, Alvord inserted his own arms between them and snapped them outward. This broke Volkmar's hold, and in the next moment Alvord drove the heel of his left hand upwards into the man's chin whilst he freed one leg with which to kick the giant off of him in a herculean effort.

Volkmar soared through the air and landed hard. Both men rose, took a moment to snatch a few ragged breaths, and then met again, punching, kicking, and elbowing with everything they had left, each determined to finish on top.

The remaining slave charged Marcel, having just put Finnbar through a table. The mountain man gamely stood his ground and at the last moment dipped left. Knife in a reverse grip, he sliced the blade across the hollow where the leg met the pelvis. In doing this he severed the femoral artery and much connecting tissue, but still the thing hobbled around, trying desperately to get its hands on him. He lobbed off several of its outstretched fingers just as Finnbar launched himself off a chair to shove his knife through the back of its neck. The man came crashing down, bleeding in dozens of places. Stabbing madly, Marcel severed what remained of its neck.

That accomplished, he sat back and panted. "Damn, but that was some kinda frantic."

Wincing as he walked over to help his friend up, Finnbar added, "Bastard nearly finished me there. Let's check on Deas and then see if we can't find Alvord."

But Deas was already up and staring around the room

calmly.

"Charles, you alright?"

Deas stared at Finnbar quite blankly.

"Deas," Marcel said gruffly, "What's wrong, son?"

"Not sure," the painter murmured.

"We don't have time for this," Finnbar said urgently.

"Listen, boy. You go wait outside the manor fer us, got it? We'll come get you soon. Sound good?"

"Sure Marcel," Deas responded, eyes unfocused. "That'd be just fine, thanks."

He began walking away mechanically.

Marcel shook his shaggy head. "That boy ain't right."

"Can't worry about that now, unfortunately."

They pushed open the door to reveal Alvord and Volkmar going at it hammer and tongs across the room. They rushed in to aid their friend.

Alvord, who was doggedly going punch for punch with his hulking enemy, saw them coming and tried to tell them to stop and let he and Volkmar finish this. But he simply could not find the breath.

Marcel came in, knife held low, but Volkmar's massive hand shot out to grab him by the collar and hurl him into Alvord.

Finnbar came in slashing back and forth like a dervish. Volkmar received two small cuts to the arm before he managed to grab hold of his assailant's knife hand, which he twisted until the blade dropped from it. He kneed the Irishman in the gut and sent doubled-up overhand fists into his back when he bent over.

But then he was backing up, for both Alvord and Marcel limped his way, and already the hardy Irishman was trying to get back on his feet.

Outnumbered and utterly spent, the Prussian warily gave ground.

Alvord snatched up Finnbar's fallen knife and brought his arm back to throw it.

But as he looked his enemy in the eye he slowly lowered the blade. After a fight like that, this was no way to end things.

Nodding tersely to Alvord, Volkmar hurled himself out of the open second-story window behind him.

They heard the impact of his body on the ground below,

heard the sound of pounding feet as he fled.

Alvord rushed over to the window and could just make out Volkmar's outline as he tore towards the forest.

Perhaps he had just made a dire miscalculation, but he could not help but feel that Volkmar would have accorded him the same respect had fortunes been reversed.

Content with his decision, he bent over and tried to catch his breath.

"Must've been some scrap," Marcel commented as he looked over Alvord's wounds.

"That it was, Marcel," he panted in reply.

With Volkmar gone, Alvord took a moment to bind his wounds with some shredded pieces of curtain. That would do for now, but pretty soon he would need proper medical attention.

He then picked up his pistol and limped as fast as his injured leg allowed towards the door through which Abendroth had disappeared. He could hear Finnbar and Marcel close behind him.

He opened the door; only a few candles lit the room inside.

"Otto?" Abendroth's voice inquired hoarsely.

"Not quite."

To Alvord's surprise Abendroth rushed past him, running full tilt. He ably dodged around Finnbar and Marcel as well, heading for the room containing Deas's paintings.

Alvord raised the Cutlass pistol and the gun spat eight inches of flame into the air. Normally a moving target was tough to hit with a flintlock pistol, but he had loaded the gun with birdshot. The mesmerizer screamed and stumbled, but continued moving. He slammed the door shut behind him and sought to lock it, but Finnbar slammed a shoulder into it and it swung wide.

He advanced on Abendroth slowly, driving him into the center of the room. Marcel and Alvord caught up and stood on either side of him.

Eyes narrowed, Alvord held his arms out to prevent the others from getting any closer to the mesmerizer.

"His life is not ours to take."

Abendroth extended his hand and attempted to mesmerize Alvord, who showed no reaction. He cocked his head to the side quizzically.

"You've grown completely refractory," Abendroth said in a curious tone.

"So I have."

"Break the deal you made," he suddenly implored Alvord, desperation in his words. He held one hand to his back, where the pistol's shot had struck him.

Marcel and Finnbar looked at Alvord in confusion, but did not say anything.

"No, and I doubt that it would do you much good anyway."

"Then at least concentrate and help me fend them off. Your aura is powerful; you may well be able to muster enough animal magnetism to help me. I cannot focus properly with that opium clouding my mind. Aid me here, help me keep them at bay, and I will personally instruct you in animal magnetism. You could become powerful, even as I am."

"I am decidedly uninterested."

The panic faded from Abendroth's face by slow degrees, replaced by a look of grim resignation. He nodded thoughtfully.

"A refusal of awesome power, eh? Now that's character, Alvord, and character is destiny."

The torches and candles in the room flickered, and Alvord observed a shadow descend from the ceiling. A rushing sound filled the room, as though an unseen vortex drew water towards its turbulent center; he knew the demon he'd cut a deal with was making its appearance.

Abendroth too sensed it and looked wildly around. The shadow slowly faded, and with it the rushing sound subsided. The four men stood in place, searching the room for some sign of the thing.

A slight movement caught Marcel's keen eye and he pointed, speechless.

All present followed his trembling finger until their eyes rested on the most recent addition to Abendroth's painting collection, *Lucifer Enthroned*.

The figures in the painting were moving. At first it was just barely perceptible, but as they watched the painting came to life with movement and sound. The imps around the throne gleefully tortured screaming human souls, as crackling flames of brimstone licked the top of the rocky cavern they were in.

Reactions varied. Marcel stood there dumbfounded, mouth agape. Finnbar kept shaking his head and muttering incredulously to himself. Abendroth, and Alvord really had to give him credit here, was apparently fascinated.

"How extraordinary," he exclaimed. "They've never done that before."

As Alvord watched in frozen awe, the figure representing Lucifer slowly stood up. Crushing a human skull underfoot with an all-to-realistic crunch of bone, it winked at him as it raised its spear in salute.

"It's about time, Alvord."

He knew that voice would haunt him the rest of his days, as once it had haunted his nightmares, but at the same time stubbornly thought to himself that it was about time *it* showed up. Abendroth had been drugged for a while now.

More sounds filled the room, the sounds of meat being torn from bones and bubbling flesh and demonic howls along with a legion of other awful noises, creating a Hellborn litany that rebounded off the walls with maddening volume.

In a scene of phantasmagoric horror all of Deas's paintings sprang to life, each one enacting what the human imagination would generally be left to speculate about.

"Ye've got to be shittin' me," breathed Finnbar in disbelief.

"Let's go!" shouted Alvord above the ruckus, taking a moment to snatch up his fallen truncheon, knife, and Colt. "It's their turn now and I sure as hell don't want to be around here for it."

His friends required no second bidding and raced each other towards the door.

Alvord limped after them but ventured a backwards glance as he reached the door to the hallway.

Mesmer's disciple stared at him with narrowed eyes, arms flung out to the sides.

"Such is the price of taking a glimpse beyond the veil," Abendroth stated quietly, with a sad little smile.

Alvord saw the shadows descend upon him from the paintings. He left the room and slammed shut the door, but not in time to drown out the screams of a soul being dragged to some new dimension of horror.

Deas was waiting for them outside. Alvord limped out of the manor last, hindered by his leg wound. Seeing this, Finnbar and Marcel rushed over to support him, though they themselves could have used a shoulder to lean on.

Deas looked past them blankly.

"Charles," Alvord asked him, "Charles, are you alright?"

"I don't think so," replied the artist hollowly.

Alvord clapped him on the shoulder. "You did well in there, son. You fought bravely."

"Oh," he said vacantly. "Well that's good."

Something was not right with him, but it might just have been the stress of a night chock-full of insanity. Alvord found himself hoping so because after what the painter had endured, permanent mental damage would not be surprising.

They began making their way back towards town, but a sharp cracking sound issued from the manor behind them, echoing off the nearby hills.

Turning in curiosity, they listened in silence. Another crack hit their ears, followed by many more. These combined into the thunderous sound of collapse, and they all watched incredulously as the manor of Count Abendroth imploded in a billowing shower of stone. And it did not just fall apart; it was reduced to fine powder, like grain in a gristmill, so all that remained atop the hill where it once stood was a slowly settling cloud of dust.

"This will certainly be something for the memoirs," Finnbar whispered in utter wonderment.

Chapter 33

It was early yet, so neither the heat nor the crowds were unmanageable on the docks of St. Louis. A mist shrouded the Mississippi, through which boats glided phantomlike. Men and boys fished from the docks, their occasional yells heralding a catch. Porters trudged sluggishly towards their appointed posts, yawning and complaining about life in general.

Alvord, leaning on a cane, stood with Deas, Finnbar, and Marcel, staring into the obfuscating mists that cast their tendrils over the wharves. He and Deas were due to board their steamship soon.

He had needed four days of recovery before departing for New York, and even now the stings and aches served as painful reminders of a desperately fought battle against an unspeakable evil and one tough Prussian bastard…

He was worried about Deas. The painter stared at the swirling water below them, eyes unfocused and features blank. Rare were the times when he chose to speak, and the responses he gave to questions posed were brief and often unrelated to the topic.

And, Alvord had noticed, every once in a while Deas's head would snap to attention and he would stare at something that wasn't there, terror consuming his face. At least, nothing *seemed* to be there. But Alvord was not so quick to dismiss things that he could not see anymore. He now knew what horrors lurked just beyond the boundaries of human perception.

As for himself, he figured that the demon had kept its promise. No thoughts of doom and gloom drove him to contemplations of suicide, no specters appeared to him. He felt normal, aside from the pain he experienced. Somehow he felt that the dark being he had dealt with, while evil in ways he probably couldn't grasp, had a sense of honor. He knew not why, but his instincts generally served him well.

Like himself, Finnbar and Marcel both walked with noticeable limps, faces marred with nasty bruises and cuts. But Alvord knew their spirits soared with the elation that follows a hard-won victory, and rightly so. What they had overcome on that wild night at the manor of Count Abendroth...

These were men he was proud to know, proud to have fought and bled alongside. Men like these were few and far between, he knew.

They hadn't told a soul about the events leading up to Abendroth's death (aside from Valda and her father, who had eagerly sought them out), but just a day later St. Louis was abuzz with talk of the mysterious and powerful Count Abendroth and his obliterated manor on the hill. False stories were in fast circulation; Alvord could not help but smile each time he heard that an earthquake or twister had done it, or God himself had smote the man and mansion.

"So Al," Marcel said, "You given much thought to that trappin' expedition up Michigan way?"

"I have been thinking about it quite a bit, actually. I have some things to attend to back in New York, but after my affairs are settled I will meet you back out here as soon as possible. I'm in."

He had been deliberating over this ever since Marcel had brought it up yesterday. There was nothing for him back in New York and the thought of relocating to some new city held no appeal. After all the reading he had done about exploration and wilderness living, after all the yearning for a life of frontier adventure, it was time for some firsthand experience. He would go to Upper Michigan and become the woodsman he'd always wanted to be. He had no family to think about, no emotional ties to sever—he could disappear into the frontier and not be missed by a soul. The time was ripe for a change, and he was hard put to think of a better one.

The mountain man smiled broadly, his beard twitching. "Glad t'hear it. We'll be waitin' right here fer you when you return. Then it's time for adventure that only the woods and wilds can offer."

"Sounds good. You have my address—send off a letter detailing how I shall find you once I return."

The captain of the steamer they would be taking began

shouting, urging people to board. Alvord had a black porter take his and Deas's belongings aboard. Many of the artist's belongings he had arranged to be shipped back separately, but he still took along a goodly sum of luggage.

"Charles," asked Finnbar with concern on his face, "you going to be alright, lad?"

"No," the painter whispered hauntingly.

Alvord exchanged worried looks with his two friends.

"Perhaps all he needs is a bit of time."

"Could do the trick," said Finnbar with unconvincing optimism.

"Well gentlemen," said Alvord shaking their hands, "See you soon enough. Probably within a month. Until then, you take care."

"Easy ridin', friend," grunted Marcel.

"*Sláinte*," Finnbar offered.

"I am not privy to that word's meaning."

"It is an old Gaelic salute to health. Have yourself a good trip. We'll have a pint waiting for you when you get back, brother," Finnbar assured him.

Alvord boarded and soon enough the steamer was chugging its way downstream. Moving to the back of the boat, he saw a rugged trapper and a wry Irish writer waving to him.

With an unrestrained grin he raised his fist in silent salute as the swirling fog enveloped them.

Three weeks later

Manhattan lay drenched in the moisture of its own humidity, although by St. Louis standards it would be considered a mild day.

It was good to walk around—their return trip had been a nightmarish affair, fraught with a host of technical difficulties and unforeseen complications.

Alvord still walked with a slight limp; he no longer needed a cane but the wound to his inner thigh was not yet fully healed. His arm had knit itself up nicely, though the wound left a sizable scar. The spot where Volkmar's sword had nicked his cheek below his ear healed as well, although no hair would grow there, leaving a thin gap in his beard.

New York was greener than it had been at the time of his departure. The elms and maples now bore fully formed leaves and a variety of flowers blossomed in the gardens and parks.

Full of happily chirping birds, a lapis sky stretched cloudlessly in all directions, but Alvord's thoughts were stormy and troubled.

He did not know what to tell Charles's mother, though long and hard had he sought the right words. In the three weeks it took them to get back to New York the painter had barely spoken, and when he did it was about mesmerism, to Alvord's profound disbelief.

Although he tried to remind the painter of the madness that resulted from mesmerism, Deas remained unmoved. He spoke of religion too, and how animal magnetism and religion could somehow be linked together. He made little sense and often stopped speaking in the middle of his sentences.

After a while, Alvord had stopped talking to him altogether.

He had an unsettling suspicion that Deas would never regain his sanity. Bringing this hollow shell of a man back to his worried mother was one of the hardest things he had ever done.

Sixty-three Franklin Street stood before them in all its stateliness. A flock of sparrows perched noisily upon the windowsills, scattering in all directions as Alvord and Deas approached.

"You are home, Charles. How does it feel?"

"Oh," murmured the painter. "Home. How nice."

His face was drawn, and the circles under his eyes hung low and dark. Sleep had rarely come to him, Alvord knew, and he muttered fiercely when he did manage to snatch some shuteye.

With a deep breath, Alvord knocked on the door.

The servant whisked it open as if he had been standing there waiting.

"Mr. Rawn, is it?"

"Yes. I have here with me—"

"Is that...?" he asked anxiously, peering around Alvord at Deas.

"It is."

"Master Deas," proclaimed the servant joyfully, "welcome home! Your mother will be overjoyed to know you are back."

Deas stared at him blankly.

"Oh."

The servant frowned slightly before he grabbed Deas's baggage and left to get the painter's mother.

Anne Izard Deas came swiftly to the door, relief flooding her face.

"*Charles*," she breathed before tightly embracing him. He did not hug her back, and noticing this she held him at arm's length and looked at him searchingly.

"Are you alright, Charles?"

"I think so, mother."

"Welcome home, my son."

"Yes, home. That's right." His voice was hollow, bereft of emotion.

"What was your trip like?" she asked of Alvord slowly, frowning at her listless son.

Alvord sighed and shook his head, looking at the ground.

"It was a descent into madness, Mrs. Deas."

She looked from him to her son and back again. Her eyes lingered on his new scar.

"What happened out there, Mr. Rawn?"

"Horrors."

She stared deeply into his eyes for some time.

"What of Count Abendroth?"

"Dead. Worse, actually."

"Killed by your hand?"

"More or less."

Her lips grew thin and she nodded at him. "You are an exceptional man, Mr. Rawn. I will not bother you for the details, but I am sure that you displayed a great amount of valor and resolve in this. Do come in, and allow me one moment to fetch the remainder of you reward money."

He put a gentle hand on her arm to restrain her as she turned to go back in the house. Mrs. Deas turned around with a look of confusion on her face.

"Yes?"

"It is Charles, Mrs. Deas."

"He is just a bit tired from your journey, is he not?" But her very tone revealed that she doubted her own words.

"Keep your money, Mrs. Deas. I... I have failed you. Had I acted faster, with greater resolution, perhaps—"

Mrs. Deas's looked him in the eye. "Mr. Rawn, I paid you to retrieve my son and bring him back to me. In that you have succeeded, and I am forever in your debt."

Alvord eyes were downcast as he spoke in a quavering voice. "That is not your son, Mrs. Deas."

She made as if to speak, but then closed her mouth and looked at her son, who stared blankly at the sky.

"Take him inside," she firmly requested of her servant before turning back to Alvord. "How? What happened to him?"

"Abendroth unleashed unspeakable evil upon him. In the end your son broke free from it, demonstrating great courage and fortitude, but the damage was done. He has been like this now for three weeks and shows no signs of improvement. I am sorry beyond the telling of it, Mrs. Deas. I don't know what to say beyond that I do not deserve this money."

She took a deep breath and closed her eyes tightly before talking. "Take it anyway. It is the very least I can do. Life is a cup we must drink to the dregs—you did as I requested and what remains to be dealt with is my affair. Had you not afforded me your services I feel quite certain that Charles would be worse off than he is now."

The servant brought out the other half of his pay.

"Take it," Mrs. Deas firmly insisted.

He did, but could not meet her gaze as he did it.

"Look at me."

He looked into her dark eyes. There was strength there, fierce resolution too, but he could discern the grief that she tried to mask.

"We cannot alter Fate. I am eternally grateful for this and I ask that you remove this burden from your conscience."

She held out her hand and Alvord shook it.

"Goodbye and good luck to you, Mr. Rawn."

"S'long, Mrs. Deas," he said miserably.

Pockets full of money he did not want and mind full of recent memories he longed to forget, he began walking away. When he reached the street, he cast a last look back and saw Charles Deas standing by a window, watching him.

With a sad little smile, Deas waved to him.

Alvord returned the gesture. As he resumed walking,

tears welled up in his eyes, and uncharacteristically he made no effort to stem their flow.

Epilogue

March 23, 1867
Bloomingdale Insane Asylum
Vandewater's Heights, upper Manhattan

On the fourth floor of the elegant Federal brownstone building known as Bloomingdale Insane Asylum, Head Physician Dorian Blaine toiled diligently under the yellow light of a large oil-lamp. Although it neared nine o'clock at night, a recent influx of new patients had augmented an already daunting workload.

One of these new inmates suffered from the worst case of catalepsy he had ever seen, and he had seen plenty in his day. Another was trapped in a perpetual state of nervous prostration and required constant supervision by day, leather restraints by night. They and the other new arrivals needed proper medical assessment, a ponderous duty that fell to him.

The incessant ticking of the clock was beginning to get to him, and his writing speed increased in his haste to be done.

A few minutes later Blaine finished his last report with a triumphant flourish of his pen. For the past five hours he had been consumed with nothing else but patient histories, lists of symptoms, potential diagnoses, and proposed treatments.

A weary sigh escaped his throat as he pulled off his glasses to rub his strained eyes. Reaching into a draw of his desk, he pulled out a half-empty bottle of brandy and poured himself a decent measure of it.

He rose from his chair with a groan and strode over to a window, stretching his back out.

Bloomingdale Asylum was the only place in the state of New York where the mentally ill could be properly hospitalized. Since 1821 the institute offered its services for all those who could afford the cost of it. Well-financed, it was a first-rate asylum and one of only a few in the entire nation. Situated on a beautiful piece of property, it was ideal for the patients—tranquil, and away from prying and judgmental eyes.

The moonlight illuminated the grounds behind the asylum, although the shadows cast by the colossal oaks and chestnuts did blot out some of it. But Blaine could still make out the tasteful walks and gardens, the two orchards, and the large green barn that sat before a field used for growing wheat. Farming and gardening were good distractions for the mentally distraught patients; indeed, some of them actually proved quite adept at it.

As he watched, two deer, a doe and its spindly-limbed fawn, began browsing along the edge of the field as a rotund raccoon rooted around in one of the gardens.

Despite the long hours and manifold responsibilities, Blaine loved what he did. The good he was able to do in a world awash in suffering and strife lent a welcome sense of validation to his existence; he was truly blessed to be in such a position.

A proud patriot, he had volunteered his services as a surgeon during the Civil War, his stiff walk serving as a token of that service—several pieces of rogue Confederate shrapnel were yet lodged in his left leg.

But his focus and specialty had always been treating ailments of the mind, so after the war he had attained this position on the recommendation of a friend and officer in the army, who had developed a great respect for Blaine during the course of the war.

Draining his glass, Blaine went back to his desk when someone rapped on his office door.

"Come in."

A young man entered the room. His name was Horatio Jones and he worked as an attendant at the asylum.

"Good evening, Mr. Blaine. I am sorry to disturb you at so late an hour, but I feel obligated to tell you—"

"Is it Charles Deas again?"

The attendant nodded wearily. "It is."

Blaine sighed wearily. Charles Deas had been admitted back in 1848 and had not been released since then. Not even once, making him one of the longest running patients Bloomingdale had ever seen. Generally he was docile and quiet enough, but there were times when his frothing insanity surpassed that of any other inmate.

Blaine rubbed the bridge of his nose as he spoke. "Listen, Jones. I realize that his talk can seem vivid and quite real, but trust me when I tell you that it is naught but the raving of a very sick man."

"But his condition has worsened these past few days. And tonight he told me that the demons he speaks of were coming for him, that they had been whispering to him all day, he fears that he cannot hold them off any longer... you should have heard him, Mr. Blaine. I think that—"

"That what?" interrupted Blaine distractedly. "That we should break out the crosses and holy water and stand guard like a flock of superstitious Catholics?"

He composed himself and heaved a haggard sigh. Jones was an enthusiastic and intelligent young man who would one day make a fine physician. The lad did not deserve to be spoken to like that.

"Forgive me. It is late, and my workload has rather strained my patience. I know better than you what a tragic case Deas's is. You probably don't know this, but there was a time when his art was recognized on a national scale. Indeed, he was hailed across the land and even toasted in Europe for his grand frontier paintings. But something happened to him when he was living out in St. Louis. This was also before your time, but in the early part of this century animal magnetism, or mesmerism as it was also known, was a very popular form of faith healing. But it was also known to induce insanity if performed improperly, and from what his mother told me before she passed, his melancholia and violent fits could be traced to improper mesmerism during his time out West. When he returned from St. Louis he was a changed man, and his art began to reflect his emotional turmoil and religious psychosis. It was a well-known fact that he was occult-obsessed and something of a monomaniac on the subject of mesmerism. In fact, that was the original diagnosis given to him upon his arrival here. Religious anxiety in combination with monomania concerning animal magnetism. He was convinced that his art would flourish if he could but fuse it with the principles of mesmerism. How one does that is rather beyond me. His talent remained intact for a bit, mind you, but his subject matter was... *unholy*. There's simply no other word for it. One work, entitled *A Vision,* was one he claimed to have lost back in St. Louis but wished to recreate. I saw it myself—a naked man suspended from a ring above a dark pit, being torn to pieces by hellish serpents and demons. Never have I seen the like. Some swooned at the very sight of it and one critic vomited, claimed the figures began to move..."

The young attendant shuddered. "I see. It makes sense, for those things he talks about—"

"Are confined to the realm of the imagination, thankfully. His mind is horribly diseased, Jones, his every waking moment is consumed by fear—frankly, death would be a mercy for him at this point."

A roar that caused both men to jump into the air tore through the night. In its wake came the alarmed howls and screeches of the inmates.

"What in the blazes was *that?*" Blaine's heart fluttered and his limbs grew weak. Another insane howl of unbelievable volume and depth assailed them, causing both to clamp their hands to their ears in an effort to escape it. Each day Blaine dealt with screeching madmen and women, but this sound was unlike anything he'd ever heard.

Suddenly, Deas's constant talk of demons and the powers of Hell seemed very real. Even to him, a skeptical man by nature.

"Someone needs help!" proclaimed the young attendant as he raced out of the room.

A human being could not make that noise, of that Blaine was positive...

Every shred of instinct told him to stay in his office, but Jones had left and if he ran into something—

Ah. He was being a fool. It was just a frightened patient with an extraordinary lung capacity, was all, but Jones might need assistance anyway.

Yet Blaine grabbed his 1858 Remington revolver all the same.

Running down the seemingly interminable hallway towards the roars as fast as his lame leg permitted him, Blaine turned a corner and spotted Jones up ahead.

"It's Deas, sir! It's coming from his cell! Quickly now!"

Jones possessed dash-fire that far exceeded his own, Blaine had to admit. The young man fumbled with his keys, but by the time Blaine caught up to him he had sprung the door's lock.

The first thing he noticed was a body falling through the air as if it had been dropped from the ceiling. It was Deas.

The former artist hit the ground with a meaty thud and began writhing and flailing in paroxysms of pain and anguish that were impossibly rapid. Mouth foaming and eyes rolling in his head, he was the very picture of madness. Although his weekly fits could be awful, Blaine had never seen Deas in such a state. Nor had he seen any person in such a state. The human body could only endure so much stress before it broke altogether...

But it was not just Deas that disturbed him, although the man's inhuman roars did set his hair on end. Something *unseen* was in that cell with him, Blaine could feel it. Something... *tainted* and unequivocally evil circulated around that room like a whirlwind, and all of a sudden he fancied that he saw an immense shadow hovering above them, blacker than the other shadows in the room. Blacker than the inkiest night.

"Back, Jones, *get back*!"

But the daring attendant dashed forward heedlessly and attempted to restrain Deas, who sent him flying back towards Blaine with a mighty sweep of his arms. Jones hit the floor hard and Blaine swiftly began dragging him out of the room.

With an odious hiss the shadow descended on the desperately struggling Deas. A moment later Blaine felt a pulse of energy pass through the room, knocking him off his feet. Jones flew into him and the two began crawling away from that scene of horror.

And then Deas's erratic movements ceased. He slumped to the floor with a rasping death rattle and gave up the ghost right then and there.

Blaine's breath came in massive gulps, and it took him a while to regain control of it. His heart ached, his limbs felt weak and rubbery.

"Are you okay, boy?"

Jones, staring at Deas, nodded and replied in a trembling voice. "Think so. But he's not. Did you see that thing, doc? Is it gone?"

"I... I don't know..."

"Sweet Mother of Christ! Look at his face! And his hair!"

Jones paused, breathing heavily.

Blaine stared at Deas's ashen face. Never had he encountered such a vivid presentment of horror. The man's contorted features were frozen in a mask of pure terror so appalling that it made Blaine's stomach knot up. Deas's hair, a glossy black just yesterday, was stark white and standing on end.

"What happened to him?"

"I am... well, I am going to call it apoplexy and leave it at that. Whatever just happened here is best left unexamined."

"You are going to lie in your report?"

Blaine ran a hand through his gray, thinning hair. "No, I shall merely omit some truths. The world at large loves to hear of such things, but in the world of science such claims would only be met with derision. Our asylum does not need bad press. So apoplexy it is. This stays between you and I, Horatio."

"Right, of course, sir..."

Jones slumped against the wall, bit his lip and put a shaking hand to his chest. "You saw it, did you not? That *thing* that got him?"

As he stared at Deas's wasted face, Blaine shook his head solemnly. "No, I did not. And neither did you, boy. Forget about this night. Though a skeptic by nature, even I concede that there are things which mankind is not meant to witness or indeed even perceive of. Working here, you sometimes sound the very depths of insanity and find that it extends far beyond the scope of the human imagination, far beyond indeed..."

The attendant's confusion was obvious—was this the same head physician who did not go to church and allegedly professed no belief in the supernatural?

"I do not understand, doctor."

Looking up towards the sky that lay beyond the asylum's ceiling, Blaine frowned. "Do you know why I am a skeptical man? It is because at my core I would rather not know what is out there. I think, Jones, that Charles Deas trespassed into a blasphemous realm and took a peek behind a door that no man should even stand before, and that we just bore witness to the dread results of that fatal curiosity."

Historical Note

An actual 19th century American painter who was quite eminent in his day, Charles Deas is now considered a quintessential, if somewhat enigmatical figure in American Western painting. Although his career spanned a mere eight years, his works came to draw critical acclaim and were much sought after, particularly his epic frontier canvases like *The Death Struggle, Prairie Fire*, and *Long Jakes*. Many of the works I describe are ones that have been either preserved throughout the years or recovered over time. A good many more have unfortunately been lost to history. However, through the tireless efforts of Carol Clark, Professor of Art and American Studies at Amherst College and foremost expert on Charles Deas, more and more of his works are being uncovered. For anyone interested on learning more about Charles Deas or the period of American history in which his art flourished, I would highly recommend her book, Charles Deas and 1840's America. Without this highly enjoyable and informative work I would have had little but a few fragmentary blurbs about Deas to work with.

By all accounts Deas went insane in St. Louis, Missouri in the mid 1840's; it is apparent that his obsession with mesmerism (the occult forerunner of hypnotism, developed by Franz Anton Mesmer) lay at the heart of his mental illness. By the spring of 1847 he was back in New York, where his condition did not improve and his new, hellish works elucidated many a startled and outraged review. Whispers of madness were well placed—by 1848 he was admitted into Bloomingdale insane asylum, where he lived out the remainder of his days.

As for mesmerism and Mesmer himself, they were both quite real and astonishing, and arguably a bit frightening. Mesmer reportedly cured everything from blindness to asthma through the use of his eponymic "science," which was somewhat akin to modern hypnosis but professed a belief in a cosmic fluid that pervaded all things and could be used in a healing capacity. What began as a European occult phenomenon soon crossed the pond, where it was seized upon, hopelessly perverted, and eventually discarded. Little is known of Mesmer's latter days, wherein he shunned the scientific community and retreated to his old home in Meersburg, Germany. Though in his later works he did admit that his science merged with the occult at times. Such a gap in knowledge presents a writer like myself with ample opportunity to speculate. And as is the case with so much regarding the mysterious life of Charles Deas, likewise is the painter's journey from St. Louis back to New York a mystery. Mesmer's Disciple is my fictional (and somewhat fanciful) take on how it could have gone down.

Hope I didn't disappoint.

Turn the page for a sneak peak at Edward Swanson's **Madoc's Legacy**, the exciting sequel to **Mesmer's Disciple**.

Prologue

Upper Michigan. Mid-October 1823

Lake Superior's southeastern coastline, the very picture of serenity just an hour ago, now writhed in elemental fury. Amidst slashing rain and a fiercely keening wind, a frothy cavalcade of nine-foot whitecaps battered the sandstone cliffs that comprised the Pictured Rocks. Only occasionally did these soaring, multi-colored walls of rock, natural arches, and sea caves give way to isolated beaches, yet the shipwrecked captain and crew of the doomed schooner *Otter* were fortunate enough to find themselves on such a beach. Had their ship gone down a bit closer to the cliffs they would surely have been drowned to a man.

Captain Elijah Thurgood acknowledged this, although he was also acutely aware that good short-term fortune would soon give way to long-term suffering. Hands clasped behind his back, he stood apart from the others, straight-backed and unflinching even as the elements tore at his coarse, rawboned face.

Drenched in icy lake water and thoroughly disgusted with his fate, Thurgood resigned to the fact that he should have stayed out among those hissing waves and gone down with his floundering ship. Many would accept a ship's captain doing so as a matter of course, and that nagged him.

In defiance of gravity, water collected at the tip of his hooked nose in a rapidly swelling drop. This he blew off with a quick, contemptuous puff of air, gritting his teeth as he continued to stare hypnotically at his forsaken vessel. From atop his vantage, a rocky promontory just above the beach, he solemnly watched his ship convulsing in her death throes.

The Hudson's Bay Company schooner *Otter*, his beloved craft, listed heavily to her starboard side eighty yards out into the heaving lake. The forty-foot vessel of fifty tons burden would not last much longer. Hammered by waves and taking on water, she continued her inexorable descent into the yawning depths of Lake Superior.

Even as he watched the waves consuming his boat, he could not help but marvel at their color. That luminous, crystalline aquamarine water was oddly tropical in appearance, totally belying the frigid water temperatures and harsh climate of Superior's southern shore. That color never failed to amaze him, even now, when almost certain death loomed on the horizon upon which his ship was currently sinking.

Yes, he should have stayed aboard. But to his credit events had transpired with astonishing speed. One moment he was struggling to pilot his crippled ship; in the next, it seemed, he was in a violently pitching birchbark canoe with the remnants of his crew. That canoe now lay hopelessly shattered on the beach, of no use to anyone. Formed from bedrock, the beach stretched out into the lake like a natural wharf, half its length submerged in shallow water. The waves had driven them headlong into the shore, a match even for the vaunted skill of the voyageurs guiding the vessel.

This late season run to Fond du Lac at Superior's southwestern corner had been routine, the return trip smooth until now. When the storm descended, their homeport of Sault Ste. Marie was but a short day away. But hopes of making that safe haven were dashed when a jagged rock from an unseen reef staved in the hull near the stern, snapping off the rudder and splintering the keel.

Silently he cursed Bechard and Alrinach, the demons of tempests and shipwrecks respectively. If he listened closely enough, he fancied that he could hear their mocking cackles amidst the wind-churned waves.

As he continued watching, the *Otter* gave a sudden lurch that submerged all but the prow, figurehead, and bowsprit. Those too began to sink; the rough-hewn, wooden otter that served as a figurehead seemed to stare with lifeless eyes at Thurgood, silently imploring him to take action and save it from so wretched a fate. Shortly thereafter the tip of the bowsprit disappeared altogether, and with that the wrathful lake was once again unsullied by the mark of man.

Sweeping off his black, tri-corner oilcloth cap, the Captain placed it over his heart with due reverence. Recalling the times, both fair and foul, that he'd known aboard the *Otter,* a void slowly expanded in his heart until it consumed his entire chest. Heralding Nature's victory, the knife-edged wind gusted with a hollow roar, setting Thurgood's voluminous overcoat to billowing.

"Ave atque Vale," he muttered softly. Hail and Farwell. Nodding gently to himself, one corner of his mouth slowly lifted and curled into what might have passed for a self-deprecating smirk.

He had made a serious miscalculation in his effort to survive; life was only to be treasured when sustainable. And here, on a cold, rugged wilderness shoreline that rarely saw the presence of man, with exceedingly limited supplies and winter fast approaching, how sustainable could life possibly be? Hope had taken wing, leaving them for the vultures.

Yes, he'd miscalculated for sure.

The smile faded by slow degrees, leaving Thurgood's wind and rain-lashed face stony.

Huddled together in a ragged assemblage, the twelve surviving crewmen all stared intently at their captain as he turned to address them.

"Well lads, another one lost to old *Gitchi Gummi.*"

The Hudson's Bay Company had first conceived of the idea for a fleet of fur-trading ships on Superior around the turn of the century, so as to combat increased competition from their hated Northwest Company rivals. And sure, the HBC might have outlived the Northwest Company by dint of absorption in part because of Superior's streamlined trade, but was it worth the price? The better part of the fleet lost along with the lives of their crewmen?

For of the five ships, the *Speedwell* alone now plied the untamed waters. And with a mistress as tempestuous and capricious as *Gitchi Gummi*, how long could the *Speedwell* hope to last? The legacy of the Superior fur schooners would come to rest on the mighty lake's bottom along with the ships themselves.

As one of the few Company employees with any serious sailing experience, Thurgood had been swiftly (and perhaps impetuously) installed as a captain at the tender age of twenty-one. The life had been lonely and dangerous, with no reliable charts to guide him (his own attempts were now lost to the lake), none but a few irregularly shaped natural harbors to seek refuge in.

"What now?" inquired a swarthy half-breed named Henry in a hollow voice.

Thurgood's dark eyes took in his crew at a glance. Most of these men were not proper sailors. That had not helped matters. Six of his eight able seamen had been lost along with some trappers and their entire cargo. He, a Liverpool lad whose scouse accent attested to his maritime heritage, was a proper son of Neptune who could hold his own aboard most any vessel. But the majority of these men were trappers by trade. Trappers merely heading east from Fond du Lac who were expected to lend a hand on the ship while they hitched a ride.

Yet looking more carefully at them, he reminded himself that yes, most of these remaining men were indeed trappers, hardened *voyageurs*: resilient men accustomed to hardship and wilderness survival. Some among them had probably survived worse situations. Perhaps they needed only a bit of leadership to overcome the deadening shock of shipwreck. As if stirred by wind, a spark of optimism swiftly rekindled in his breast. It was time to take charge.

"What have we for provisions?"

A towheaded man rooted through a sopping hemp bag. "Mmm, not much, Ol' Hoss. Some sowbelly, hardtack... bit o' pemmican."

Thurgood snorted sardonically. "Well, that caps the bloody climax. Is that fowling piece serviceable?"

"Somehow stayed pretty dry. She's loaded with swan shot, should be able to take down something with it. I can tend to that, if'n you like."

"A sound idea." He observed that most of them still had knives in their belts, which would be a big help. A bunch of knife-toting voyageurs at his side- he had been far too quick to dismiss this situation as lost.

"Do any of you have knowledge of nearby trails, however old or unused, that we might take to Sault Ste. Marie? I realize that this place is little traveled, but mayhap one of you knows something?"

The men looked at each other as if he'd just made a rather lame attempt at a joke.

"Sorry boss," replied Fisher, "none of us have ever trapped this ground. Hell, only one crazy young bastard named Marcel Durand would dare that. Bad things happened to the early voyageurs who strayed into this area. Rumor has it some Jesuits went missin' back in the day too. Injuns fight shy of it, have for some time. Cursed land, they say. Hell, there are probably some well-defined game trails, but we're all going in blind if we take a land route. Best bet might be to try and lash a raft together, but storms is awful common this time o' year..."

Henry pursed his lips. "Well, let's get a raft thrown together, then we study the clouds and winds, see if decent weather is likely. Although hell, this storm sure came outta nowhere. But if it looks good, then the Soo will be our best bet."

"Very well. Sault Ste. Marie it is. Let's get moving, men."

Stepping off of his rocky perch, he led the way towards a sandy beach that lay on the other side of a narrow river. Crossing the shallow river mouth with authoritative stride, Thurgood suddenly caught sight of Migizi, a Chippewa brave, kneeling on the sand. It appeared that he was fiddling with something in front of him.

"Migizi! What's the matter, man?"

Migizi rose, his sodden black hair obscuring his face as he solemnly turned towards his captain.

"Make offer," he explained in highly accented English.

"To what end?" demanded Thurgood. He could see it now, a low altar of driftwood, atop which were carefully arranged bits of copper, vermillion, carnelian, and tobacco.

The Indian tried to explain in English, but ended up lapsing into Chippewa, a tongue in which Thurgood could claim little comprehension.

"Christ's wounds! English, man! Or French, if you must."

Slocum, a veteran trapper of considerable renown, translated. Thurgood did not much like the growing look of concern on his grizzled face.

"He's making an offering to appease the *manitous* that haunt these shores. Bad *manitous*, Cap'n. Malevolent gods of the copper, he says. An offering must be made- damn, he even wants to leave his knife."

Upon hearing this, the rest of the crew began staring into the dark, fog-festooned aisles of the blazing maples and massive, gloomy hemlocks that marked the beach's edge. As they watched, a deep, howling sound tore through the shaking trees, quite unlike the shrieking of the wind.

The men exchanged grim looks, obviously rattled. Thurgood himself felt a chill- that had been a most abnormal sound...

"You know," muttered Slocum uneasily, "I coulda sworn I saw a figure up on the rocks wachin' us 'fore we went down, thought I was just seein' things..."

Thurgood spat bitterly. He had seen how Indian legends could rattle half-breeds and even seasoned white trappers. This was the last thing he needed now, a spooked crew... especially when the rugged, virtually unexplored territory around the Pictured Rocks offered little in the way of comfort. This was *terra incognita* for men both red and white. Of all the places to go down, it had to be here, the place avoided by Indians and trappers alike due to rumors of an ancient evil lurking amidst the cliffs...

"These people and their bleeding superstitions... tell him to pick up the shit he has arranged there, we may need it to trade. And you lot, grab a hold of your codpieces and stop quaking, that was the bloody wind and you know it."

His voice increased in volume as he began rapping out orders. "We need to get a fire going and get out of these clothes posthaste. Perkins and Fisher, you're in charge of that. The fire, that is." Chuckles broke out, an encouraging sign. "Henry, as they collect wood, you look for a decent spot to erect a shelter."

The men began straightening up, putting on brave faces as they strove to impress their admittedly young, but undeniably game captain whose leadership now extended beyond the decks of his ship.

But still they kept one eye on the dim forest.

"And we'll need- blimey! What in God's name are you doing, Migizi? Eh? What did I just tell you?"

He tipped over the altar with a fierce kick, yanking the intractable Indian up at the same time. "You will follow my orders, damn you-"

Migizi groaned suddenly, and Thurgood wondered if he had hurt the man. Then a spear hissed past his face, leaving a thin trail of blood on his cheek before slicing into the waves beyond. He swore bitterly and, throwing himself into a sideways roll, sprang up by his men.

Now he could see the arrow jutting from Migizi's chest; had he not lifted the man, that arrow would have taken him instead. Indians! He did not understand why Chippewa Indians, the dominant tribe of this region, would attack them. They were on good terms with whites, but obviously this rogue band sought blood. Although maybe this was a Sioux war party come far east, but that was unlikely. And wait- did not Indians avoid this area altogether? It simply did not add up, but reaction, not deliberation, was the order of the day.

That demoniac howling sound again tore through the air, above even the shrieking wind, and in its wake a hair-raising, barbaric shout went up. Figures could be seen flitting between the trees, figures that seemed to move awfully fast for men, even Indians.

A fusillade of arrows and spears poured out of the wood line, some finding their mark among the momentarily stunned men. Recovering, they began racing down the shoreline, but dark figures poured out of the forest and onto the sands about a hundred yards away. Mindlessly, in primal panic, two of the men sprinted straight into the raging hell that was the lake, as if they hoped to find deliverance in the embrace of glacial waves. Perhaps, in a way, they did; as he spared them a half-glance Thurgood saw their dwarfed, pathetic forms swallowed up, *consumed*, by the unrelenting surf.

There was nowhere to go, nowhere that safety might be found. Hopelessly exposed, outnumbered, and outgunned, they were caught between the Devil and the deep, blue sea.

He could not speak for the others, but Captain Elijah Thurgood was not going out on a passive note. Blood rushed into his head and with a wild roar of his own he drew his short sword and rushed out to meet his concealed foes. He was heartened to hear some of the men follow.

Bursting into the ill-lit forest they were immediately engaged by their assailants. To his left Thurgood saw Henry, a man of considerable strength, hurled like a ragdoll into a tree. It was damnably hard to see, as the giant hemlocks blotted out most light. But he could discern well enough the hulking, man-like form as it rounded on him. The ship's captain thrust hard with his weapon, sticking his enemy squarely in the throat until he felt the blade scratch against bone.

He then spun around, jerking the blade out to viciously slash another comer across the face, but after that the sword was batted aside by a copper-tipped club, which slammed into his gut on its next swing. Then powerful, tattooed hands seized him, swung him aloft, and tossed him a considerable distance.

He fair flew for a second or two before coming down hard upon a rotting log.

Screams of pain, roars of anger, the clash of weapons; the sounds melded into a dreadful cacophony as the fight raged on. Few of his men remained standing and all faced multiple opponents. Through vision blurred and spotty, Thurgood could make out Perkins as he fired the shotgun. A clanging sound accompanied the resultant shriek of agony, as if the shot had struck metal.

Two dark forms came up from behind the voyageur, pinning Perkins' arms behind his back as a third figure slashed viciously with a long sword, spilling his organs onto the leaf litter.

A sword? What manner of Indians were these?

Thurgood staggered to his feet and began stumbling through the woods, where to he did not know. But the fight was knocked out of him and he simply to get away from this scene of butchery.

Turning to look behind him, he saw an Indian in pursuit-but how could it be? Torso clad in copper, his pale skin stood out starkly against the saturated bark of the trees. Beard hanging long and shaggy off his black-painted face, he leered evilly as Thurgood gazed upon him in abject horror.

He had never known Great Lakes Indians to sport metal breastplates. And they sure as hell didn't grow beards. A disturbing sense of unreality set in as he sped through the dank woods. While his legs pumped furiously, Thurgood's mind tried in vain to formulate a plausible explanation for this madness. He chanced another backward glance and beheld a veritable horde in hot pursuit. Then the ground abruptly gave way beneath him and he was falling, falling... finally coming to a bone-crunching halt next to a stream at the base of a small cliff. Shadow-dappled figures gathered at the cliff's edge, silently staring down at his supine form.

The Indian legends were true, then. Imagine that. As the darkness embraced him, Elijah Thurgood grudgingly arrived at this conclusion.

The legends were true and may Heaven help those who invoked the wrath of the copper gods.

About the Author

Edward Swanson is a twenty-four year old, first time author from New Hampshire. Having graduated from Plymouth State University with a Major in History and Minor in Art History, he is now pursuing a Master's Degree in History.

An avid outdoorsman, he enjoys fishing, hunting, canoeing and horse packing. He has undertaken several unguided horseback trips through the Rocky Mountains. Hopelessly infected with wanderlust, he can often be found traveling the country. He divides his time between New Hampshire and Minnesota.

Made in the USA
Lexington, KY
11 February 2015